MPLS sound

ILLIDGE • TABU • LAXTON

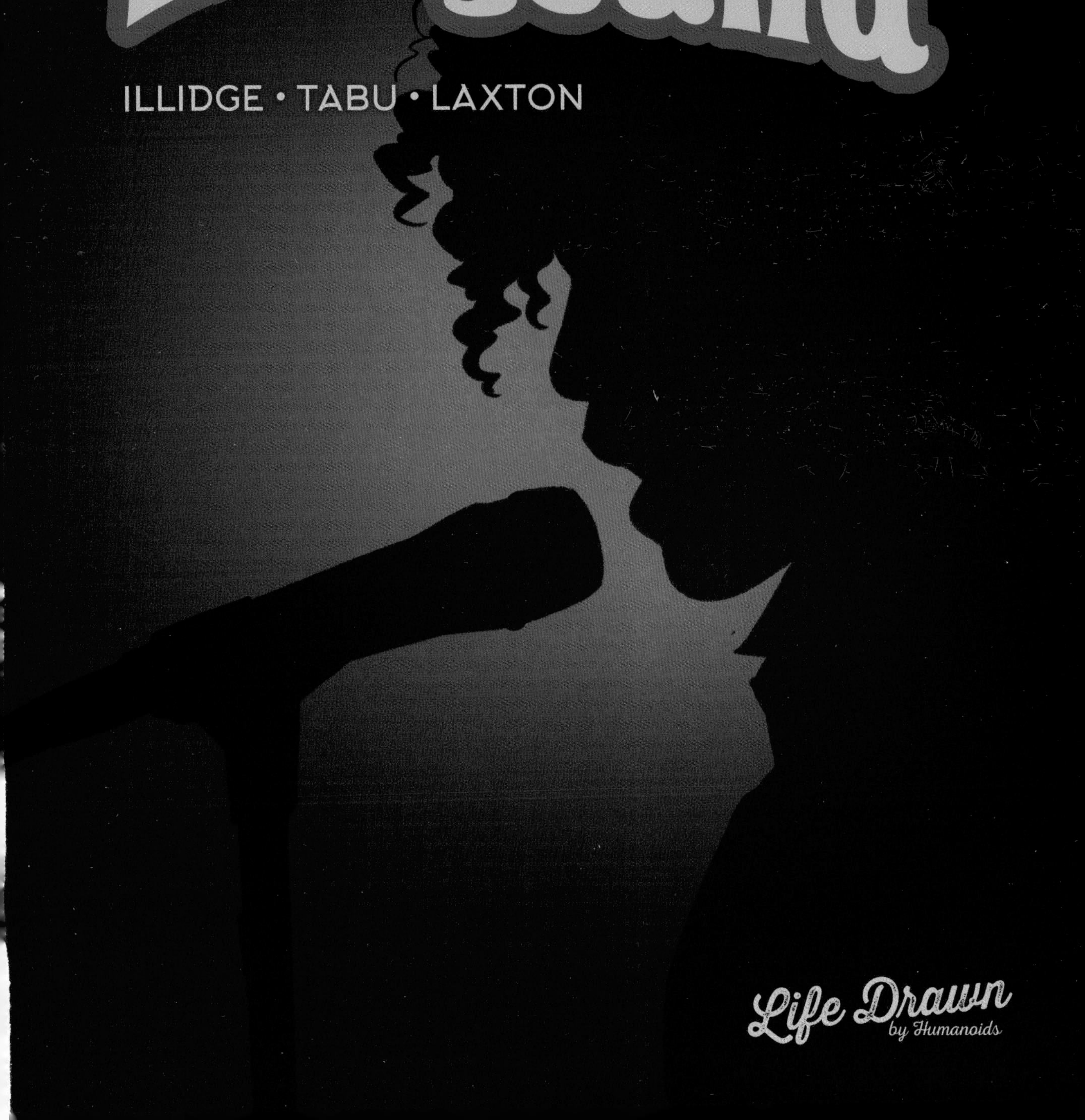

Life Drawn
by Humanoids

**JOSEPH P. ILLIDGE
& HANNIBAL TABU**
Writers

MEREDITH LAXTON
Artist

TAN SHU
Color Artist

ALW'S TROY PETERI
with **RYAN LEWIS**
Letters

JEN BARTEL
Cover Artist

AMANDA LUCIDO
Assistant Editor

ROB LEVIN & **FABRICE SAPOLSKY**
Editors

JERRY FRISSEN
Senior Art Director

RYAN LEWIS
Junior Designer

MARK WAID
Publisher

Rights and Licensing: licensing@humanoids.com
Press and Social Media: pr@humanoids.com

MPLS SOUND
First Edition. This title is a publication of Humanoids, Inc.
8033 Sunset Blvd. #628, Los Angeles, CA 90046. Copyright
© 2021 Humanoids, Inc., Los Angeles (USA). All rights reserved.
Humanoids and its logos are ® and © 2021 Humanoids, Inc.
Library of Congress Control Number: 2020944577

Life Drawn is an imprint of Humanoids, Inc.

*To every woman who lives in defiance of being
told they cannot be extraordinary and achieve
amazing things, and to Pauline Illidge, the first
woman I met who never gave up on her dreams.*

    – Joseph

*For Alek and Ella, my own new power generation.
For Myshell, the most beautiful girl in the world.
For Christopher Priest, showing me how to fight
thieves in the temple.*

    – Hannibal

For my dad, who loved music and stories.

    – Meredith

FOREWORD
By **Josh Jackson**

The story of Starchild is the story of Prince. It's the story of the Revolution. It's the story of every band from Minneapolis, Seattle, or Athens, Ga., dreaming of making it in an often-cruel business that demands more than just the love of music that many of us feel. It demands hustle, a drive to push through near-impossible barriers, and a vision to create something new. That hustle took four young Scousers off to Hamburg to refine their sound night after night. That single-mindedness and drive has alienated more bandmates than history can chronicle, including Prince's childhood friend and original bassist, André Cymone. And that vision has to be guarded like the most precious secret, even when temptations promise a shortcut to stardom.

Prince had that hustle and desire, but it was his vision that inexplicably put Minneapolis on the map for a fusion of funk, New Wave, R&B and art pop. Minneapolis was primarily a rock 'n' roll town when the singer/songwriter/guitar virtuoso released his self-titled album just as the decade drew to a close. The Replacements and Hüsker Dü would help define alternative rock in the '80s, but Prince would revolutionize pop music across the globe.

His 39 studio albums would sell more than 100 million copies. His tours would take him around the world. When he couldn't put out albums fast enough for all the songs that were pouring out of him, some would become hits for others, like Sinéad O'Connor's *"Nothing Compares 2 U"* or The Bangles' *"Manic Monday."* He would release five different feature films and put on the best Super Bowl halftime performance of all time. And that kid listening to his music in Sao Paolo, Brazil or Osaka, Japan would have no idea that his hometown of Minneapolis was more than 98% white when he was born or about the city's mixed history of addressing racial discrimination.

Prince strove to move past definitions, surrounding himself with a rainbow of artists and presenting himself as an androgynous, genre-defying enigma. It wasn't always an easy path to follow—he was once booed off the stage in Los Angeles while opening for The Rolling Stones. But he never wavered from his own creative instincts, even when it put him at odds with his record label and took him out of the spotlight for a while. What he created was unique.

The Minneapolis Sound was bigger than Prince, but most of its hitmakers were his hand-picked acolytes, beneficiaries of his purple coattails: Morris Day and the Time, Sheila E., Wendy & Lisa all made some memorable music, but the diminutive Prince's shadow was impossible to escape.

Starchild's Theresa is another visionary, one who saw Jimi Hendrix, saw Prince, and saw a future, even in a city that made a habit of overlooking those who looked like her. Her story may mirror that of Prince's longtime band The Revolution, but she's nobody's acolyte. Her story is an important one, even as Minneapolis once again sparks a global movement—this time through a shocking act of violence that finally pushed police brutality into the consciousness of those who ignored it for far too long.

Minneapolis is a much more diverse place than it was when Prince was young Prince Rogers Nelson, son of jazz musicians. Its music scene is more diverse than ever, but it's been indelibly touched by the Minneapolis Sound.

Josh Jackson is the co-founder, President, and Editor-in-Chief of the award-winning *Paste* magazine.

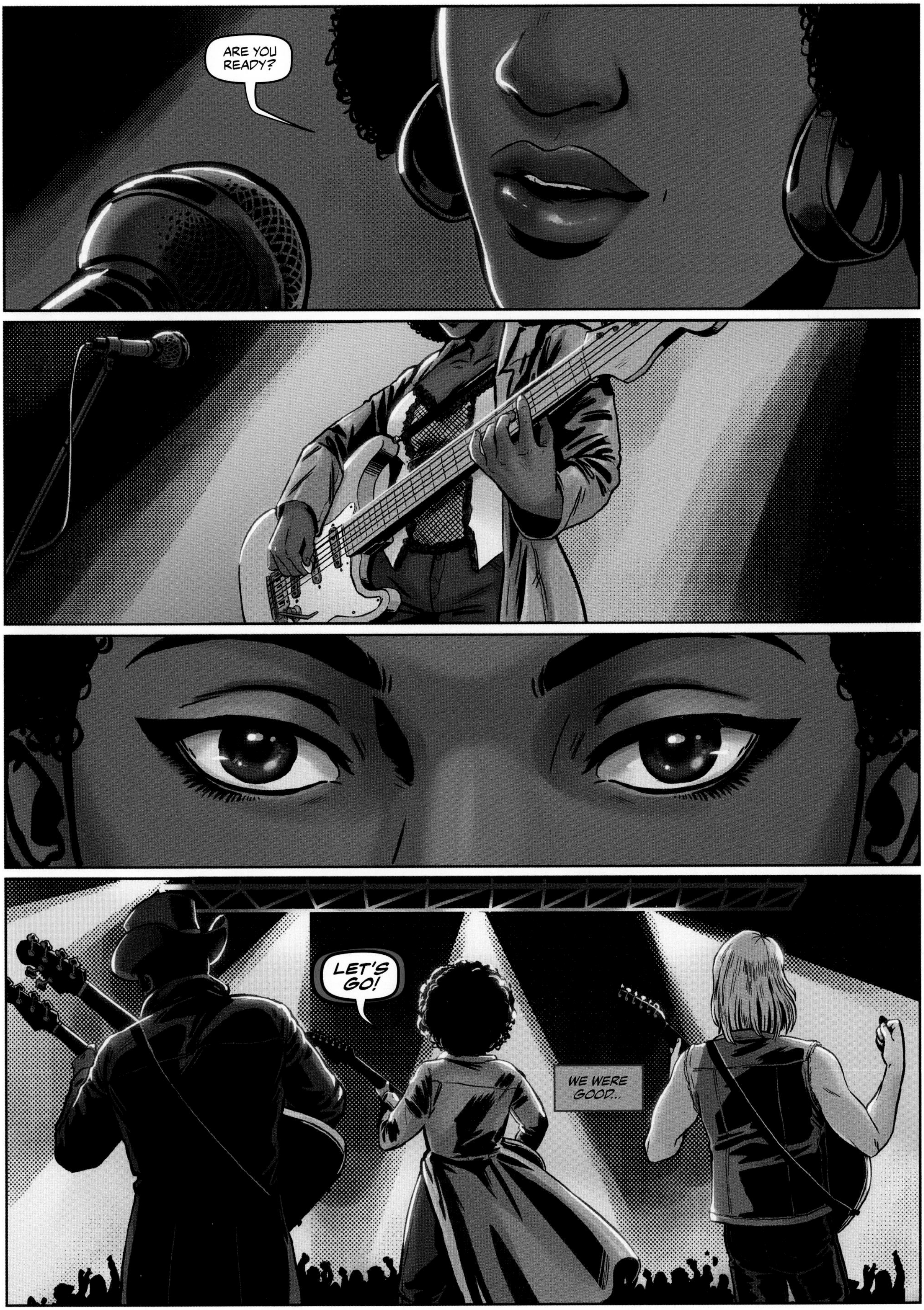
ARE YOU READY?
LET'S GO!
WE WERE GOOD...

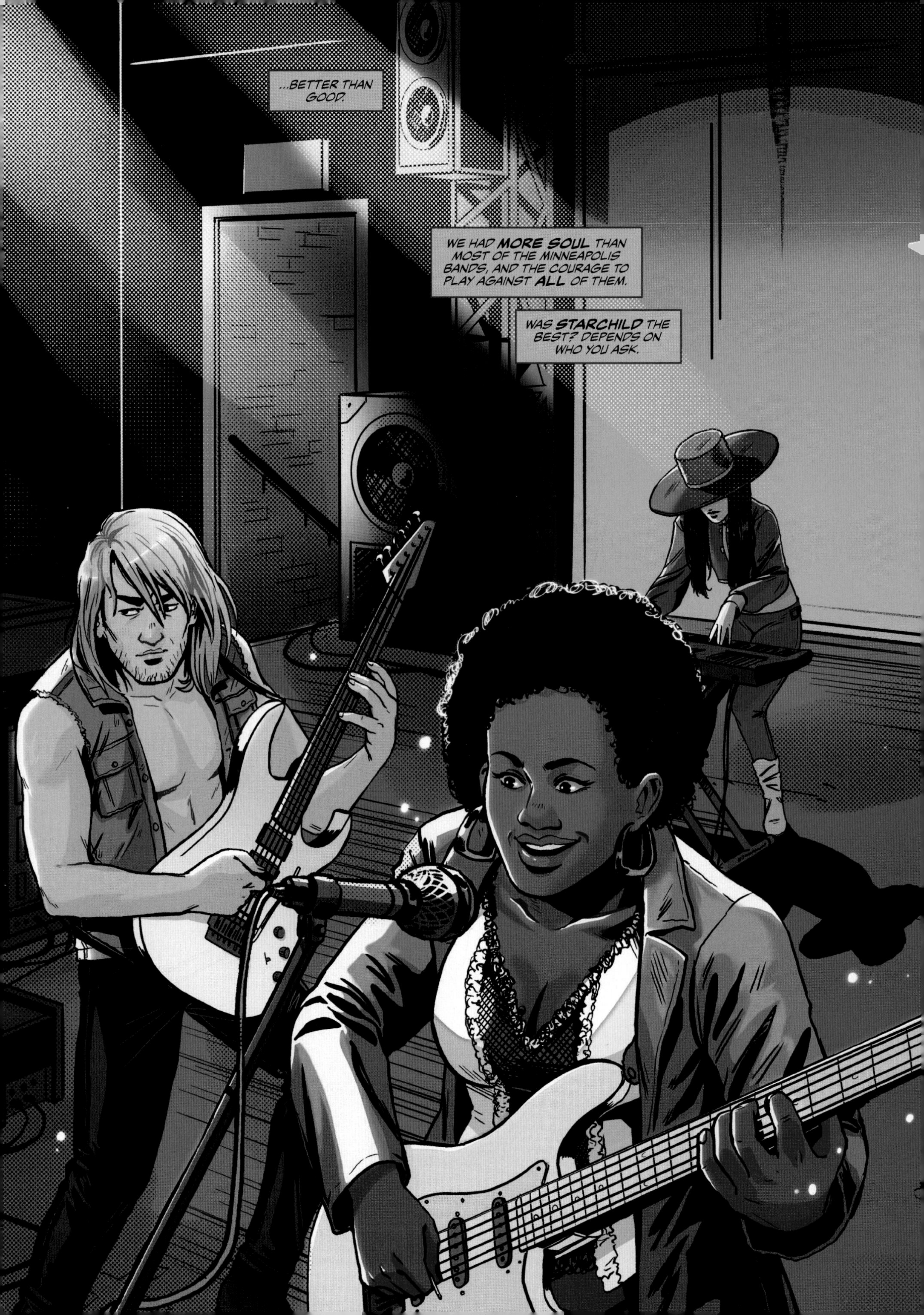
...BETTER THAN GOOD.
WE HAD MORE SOUL THAN MOST OF THE MINNEAPOLIS BANDS, AND THE COURAGE TO PLAY AGAINST ALL OF THEM.
WAS STARCHILD THE BEST? DEPENDS ON WHO YOU ASK.

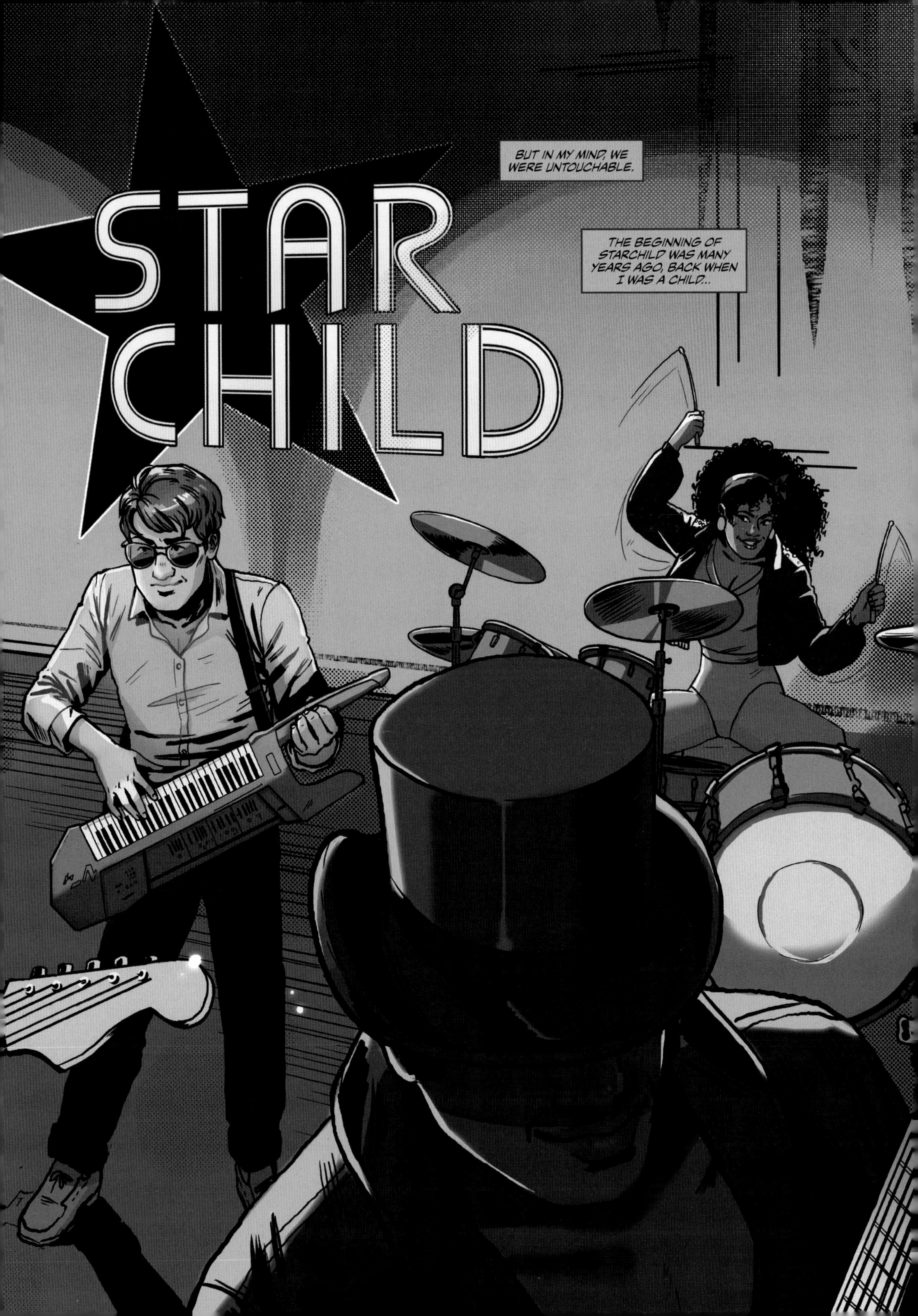

BUT IN MY MIND, WE WERE UNTOUCHABLE.
THE BEGINNING OF STARCHILD WAS MANY YEARS AGO, BACK WHEN I WAS A CHILD...
STAR CHILD

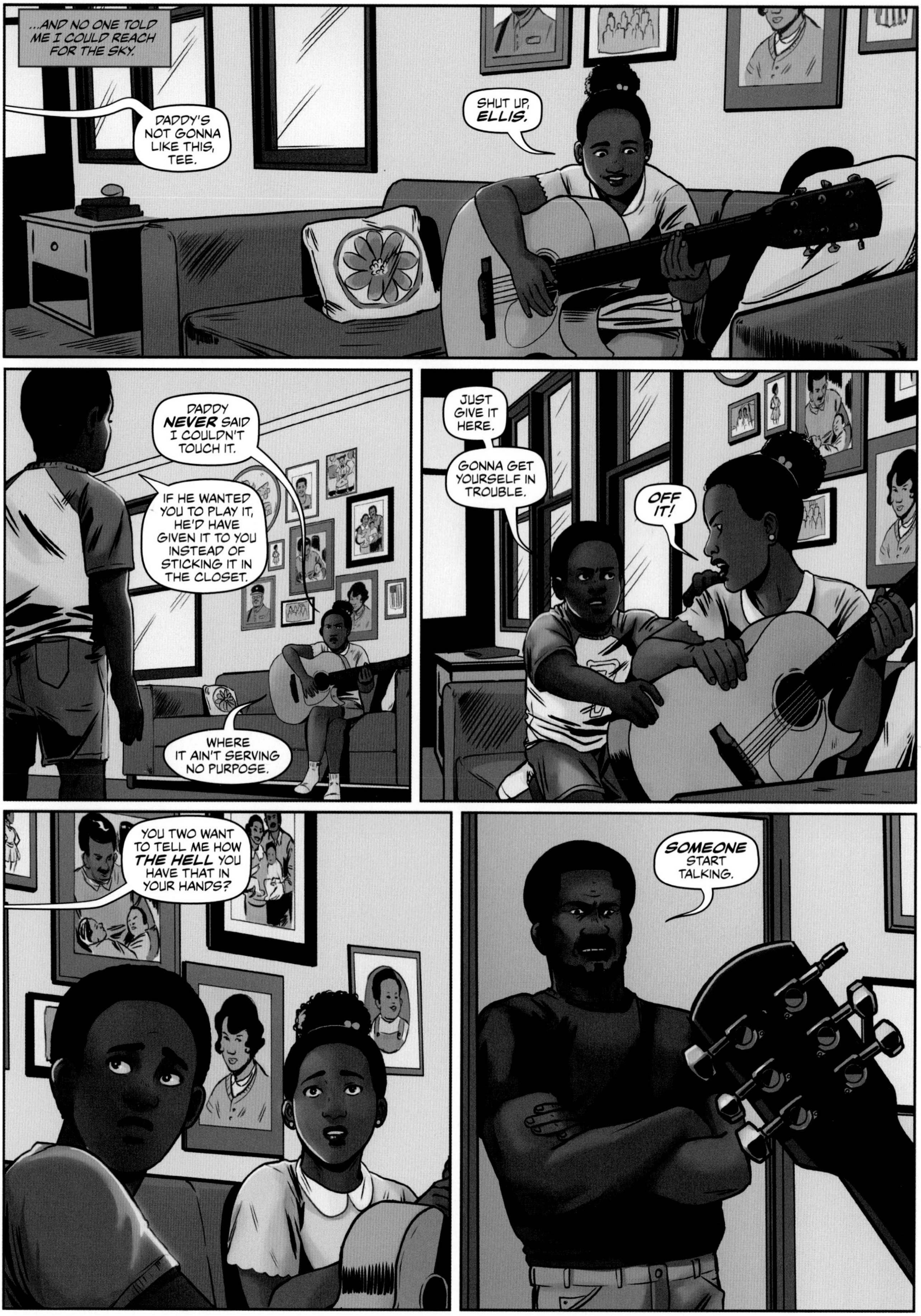
...AND NO ONE TOLD ME I COULD REACH FOR THE SKY.
DADDY'S NOT GONNA LIKE THIS, TEE.
SHUT UP, ELLIS.
DADDY NEVER SAID I COULDN'T TOUCH IT.
IF HE WANTED YOU TO PLAY IT, HE'D HAVE GIVEN IT TO YOU INSTEAD OF STICKING IT IN THE CLOSET.
WHERE IT AIN'T SERVING NO PURPOSE.
JUST GIVE IT HERE.
GONNA GET YOURSELF IN TROUBLE.
OFF IT!
YOU TWO WANT TO TELL ME HOW THE HELL YOU HAVE THAT IN YOUR HANDS?
SOMEONE START TALKING.

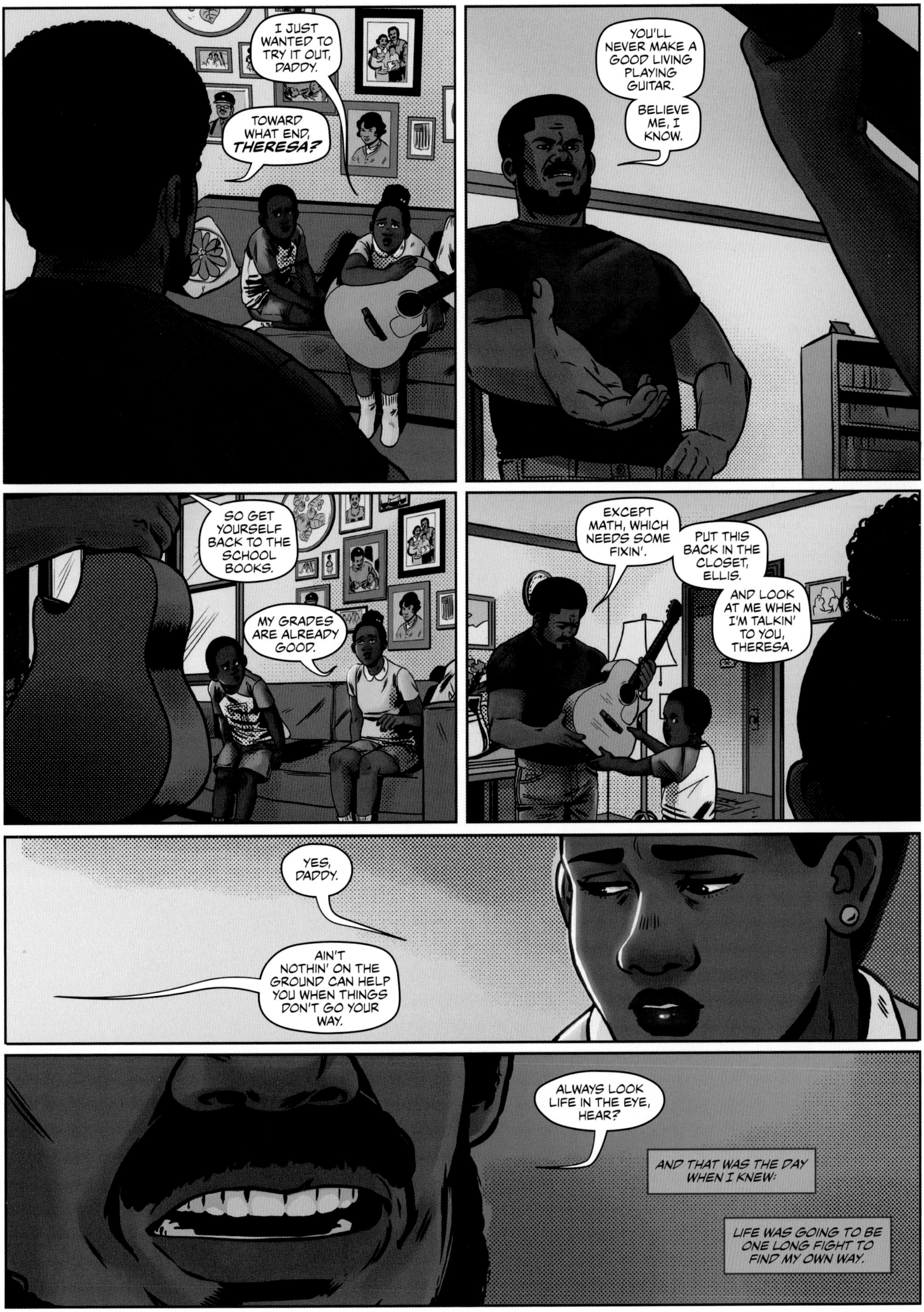
I JUST WANTED TO TRY IT OUT, DADDY.
TOWARD WHAT END, THERESA?
YOU'LL NEVER MAKE A GOOD LIVING PLAYING GUITAR.
BELIEVE ME, I KNOW.
SO GET YOURSELF BACK TO THE SCHOOL BOOKS.
MY GRADES ARE ALREADY GOOD.
EXCEPT MATH, WHICH NEEDS SOME FIXIN'.
PUT THIS BACK IN THE CLOSET, ELLIS.
AND LOOK AT ME WHEN I'M TALKIN' TO YOU, THERESA.
YES, DADDY.
AIN'T NOTHIN' ON THE GROUND CAN HELP YOU WHEN THINGS DON'T GO YOUR WAY.
ALWAYS LOOK LIFE IN THE EYE, HEAR?
AND THAT WAS THE DAY WHEN I KNEW:
LIFE WAS GOING TO BE ONE LONG FIGHT TO FIND MY OWN WAY.

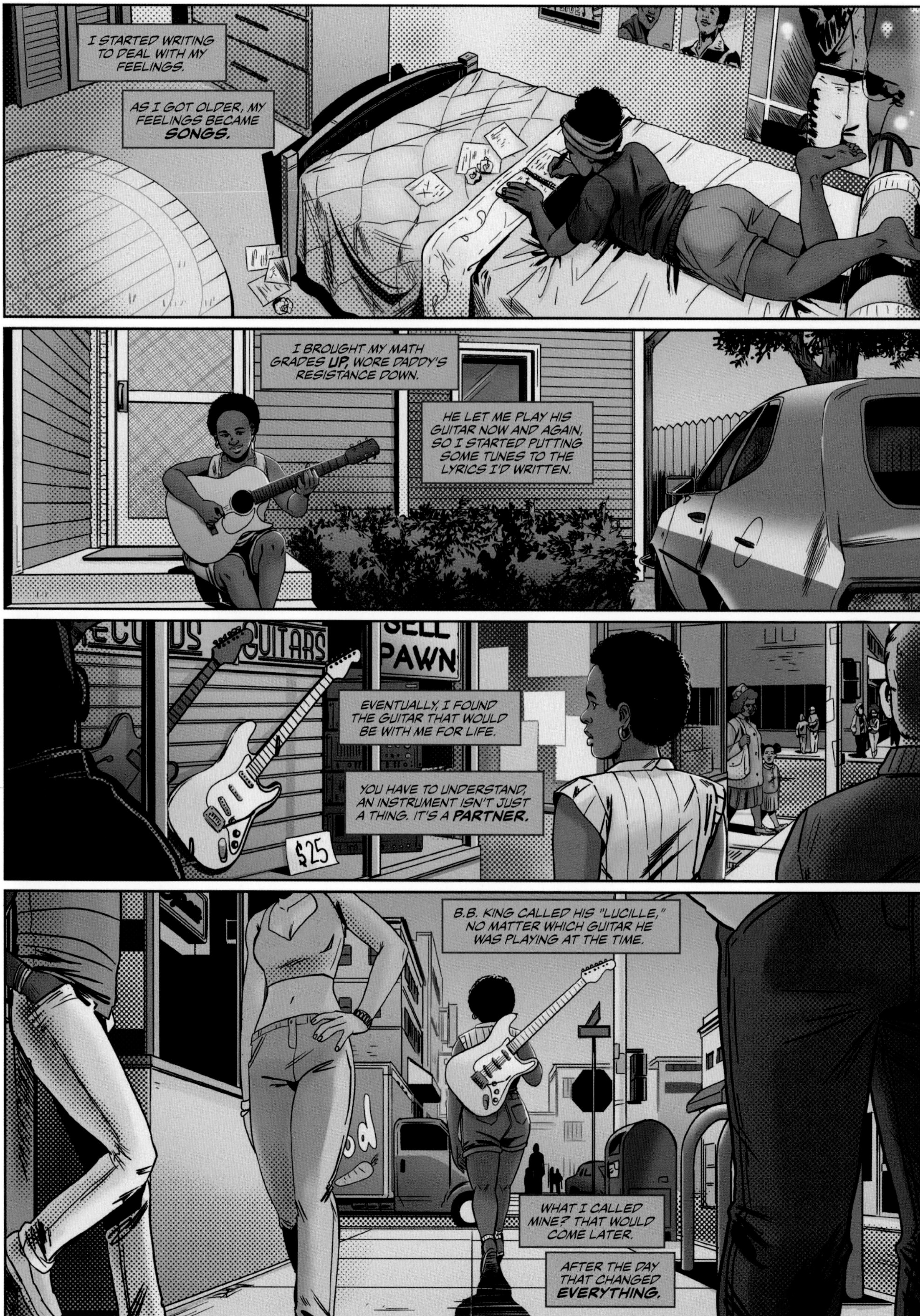
I STARTED WRITING TO DEAL WITH MY FEELINGS.
AS I GOT OLDER, MY FEELINGS BECAME SONGS.
I BROUGHT MY MATH GRADES UP, WORE DADDY'S RESISTANCE DOWN.
HE LET ME PLAY HIS GUITAR NOW AND AGAIN, SO I STARTED PUTTING SOME TUNES TO THE LYRICS I'D WRITTEN.
RECORDS
GUITARS
SELL
PAWN
EVENTUALLY, I FOUND THE GUITAR THAT WOULD BE WITH ME FOR LIFE.
YOU HAVE TO UNDERSTAND, AN INSTRUMENT ISN'T JUST A THING. IT'S A PARTNER.
$25
B.B. KING CALLED HIS "LUCILLE," NO MATTER WHICH GUITAR HE WAS PLAYING AT THE TIME.
WHAT I CALLED MINE? THAT WOULD COME LATER.
AFTER THE DAY THAT CHANGED EVERYTHING.

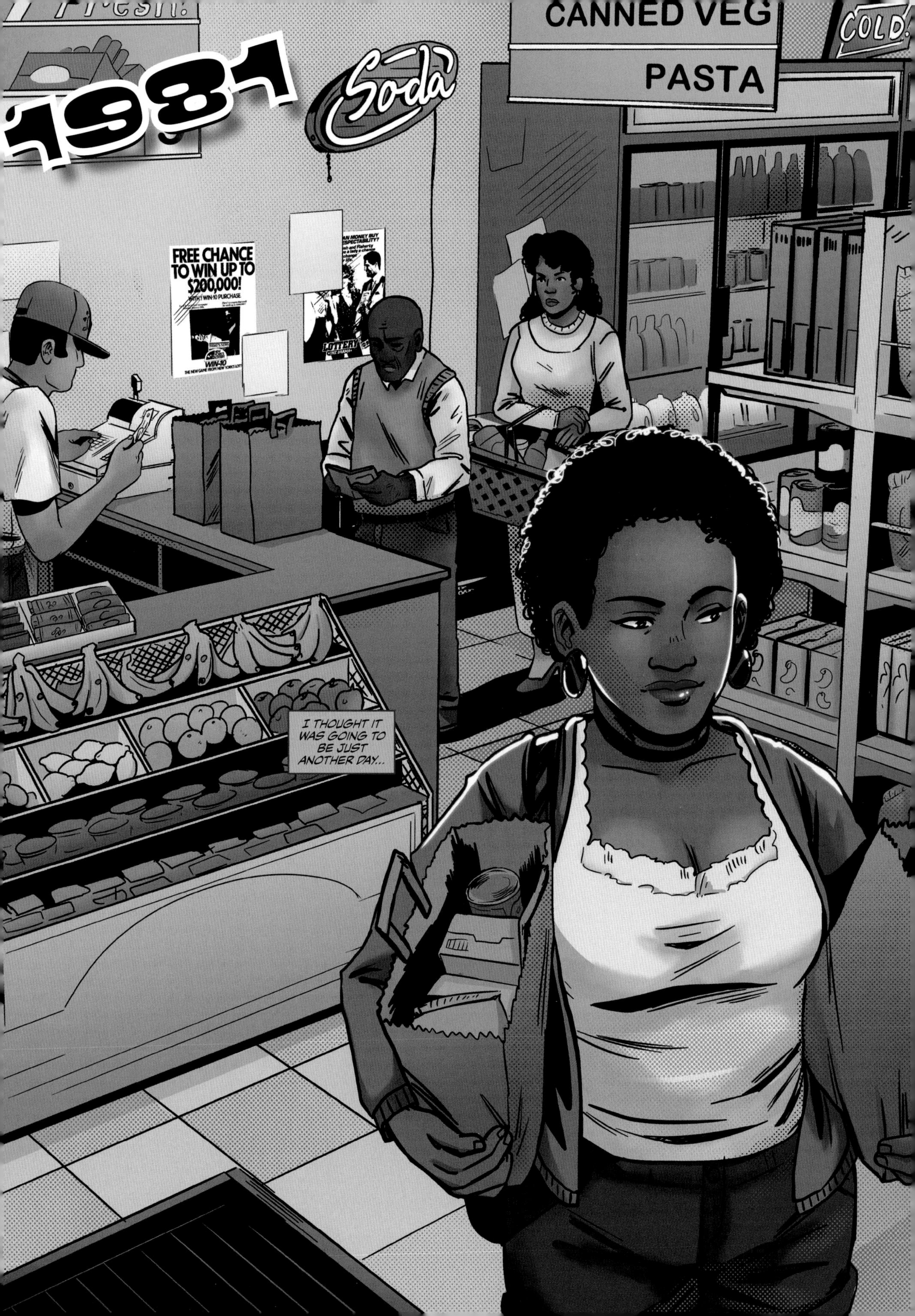
1981
Soda
CANNED VEG
PASTA
COLD!
FREE CHANCE TO WIN UP TO $200,000!
WITH 1 WIN-10 PURCHASE
WIN-10
LOTTERY
I THOUGHT IT WAS GOING TO BE JUST ANOTHER DAY...

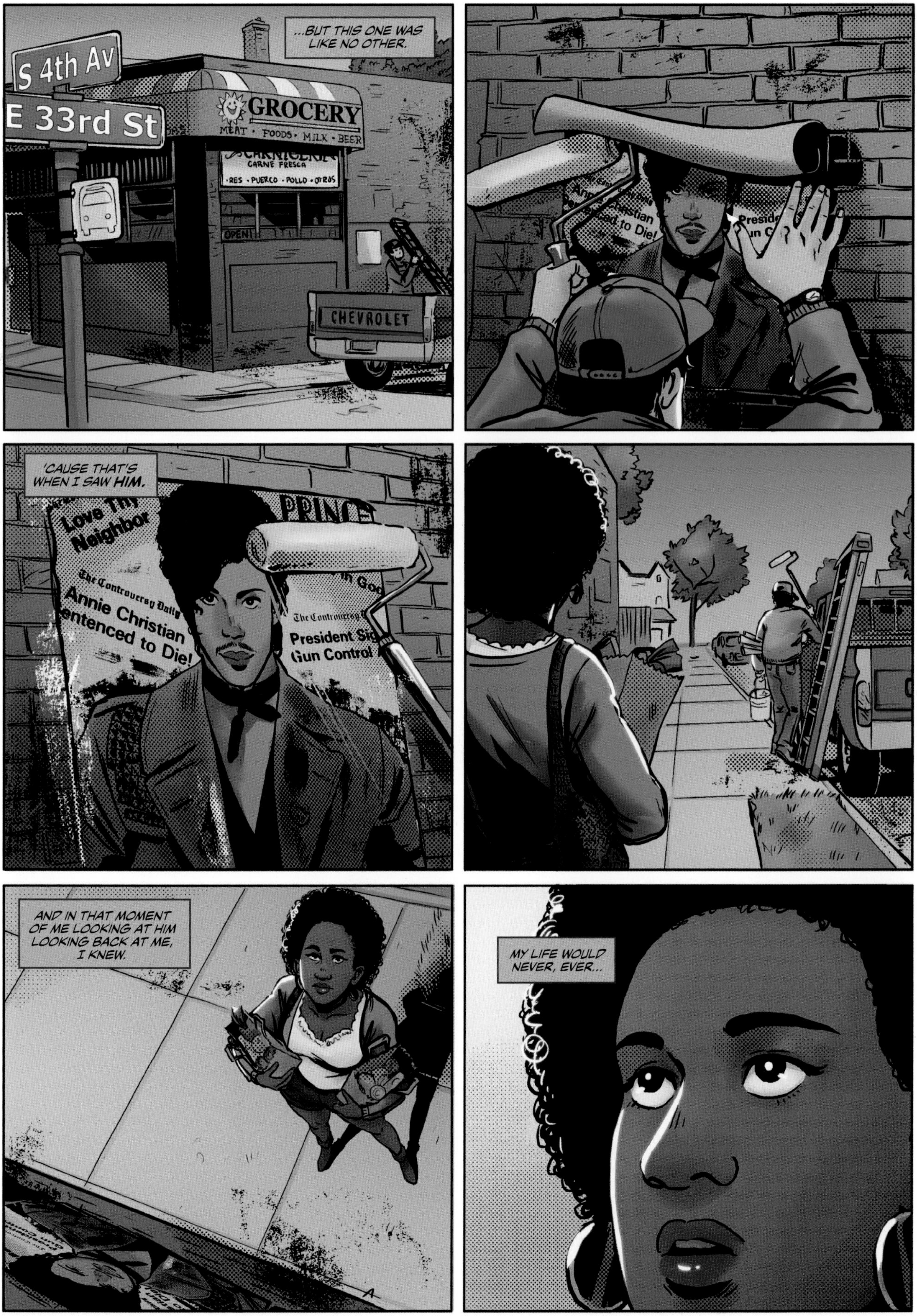
S 4th Av
E 33rd St
...BUT THIS ONE WAS LIKE NO OTHER.
GROCERY
MEAT • FOODS • MILK • BEER
CARNE FRESCA
RES • PUERCO • POLLO • OTRAS
OPEN
CHEVROLET
'CAUSE THAT'S WHEN I SAW HIM.
Love Thy Neighbor
PRINCE
The Controversy Daily
Annie Christian entenced to Die!
President Sig Gun Control
AND IN THAT MOMENT OF ME LOOKING AT HIM LOOKING BACK AT ME, I KNEW.
MY LIFE WOULD NEVER, EVER...

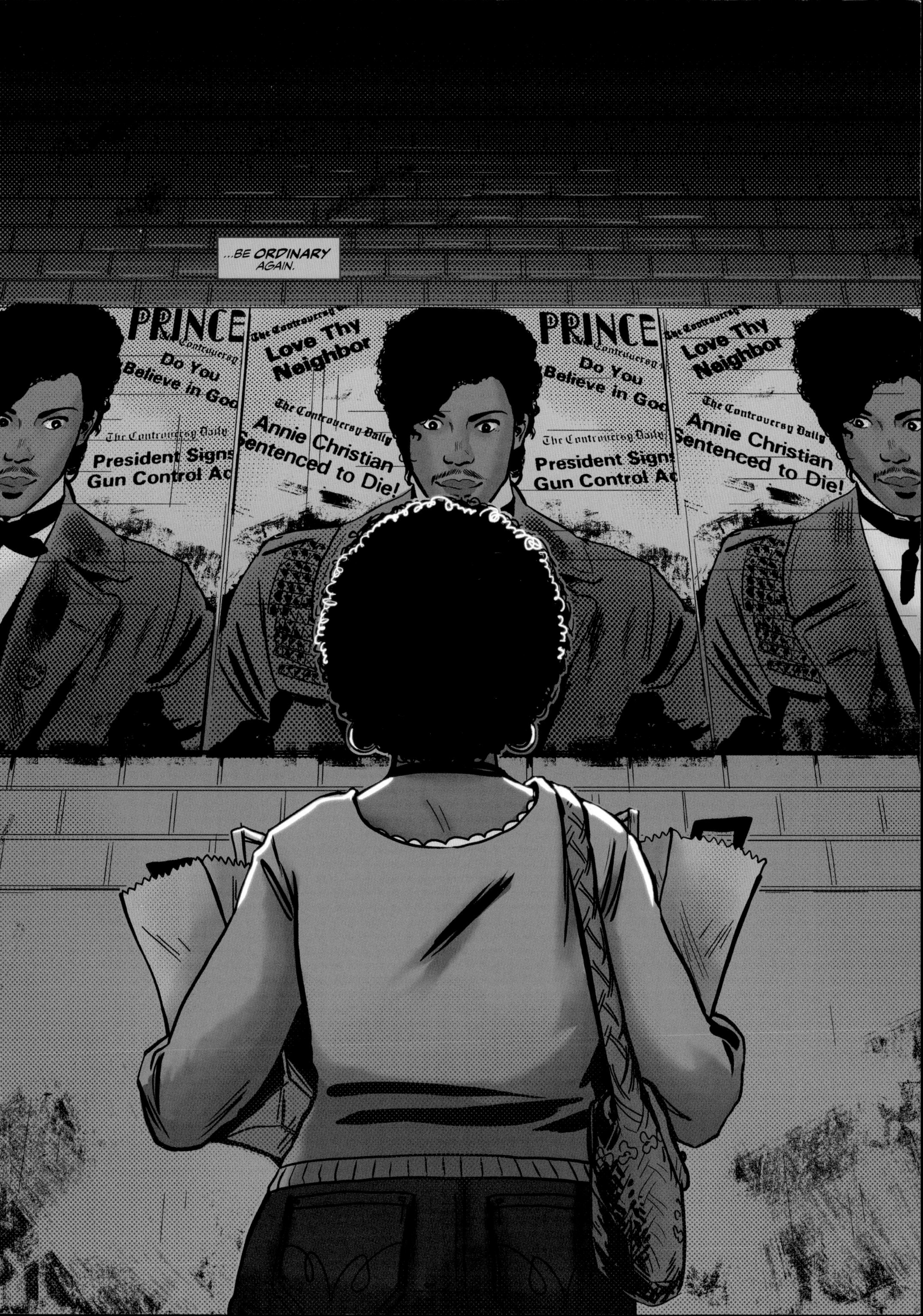

...BE ORDINARY AGAIN.
PRINCE
Do You Believe in God
President Signs Gun Control Ac
Love Thy Neighbor
Annie Christian Sentenced to Die!

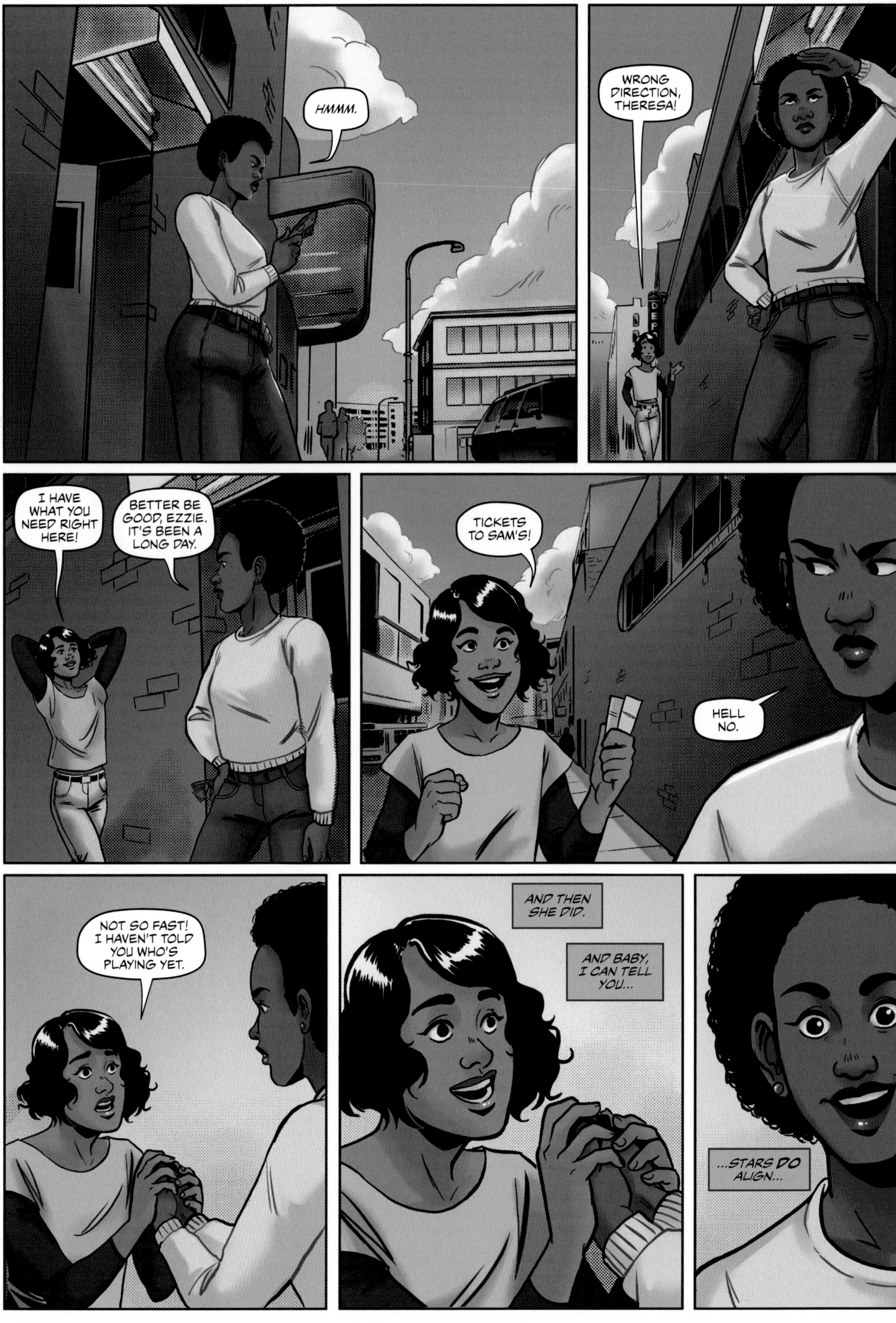
HMMM.
WRONG DIRECTION, THERESA!
I HAVE WHAT YOU NEED RIGHT HERE!
BETTER BE GOOD, EZZIE. IT'S BEEN A LONG DAY.
TICKETS TO SAM'S!
HELL NO.
NOT SO FAST! I HAVEN'T TOLD YOU WHO'S PLAYING YET.
AND THEN SHE DID.
AND BABY, I CAN TELL YOU...
...STARS DO ALIGN...

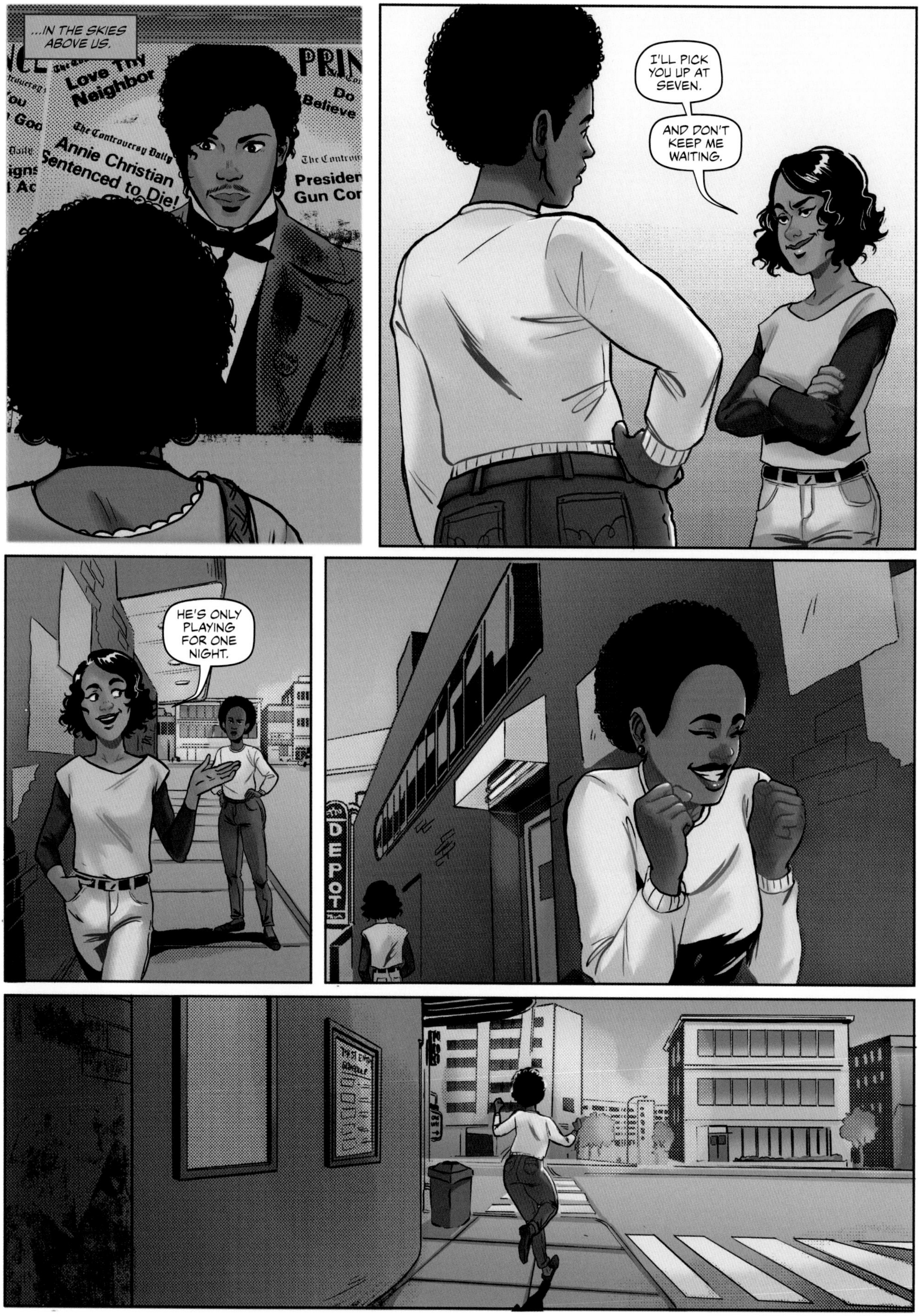
...IN THE SKIES ABOVE US.
Love Thy Neighbor
Do Believe
The Controversy Daily
Annie Christian Sentenced to Die!
I'LL PICK YOU UP AT SEVEN.
AND DON'T KEEP ME WAITING.
HE'S ONLY PLAYING FOR ONE NIGHT.
DEPOT

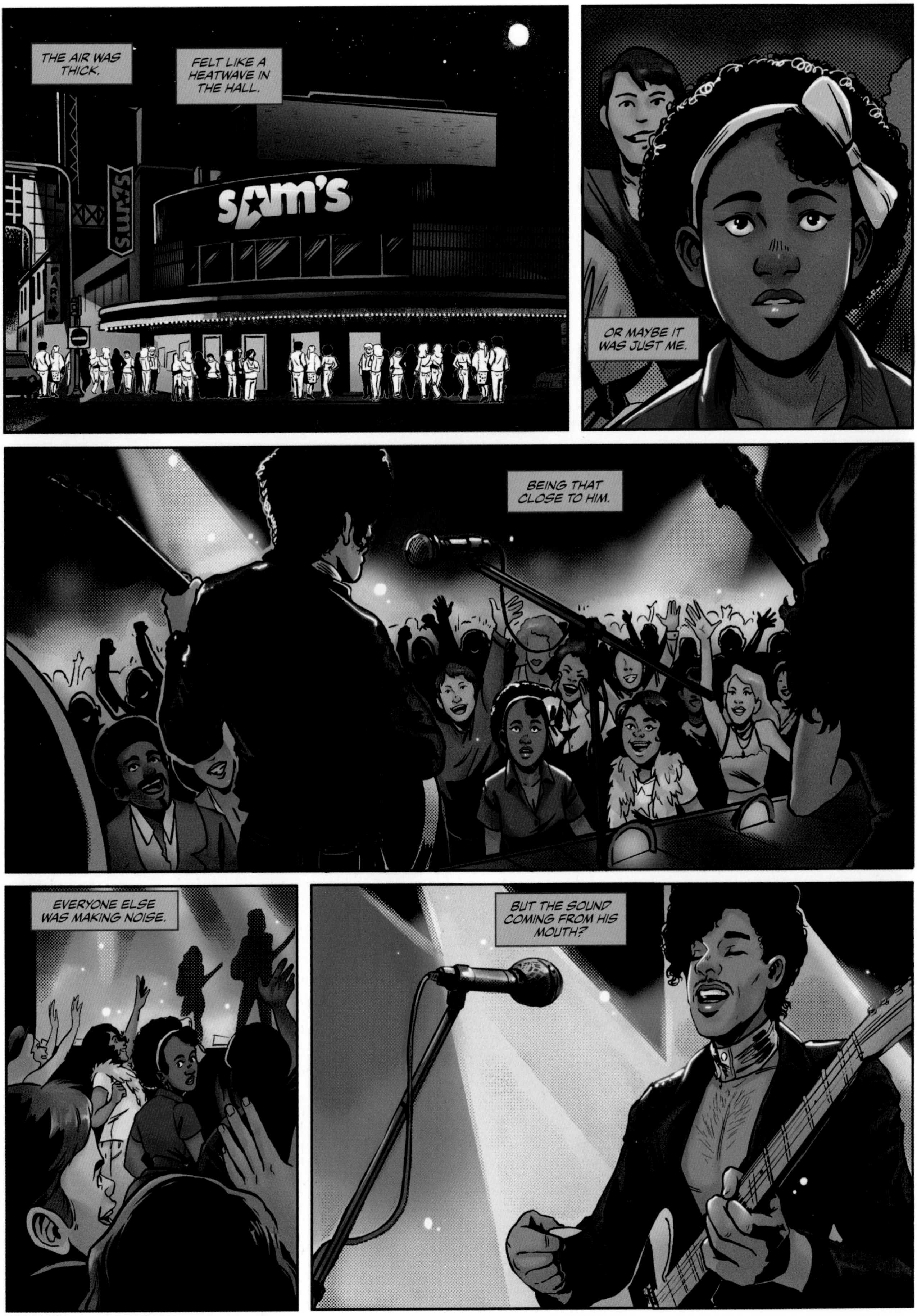
THE AIR WAS THICK.
FELT LIKE A HEATWAVE IN THE HALL.
SAM'S
OR MAYBE IT WAS JUST ME.
BEING THAT CLOSE TO HIM.
EVERYONE ELSE WAS MAKING NOISE.
BUT THE SOUND COMING FROM HIS MOUTH?

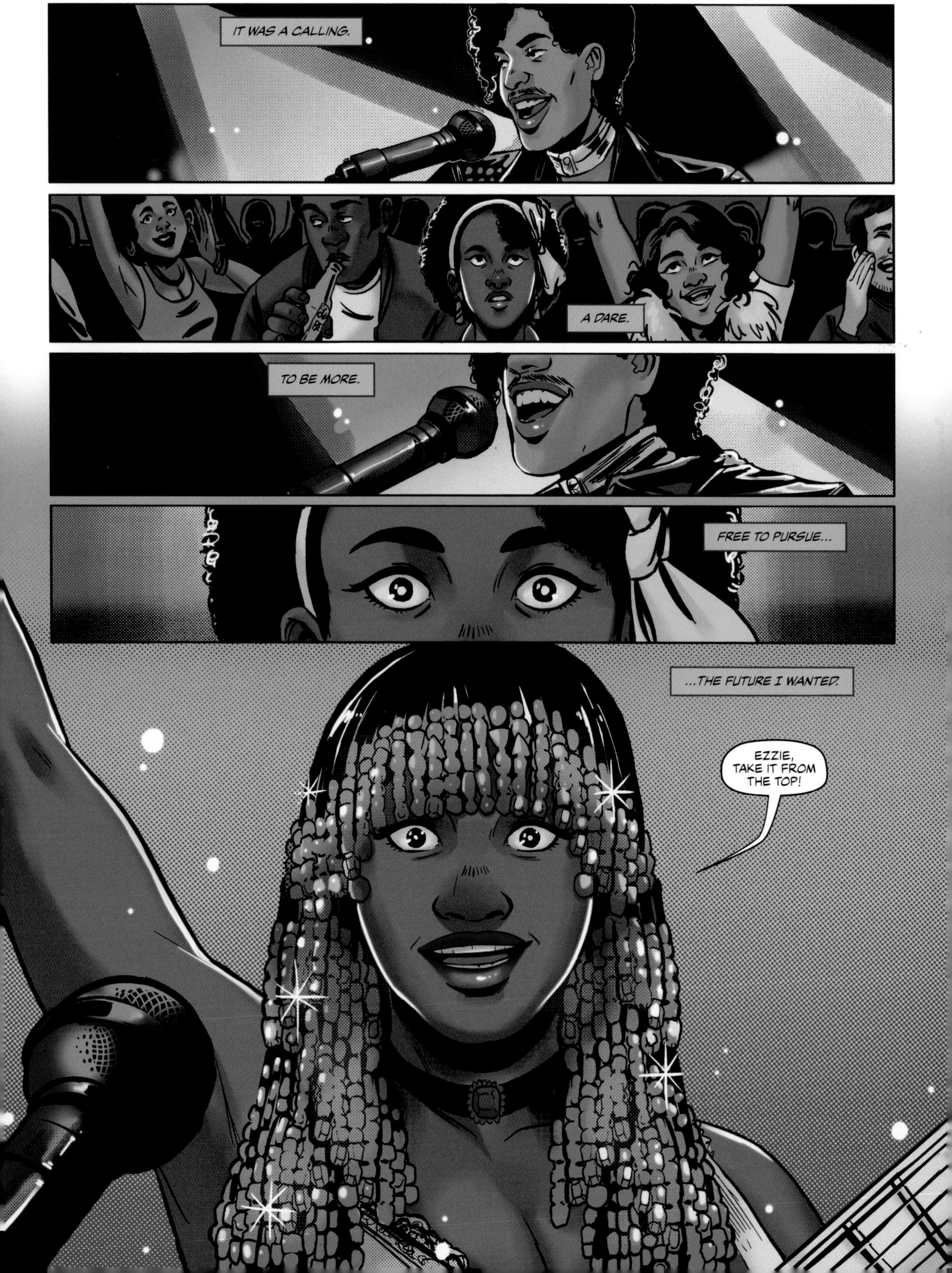
IT WAS A CALLING.
A DARE.
TO BE MORE.
FREE TO PURSUE...
...THE FUTURE I WANTED.
EZZIE, TAKE IT FROM THE TOP!

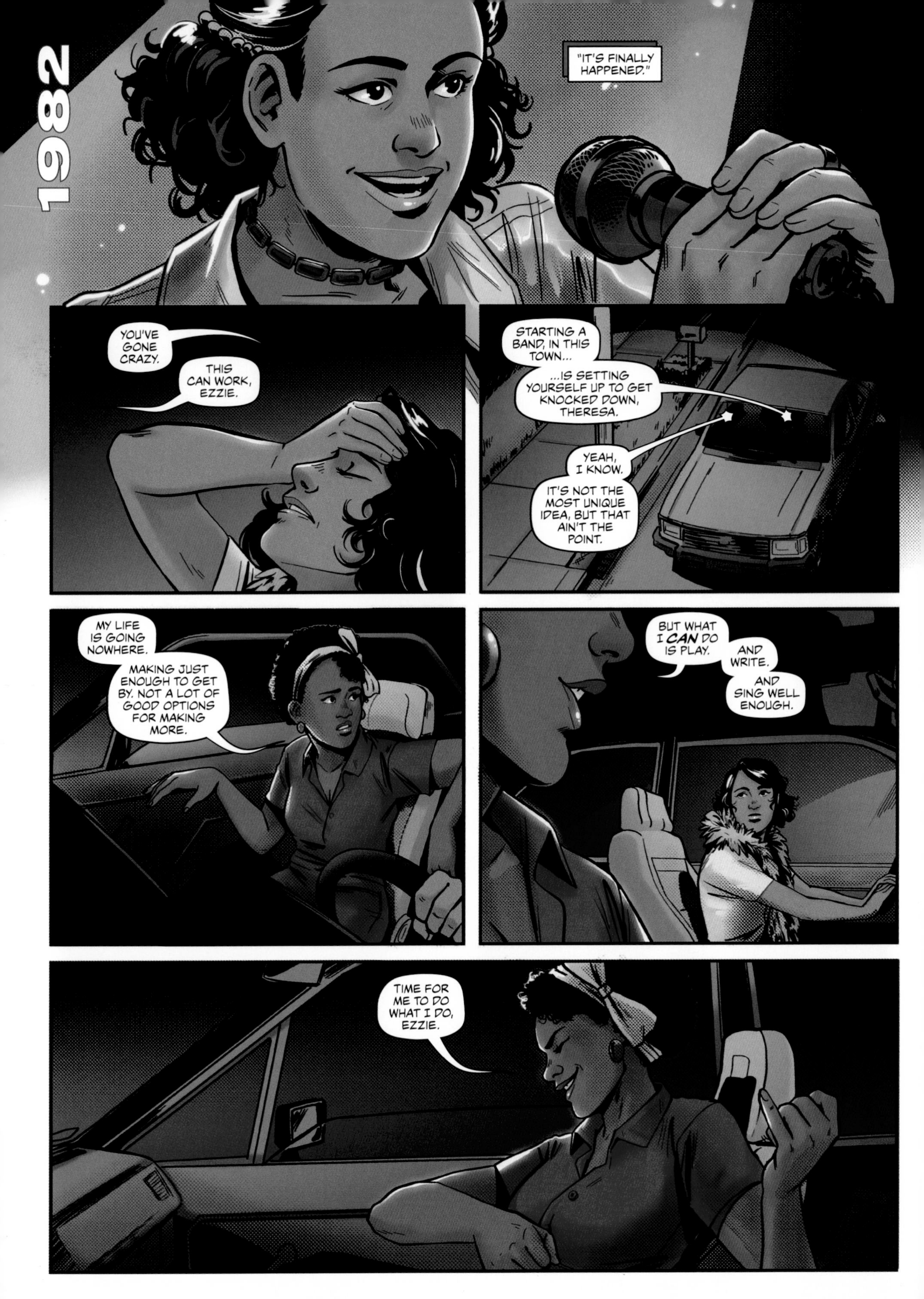
1982
"IT'S FINALLY HAPPENED."
YOU'VE GONE CRAZY.
THIS CAN WORK, EZZIE.
STARTING A BAND, IN THIS TOWN...
...IS SETTING YOURSELF UP TO GET KNOCKED DOWN, THERESA.
YEAH, I KNOW.
IT'S NOT THE MOST UNIQUE IDEA, BUT THAT AIN'T THE POINT.
MY LIFE IS GOING NOWHERE.
MAKING JUST ENOUGH TO GET BY. NOT A LOT OF GOOD OPTIONS FOR MAKING MORE.
BUT WHAT I CAN DO IS PLAY.
AND WRITE.
AND SING WELL ENOUGH.
TIME FOR ME TO DO WHAT I DO, EZZIE.

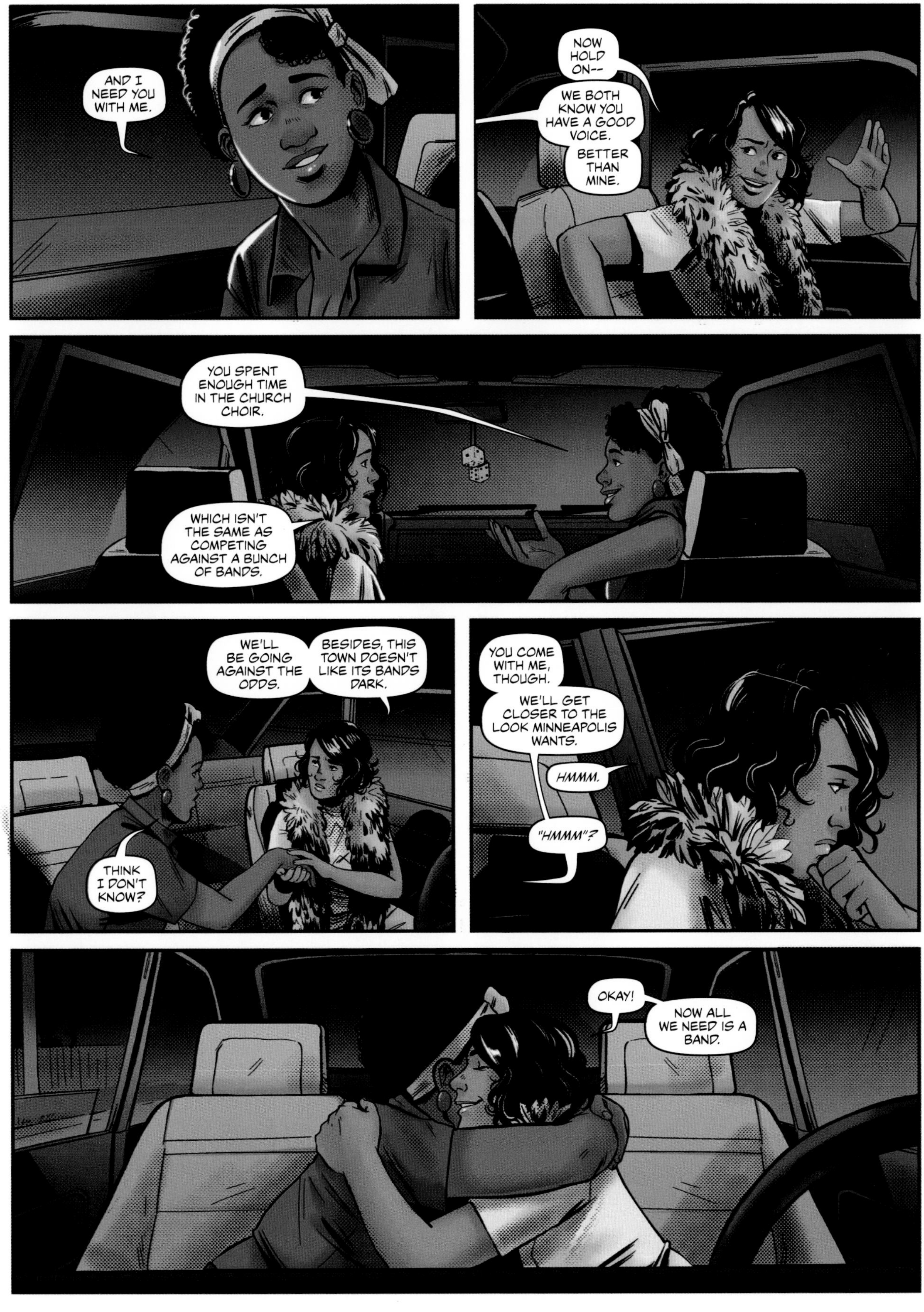
AND I NEED YOU WITH ME.
NOW HOLD ON--
WE BOTH KNOW YOU HAVE A GOOD VOICE.
BETTER THAN MINE.
YOU SPENT ENOUGH TIME IN THE CHURCH CHOIR.
WHICH ISN'T THE SAME AS COMPETING AGAINST A BUNCH OF BANDS.
WE'LL BE GOING AGAINST THE ODDS.
BESIDES, THIS TOWN DOESN'T LIKE ITS BANDS DARK.
THINK I DON'T KNOW?
YOU COME WITH ME, THOUGH.
WE'LL GET CLOSER TO THE LOOK MINNEAPOLIS WANTS.
HMMM.
"HMMM"?
OKAY!
NOW ALL WE NEED IS A BAND.

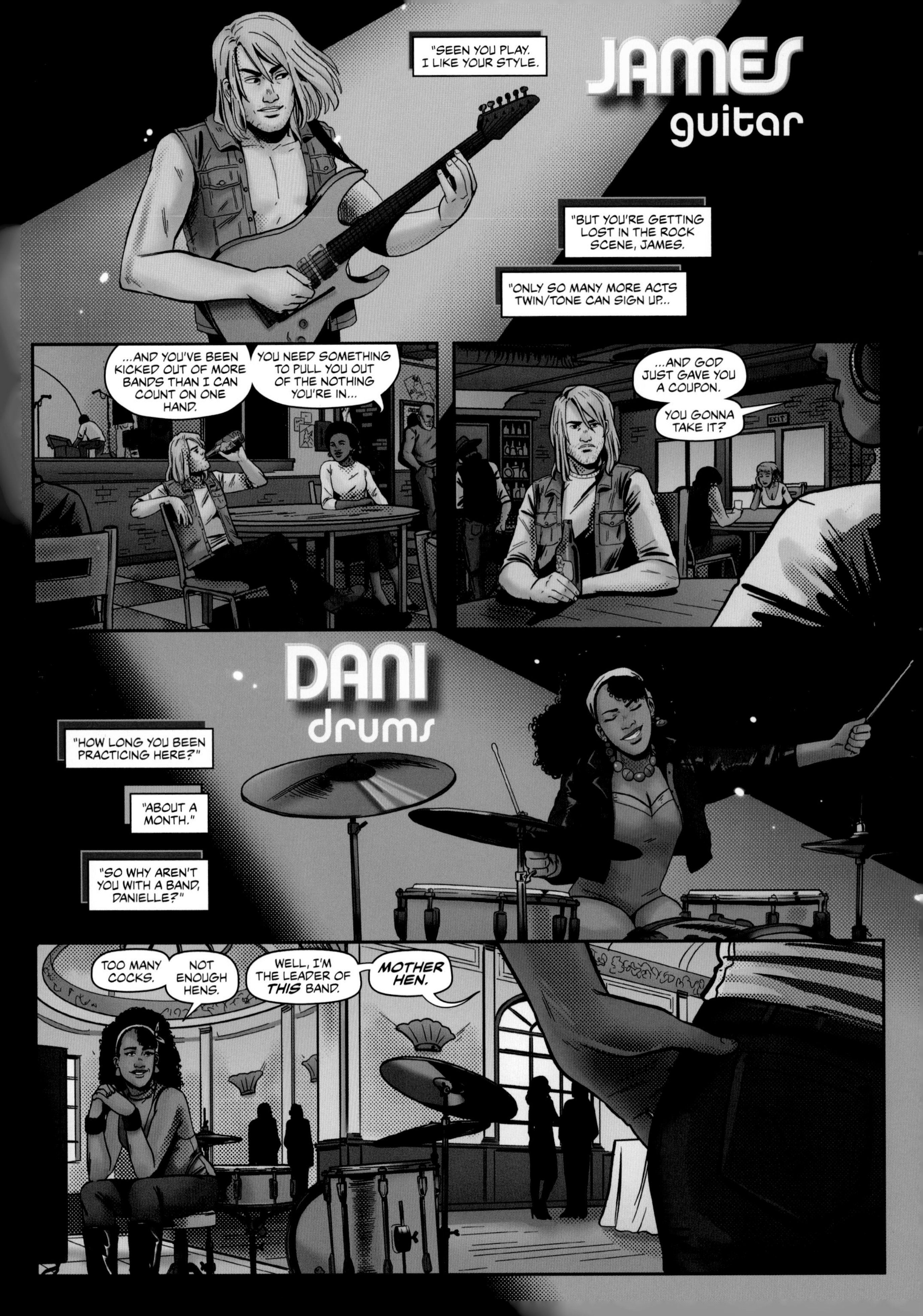
"SEEN YOU PLAY. I LIKE YOUR STYLE.
JAMES
guitar
"BUT YOU'RE GETTING LOST IN THE ROCK SCENE, JAMES.
"ONLY SO MANY MORE ACTS TWIN/TONE CAN SIGN UP...
...AND YOU'VE BEEN KICKED OUT OF MORE BANDS THAN I CAN COUNT ON ONE HAND.
YOU NEED SOMETHING TO PULL YOU OUT OF THE NOTHING YOU'RE IN...
...AND GOD JUST GAVE YOU A COUPON.
YOU GONNA TAKE IT?
EXIT
DANI
drums
"HOW LONG YOU BEEN PRACTICING HERE?"
"ABOUT A MONTH."
"SO WHY AREN'T YOU WITH A BAND, DANIELLE?"
TOO MANY COCKS.
NOT ENOUGH HENS.
WELL, I'M THE LEADER OF *THIS* BAND.
MOTHER HEN.

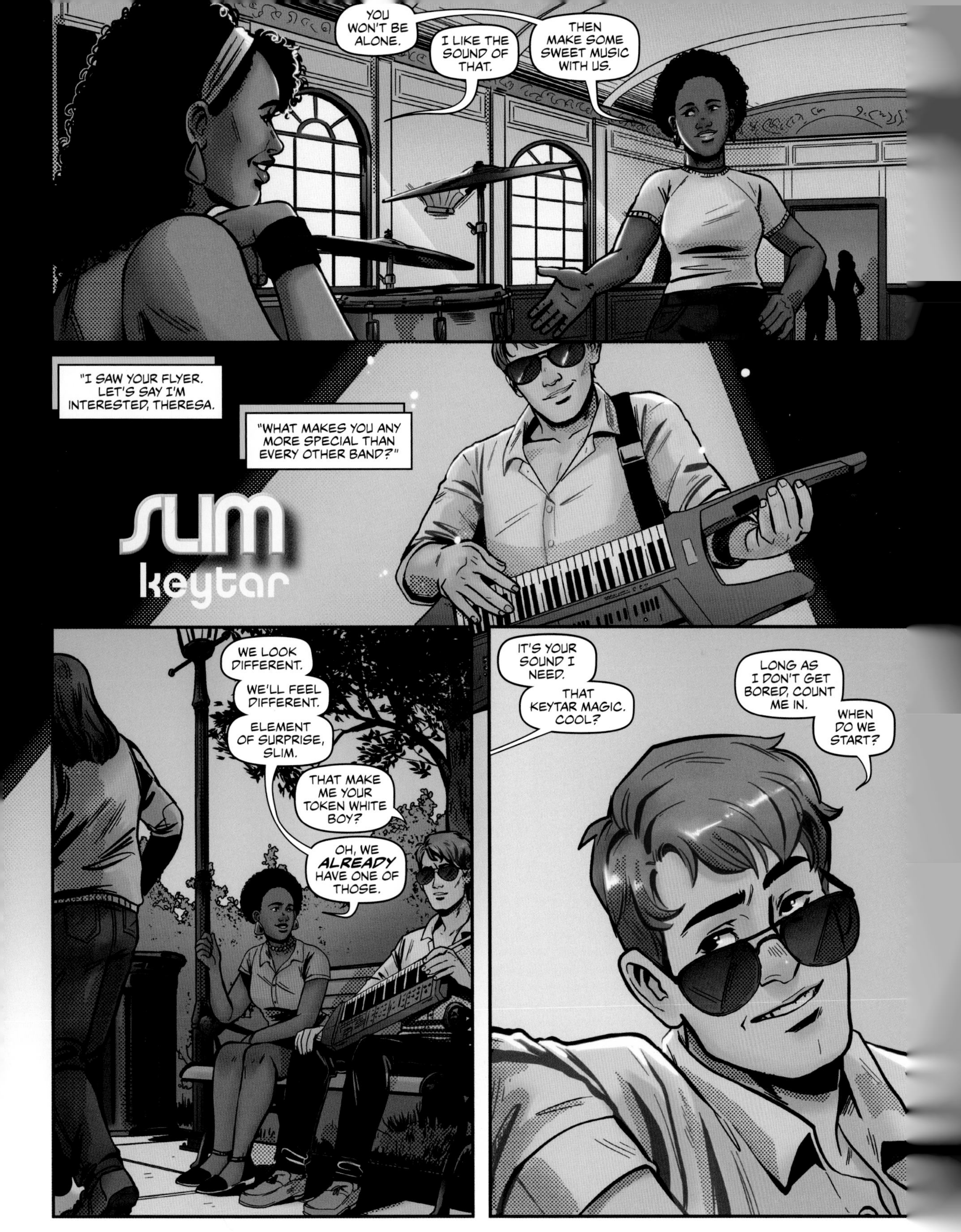
YOU WON'T BE ALONE.
I LIKE THE SOUND OF THAT.
THEN MAKE SOME SWEET MUSIC WITH US.
"I SAW YOUR FLYER. LET'S SAY I'M INTERESTED, THERESA.
"WHAT MAKES YOU ANY MORE SPECIAL THAN EVERY OTHER BAND?"
SLIM
keytar
WE LOOK DIFFERENT.
WE'LL FEEL DIFFERENT.
ELEMENT OF SURPRISE, SLIM.
THAT MAKE ME YOUR TOKEN WHITE BOY?
OH, WE ***ALREADY*** HAVE ONE OF THOSE.
IT'S YOUR SOUND I NEED.
THAT KEYTAR MAGIC. COOL?
LONG AS I DON'T GET BORED, COUNT ME IN.
WHEN DO WE START?

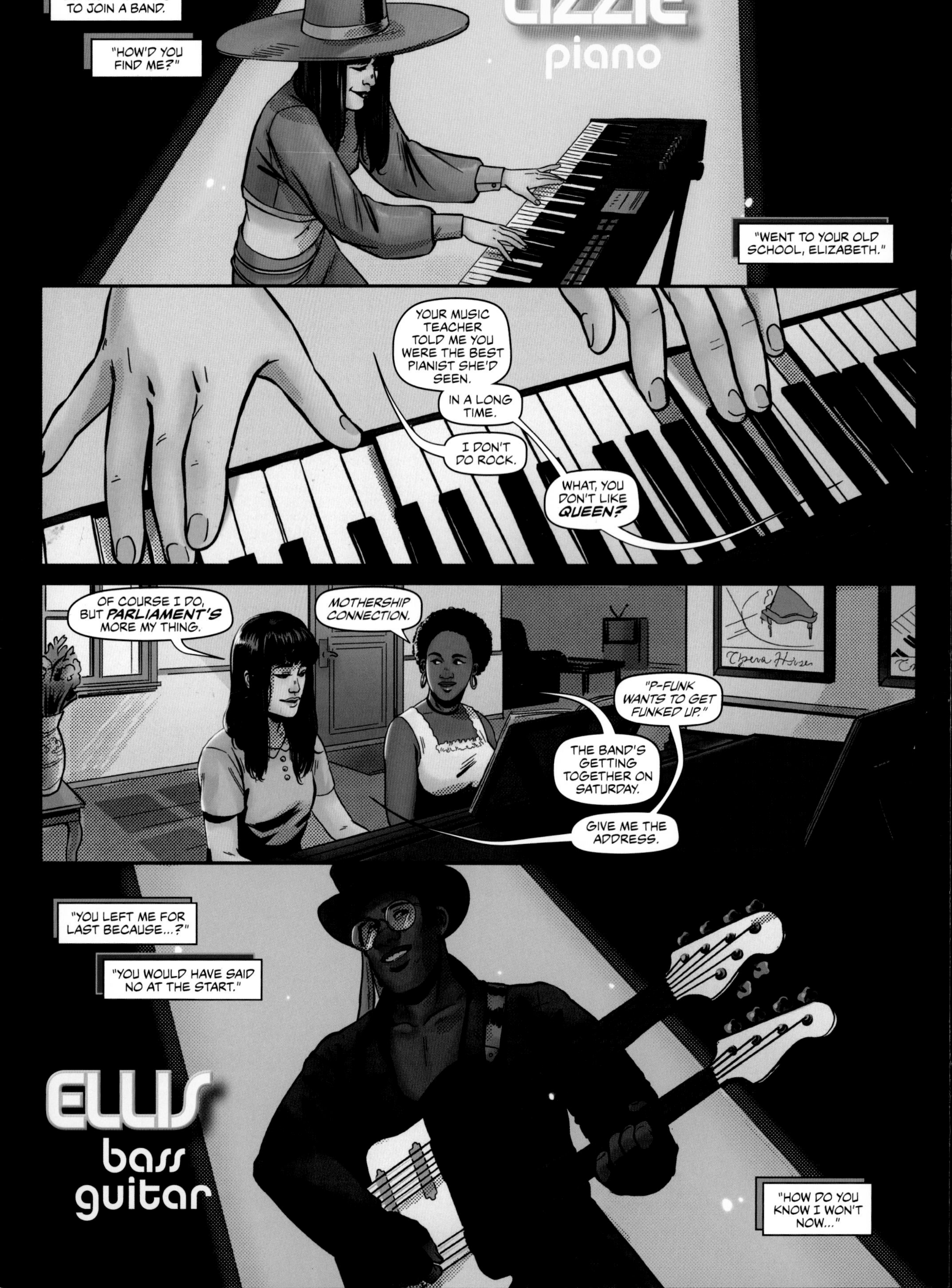
TO JOIN A BAND.
"HOW'D YOU FIND ME?"
LIZZIE
piano
"WENT TO YOUR OLD SCHOOL, ELIZABETH."
YOUR MUSIC TEACHER TOLD ME YOU WERE THE BEST PIANIST SHE'D SEEN.
IN A LONG TIME.
I DON'T DO ROCK.
WHAT, YOU DON'T LIKE QUEEN?
OF COURSE I DO, BUT PARLIAMENT'S MORE MY THING.
MOTHERSHIP CONNECTION.
"P-FUNK WANTS TO GET FUNKED UP."
THE BAND'S GETTING TOGETHER ON SATURDAY.
GIVE ME THE ADDRESS.
"YOU LEFT ME FOR LAST BECAUSE...?"
"YOU WOULD HAVE SAID NO AT THE START."
ELLIS
bass guitar
"HOW DO YOU KNOW I WON'T NOW..."

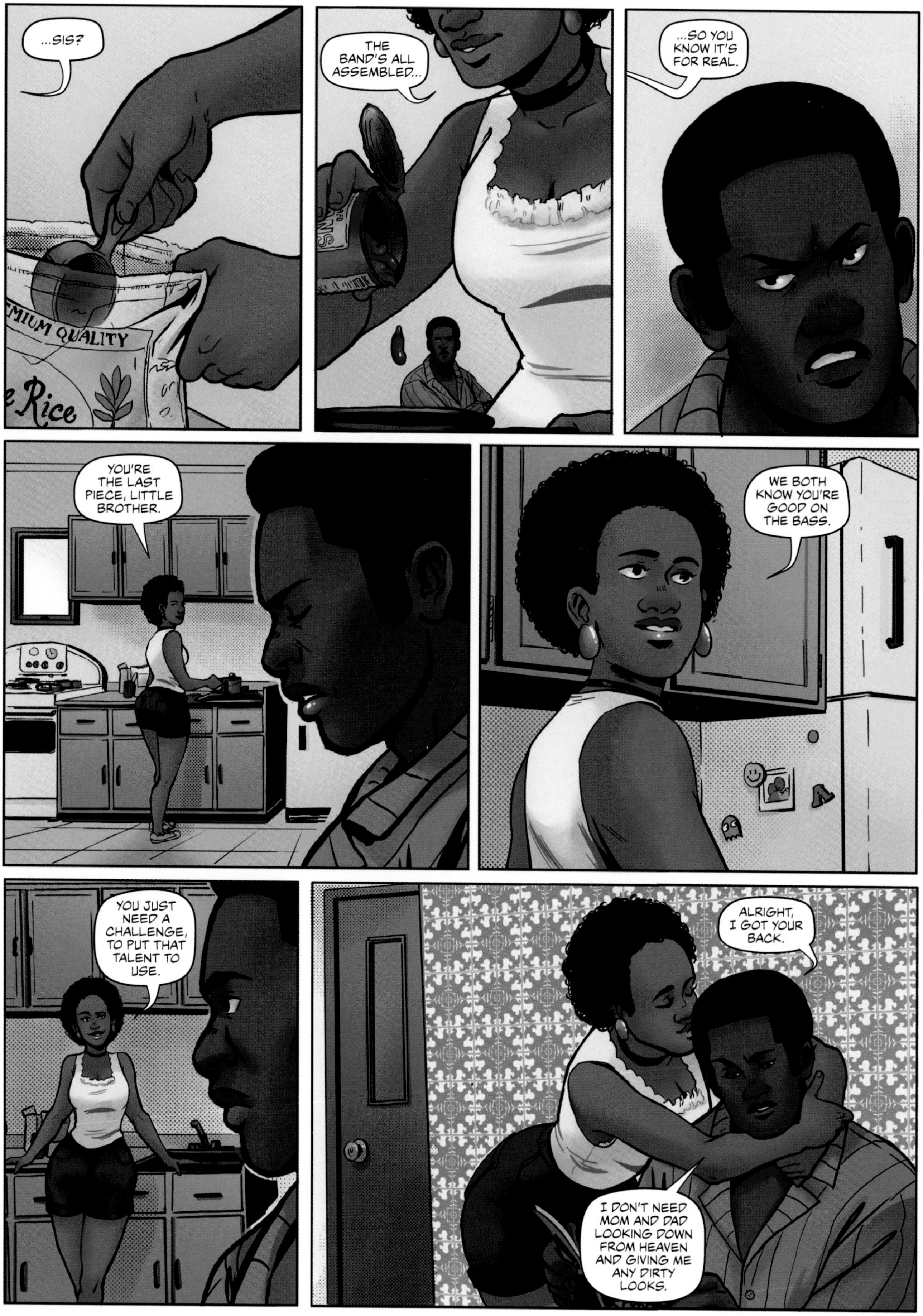
...SIS?
THE BAND'S ALL ASSEMBLED...
...SO YOU KNOW IT'S FOR REAL.
YOU'RE THE LAST PIECE, LITTLE BROTHER.
WE BOTH KNOW YOU'RE GOOD ON THE BASS.
YOU JUST NEED A CHALLENGE, TO PUT THAT TALENT TO USE.
ALRIGHT, I GOT YOUR BACK.
I DON'T NEED MOM AND DAD LOOKING DOWN FROM HEAVEN AND GIVING ME ANY DIRTY LOOKS.

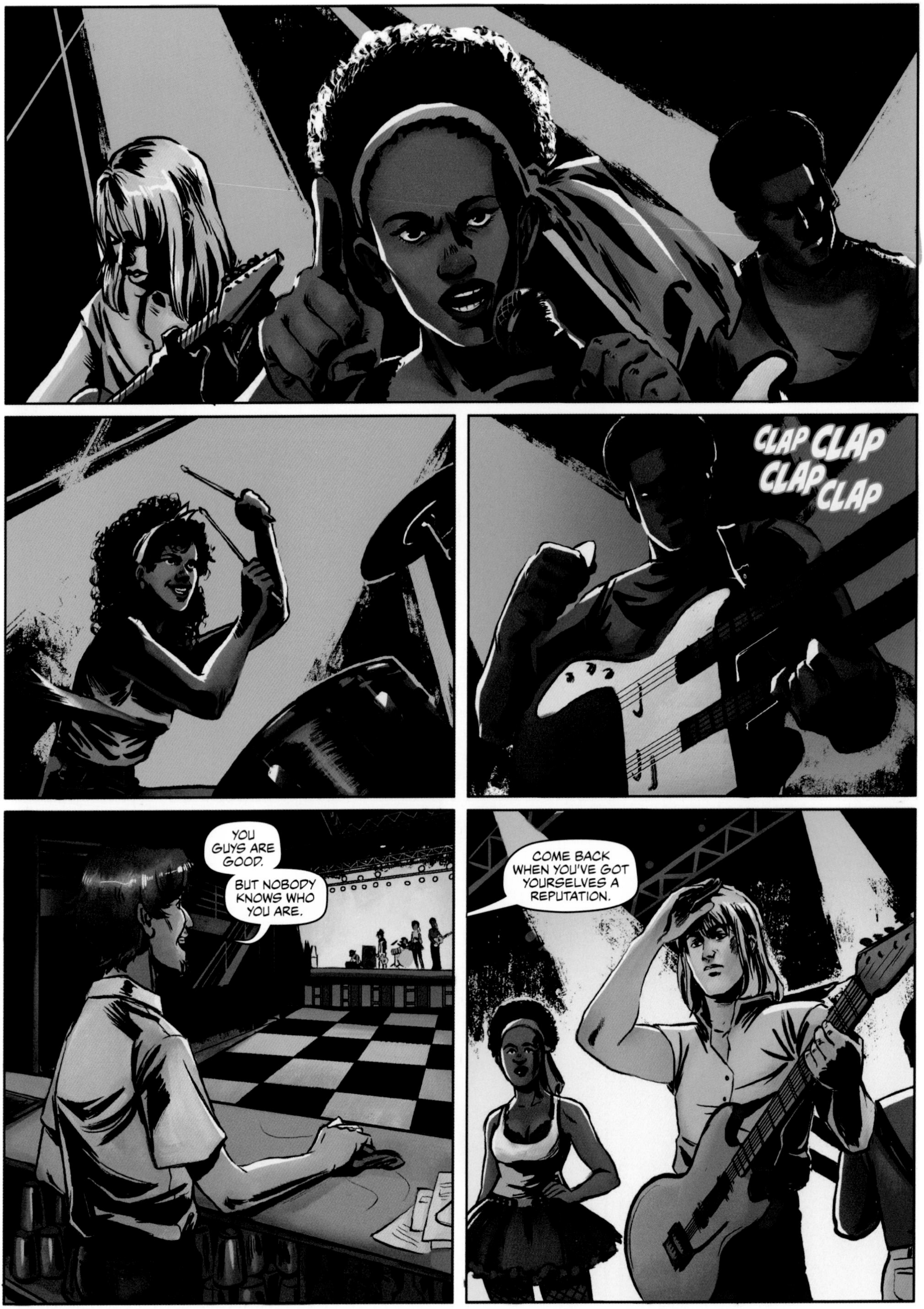
CLAP CLAP
CLAP CLAP
YOU GUYS ARE GOOD.
BUT NOBODY KNOWS WHO YOU ARE.
COME BACK WHEN YOU'VE GOT YOURSELVES A REPUTATION.

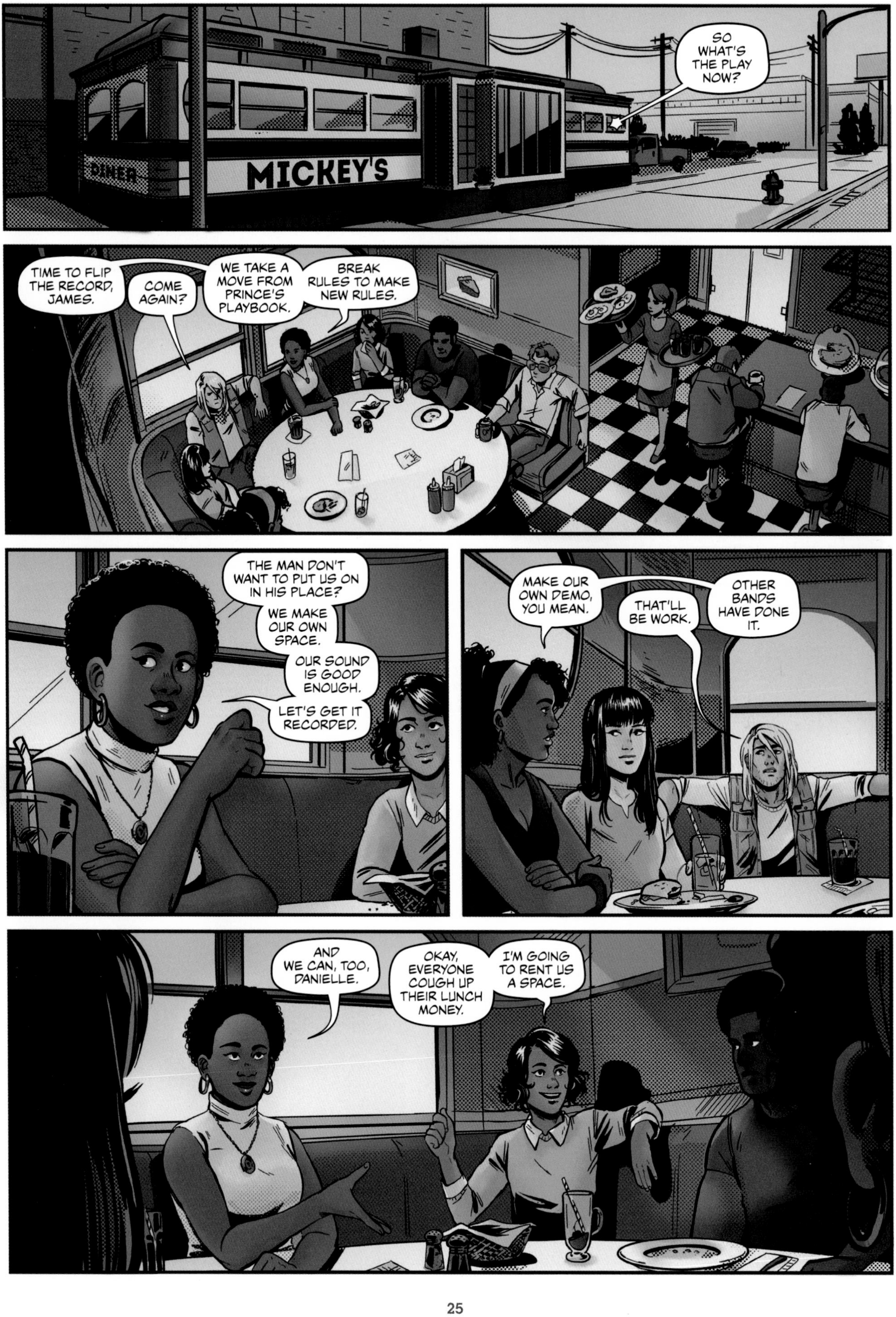
DINER
MICKEY'S
SO WHAT'S THE PLAY NOW?
TIME TO FLIP THE RECORD, JAMES.
COME AGAIN?
WE TAKE A MOVE FROM PRINCE'S PLAYBOOK.
BREAK RULES TO MAKE NEW RULES.
THE MAN DON'T WANT TO PUT US ON IN HIS PLACE?
WE MAKE OUR OWN SPACE.
OUR SOUND IS GOOD ENOUGH.
LET'S GET IT RECORDED.
MAKE OUR OWN DEMO, YOU MEAN.
THAT'LL BE WORK.
OTHER BANDS HAVE DONE IT.
AND WE CAN, TOO, DANIELLE.
OKAY, EVERYONE COUGH UP THEIR LUNCH MONEY.
I'M GOING TO RENT US A SPACE.

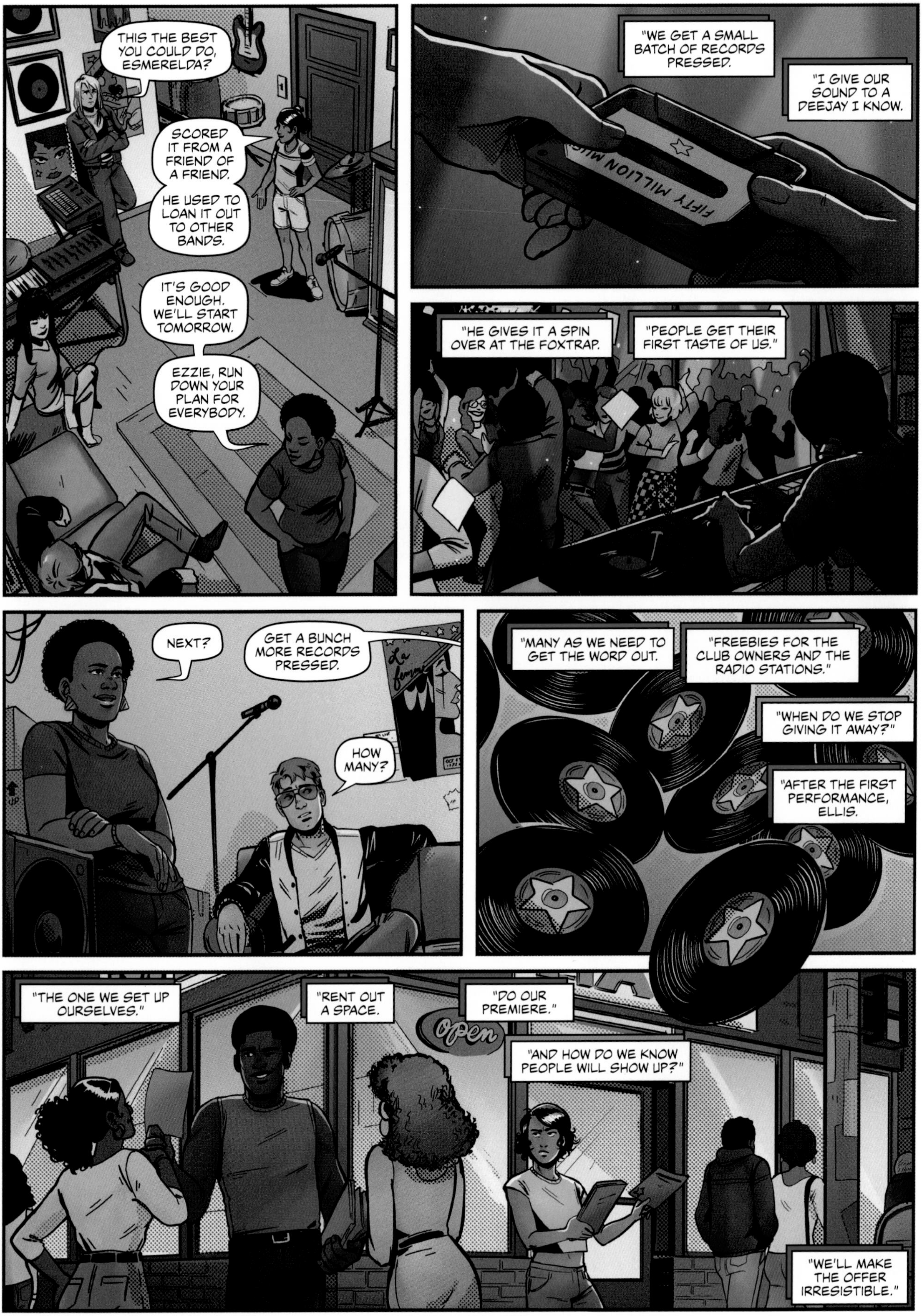
THIS THE BEST YOU COULD DO, ESMERELDA?
SCORED IT FROM A FRIEND OF A FRIEND.
HE USED TO LOAN IT OUT TO OTHER BANDS.
IT'S GOOD ENOUGH. WE'LL START TOMORROW.
EZZIE, RUN DOWN YOUR PLAN FOR EVERYBODY.
"WE GET A SMALL BATCH OF RECORDS PRESSED.
FIFTY MILLION
"I GIVE OUR SOUND TO A DEEJAY I KNOW.
"HE GIVES IT A SPIN OVER AT THE FOXTRAP.
"PEOPLE GET THEIR FIRST TASTE OF US."
NEXT?
GET A BUNCH MORE RECORDS PRESSED.
HOW MANY?
"MANY AS WE NEED TO GET THE WORD OUT.
"FREEBIES FOR THE CLUB OWNERS AND THE RADIO STATIONS."
"WHEN DO WE STOP GIVING IT AWAY?"
"AFTER THE FIRST PERFORMANCE, ELLIS.
"THE ONE WE SET UP OURSELVES."
"RENT OUT A SPACE.
"DO OUR PREMIERE."
Open
"AND HOW DO WE KNOW PEOPLE WILL SHOW UP?"
"WE'LL MAKE THE OFFER IRRESISTIBLE."

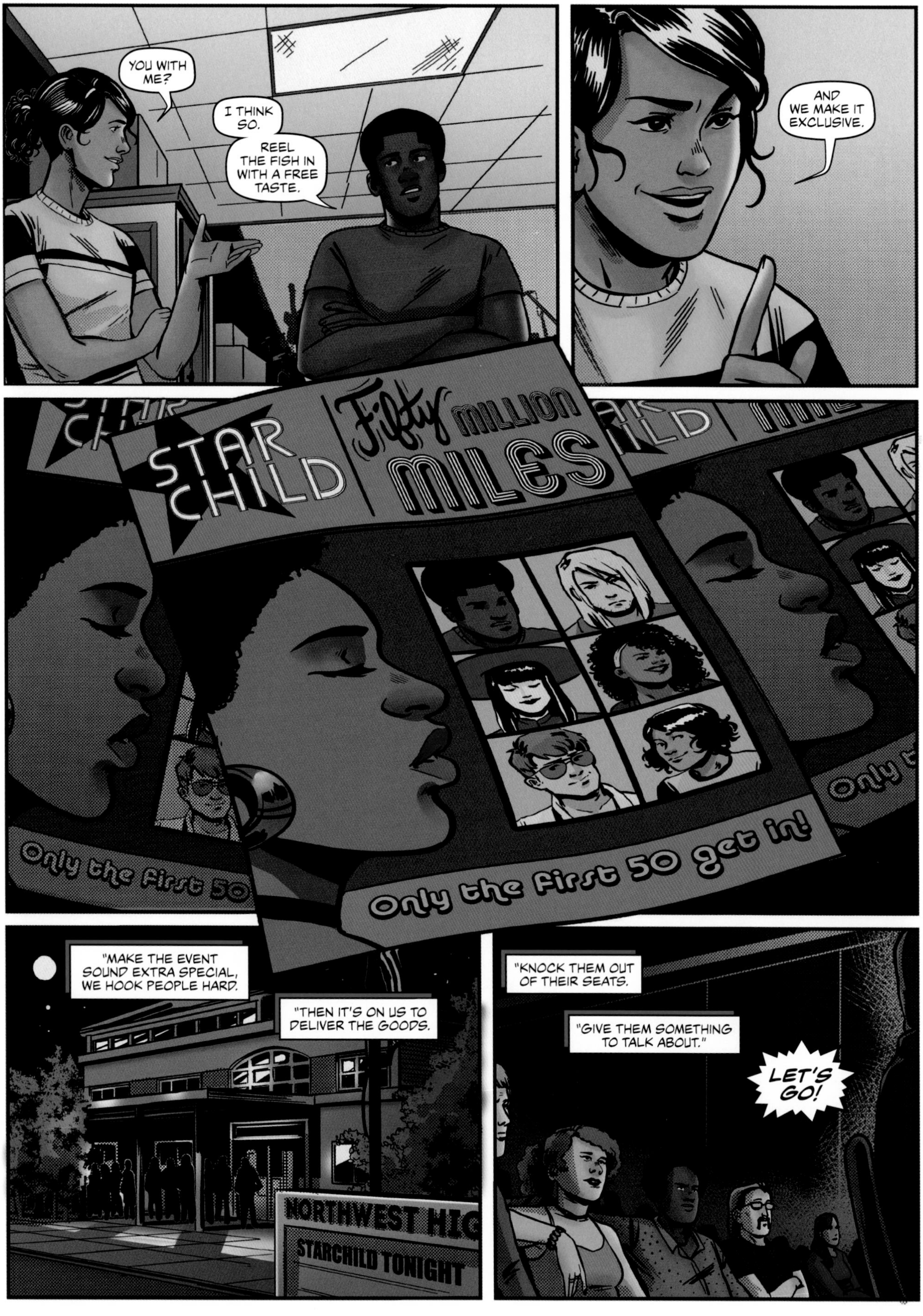
YOU WITH ME?
I THINK SO.
REEL THE FISH IN WITH A FREE TASTE.
AND WE MAKE IT EXCLUSIVE.
STAR CHILD
Fifty MILLION MILES
Only the first 50 get in!
"MAKE THE EVENT SOUND EXTRA SPECIAL, WE HOOK PEOPLE HARD.
"THEN IT'S ON US TO DELIVER THE GOODS.
NORTHWEST HIG
STARCHILD TONIGHT
"KNOCK THEM OUT OF THEIR SEATS.
"GIVE THEM SOMETHING TO TALK ABOUT."
LET'S GO!

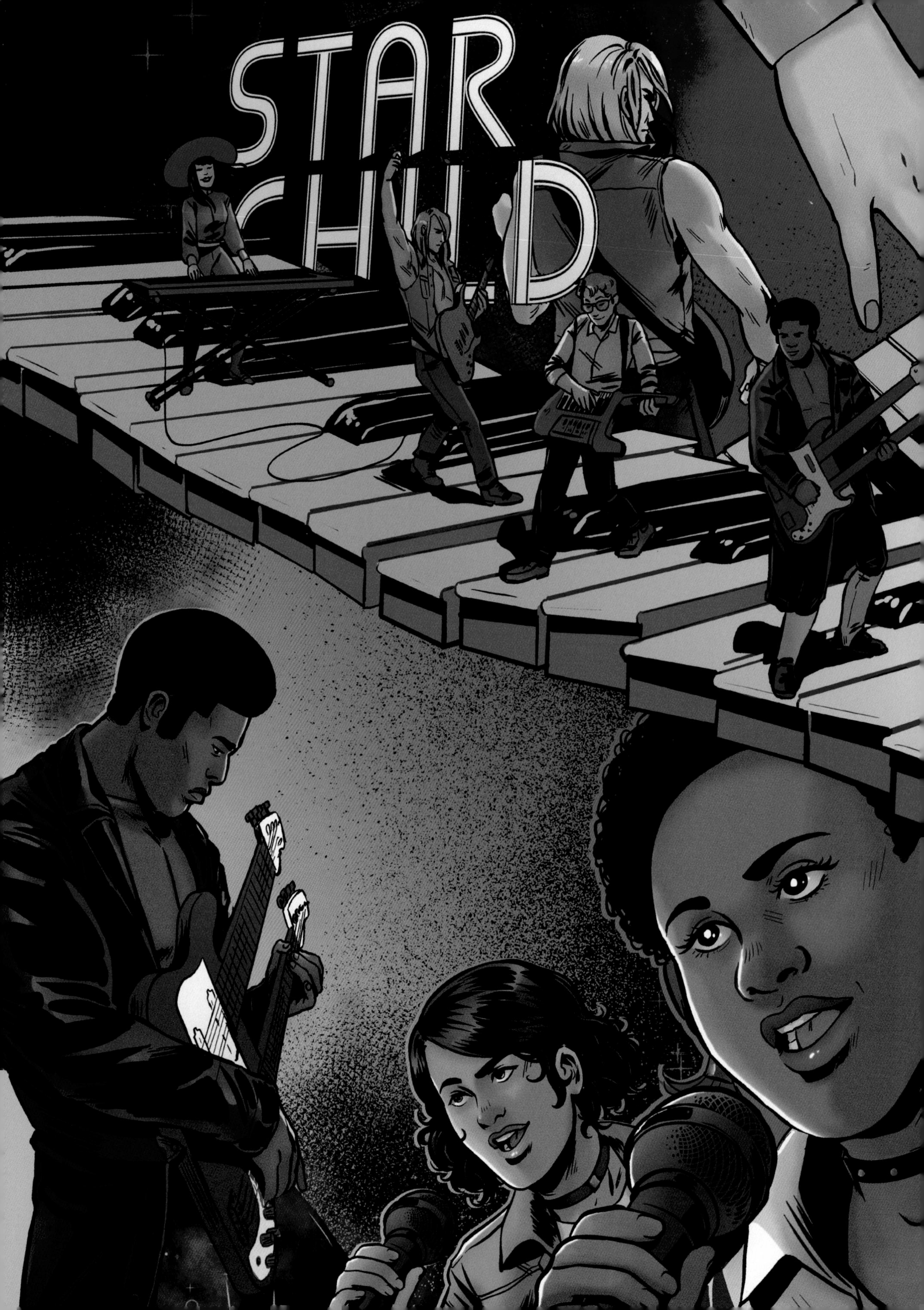
STAR
CHILD

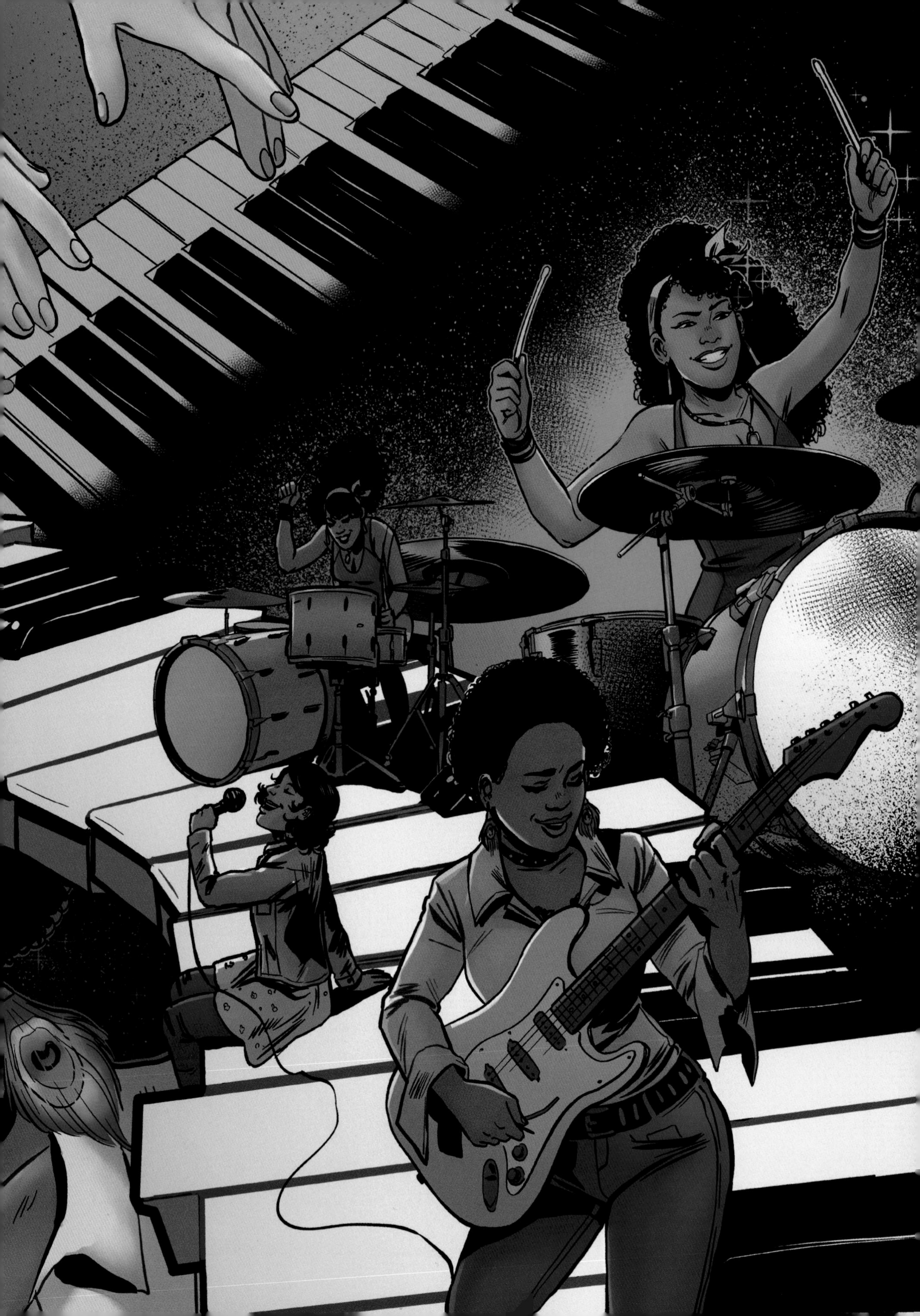

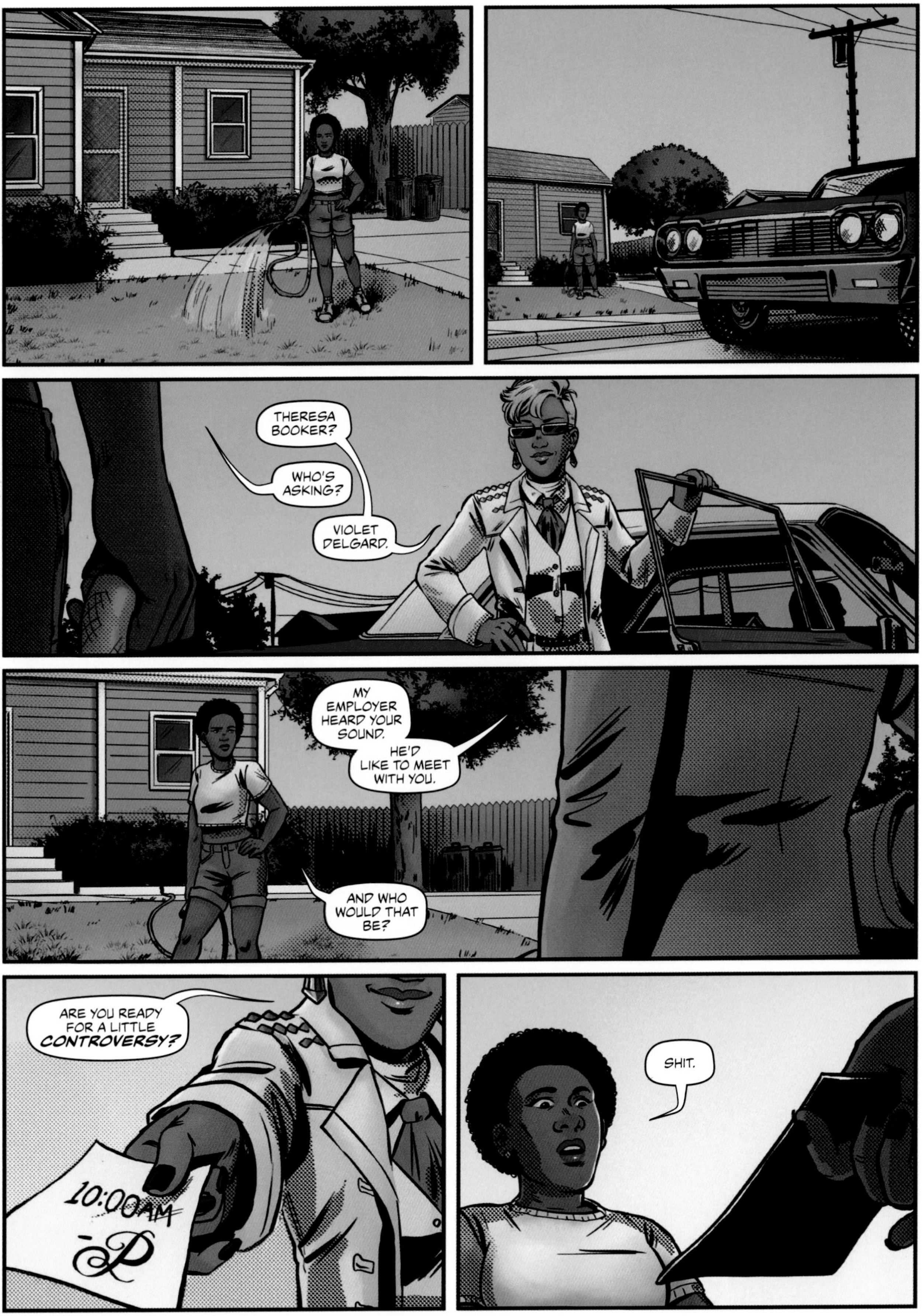

THERESA BOOKER?
WHO'S ASKING?
VIOLET DELGARD.
MY EMPLOYER HEARD YOUR SOUND.
HE'D LIKE TO MEET WITH YOU.
AND WHO WOULD THAT BE?
ARE YOU READY FOR A LITTLE CONTROVERSY?
10:00AM -P
SHIT.

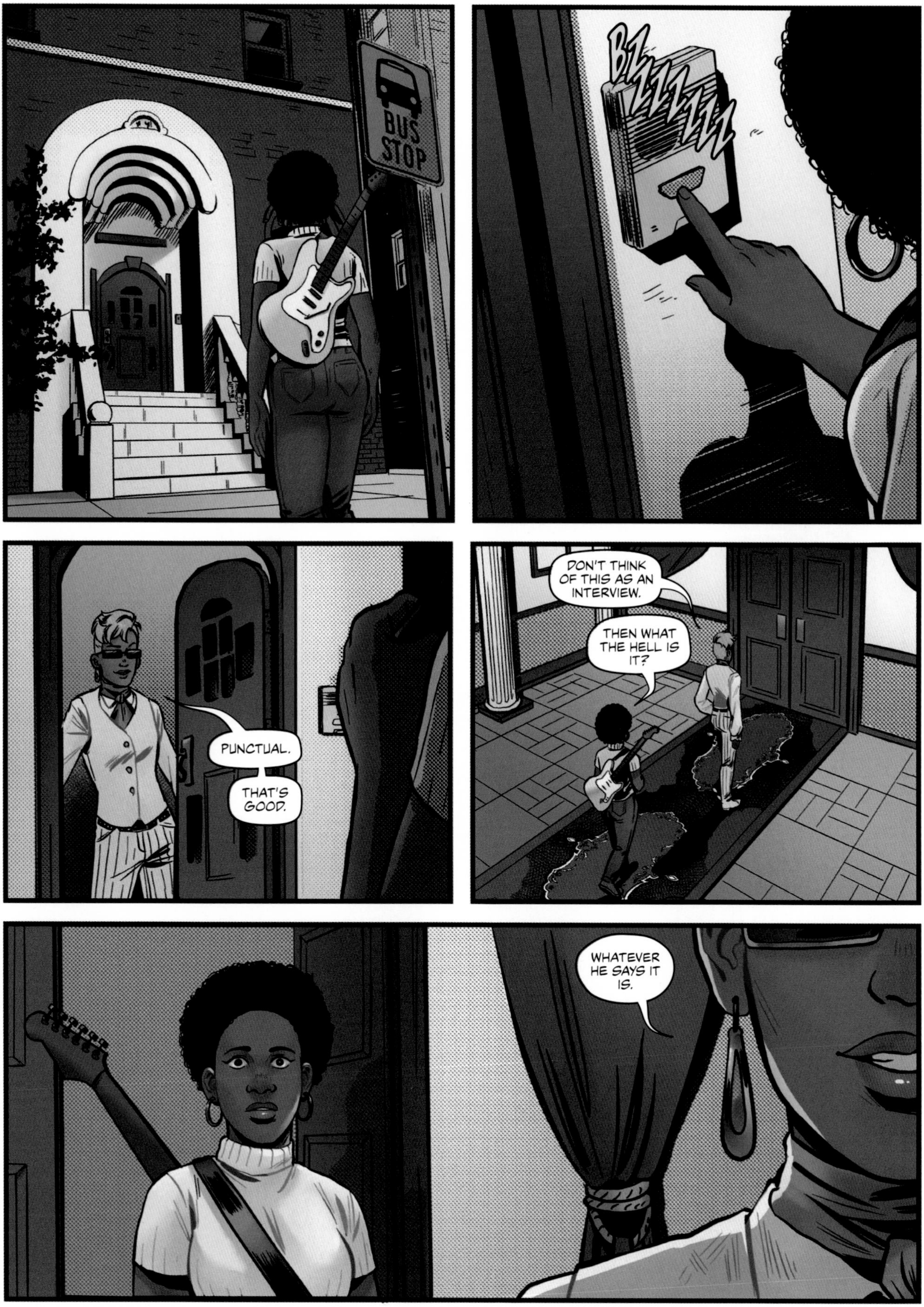
BUS STOP
BZZZZZZZ
PUNCTUAL.
THAT'S GOOD.
DON'T THINK OF THIS AS AN INTERVIEW.
THEN WHAT THE HELL IS IT?
WHATEVER HE SAYS IT IS.

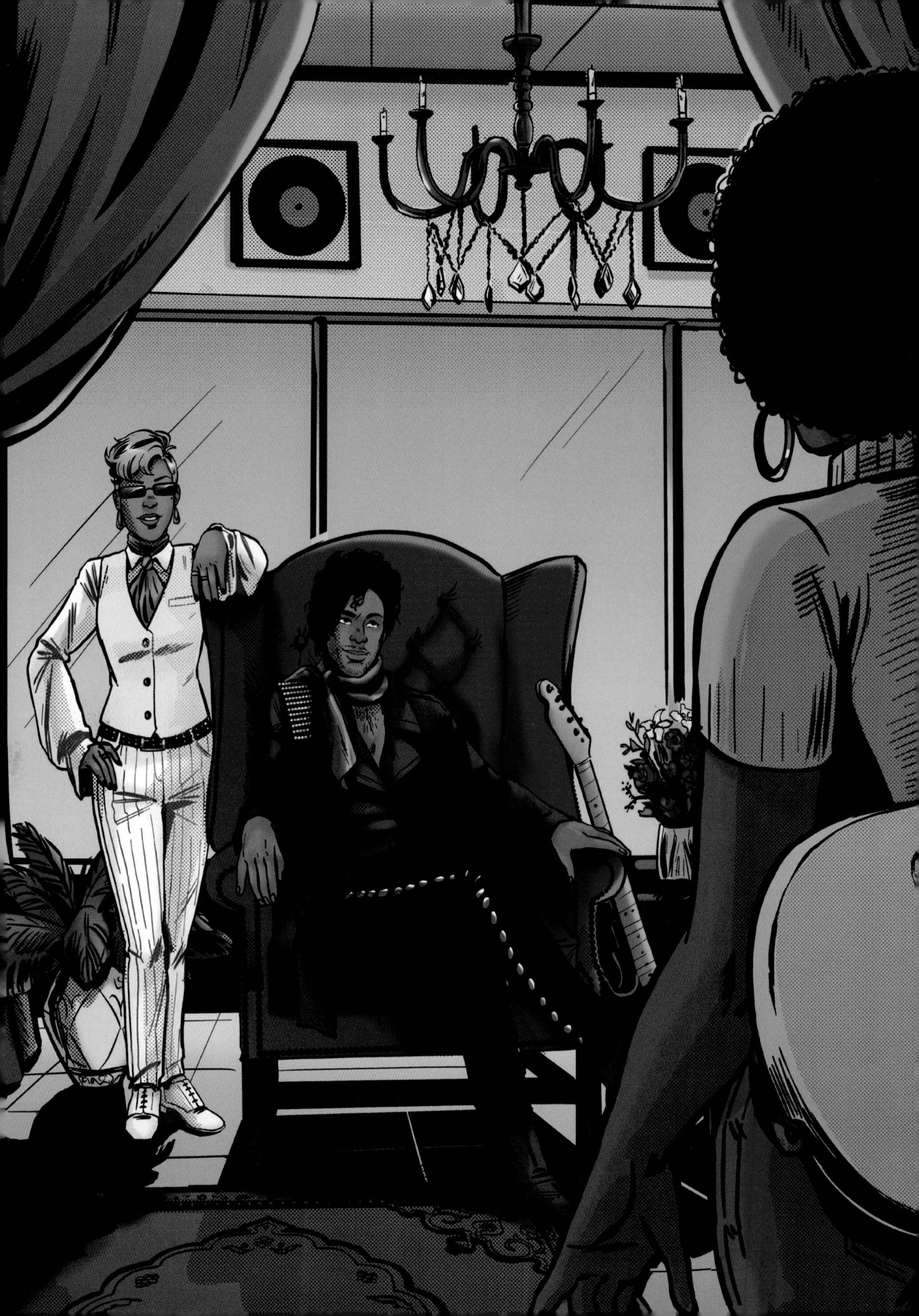

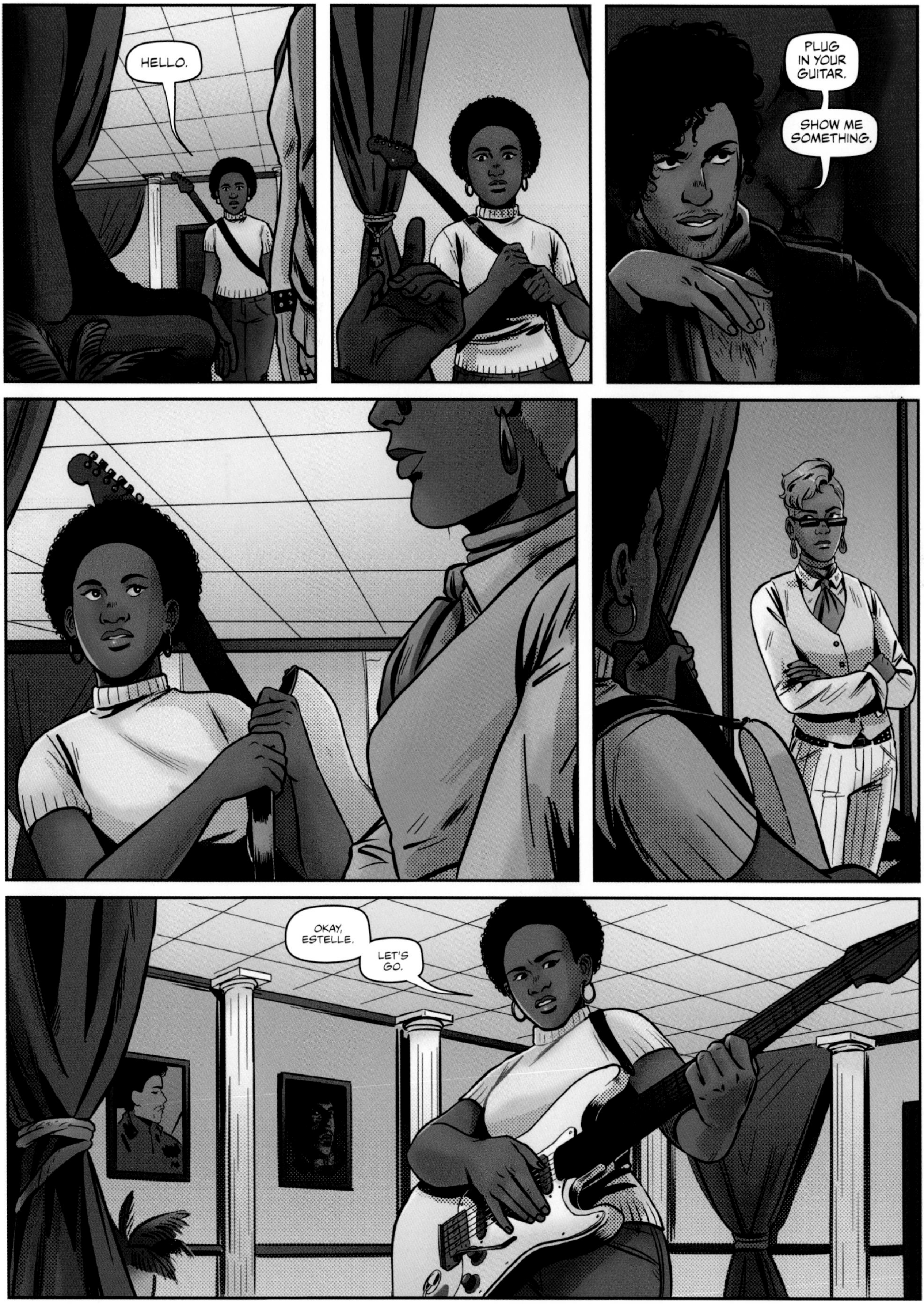
HELLO.
PLUG IN YOUR GUITAR.
SHOW ME SOMETHING.
OKAY, ESTELLE.
LET'S GO.

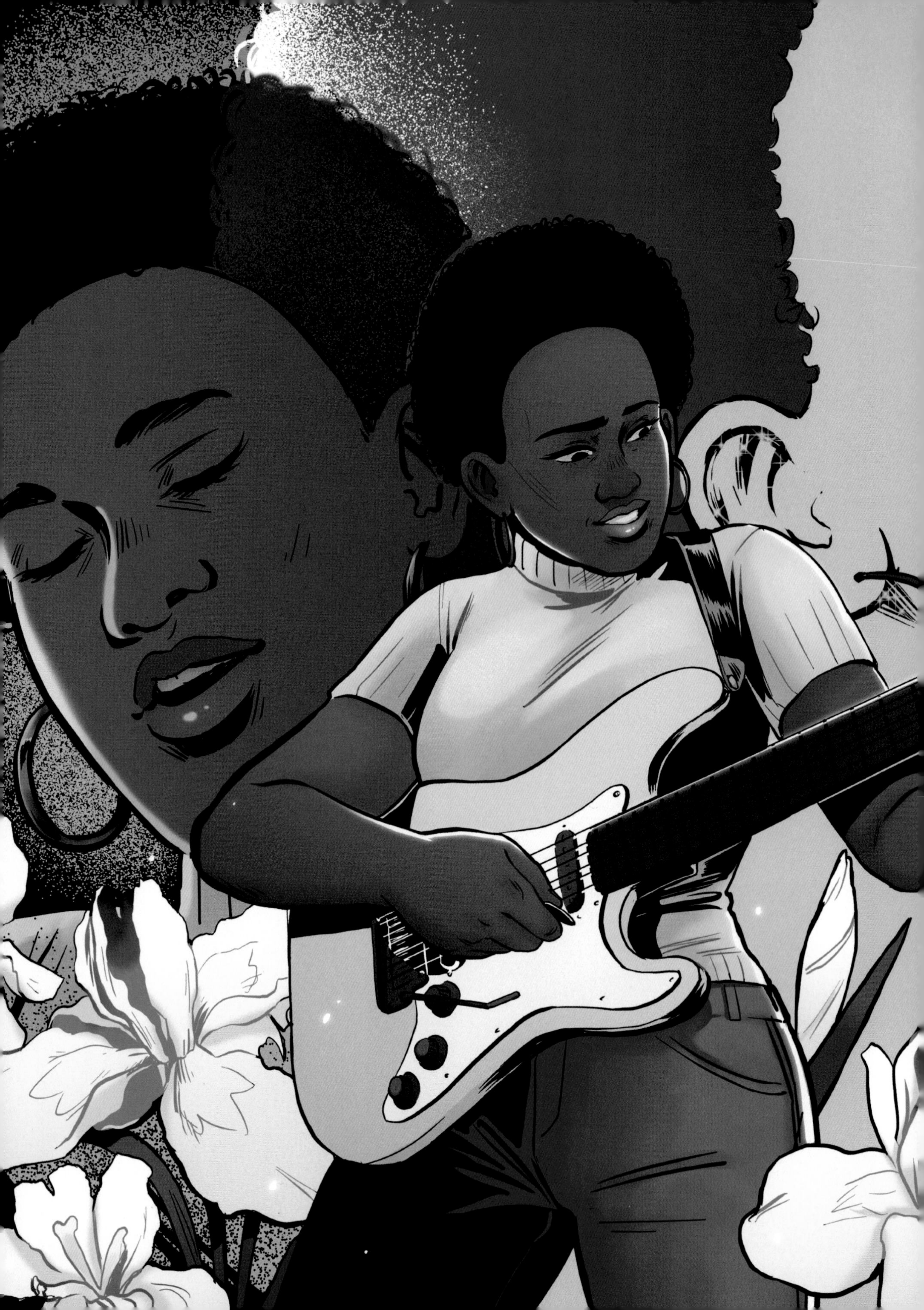

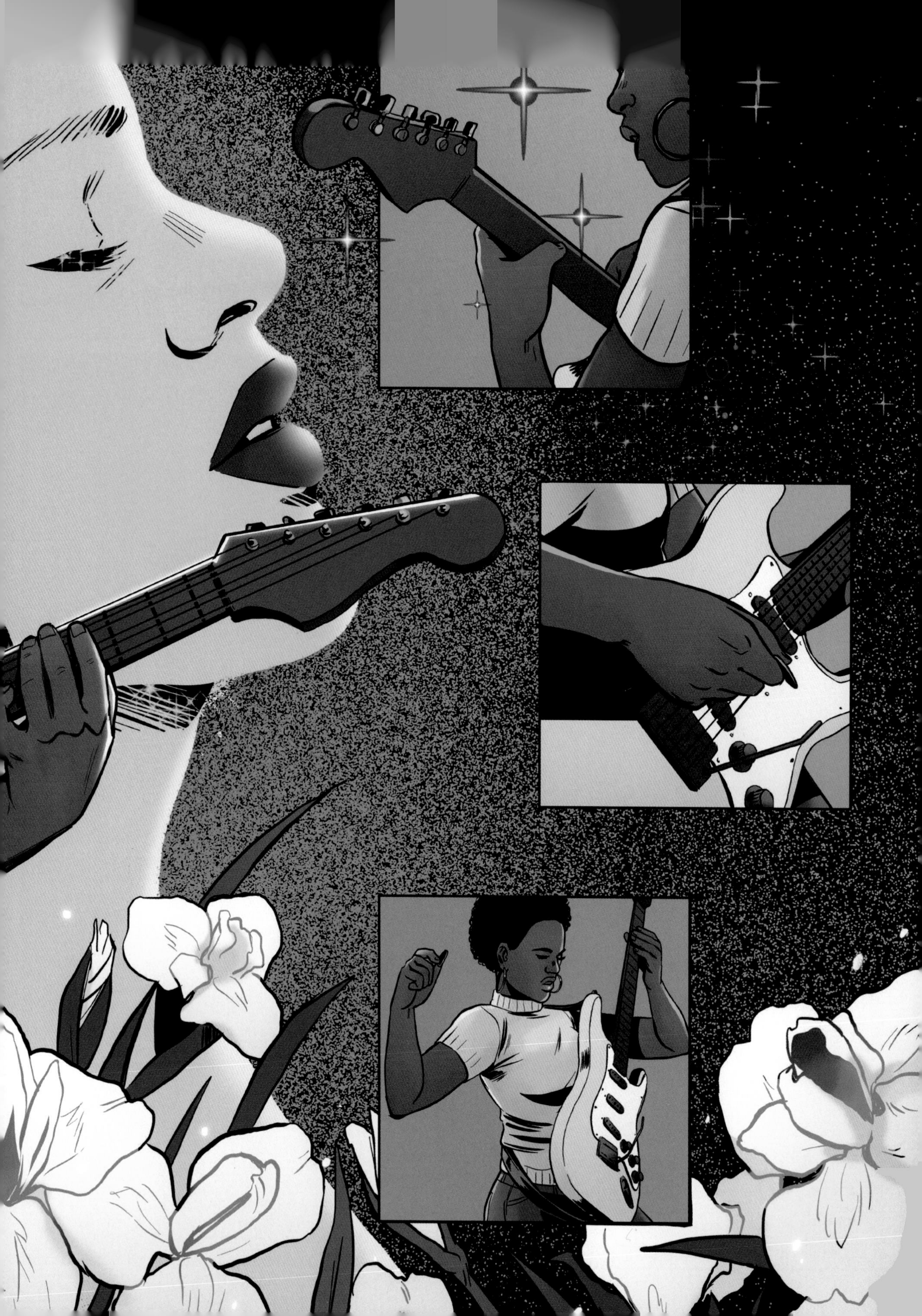

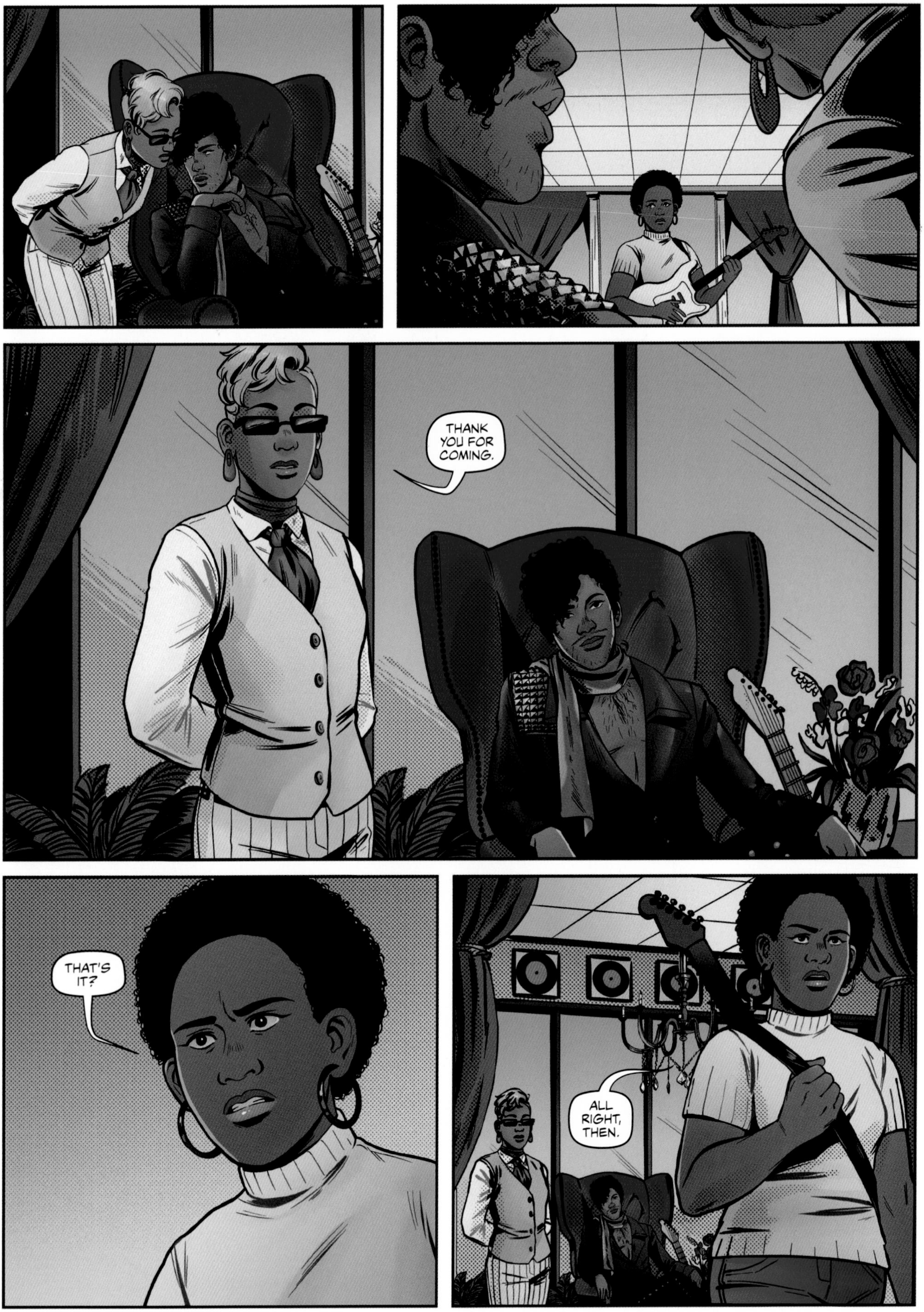
THANK YOU FOR COMING.
THAT'S IT?
ALL RIGHT, THEN.

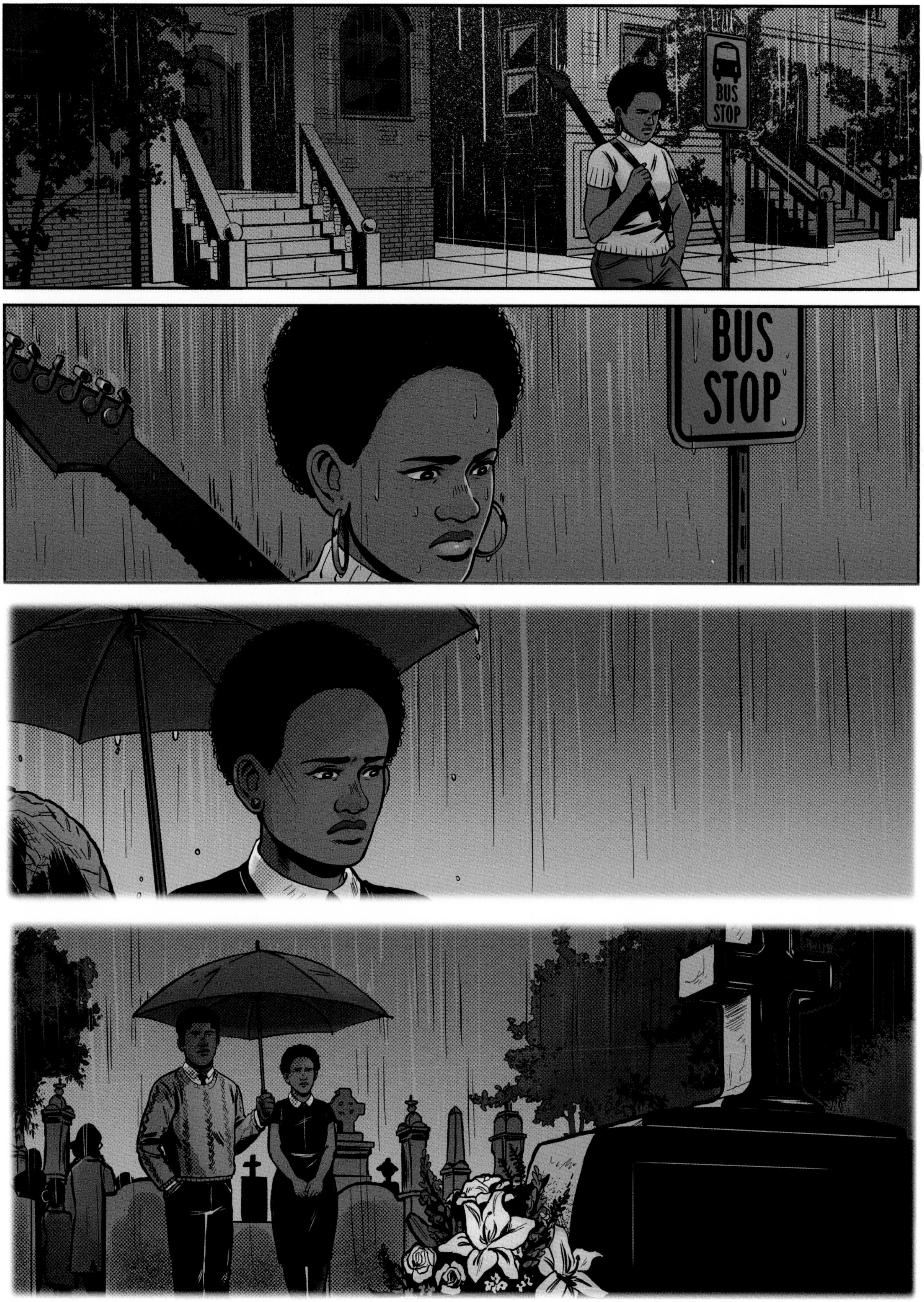
BUS STOP
BUS STOP

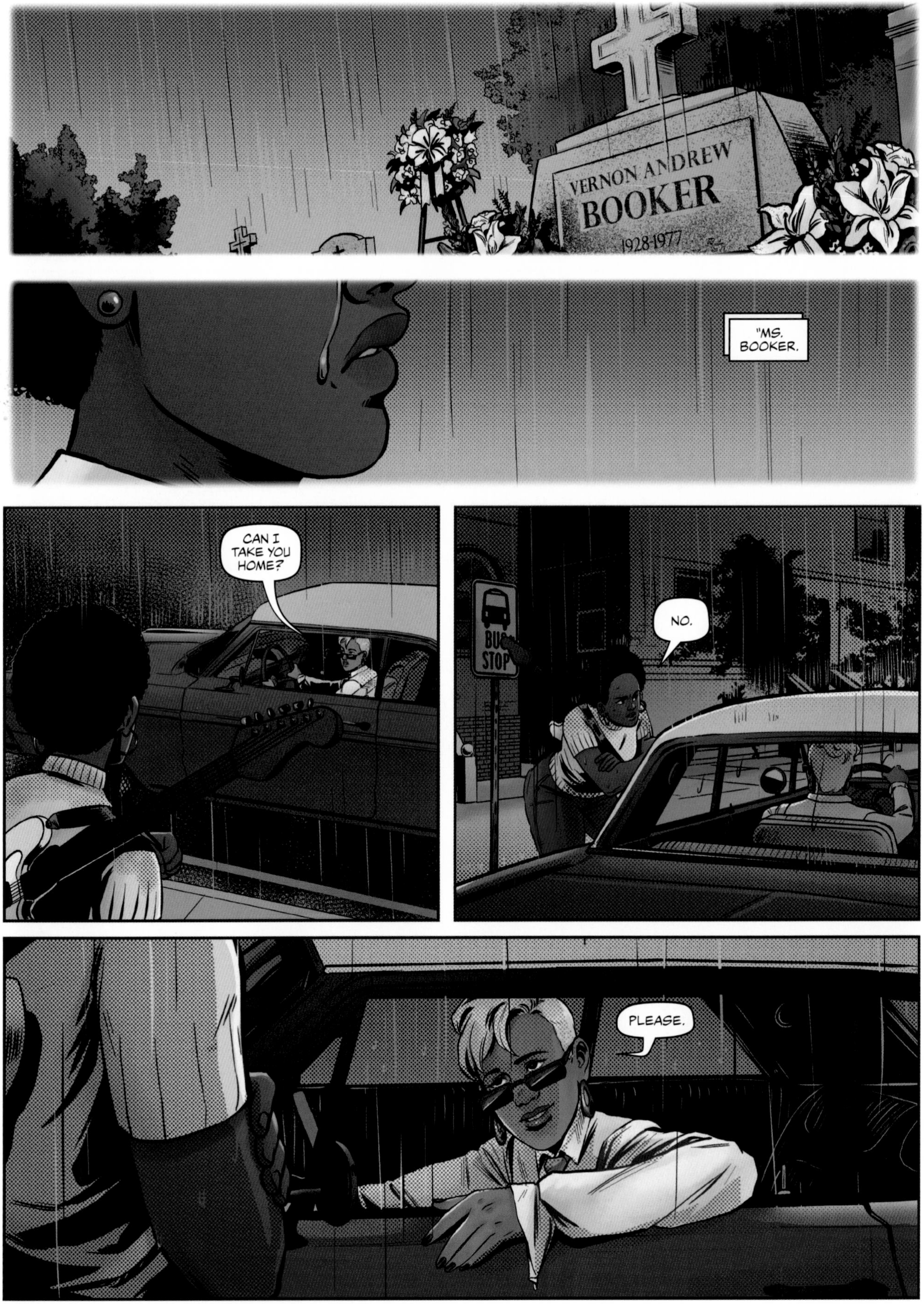
VERNON ANDREW
BOOKER
1928-1977
"MS. BOOKER.
CAN I TAKE YOU HOME?
STOP
NO.
PLEASE.

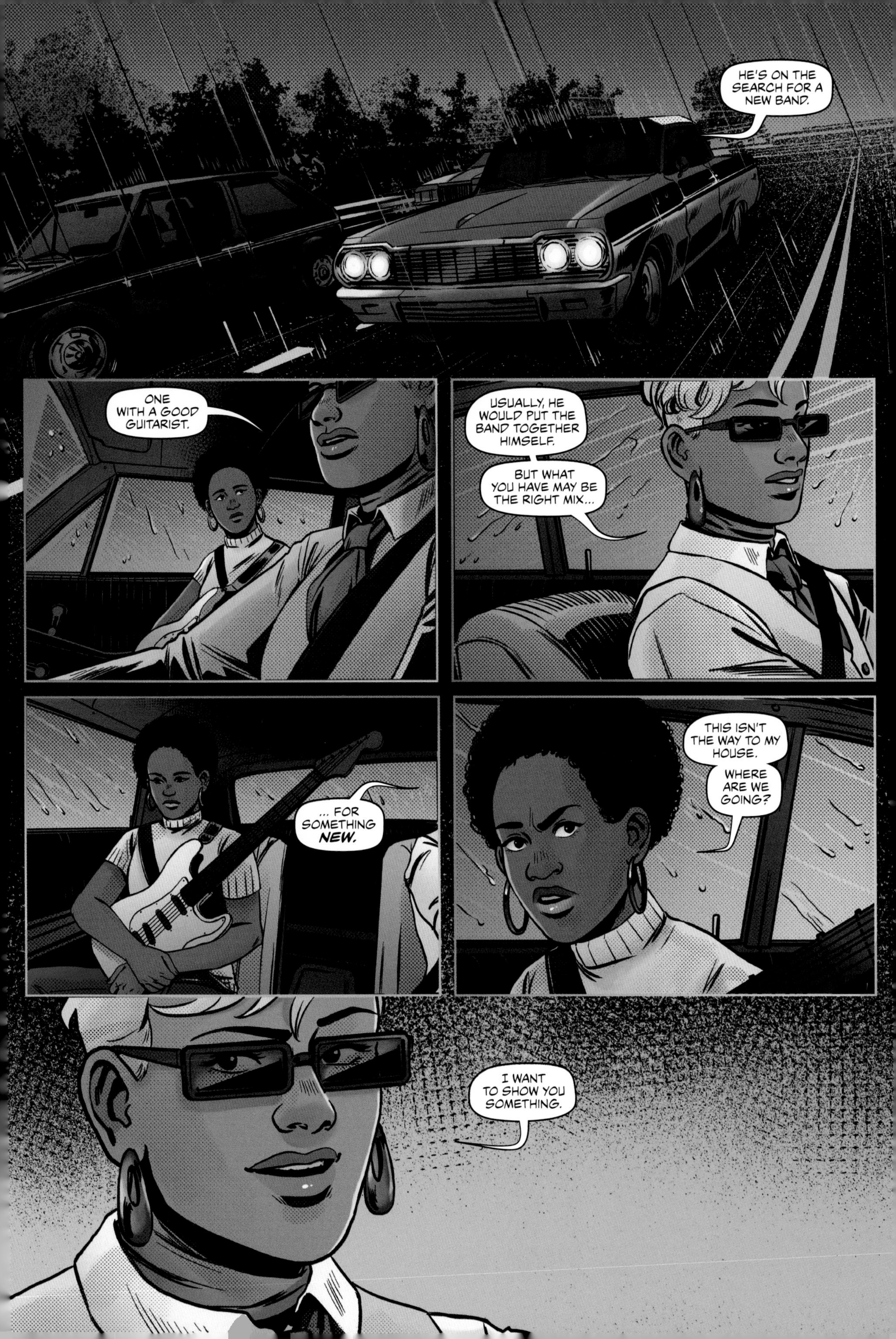
HE'S ON THE SEARCH FOR A NEW BAND.
ONE WITH A GOOD GUITARIST.
USUALLY, HE WOULD PUT THE BAND TOGETHER HIMSELF.
BUT WHAT YOU HAVE MAY BE THE RIGHT MIX...
... FOR SOMETHING *NEW.*
THIS ISN'T THE WAY TO MY HOUSE.
WHERE ARE WE GOING?
I WANT TO SHOW YOU SOMETHING.

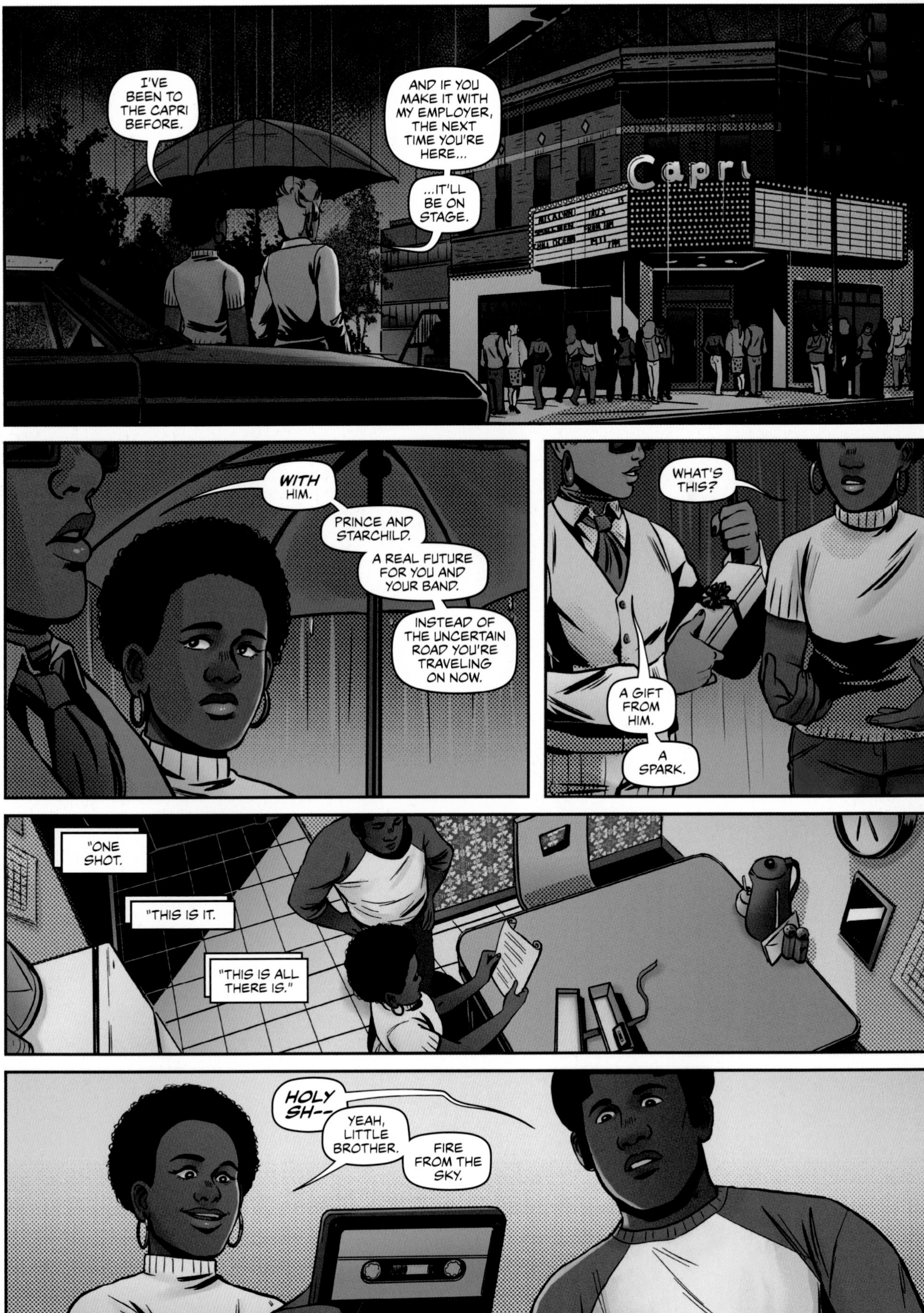
I'VE BEEN TO THE CAPRI BEFORE.
AND IF YOU MAKE IT WITH MY EMPLOYER, THE NEXT TIME YOU'RE HERE...
...IT'LL BE ON STAGE.
Capri
WITH HIM.
PRINCE AND STARCHILD.
A REAL FUTURE FOR YOU AND YOUR BAND.
INSTEAD OF THE UNCERTAIN ROAD YOU'RE TRAVELING ON NOW.
WHAT'S THIS?
A GIFT FROM HIM.
A SPARK.
"ONE SHOT.
"THIS IS IT.
"THIS IS ALL THERE IS."
HOLY SH--
YEAH, LITTLE BROTHER.
FIRE FROM THE SKY.

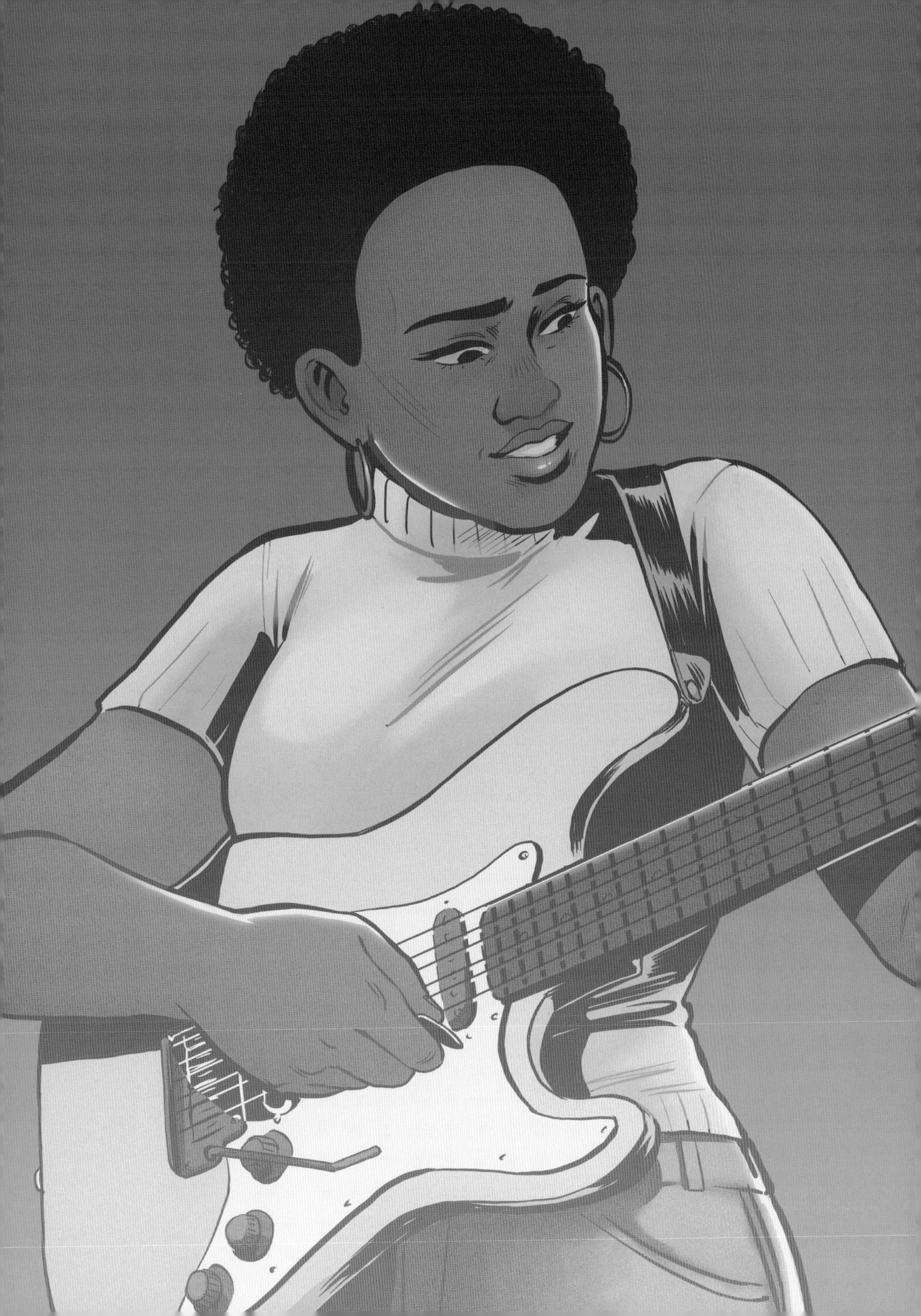

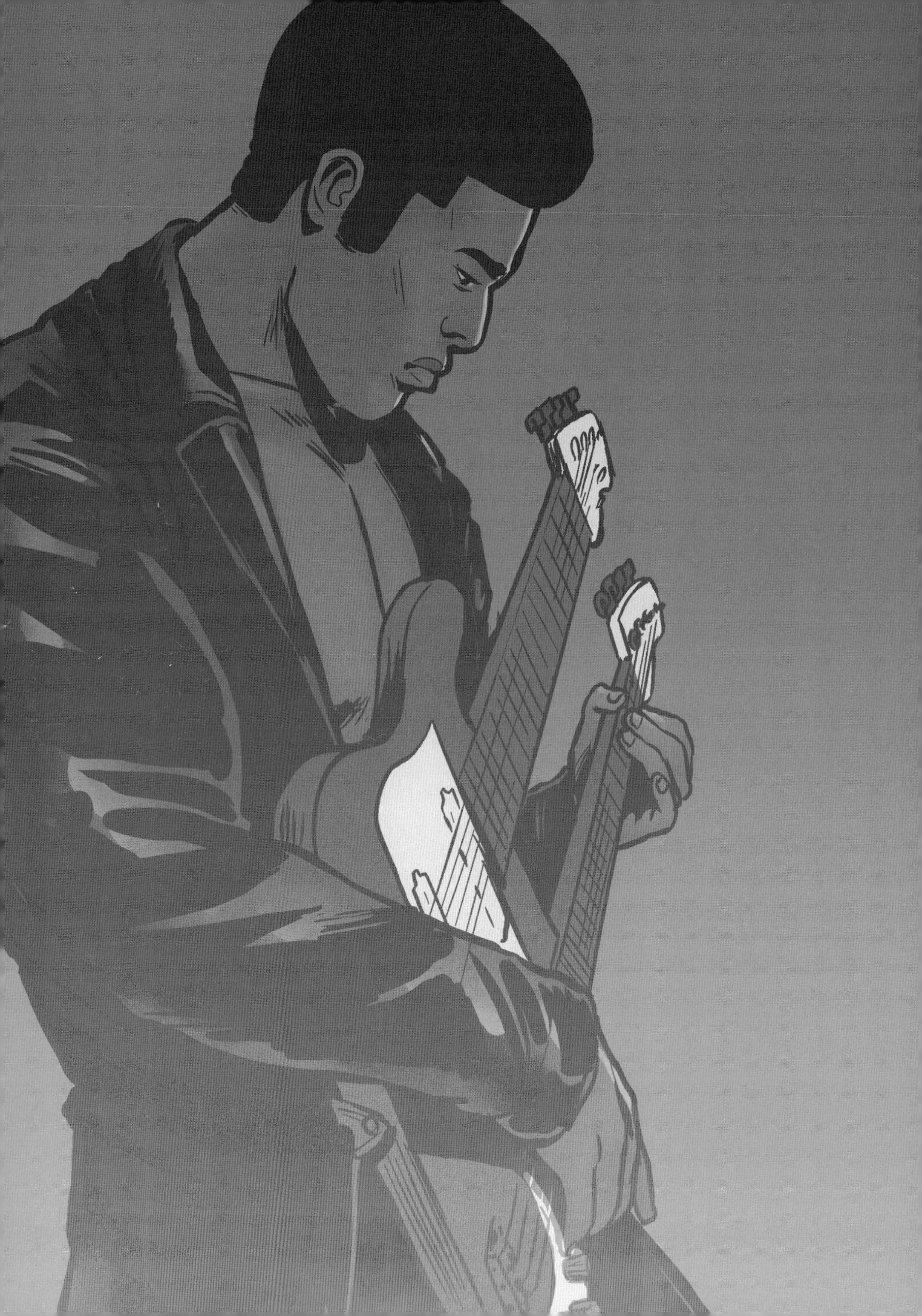

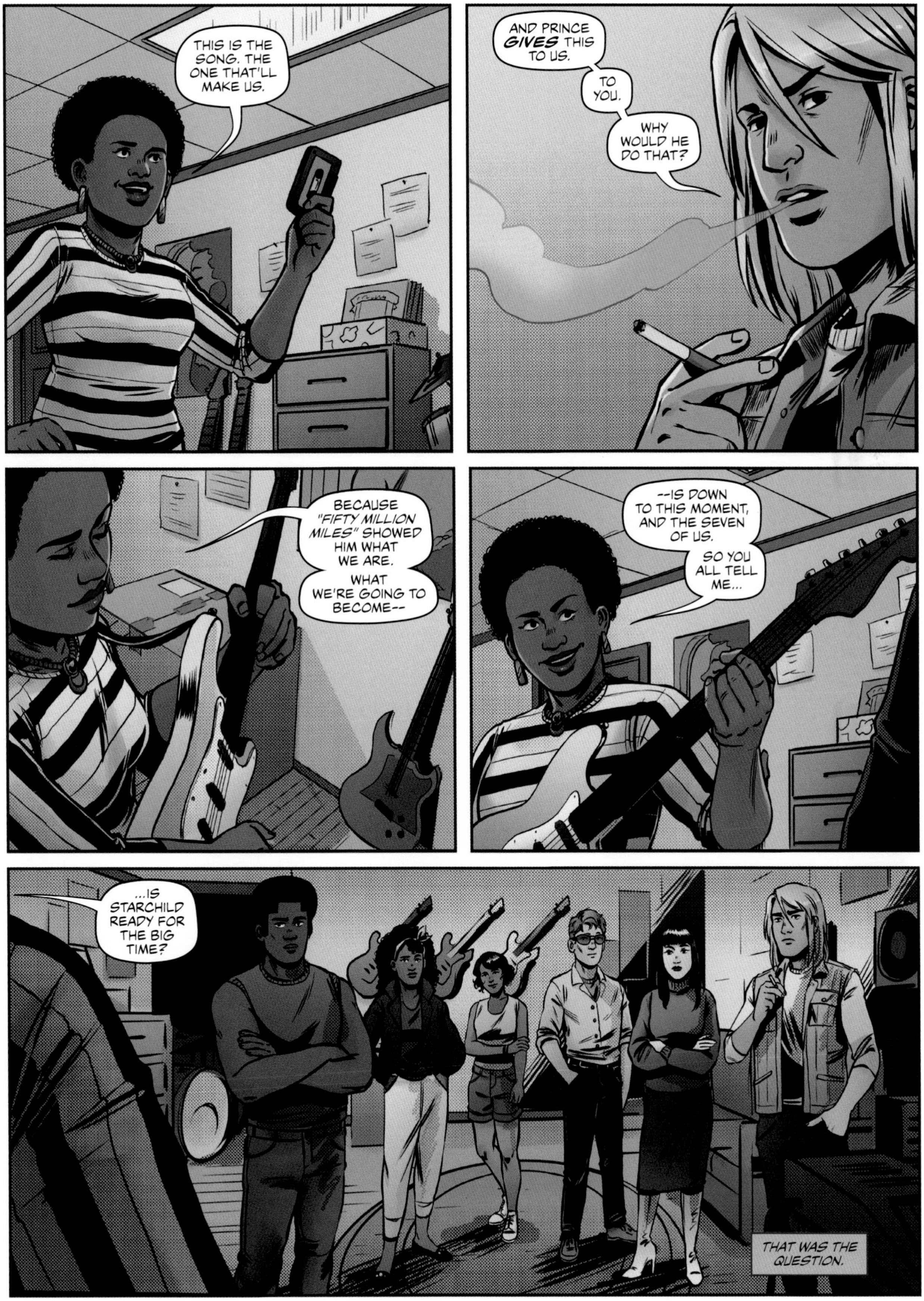
THIS IS THE SONG. THE ONE THAT'LL MAKE US.
AND PRINCE GIVES THIS TO US.
TO YOU.
WHY WOULD HE DO THAT?
BECAUSE "FIFTY MILLION MILES" SHOWED HIM WHAT WE ARE.
WHAT WE'RE GOING TO BECOME--
--IS DOWN TO THIS MOMENT, AND THE SEVEN OF US.
SO YOU ALL TELL ME...
...IS STARCHILD READY FOR THE BIG TIME?
THAT WAS THE QUESTION.

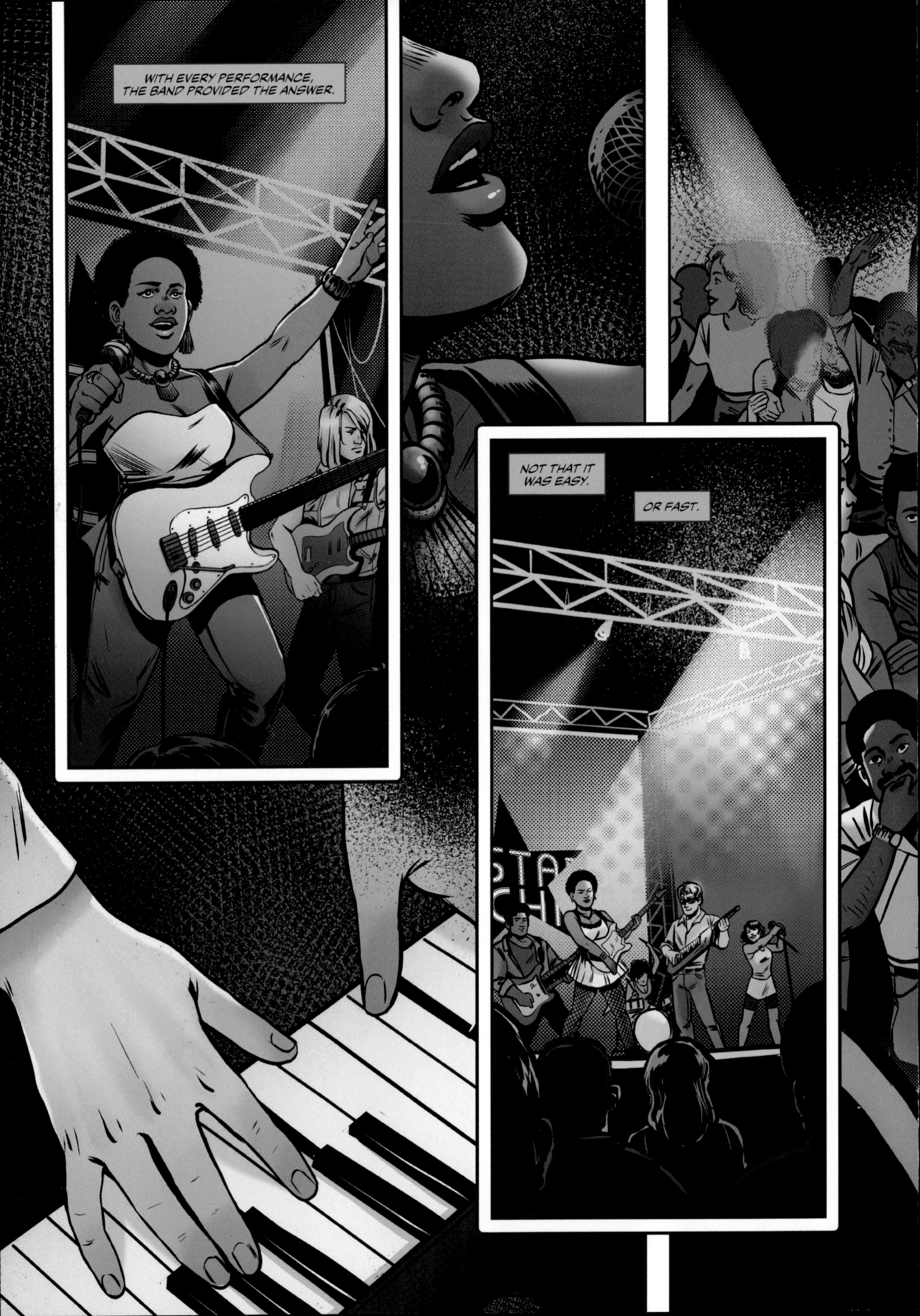
WITH EVERY PERFORMANCE, THE BAND PROVIDED THE ANSWER.
NOT THAT IT WAS EASY.
OR FAST.

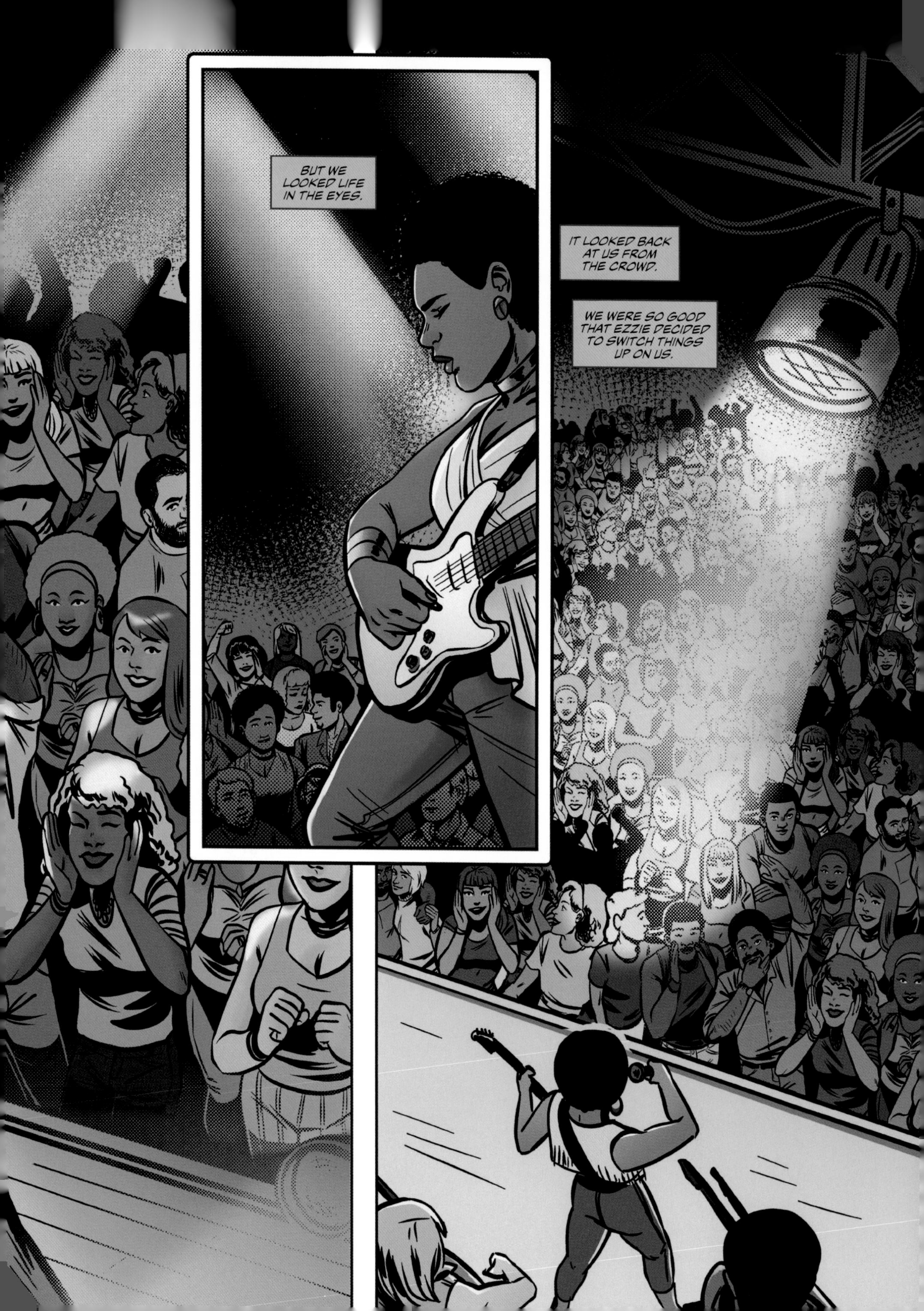
BUT WE LOOKED LIFE IN THE EYES.
IT LOOKED BACK AT US FROM THE CROWD.
WE WERE SO GOOD THAT EZZIE DECIDED TO SWITCH THINGS UP ON US.

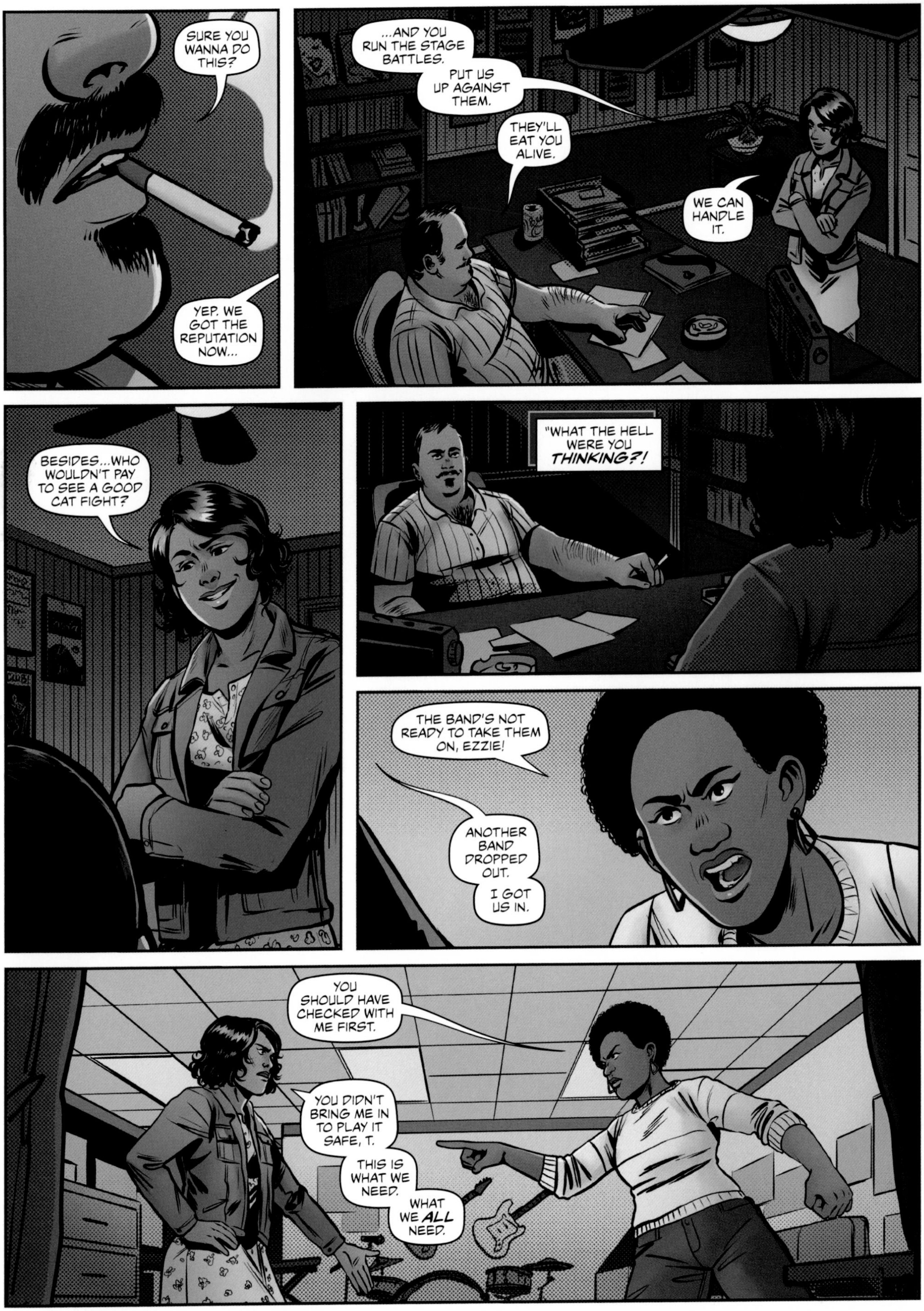
SURE YOU WANNA DO THIS?
YEP. WE GOT THE REPUTATION NOW...
...AND YOU RUN THE STAGE BATTLES.
PUT US UP AGAINST THEM.
THEY'LL EAT YOU ALIVE.
WE CAN HANDLE IT.
BESIDES...WHO WOULDN'T PAY TO SEE A GOOD CAT FIGHT?
"WHAT THE HELL WERE YOU *THINKING?!*
THE BAND'S NOT READY TO TAKE THEM ON, EZZIE!
ANOTHER BAND DROPPED OUT.
I GOT US IN.
YOU SHOULD HAVE CHECKED WITH ME FIRST.
YOU DIDN'T BRING ME IN TO PLAY IT SAFE, T.
THIS IS WHAT WE NEED.
WHAT WE *ALL* NEED.

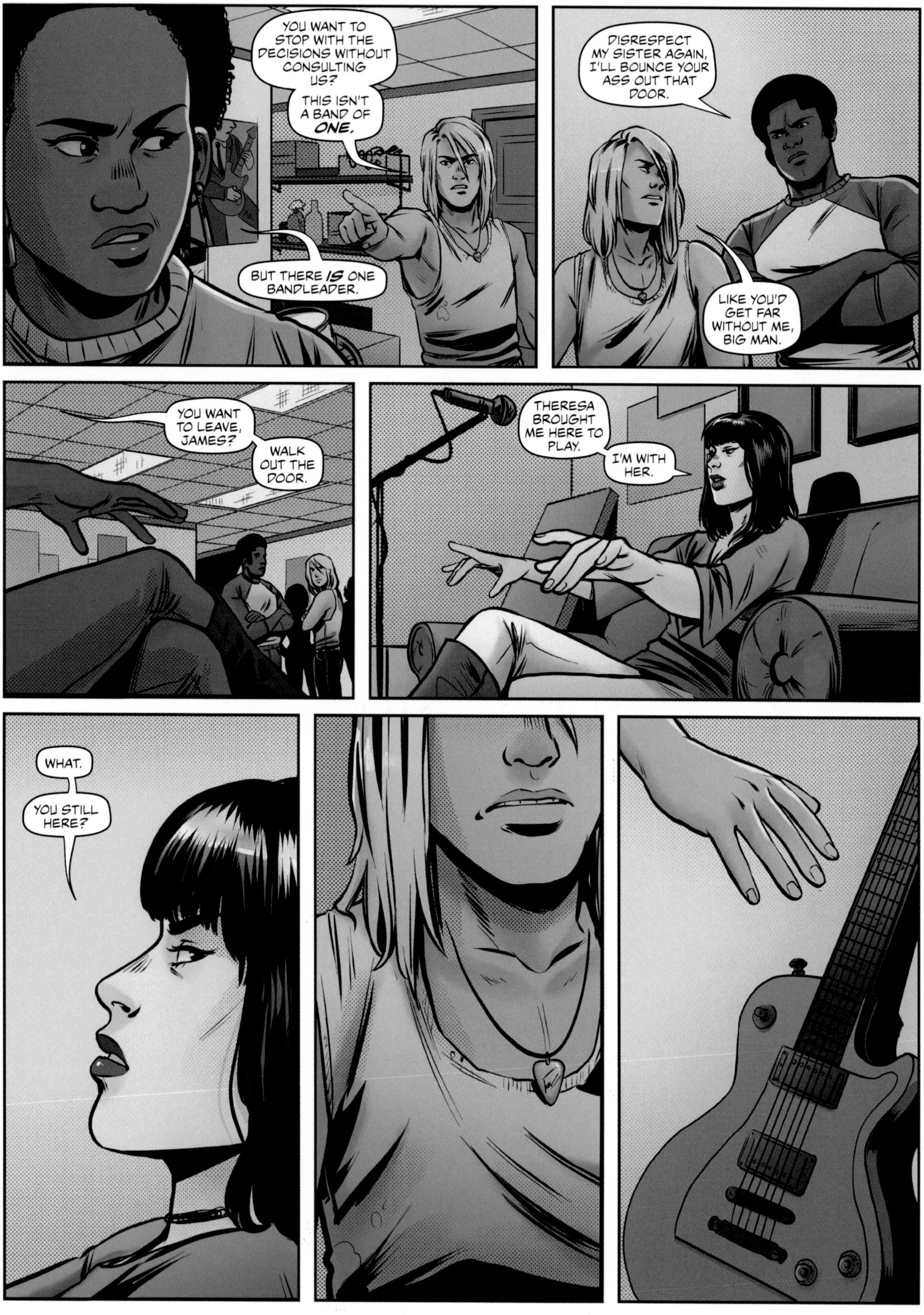
YOU WANT TO STOP WITH THE DECISIONS WITHOUT CONSULTING US?
THIS ISN'T A BAND OF *ONE.*
BUT THERE *IS* ONE BANDLEADER.
DISRESPECT MY SISTER AGAIN, I'LL BOUNCE YOUR ASS OUT THAT DOOR.
LIKE YOU'D GET FAR WITHOUT ME, BIG MAN.
YOU WANT TO LEAVE, JAMES?
WALK OUT THE DOOR.
THERESA BROUGHT ME HERE TO PLAY.
I'M WITH HER.
WHAT.
YOU STILL HERE?

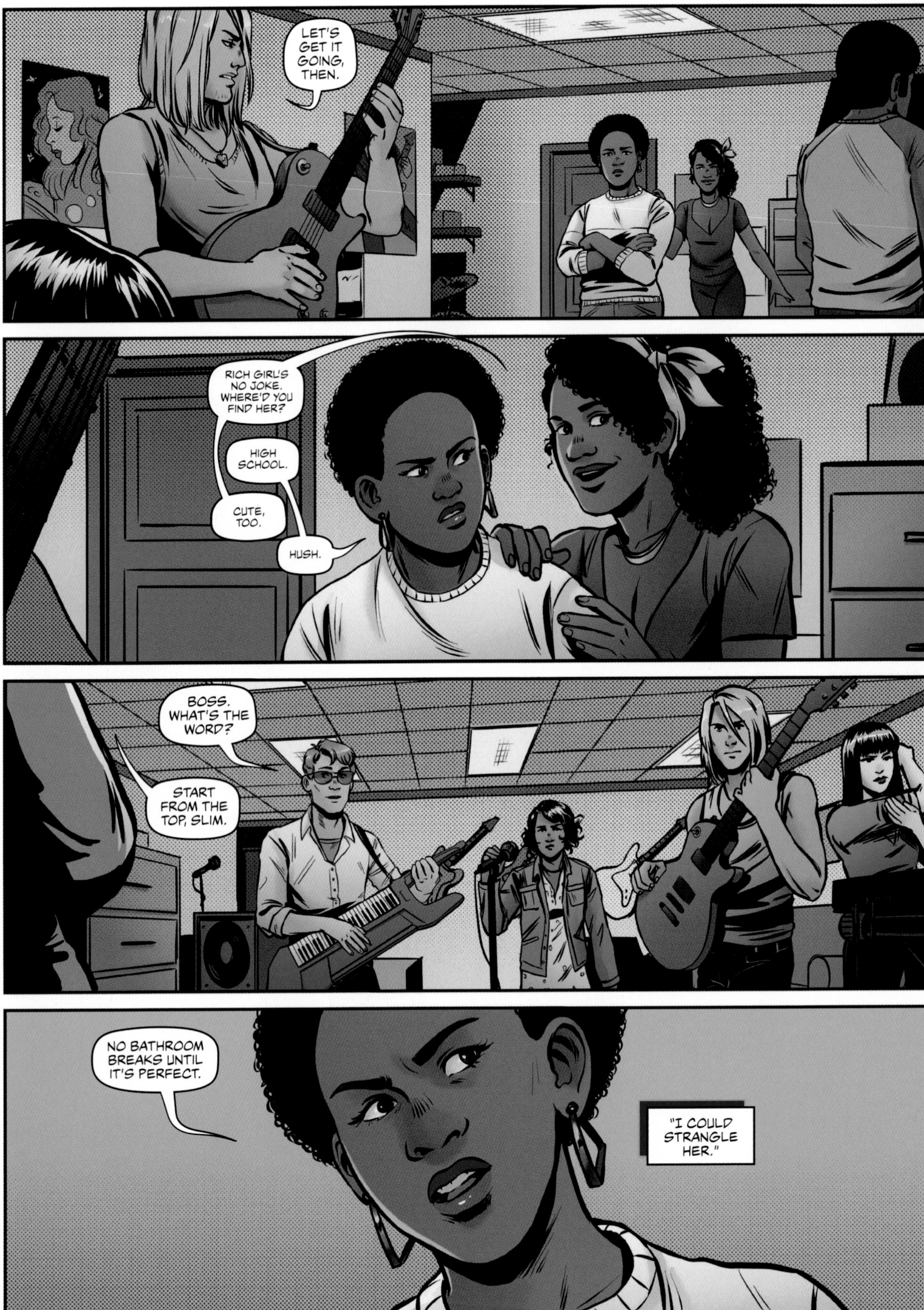
LET'S GET IT GOING, THEN.
RICH GIRL'S NO JOKE. WHERE'D YOU FIND HER?
HIGH SCHOOL.
CUTE, TOO.
HUSH.
BOSS. WHAT'S THE WORD?
START FROM THE TOP, SLIM.
NO BATHROOM BREAKS UNTIL IT'S PERFECT.
"I COULD STRANGLE HER."

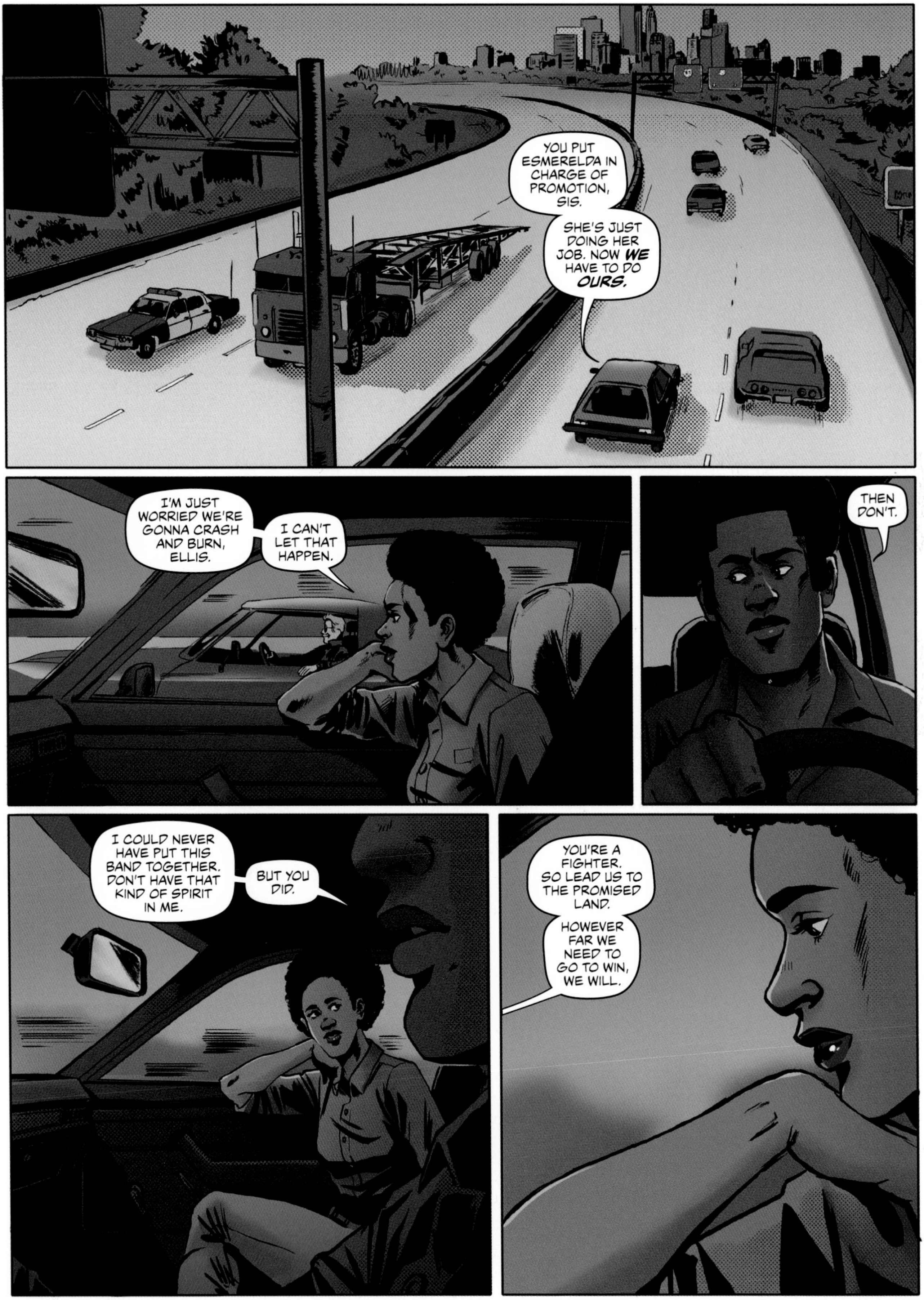
YOU PUT ESMERELDA IN CHARGE OF PROMOTION, SIS.
SHE'S JUST DOING HER JOB. NOW ***WE*** HAVE TO DO ***OURS.***
I'M JUST WORRIED WE'RE GONNA CRASH AND BURN, ELLIS.
I CAN'T LET THAT HAPPEN.
THEN DON'T.
I COULD NEVER HAVE PUT THIS BAND TOGETHER. DON'T HAVE THAT KIND OF SPIRIT IN ME.
BUT YOU DID.
YOU'RE A FIGHTER. SO LEAD US TO THE PROMISED LAND.
HOWEVER FAR WE NEED TO GO TO WIN, WE WILL.

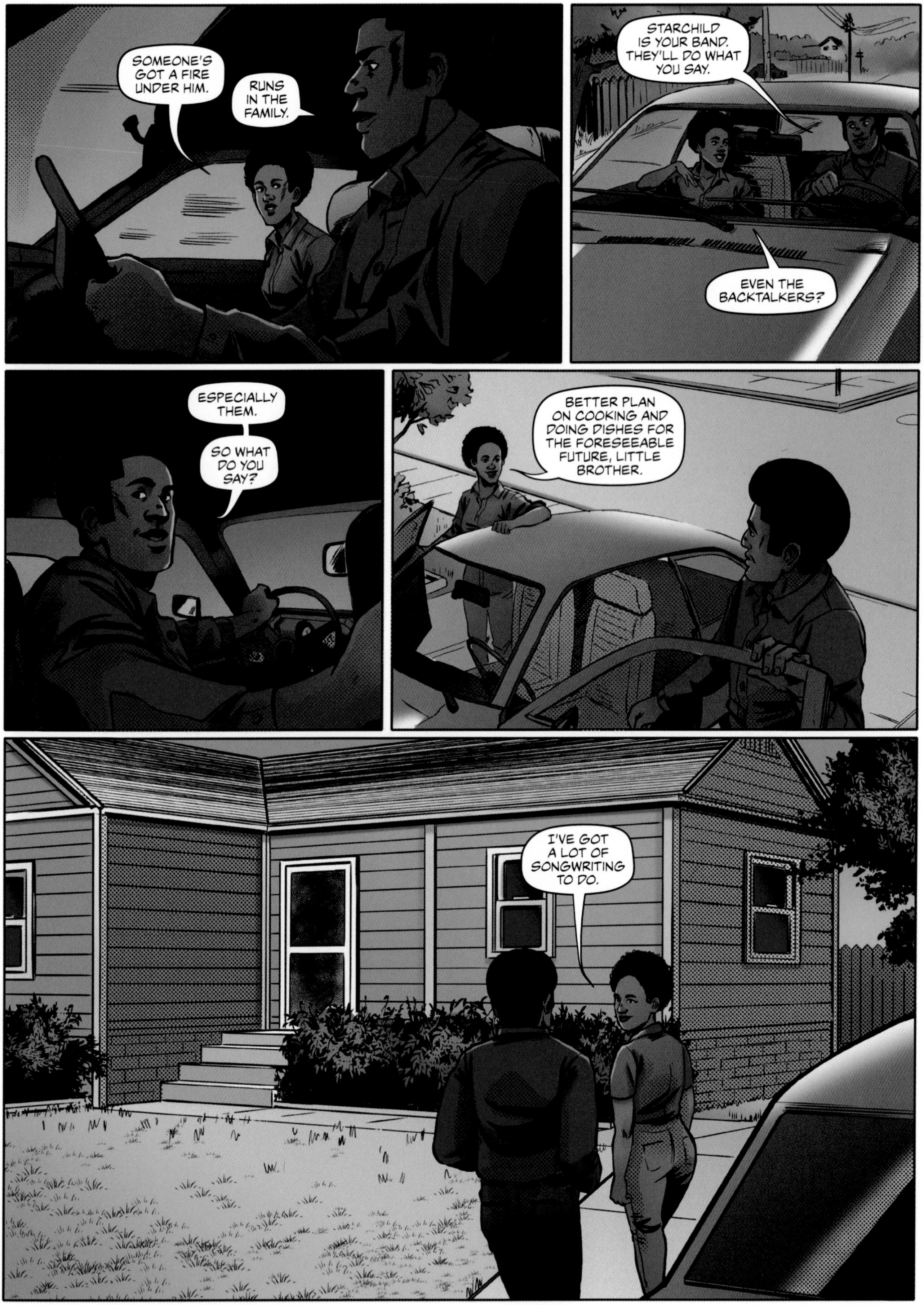
SOMEONE'S GOT A FIRE UNDER HIM.
RUNS IN THE FAMILY.
STARCHILD IS YOUR BAND. THEY'LL DO WHAT YOU SAY.
EVEN THE BACKTALKERS?
ESPECIALLY THEM.
SO WHAT DO YOU SAY?
BETTER PLAN ON COOKING AND DOING DISHES FOR THE FORESEEABLE FUTURE, LITTLE BROTHER.
I'VE GOT A LOT OF SONGWRITING TO DO.

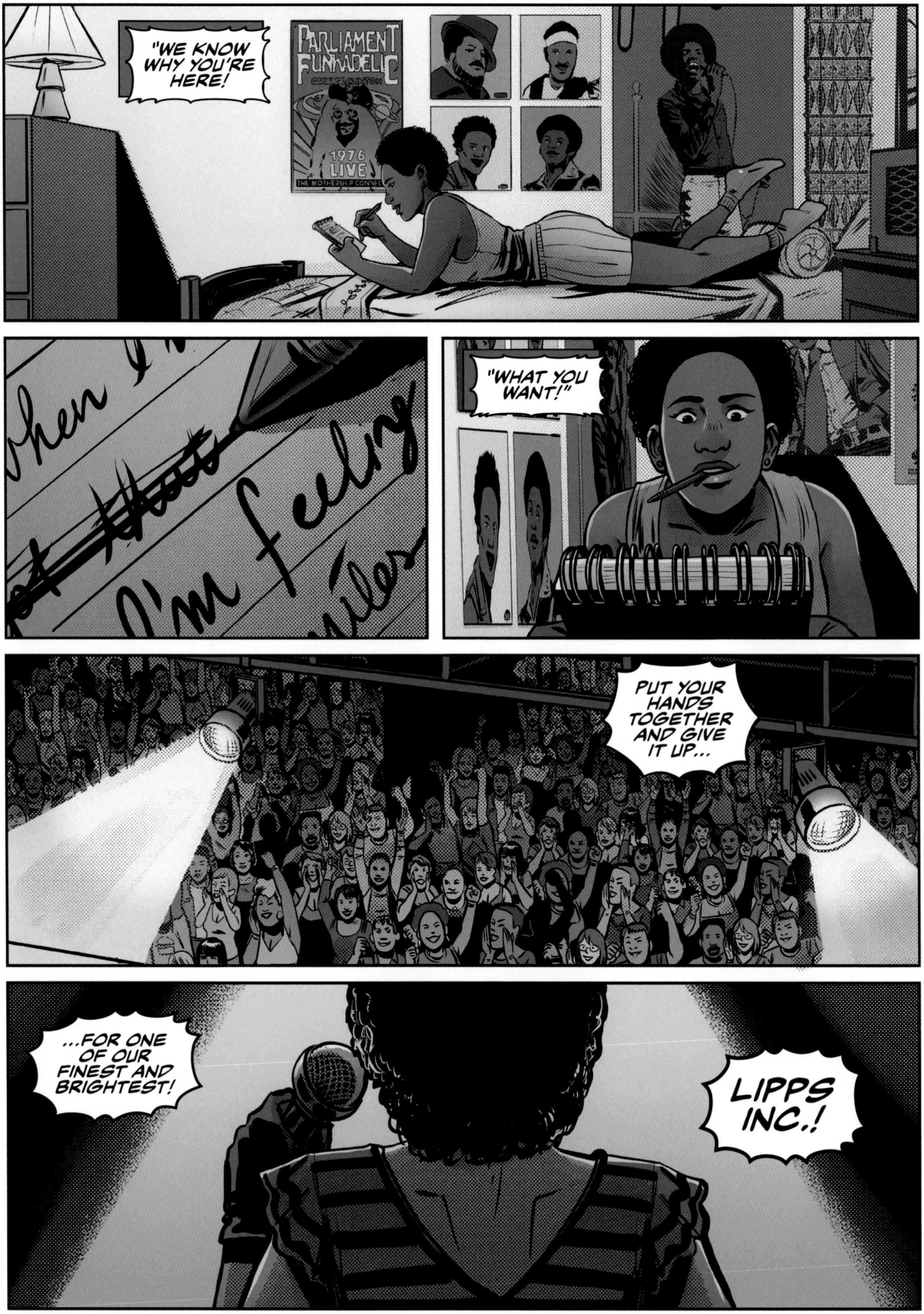
"WE KNOW WHY YOU'RE HERE!
PARLIAMENT FUNKADELIC
1976 LIVE
THE MOTHERSHIP CONNEC
"WHAT YOU WANT!"
PUT YOUR HANDS TOGETHER AND GIVE IT UP...
...FOR ONE OF OUR FINEST AND BRIGHTEST!
LIPPS INC.!

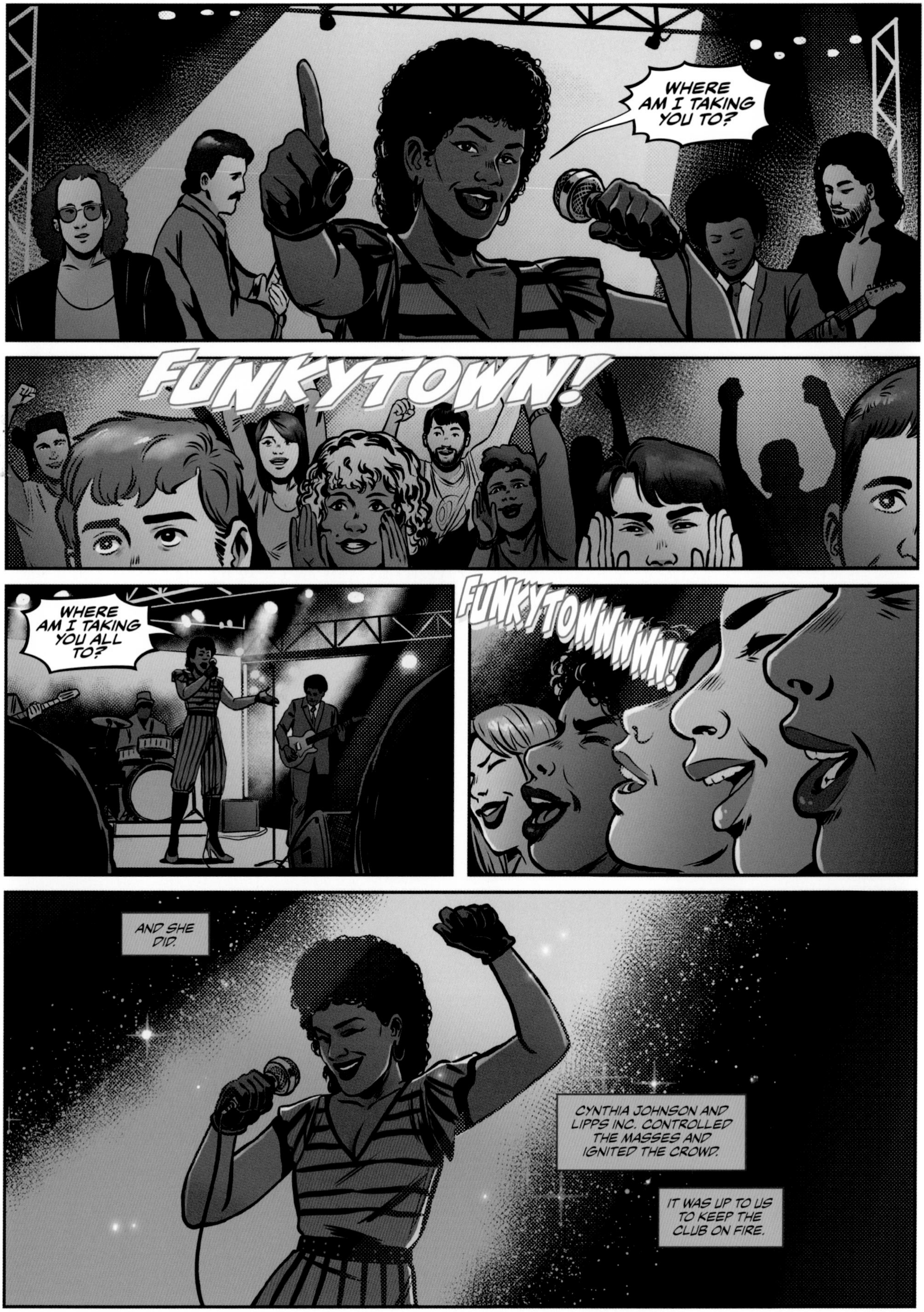
WHERE AM I TAKING YOU TO?
FUNKYTOWN!
WHERE AM I TAKING YOU ALL TO?
FUNKYTOWWWWN!
AND SHE DID.
CYNTHIA JOHNSON AND LIPPS INC. CONTROLLED THE MASSES AND IGNITED THE CROWD.
IT WAS UP TO US TO KEEP THE CLUB ON FIRE.

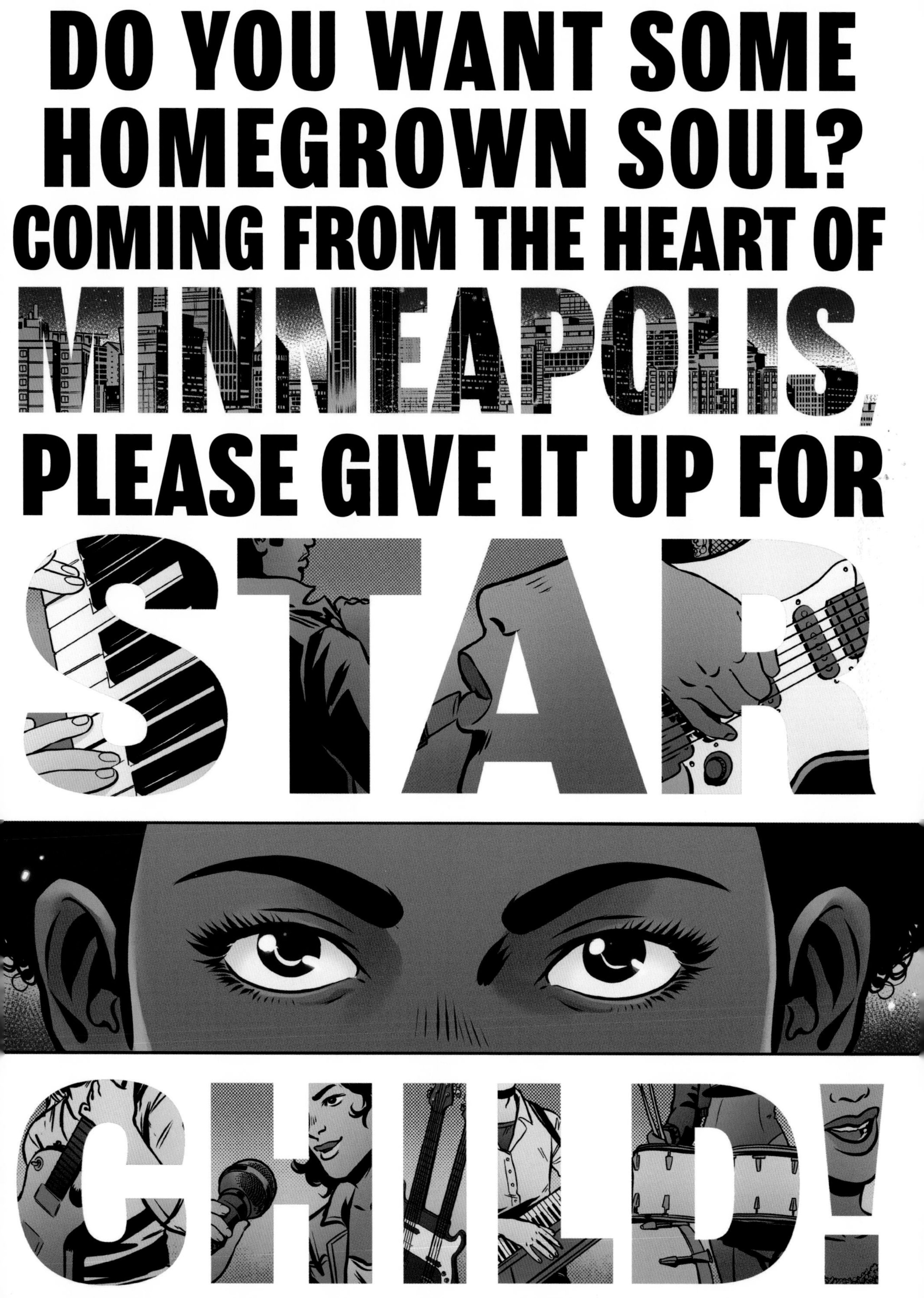
DO YOU WANT SOME HOMEGROWN SOUL?
COMING FROM THE HEART OF
MINNEAPOLIS,
PLEASE GIVE IT UP FOR
STAR
CHILD!

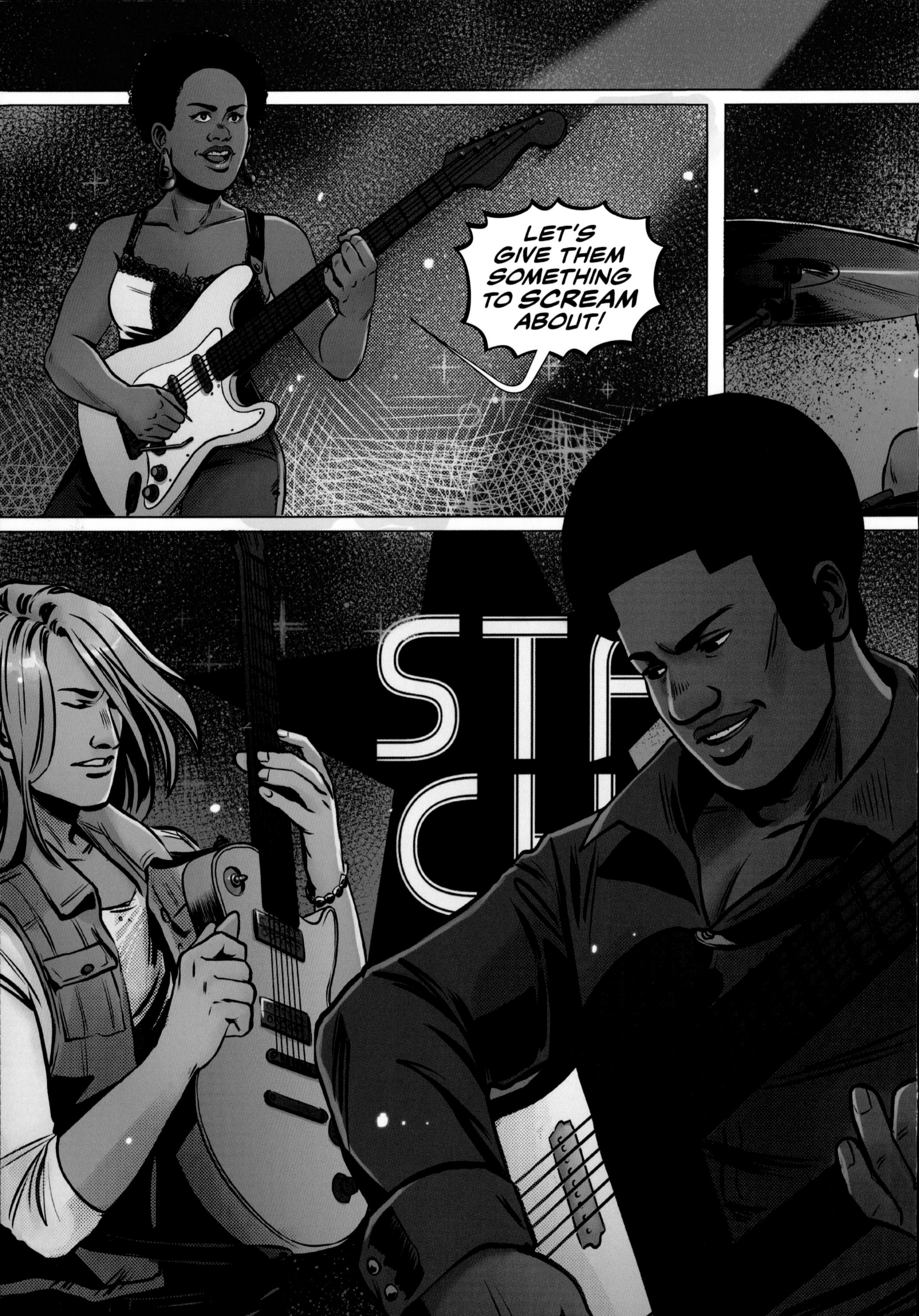
LET'S GIVE THEM SOMETHING TO SCREAM ABOUT!

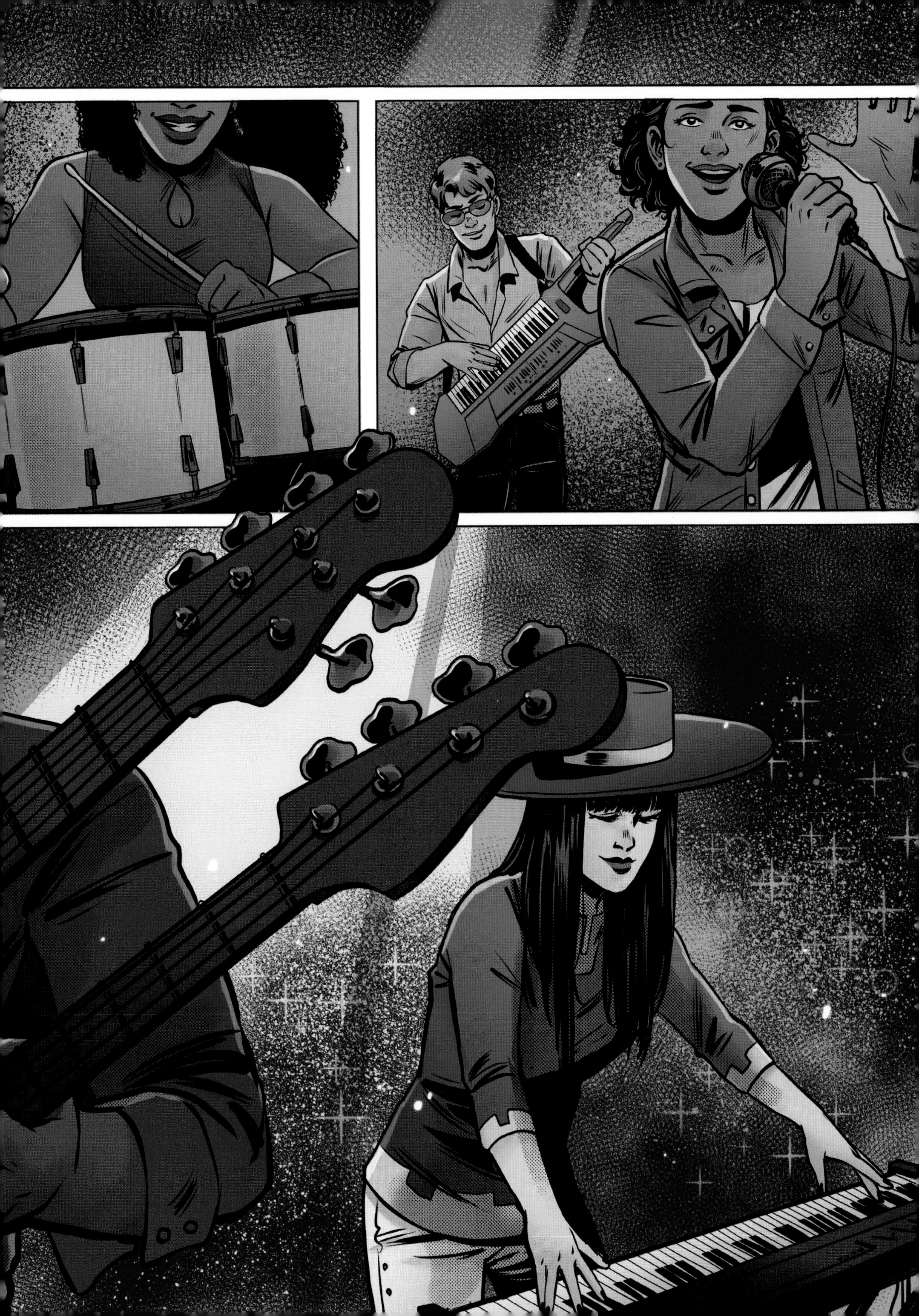

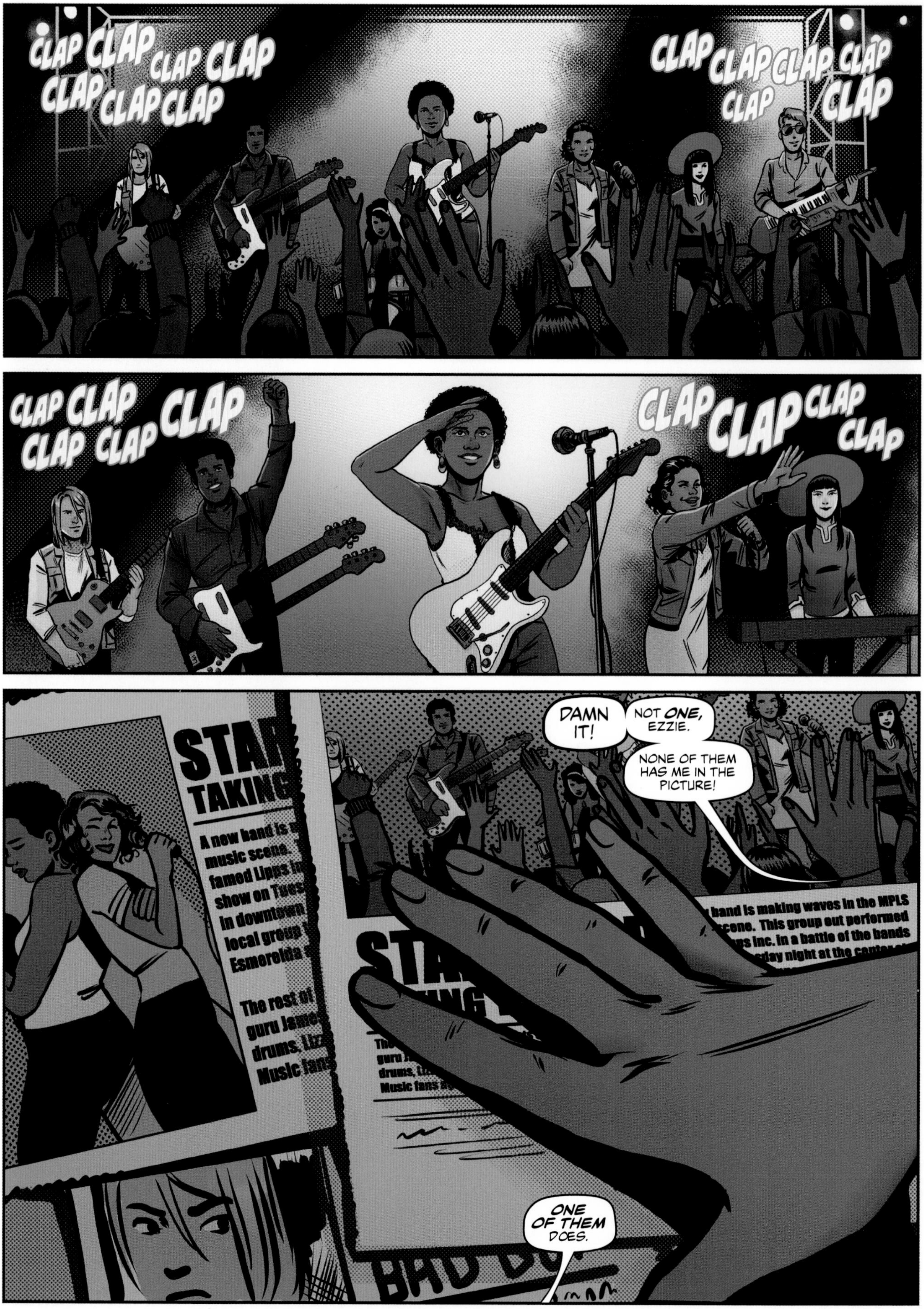

CLAP CLAP CLAP CLAP
CLAP CLAP CLAP
CLAP CLAP CLAP CLAP
CLAP CLAP
CLAP CLAP
CLAP CLAP CLAP
CLAP CLAP CLAP
CLAP
STAR
TAKING
A new band is
music scene.
famed Lipps In
show on Tues
in downtown
local group
Esmerelda
DAMN IT!
NOT ONE, EZZIE.
NONE OF THEM HAS ME IN THE PICTURE!
band is making waves in the MPLS
scene. This group out performed
inc. in a battle of the bands
day night at the center
ONE OF THEM DOES.

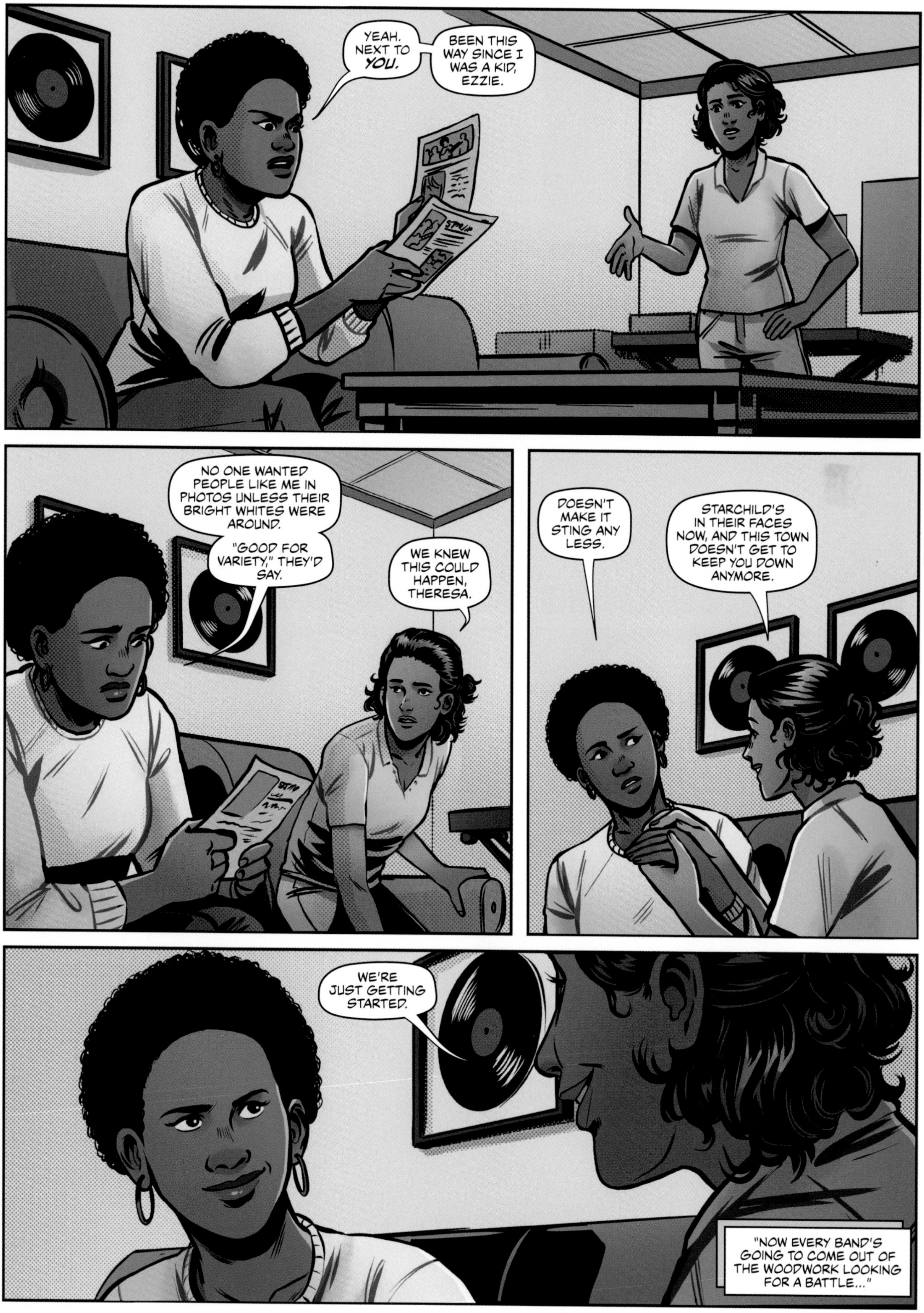
YEAH. NEXT TO YOU.
BEEN THIS WAY SINCE I WAS A KID, EZZIE.
NO ONE WANTED PEOPLE LIKE ME IN PHOTOS UNLESS THEIR BRIGHT WHITES WERE AROUND.
"GOOD FOR VARIETY," THEY'D SAY.
WE KNEW THIS COULD HAPPEN, THERESA.
DOESN'T MAKE IT STING ANY LESS.
STARCHILD'S IN THEIR FACES NOW, AND THIS TOWN DOESN'T GET TO KEEP YOU DOWN ANYMORE.
WE'RE JUST GETTING STARTED.
"NOW EVERY BAND'S GOING TO COME OUT OF THE WOODWORK LOOKING FOR A BATTLE..."

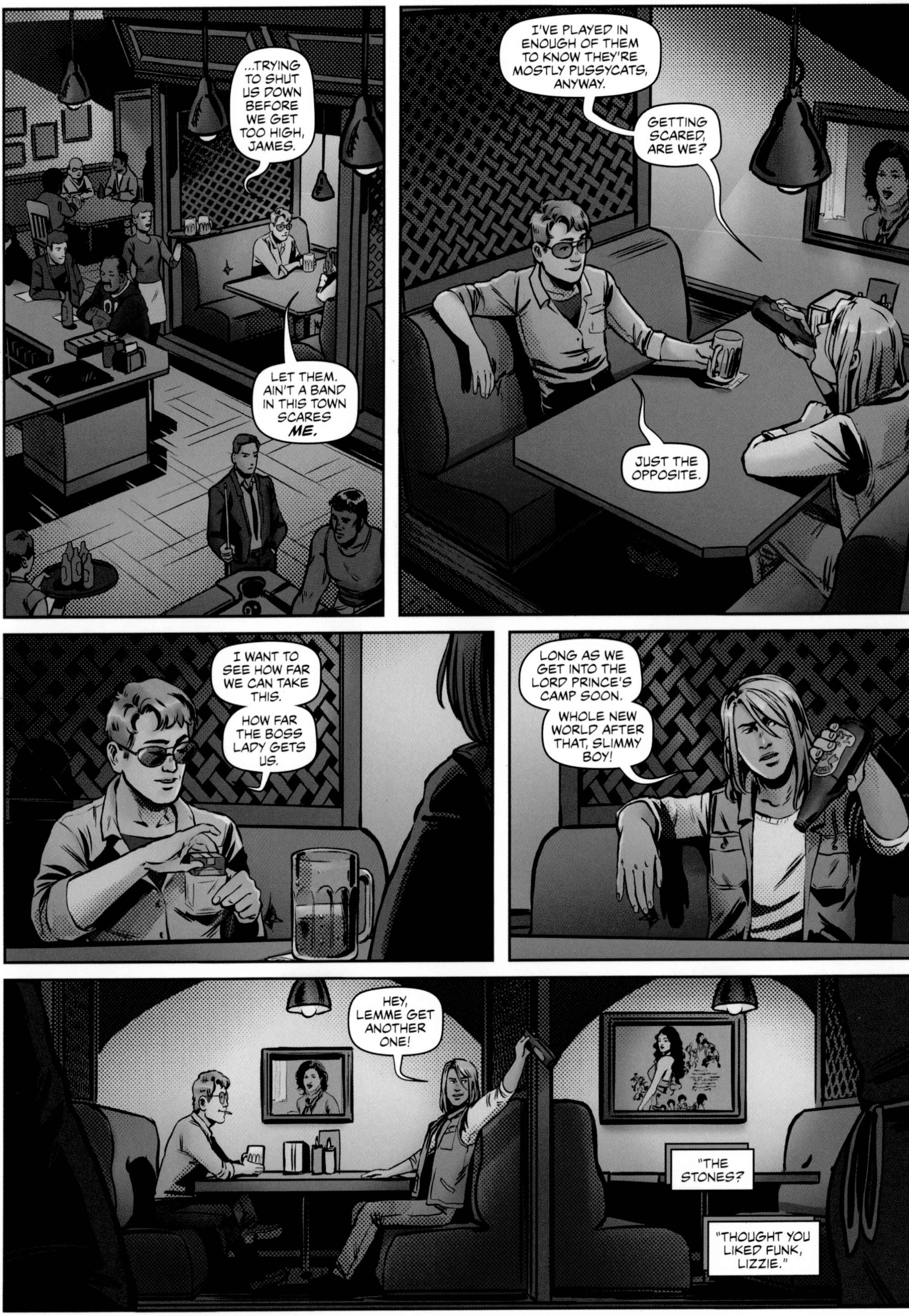

...TRYING TO SHUT US DOWN BEFORE WE GET TOO HIGH, JAMES.
LET THEM. AIN'T A BAND IN THIS TOWN SCARES *ME.*
I'VE PLAYED IN ENOUGH OF THEM TO KNOW THEY'RE MOSTLY PUSSYCATS, ANYWAY.
GETTING SCARED, ARE WE?
JUST THE OPPOSITE.
I WANT TO SEE HOW FAR WE CAN TAKE THIS.
HOW FAR THE BOSS LADY GETS US.
LONG AS WE GET INTO THE LORD PRINCE'S CAMP SOON.
WHOLE NEW WORLD AFTER THAT, SLIMMY BOY!
HEY, LEMME GET ANOTHER ONE!
"THE STONES?
"THOUGHT YOU LIKED FUNK, LIZZIE."

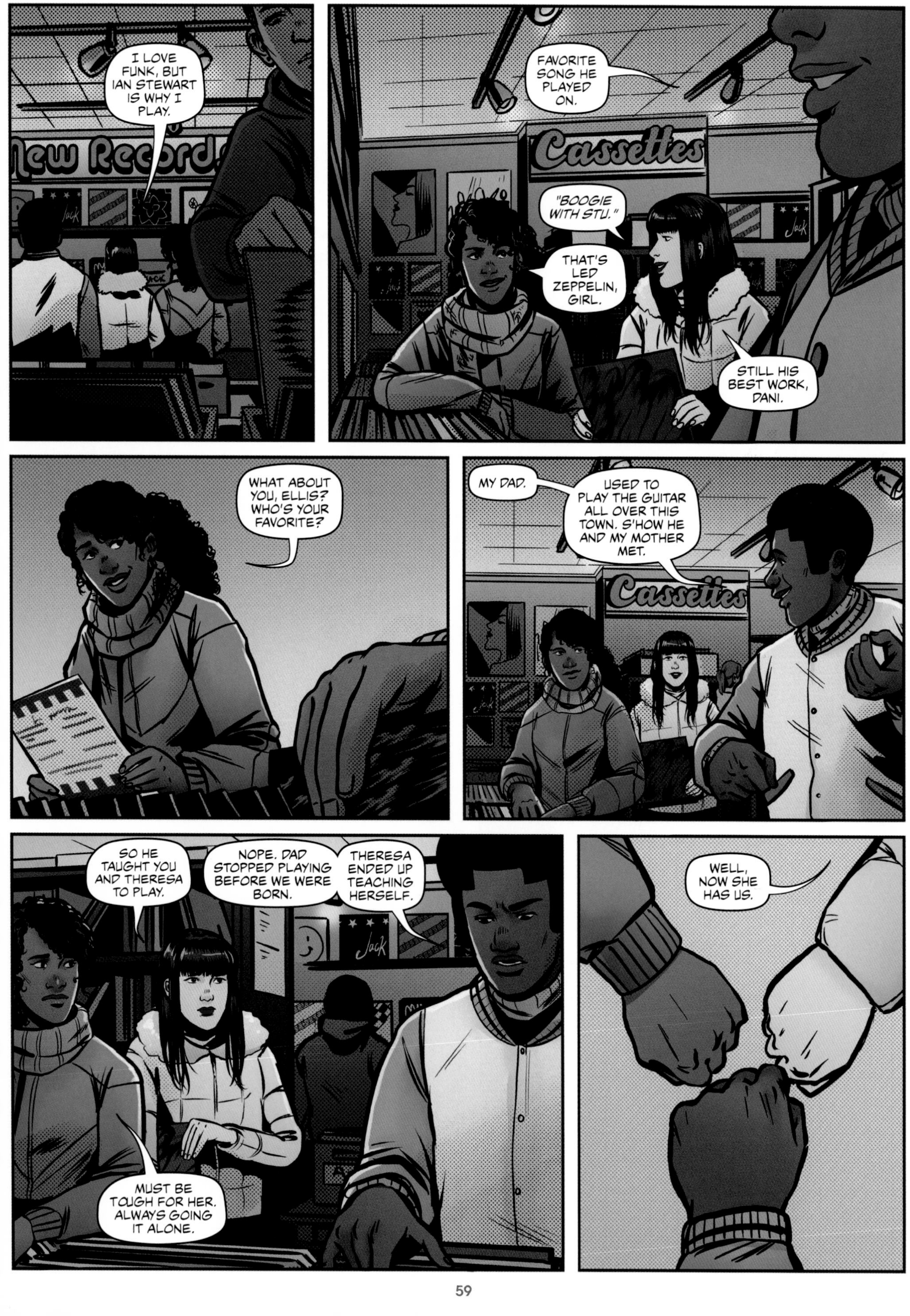
I LOVE FUNK, BUT IAN STEWART IS WHY I PLAY.
FAVORITE SONG HE PLAYED ON.
Cassettes
"BOOGIE WITH STU."
THAT'S LED ZEPPELIN, GIRL.
STILL HIS BEST WORK, DANI.
WHAT ABOUT YOU, ELLIS? WHO'S YOUR FAVORITE?
MY DAD.
USED TO PLAY THE GUITAR ALL OVER THIS TOWN. S'HOW HE AND MY MOTHER MET.
Cassettes
SO HE TAUGHT YOU AND THERESA TO PLAY.
NOPE. DAD STOPPED PLAYING BEFORE WE WERE BORN.
THERESA ENDED UP TEACHING HERSELF.
MUST BE TOUGH FOR HER. ALWAYS GOING IT ALONE.
WELL, NOW SHE HAS US.

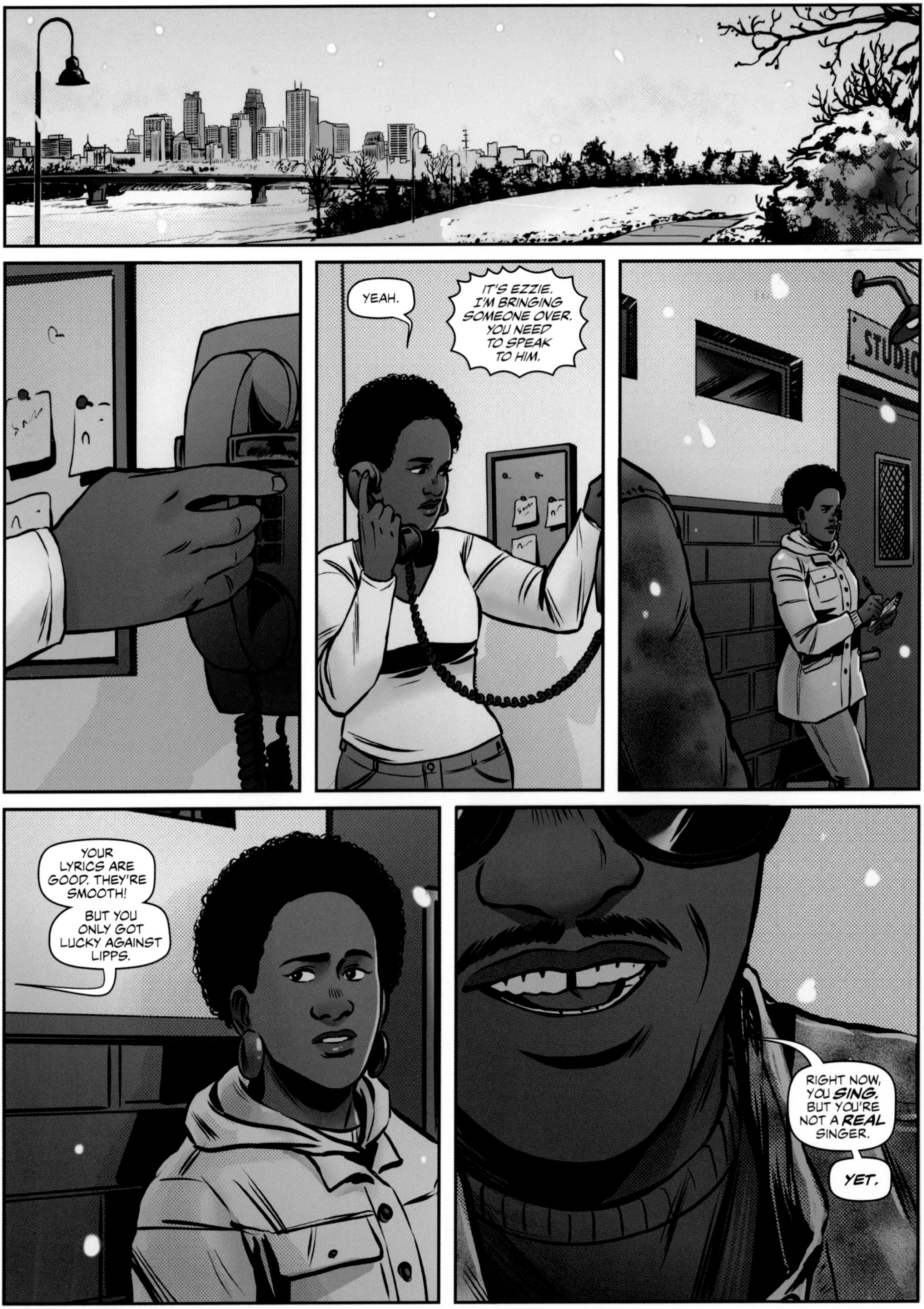
YEAH.
IT'S EZZIE. I'M BRINGING SOMEONE OVER. YOU NEED TO SPEAK TO HIM.
STUDIO
YOUR LYRICS ARE GOOD. THEY'RE SMOOTH!
BUT YOU ONLY GOT LUCKY AGAINST LIPPS.
RIGHT NOW, YOU **SING.** BUT YOU'RE NOT A **REAL** SINGER.
YET.

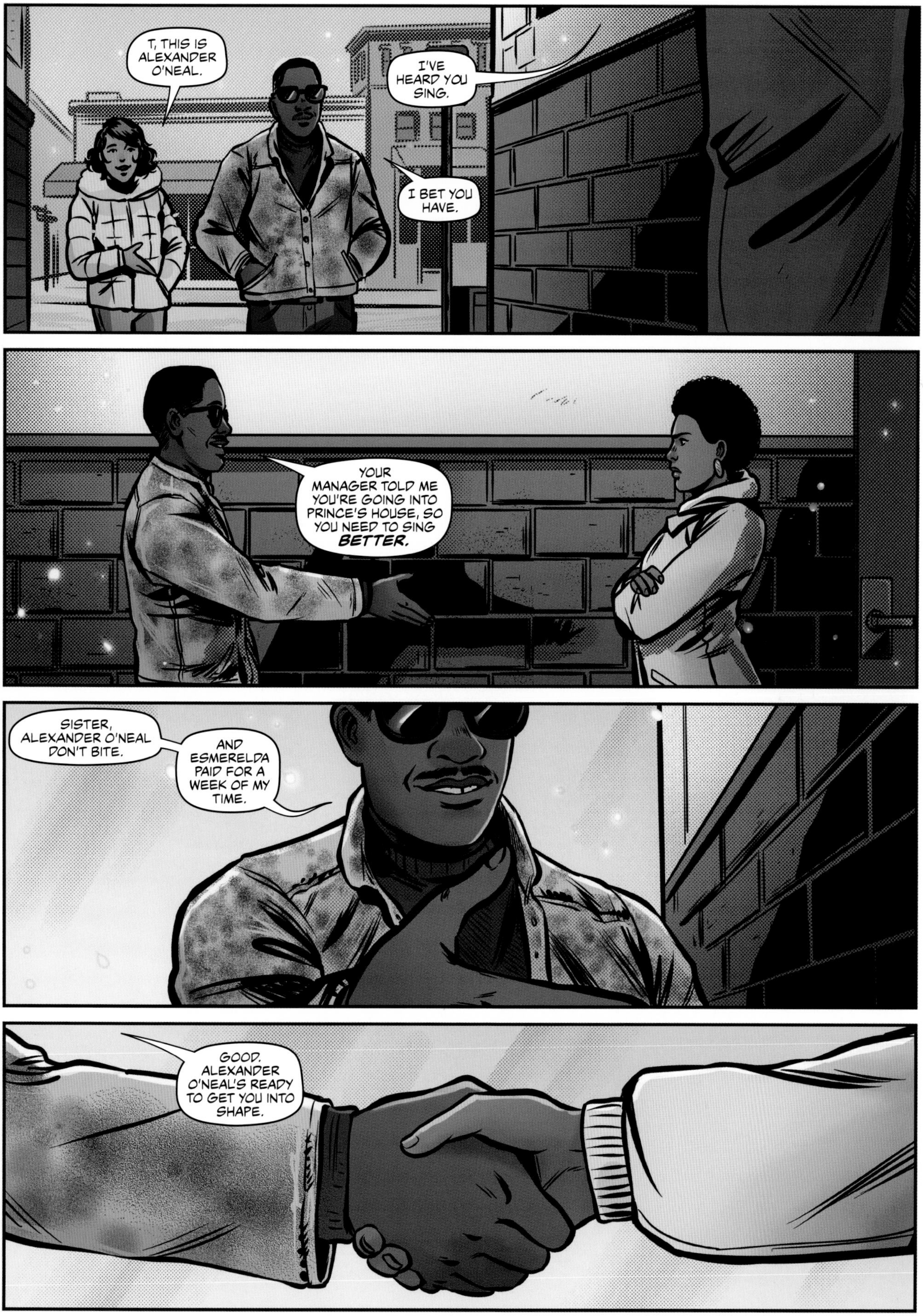
T, THIS IS ALEXANDER O'NEAL.
I'VE HEARD YOU SING.
I BET YOU HAVE.
YOUR MANAGER TOLD ME YOU'RE GOING INTO PRINCE'S HOUSE, SO YOU NEED TO SING **BETTER.**
SISTER, ALEXANDER O'NEAL DON'T BITE.
AND ESMERELDA PAID FOR A WEEK OF MY TIME.
GOOD. ALEXANDER O'NEAL'S READY TO GET YOU INTO SHAPE.

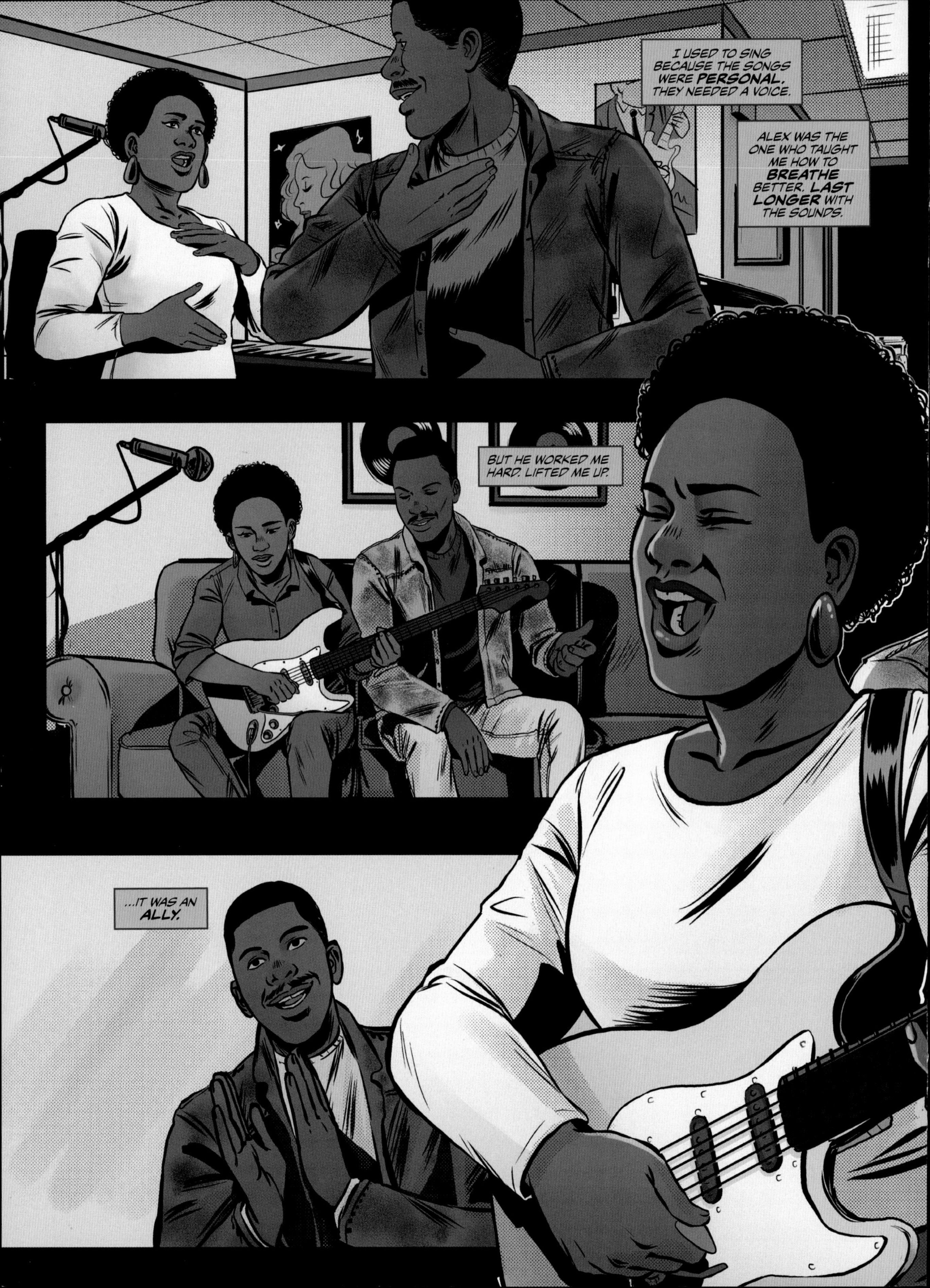
I USED TO SING BECAUSE THE SONGS WERE PERSONAL. THEY NEEDED A VOICE.
ALEX WAS THE ONE WHO TAUGHT ME HOW TO BREATHE BETTER. LAST LONGER WITH THE SOUNDS.
BUT HE WORKED ME HARD. LIFTED ME UP.
...IT WAS AN ALLY.

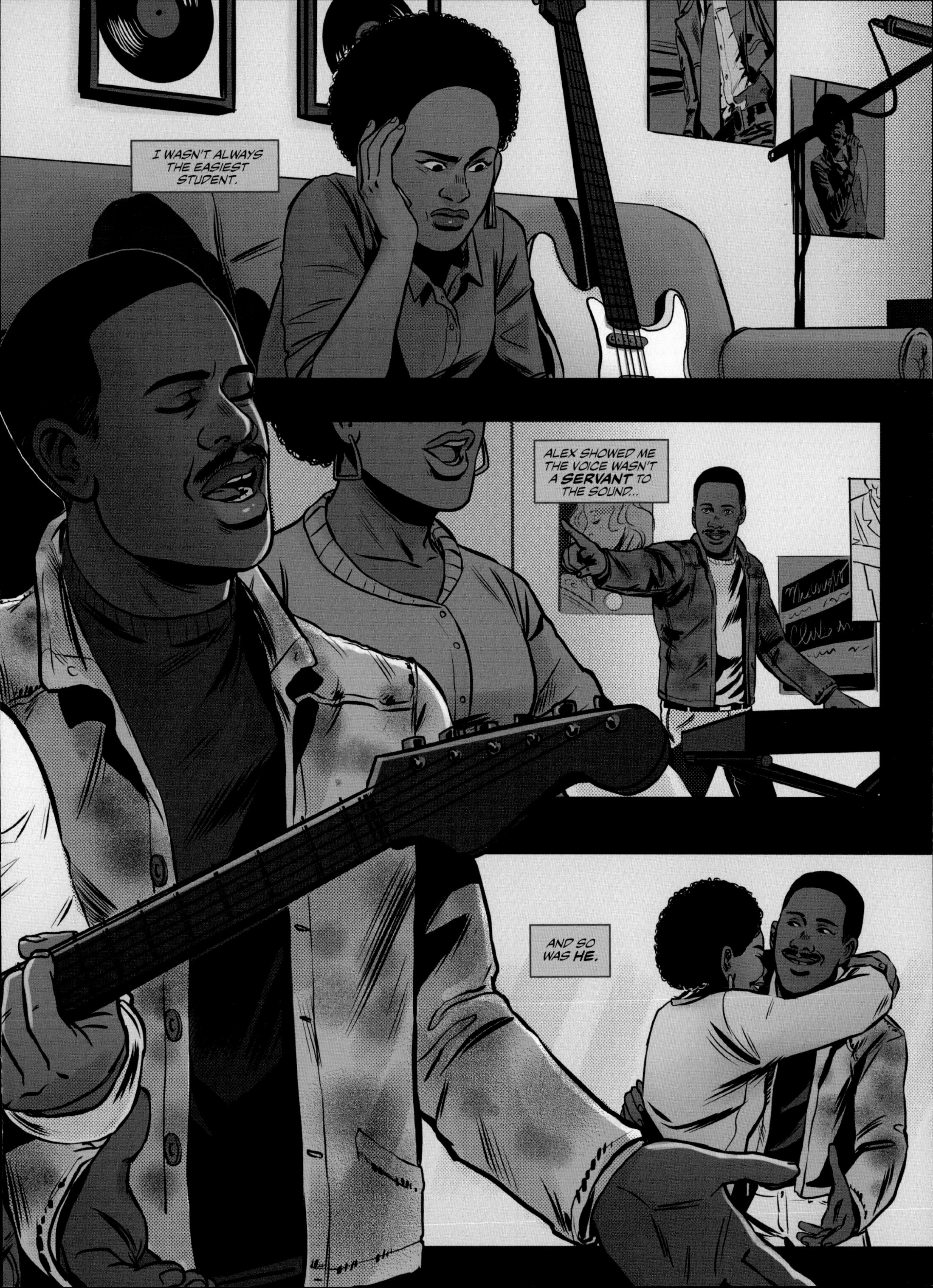

I WASN'T ALWAYS THE EASIEST STUDENT.
ALEX SHOWED ME THE VOICE WASN'T A SERVANT TO THE SOUND...
AND SO WAS HE.

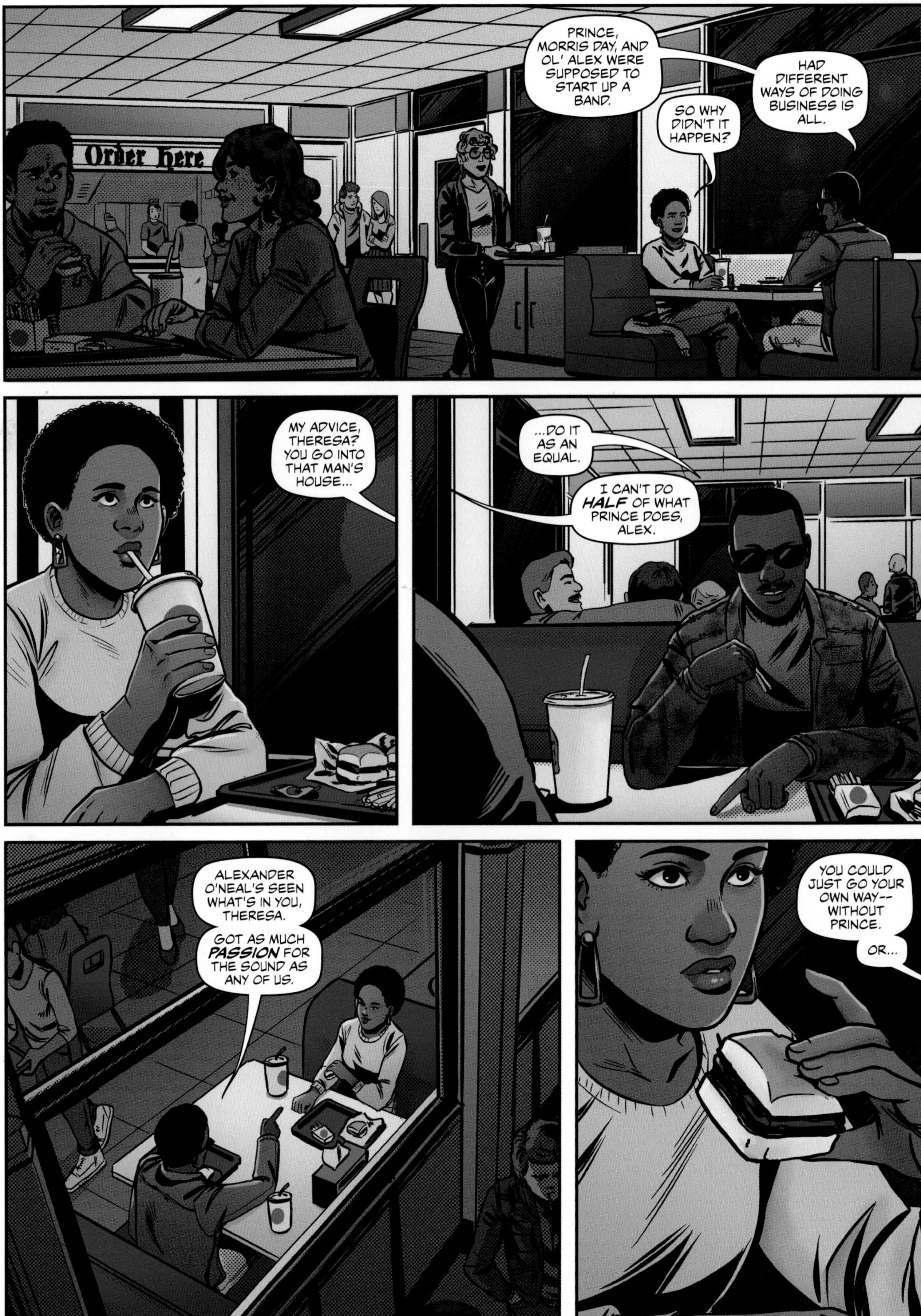
Order here
PRINCE, MORRIS DAY, AND OL' ALEX WERE SUPPOSED TO START UP A BAND.
SO WHY DIDN'T IT HAPPEN?
HAD DIFFERENT WAYS OF DOING BUSINESS IS ALL.
MY ADVICE, THERESA? YOU GO INTO THAT MAN'S HOUSE...
...DO IT AS AN EQUAL.
I CAN'T DO **HALF** OF WHAT PRINCE DOES, ALEX.
ALEXANDER O'NEAL'S SEEN WHAT'S IN YOU, THERESA.
GOT AS MUCH **PASSION** FOR THE SOUND AS ANY OF US.
YOU COULD JUST GO YOUR OWN WAY-- WITHOUT PRINCE.
OR...

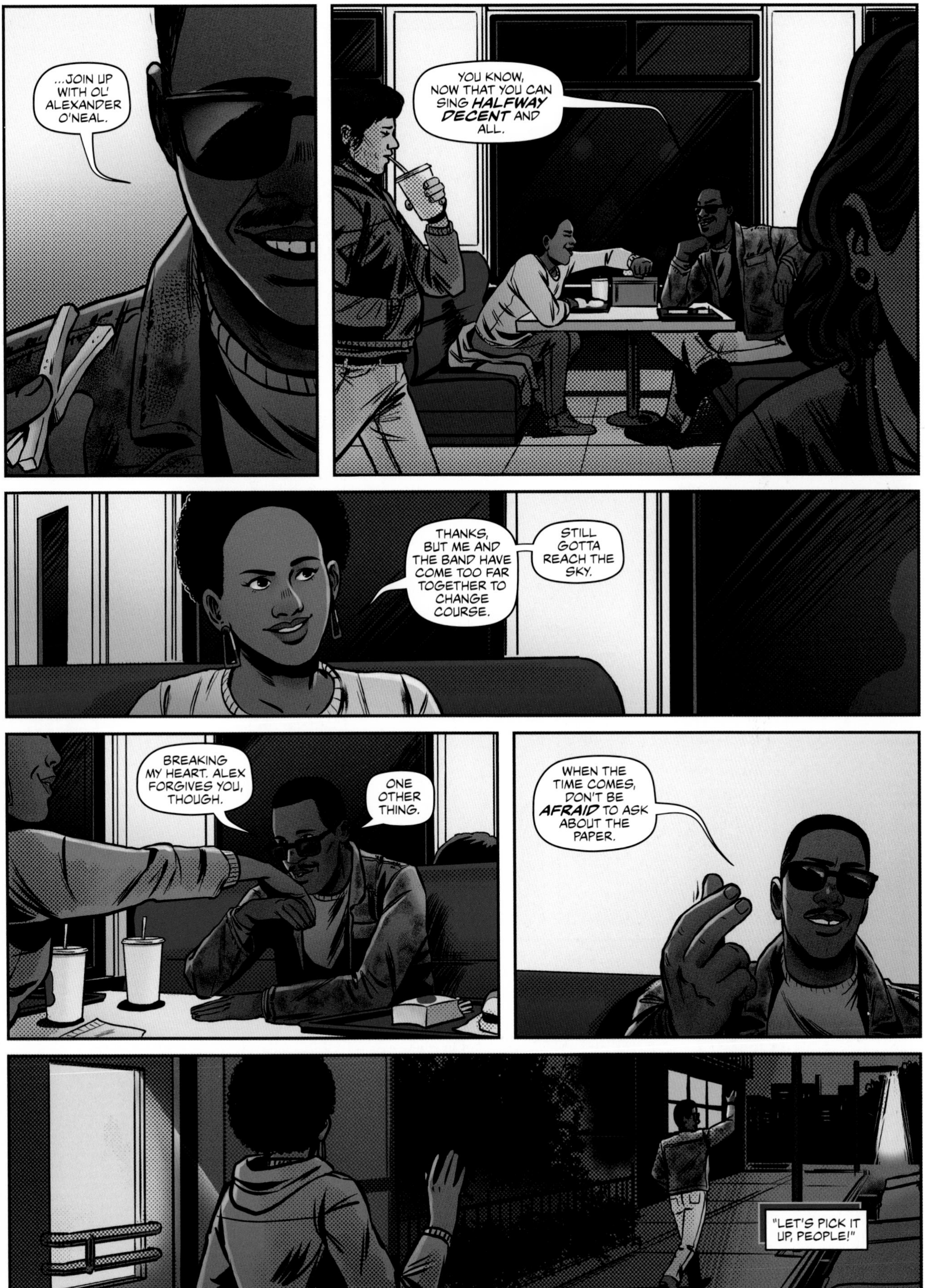
...JOIN UP WITH OL' ALEXANDER O'NEAL.
YOU KNOW, NOW THAT YOU CAN SING HALFWAY DECENT AND ALL.
THANKS, BUT ME AND THE BAND HAVE COME TOO FAR TOGETHER TO CHANGE COURSE.
STILL GOTTA REACH THE SKY.
BREAKING MY HEART. ALEX FORGIVES YOU, THOUGH.
ONE OTHER THING.
WHEN THE TIME COMES, DON'T BE AFRAID TO ASK ABOUT THE PAPER.
"LET'S PICK IT UP, PEOPLE!"

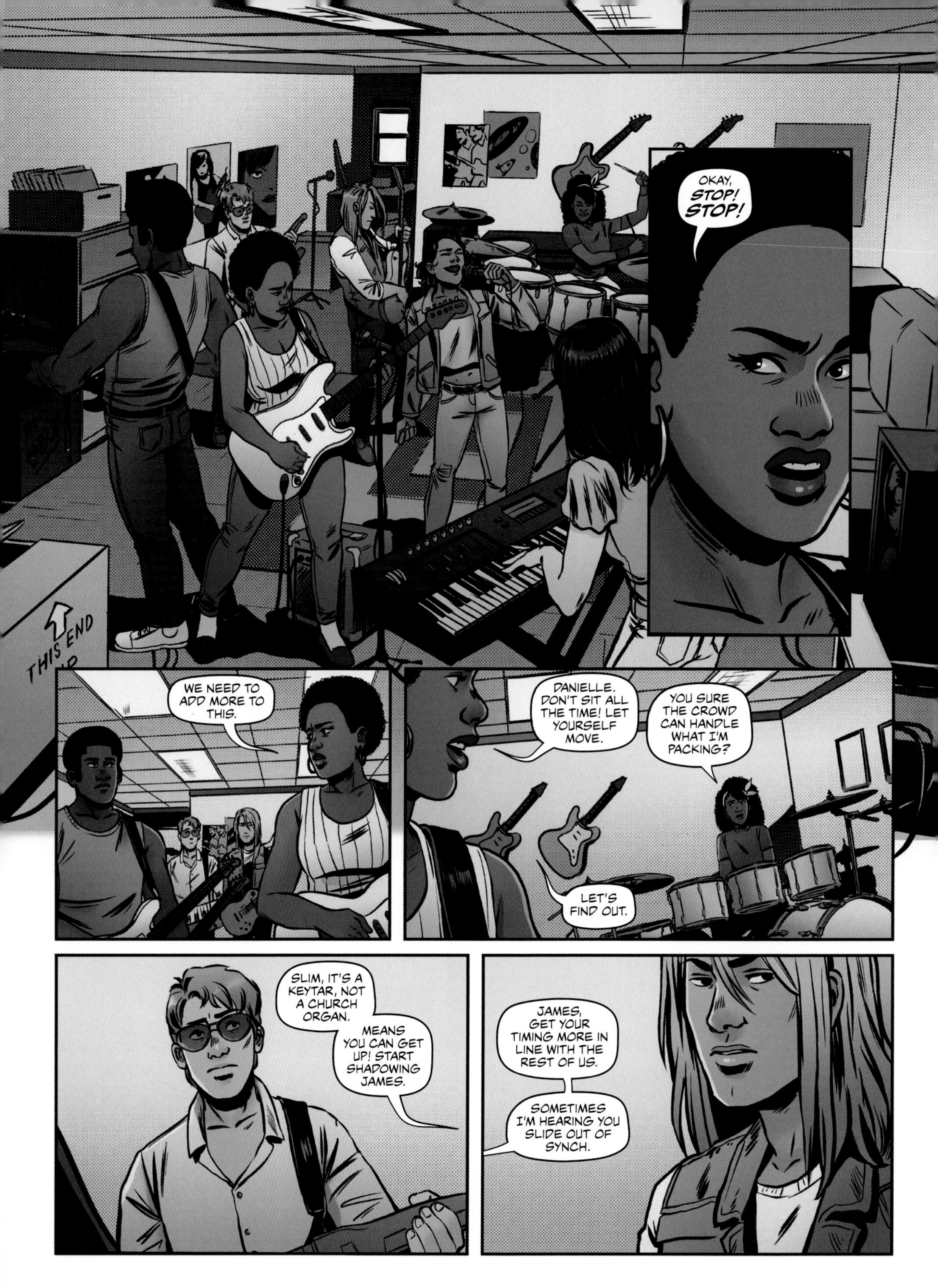
OKAY, STOP! STOP!
WE NEED TO ADD MORE TO THIS.
DANIELLE. DON'T SIT ALL THE TIME! LET YOURSELF MOVE.
YOU SURE THE CROWD CAN HANDLE WHAT I'M PACKING?
LET'S FIND OUT.
SLIM, IT'S A KEYTAR, NOT A CHURCH ORGAN.
MEANS YOU CAN GET UP! START SHADOWING JAMES.
JAMES, GET YOUR TIMING MORE IN LINE WITH THE REST OF US.
SOMETIMES I'M HEARING YOU SLIDE OUT OF SYNCH.
THIS END UP

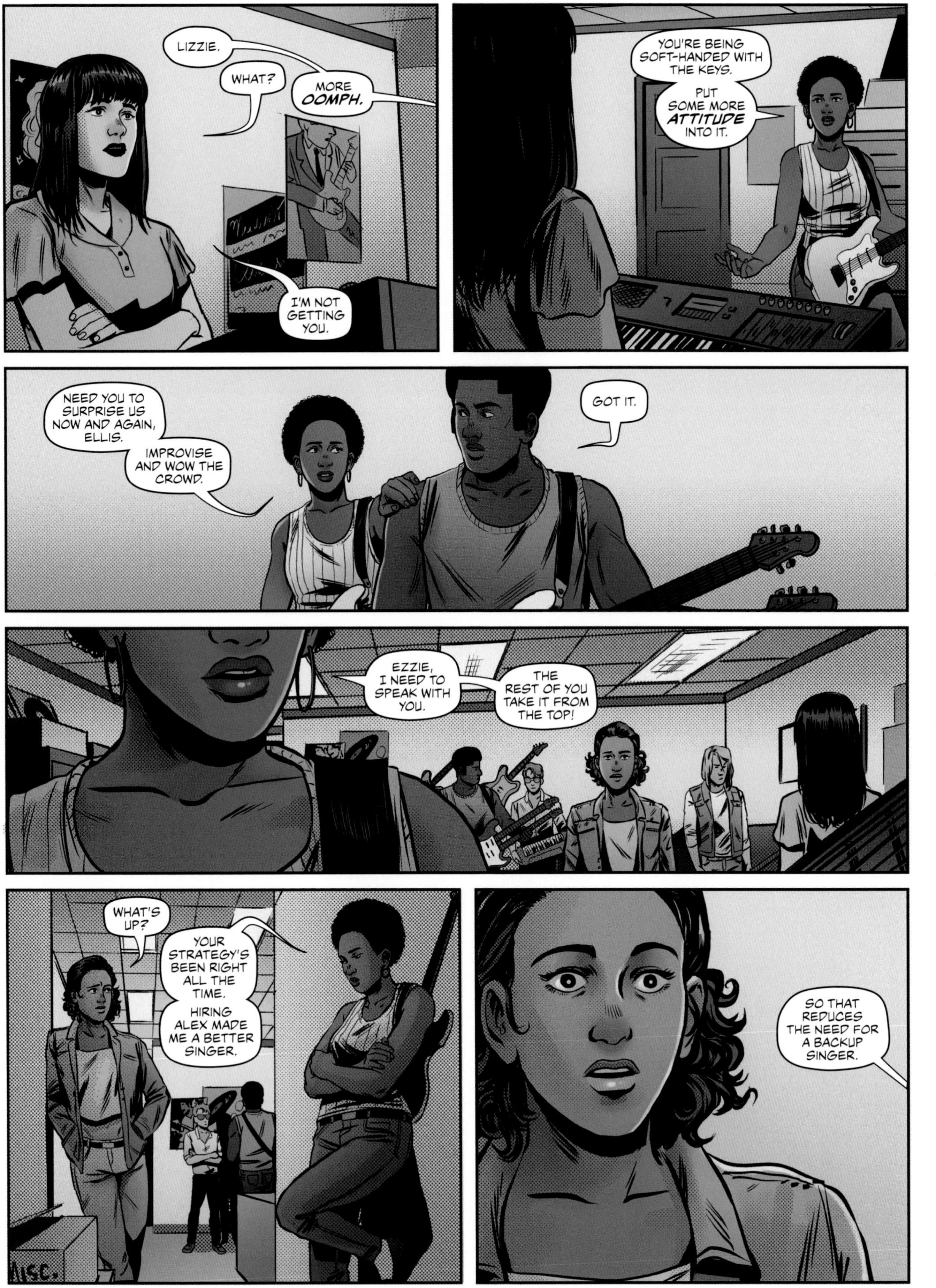

LIZZIE.
WHAT?
MORE OOMPH.
I'M NOT GETTING YOU.
YOU'RE BEING SOFT-HANDED WITH THE KEYS.
PUT SOME MORE ATTITUDE INTO IT.
NEED YOU TO SURPRISE US NOW AND AGAIN, ELLIS.
IMPROVISE AND WOW THE CROWD.
GOT IT.
EZZIE, I NEED TO SPEAK WITH YOU.
THE REST OF YOU TAKE IT FROM THE TOP!
WHAT'S UP?
YOUR STRATEGY'S BEEN RIGHT ALL THE TIME.
HIRING ALEX MADE ME A BETTER SINGER.
SO THAT REDUCES THE NEED FOR A BACKUP SINGER.

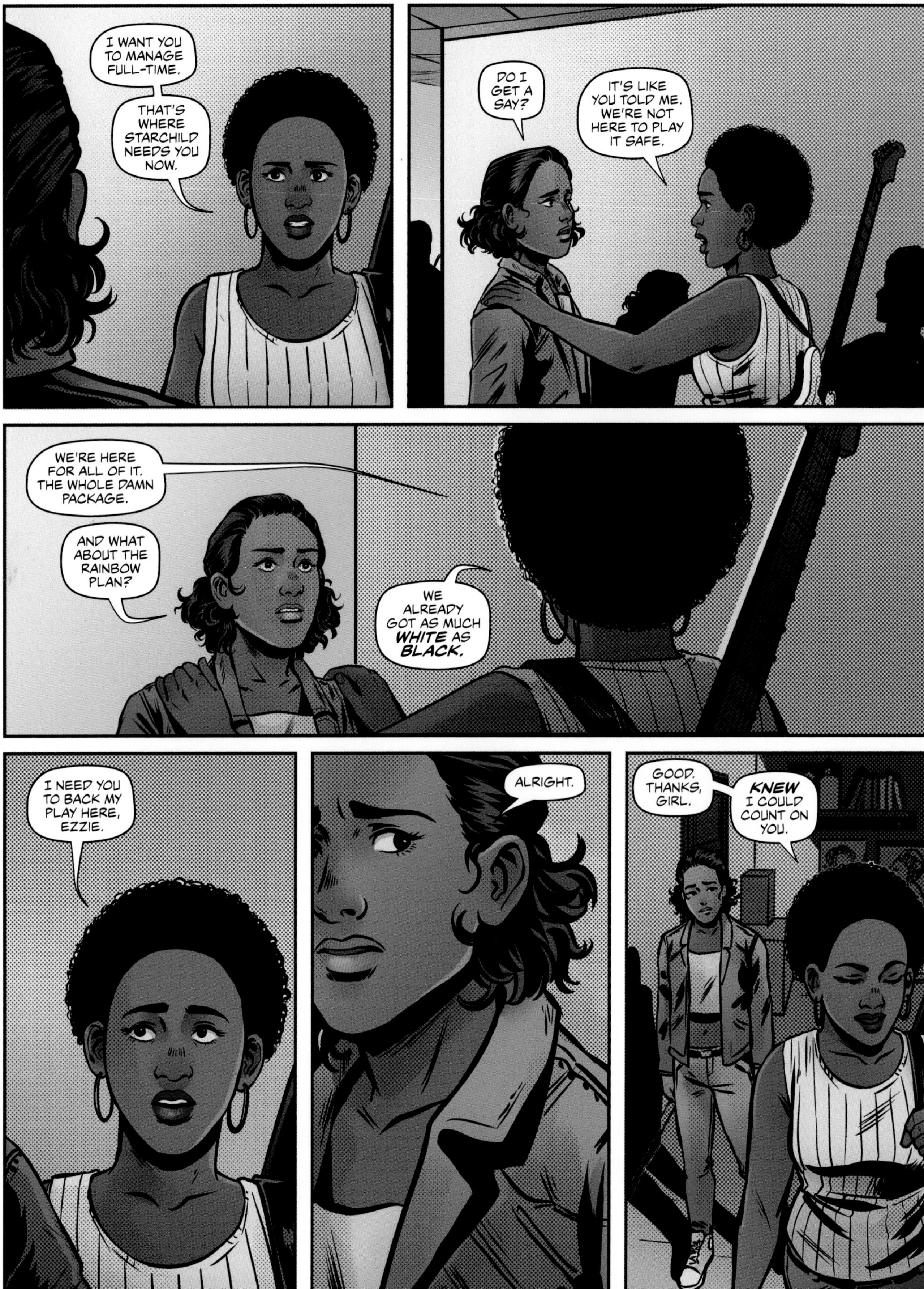
I WANT YOU TO MANAGE FULL-TIME.
THAT'S WHERE STARCHILD NEEDS YOU NOW.
DO I GET A SAY?
IT'S LIKE YOU TOLD ME. WE'RE NOT HERE TO PLAY IT SAFE.
WE'RE HERE FOR ALL OF IT. THE WHOLE DAMN PACKAGE.
AND WHAT ABOUT THE RAINBOW PLAN?
WE ALREADY GOT AS MUCH WHITE AS BLACK.
I NEED YOU TO BACK MY PLAY HERE, EZZIE.
ALRIGHT.
GOOD. THANKS, GIRL.
KNEW I COULD COUNT ON YOU.

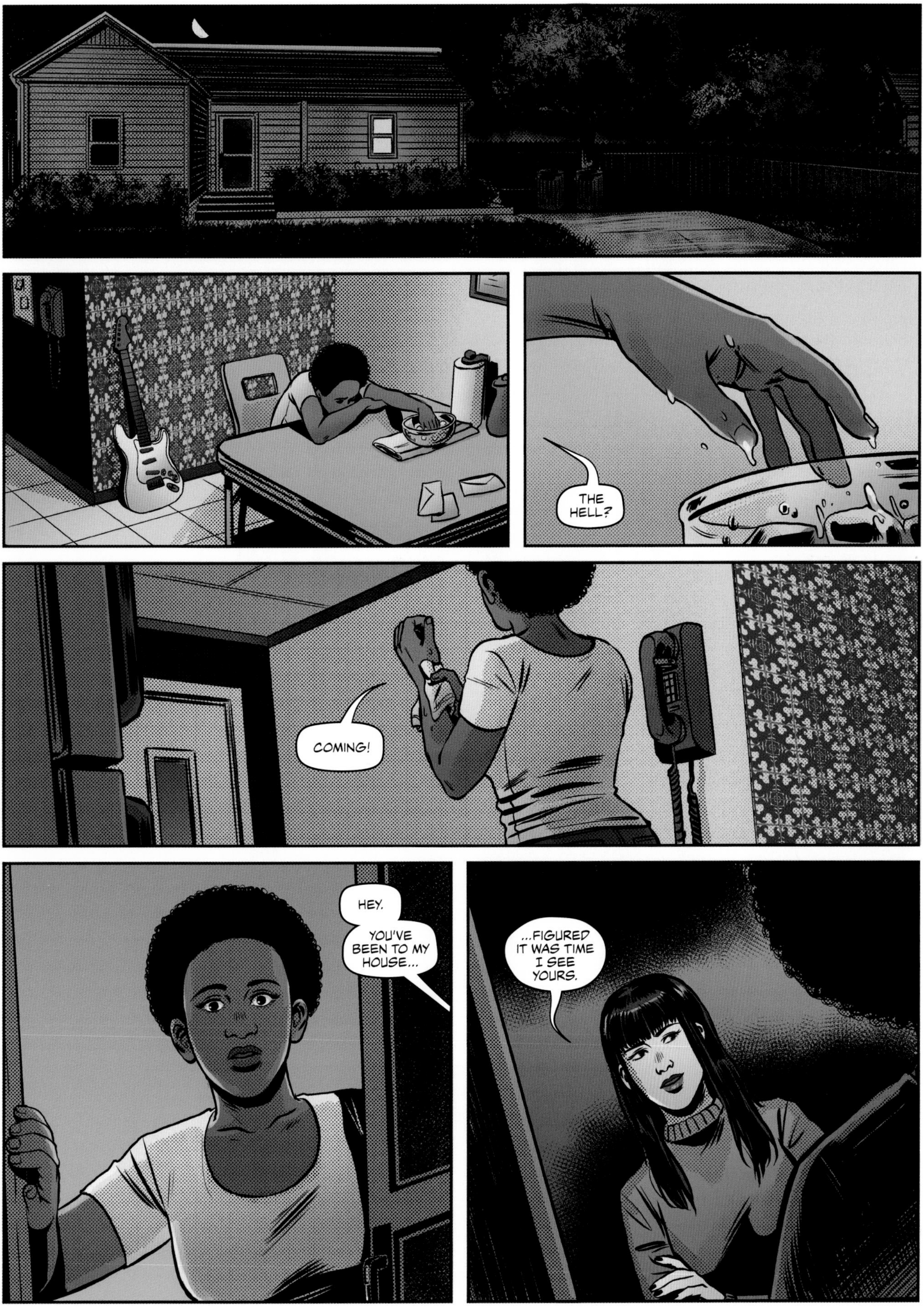
THE HELL?
COMING!
HEY.
YOU'VE BEEN TO MY HOUSE...
...FIGURED IT WAS TIME I SEE YOURS.

NICE PLACE.

BORN AND RAISED IN IT. OUR PARENTS BUSTED HUMP TO GIVE ELLIS AND ME A DECENT LIFE.

WHAT'S GOING ON, LIZZIE?

THE WAY THINGS ARE GOING WITH THE BAND--

--I DON'T LIKE IT.

I CAME ON BOARD BECAUSE OF YOU.

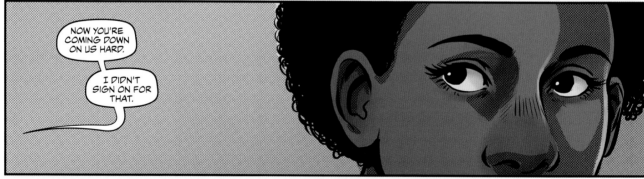

NOW YOU'RE COMING DOWN ON US HARD.

I DIDN'T SIGN ON FOR THAT.

YOU WANT TO TELL ME WHAT'S HAPPENING?

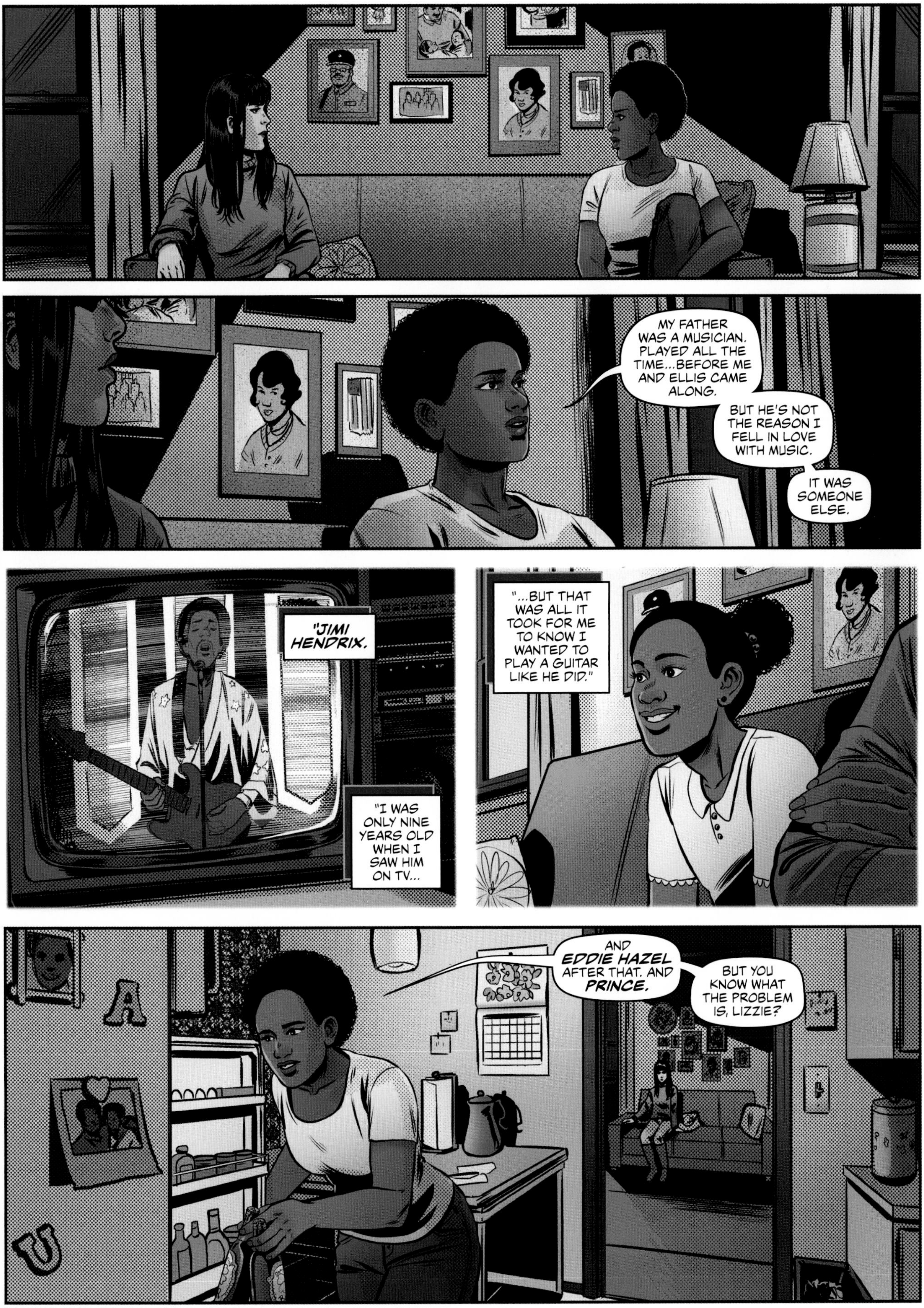
MY FATHER WAS A MUSICIAN. PLAYED ALL THE TIME...BEFORE ME AND ELLIS CAME ALONG.
BUT HE'S NOT THE REASON I FELL IN LOVE WITH MUSIC.
IT WAS SOMEONE ELSE.
"JIMI HENDRIX.
"I WAS ONLY NINE YEARS OLD WHEN I SAW HIM ON TV...
"...BUT THAT WAS ALL IT TOOK FOR ME TO KNOW I WANTED TO PLAY A GUITAR LIKE HE DID."
AND EDDIE HAZEL AFTER THAT. AND PRINCE.
BUT YOU KNOW WHAT THE PROBLEM IS, LIZZIE?

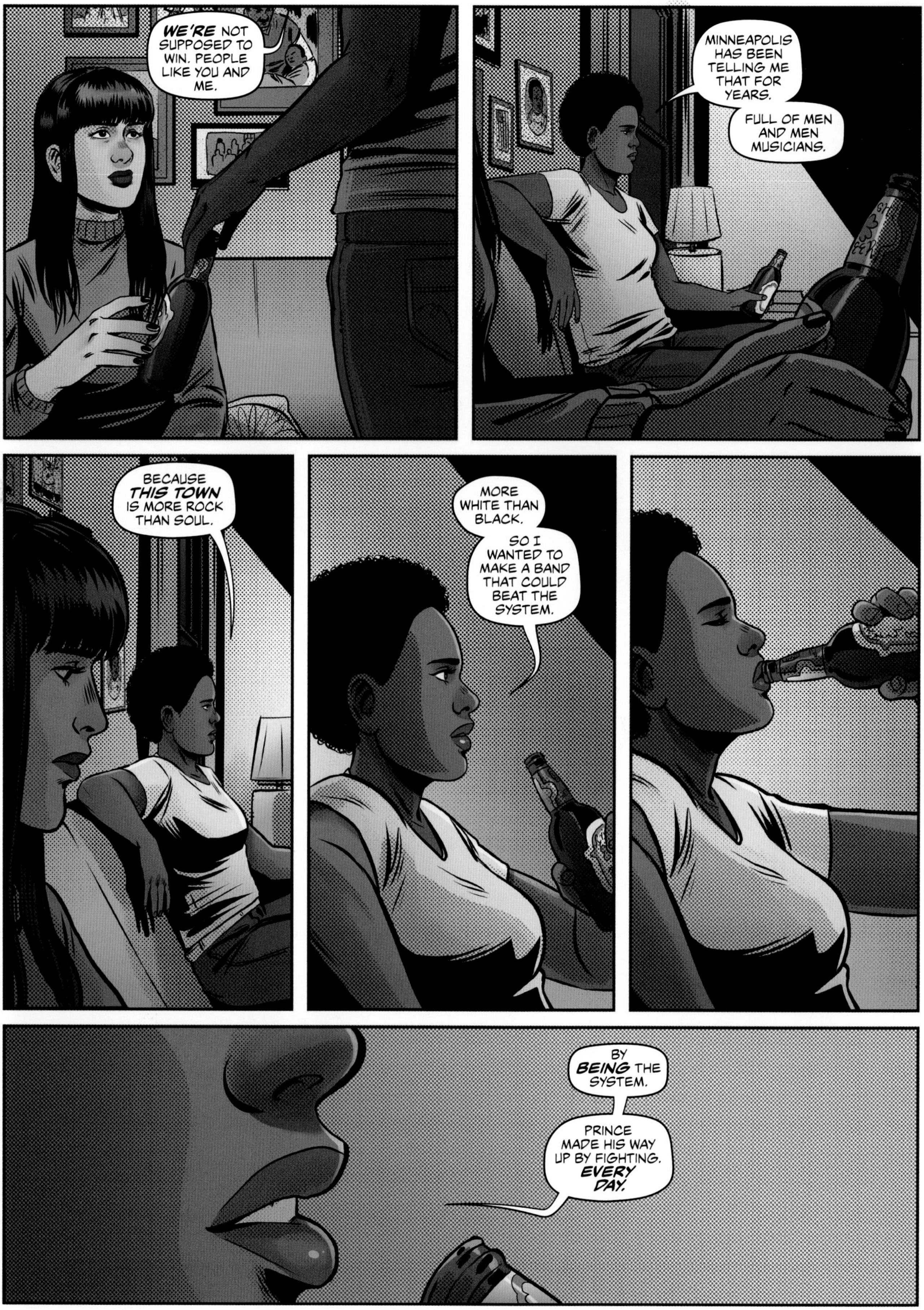
WE'RE NOT SUPPOSED TO WIN. PEOPLE LIKE YOU AND ME.
MINNEAPOLIS HAS BEEN TELLING ME THAT FOR YEARS.
FULL OF MEN AND MEN MUSICIANS.
BECAUSE THIS TOWN IS MORE ROCK THAN SOUL.
MORE WHITE THAN BLACK.
SO I WANTED TO MAKE A BAND THAT COULD BEAT THE SYSTEM.
BY BEING THE SYSTEM.
PRINCE MADE HIS WAY UP BY FIGHTING. EVERY DAY.

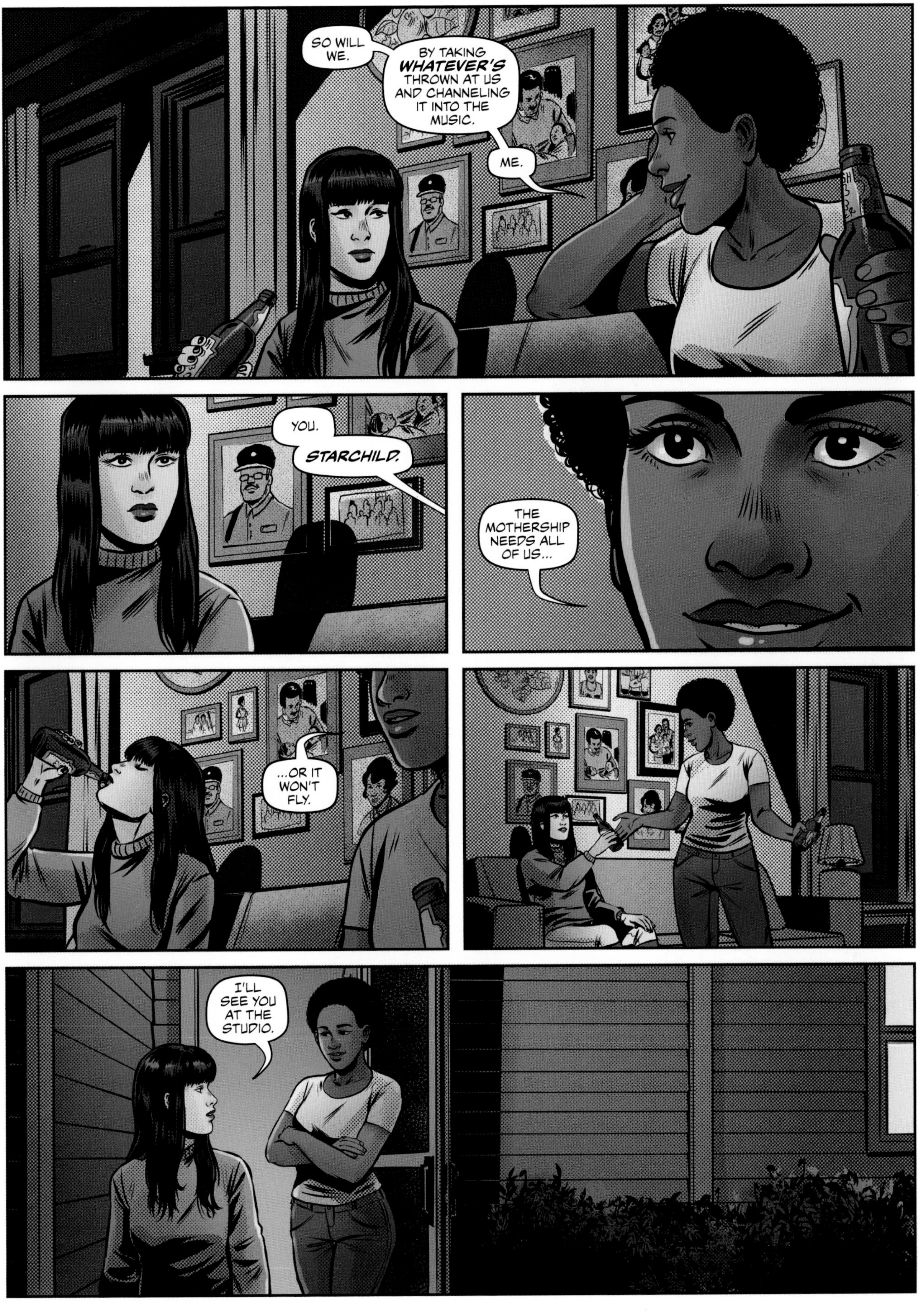

SO WILL WE.
BY TAKING WHATEVER'S THROWN AT US AND CHANNELING IT INTO THE MUSIC.
ME.
YOU.
STARCHILD.
THE MOTHERSHIP NEEDS ALL OF US...
...OR IT WON'T FLY.
I'LL SEE YOU AT THE STUDIO.

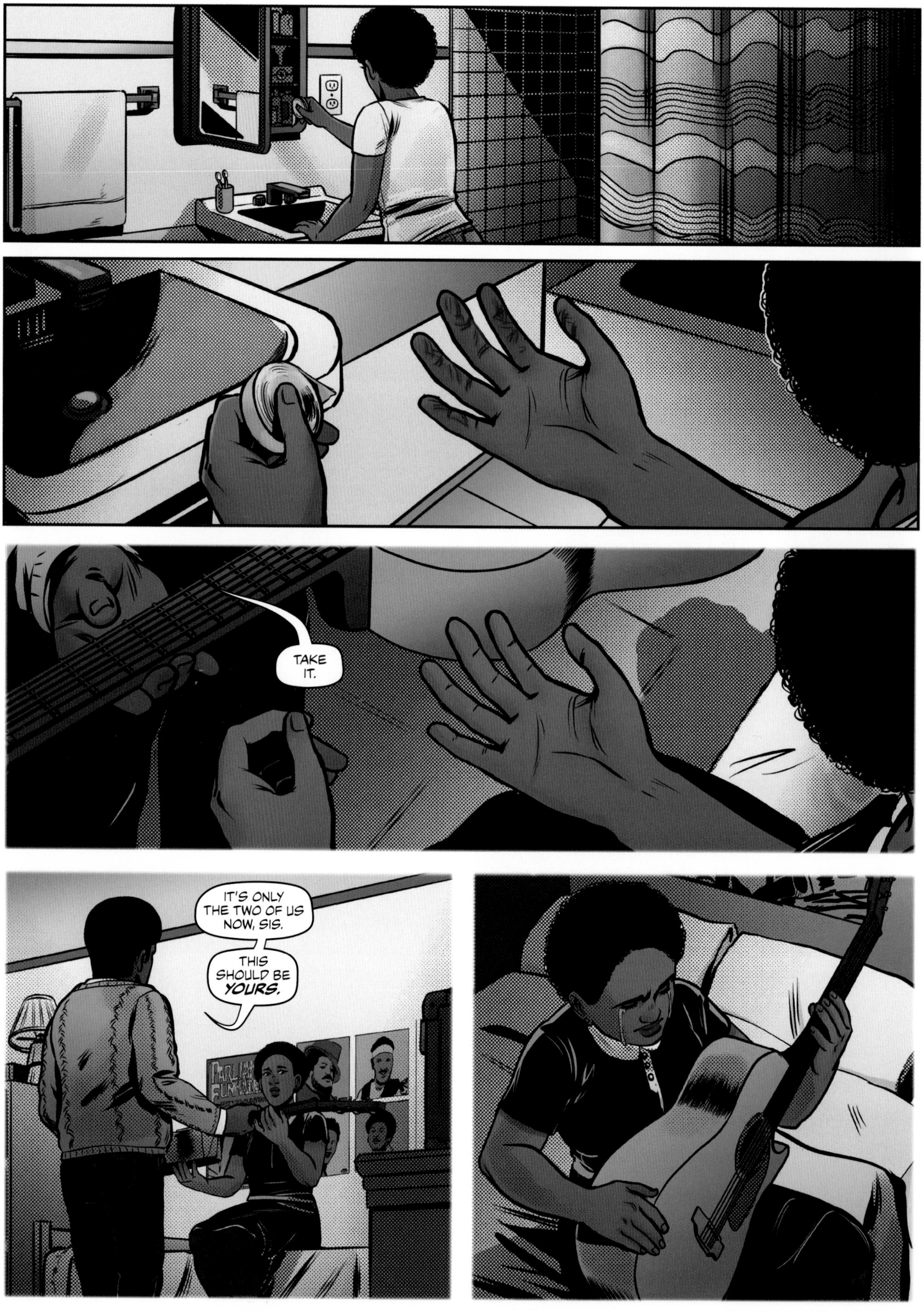
TAKE IT.
IT'S ONLY THE TWO OF US NOW, SIS.
THIS SHOULD BE ***YOURS.***

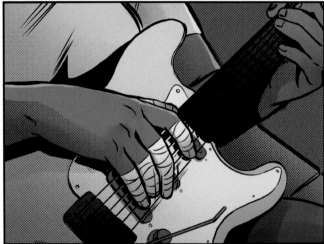

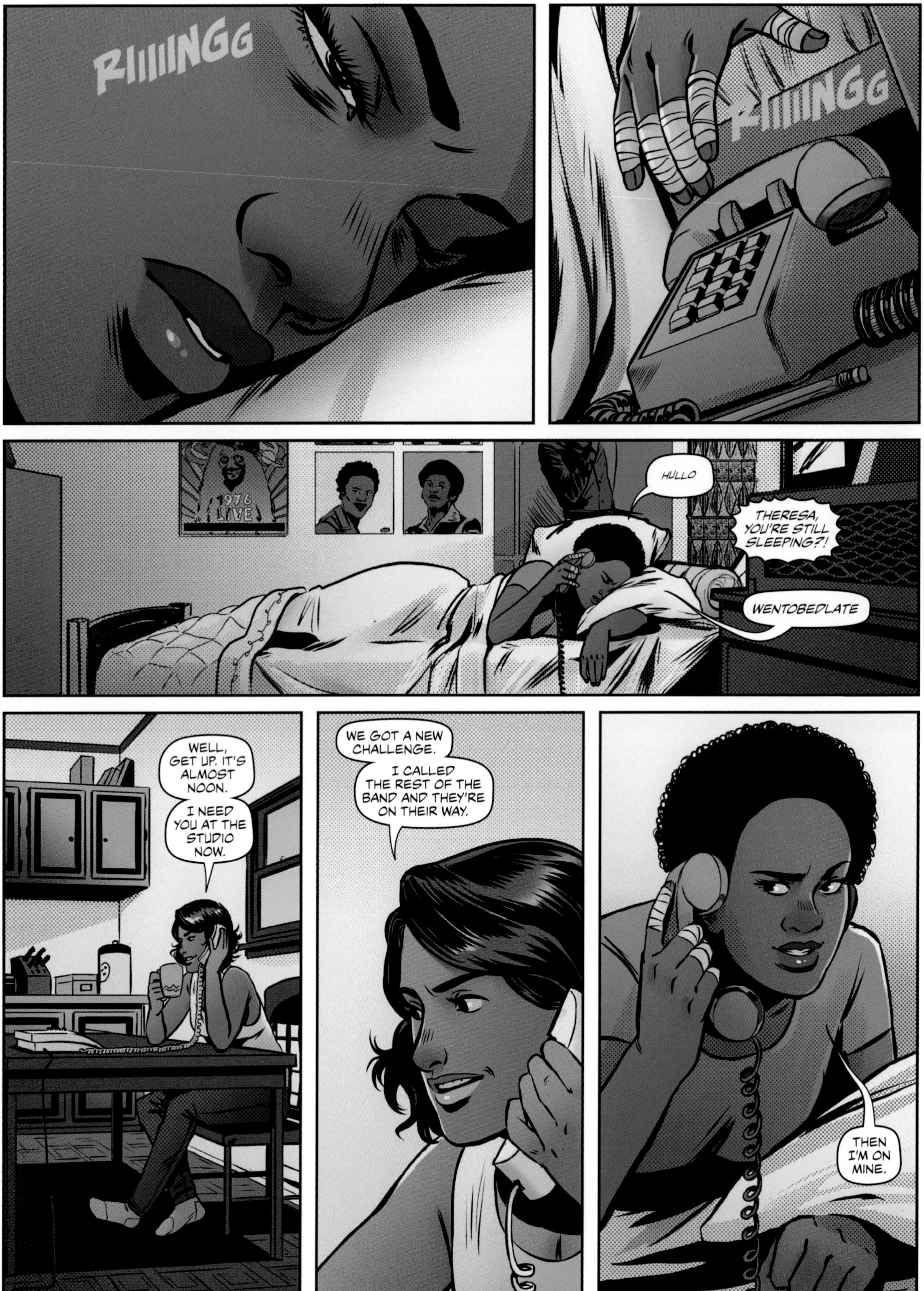
RIIIINGG
RIIIINGG
HULLO
THERESA, YOU'RE STILL SLEEPING?!
WENTOBEDLATE
WELL, GET UP. IT'S ALMOST NOON.
I NEED YOU AT THE STUDIO NOW.
WE GOT A NEW CHALLENGE.
I CALLED THE REST OF THE BAND AND THEY'RE ON THEIR WAY.
THEN I'M ON MINE.

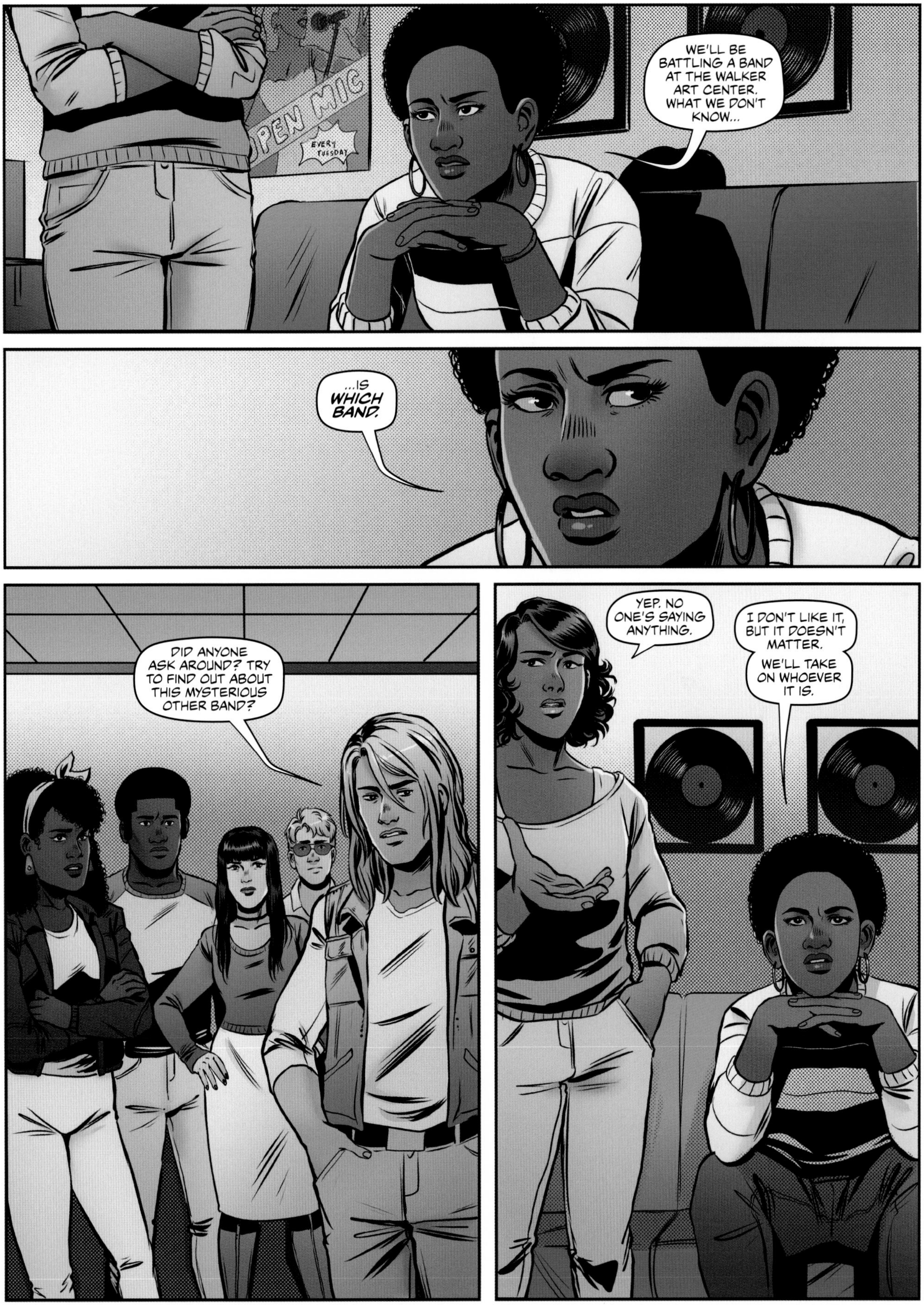

WE'LL BE BATTLING A BAND AT THE WALKER ART CENTER. WHAT WE DON'T KNOW...
OPEN MIC
EVERY TUESDAY
...IS WHICH BAND.
DID ANYONE ASK AROUND? TRY TO FIND OUT ABOUT THIS MYSTERIOUS OTHER BAND?
YEP. NO ONE'S SAYING ANYTHING.
I DON'T LIKE IT, BUT IT DOESN'T MATTER.
WE'LL TAKE ON WHOEVER IT IS.

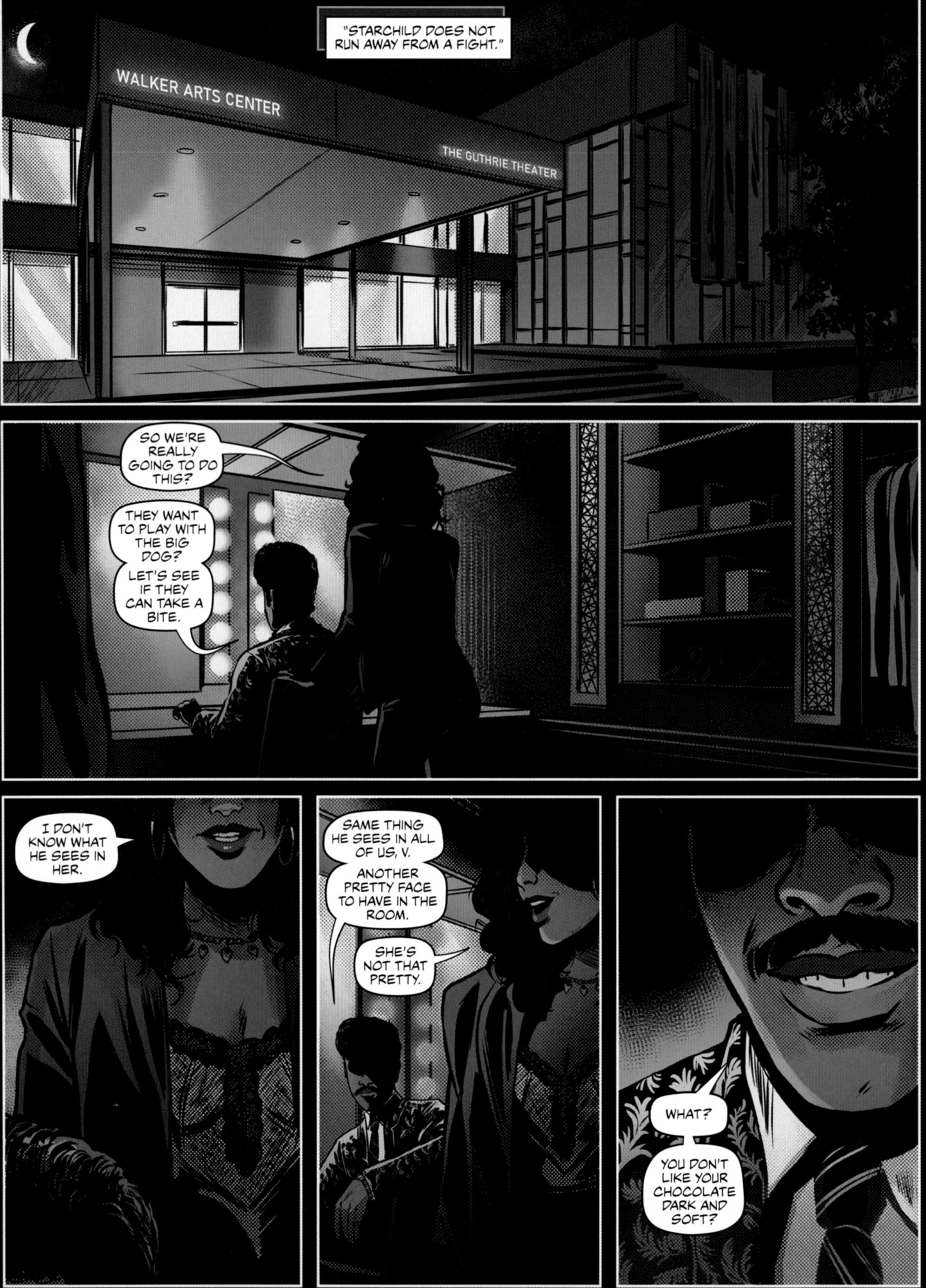
"STARCHILD DOES NOT RUN AWAY FROM A FIGHT."
WALKER ARTS CENTER
THE GUTHRIE THEATER
SO WE'RE REALLY GOING TO DO THIS?
THEY WANT TO PLAY WITH THE BIG DOG?
LET'S SEE IF THEY CAN TAKE A BITE.
I DON'T KNOW WHAT HE SEES IN HER.
SAME THING HE SEES IN ALL OF US, V.
ANOTHER PRETTY FACE TO HAVE IN THE ROOM.
SHE'S NOT THAT PRETTY.
WHAT?
YOU DON'T LIKE YOUR CHOCOLATE DARK AND SOFT?

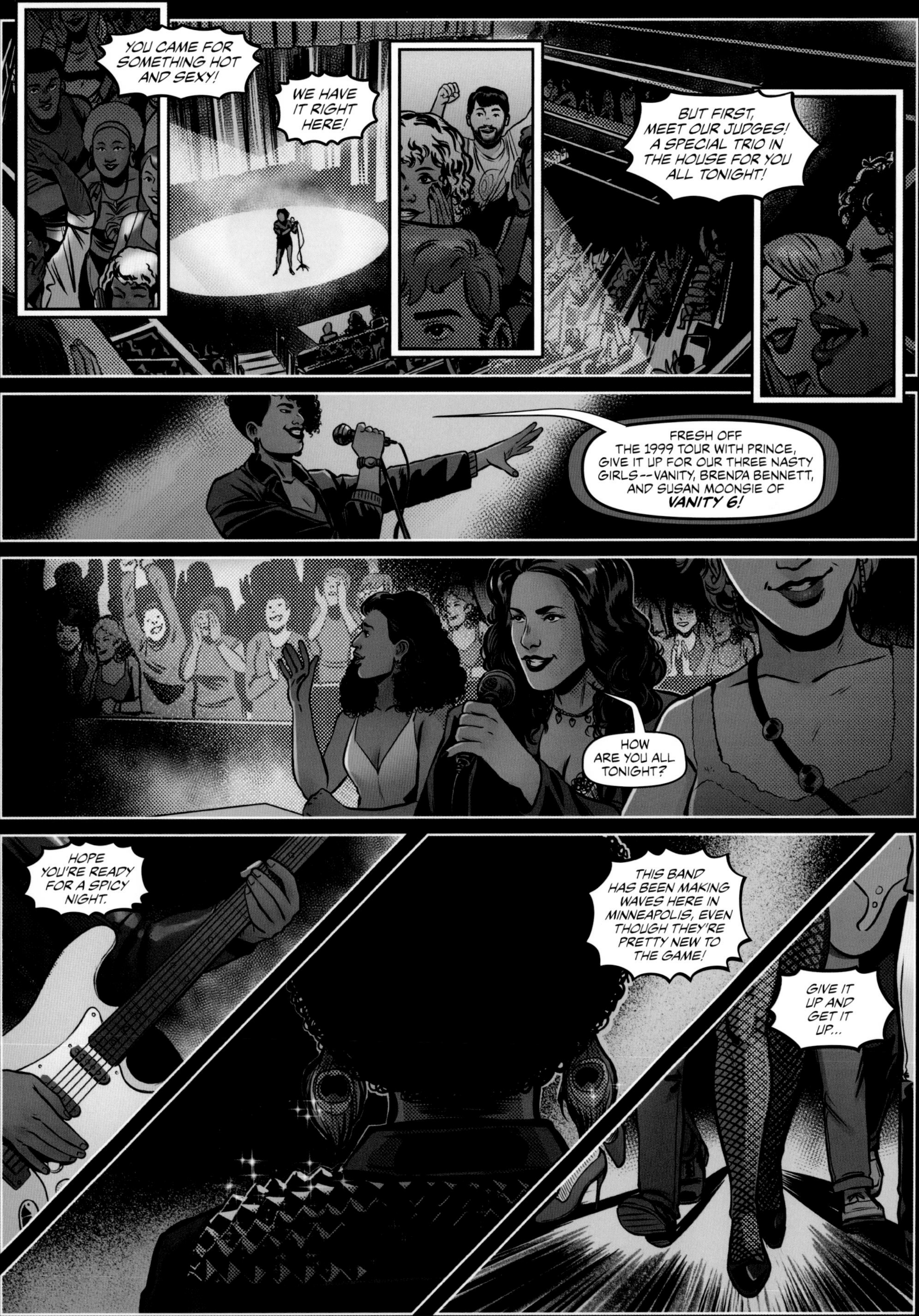
YOU CAME FOR SOMETHING HOT AND SEXY!
WE HAVE IT RIGHT HERE!
BUT FIRST, MEET OUR JUDGES! A SPECIAL TRIO IN THE HOUSE FOR YOU ALL TONIGHT!
FRESH OFF THE 1999 TOUR WITH PRINCE, GIVE IT UP FOR OUR THREE NASTY GIRLS--VANITY, BRENDA BENNETT, AND SUSAN MOONSIE OF **VANITY 6!**
HOW ARE YOU ALL TONIGHT?
HOPE YOU'RE READY FOR A SPICY NIGHT.
THIS BAND HAS BEEN MAKING WAVES HERE IN MINNEAPOLIS, EVEN THOUGH THEY'RE PRETTY NEW TO THE GAME!
GIVE IT UP AND GET IT UP...

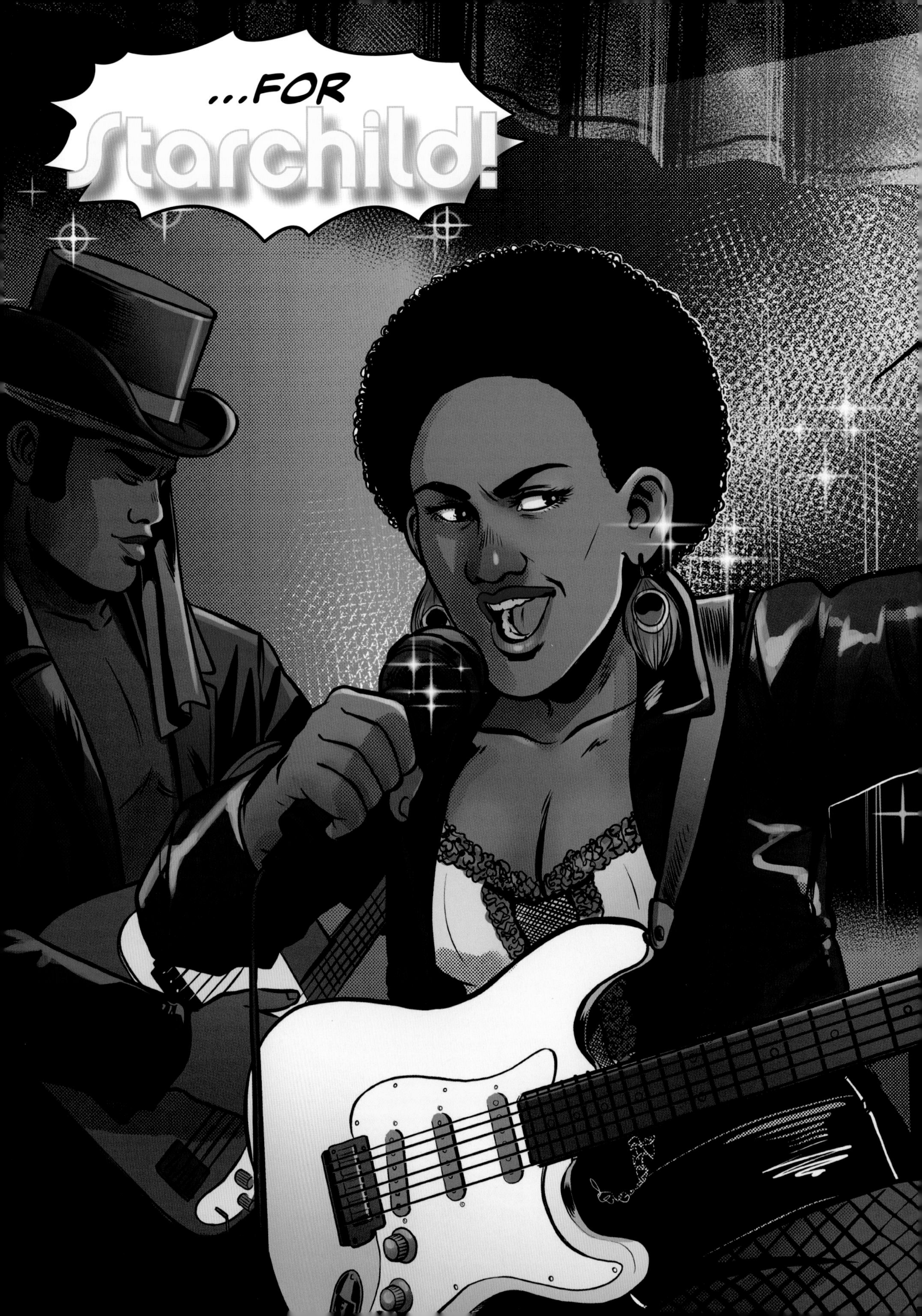
...FOR
Starchild!

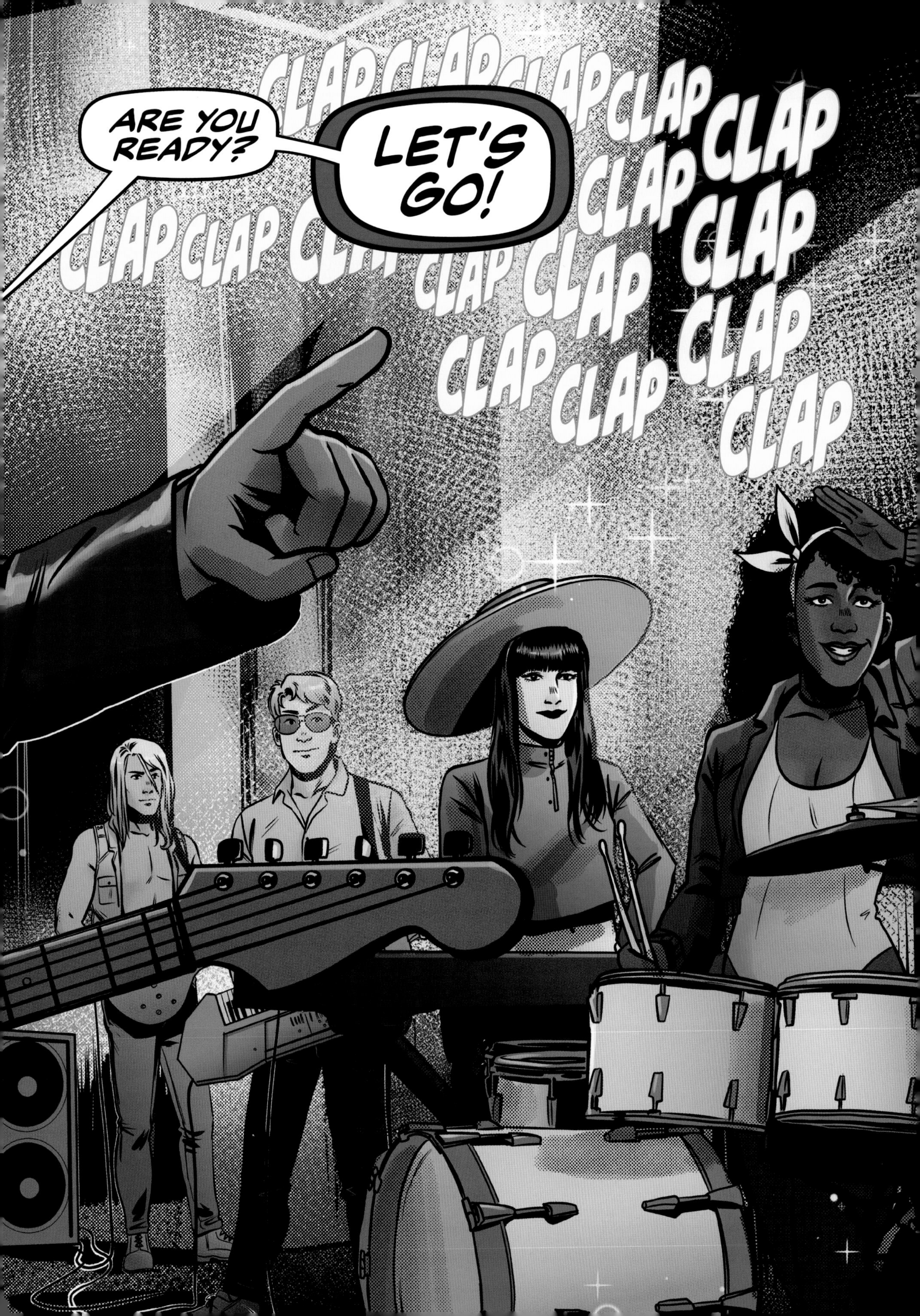
ARE YOU READY?
LET'S GO!
CLAP CLAP CLAP CLAP CLAP CLAP CLAP CLAP CLAP CLAP CLAP CLAP CLAP CLAP CLAP CLAP CLAP CLAP CLAP

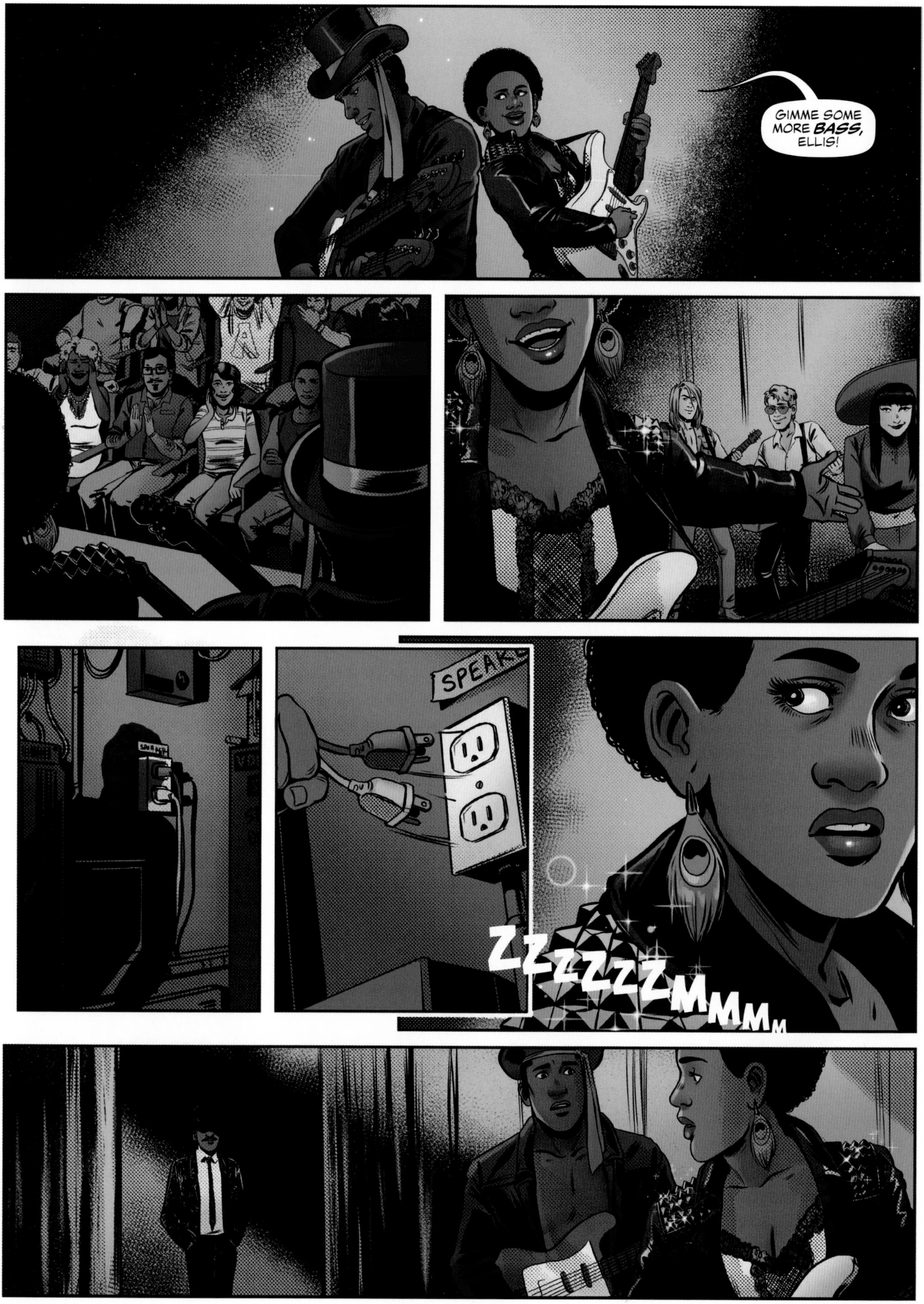
GIMME SOME MORE BASS, ELLIS!
SPEAKE
ZZZZZZZMMMM

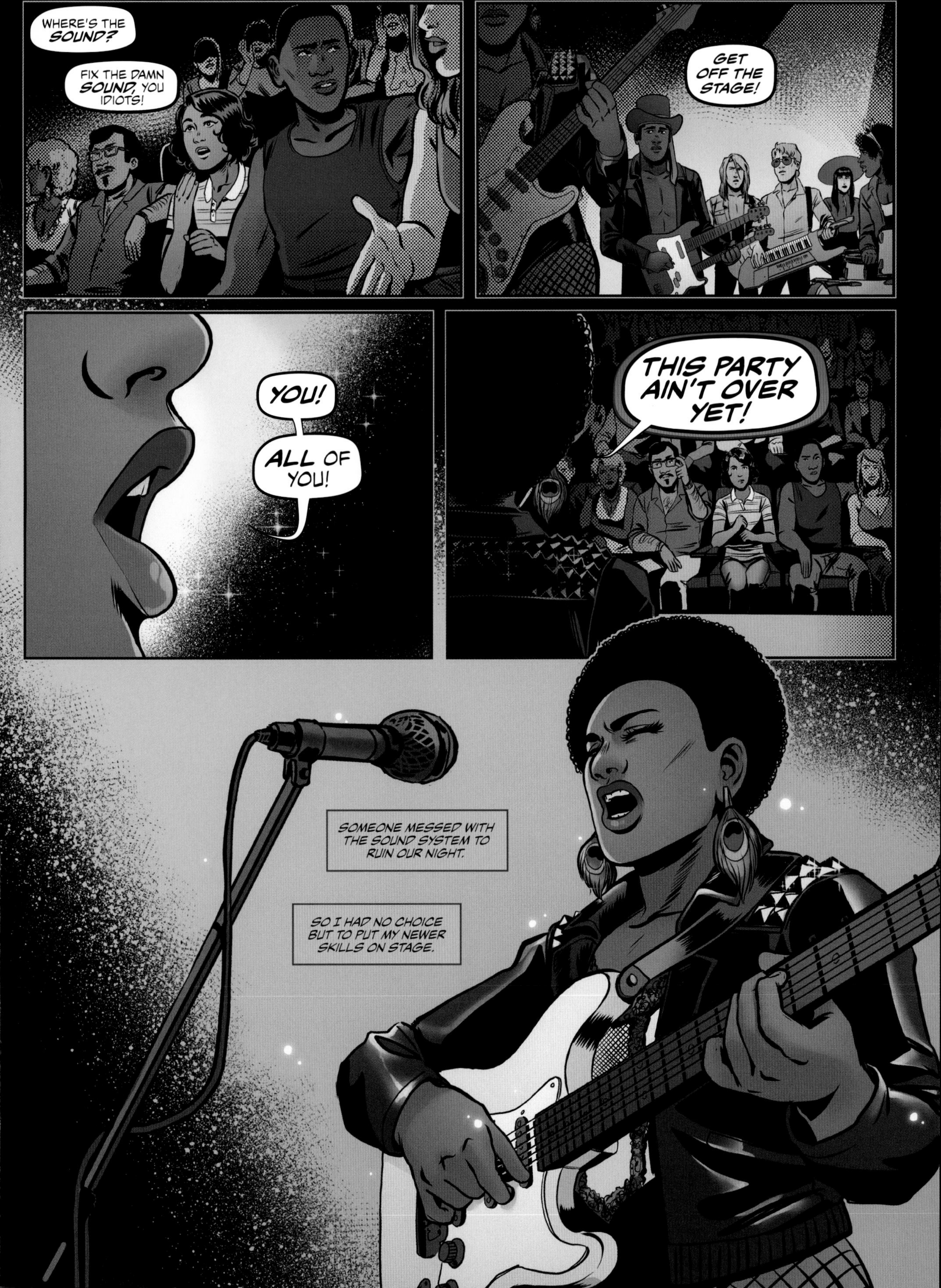
WHERE'S THE SOUND?
FIX THE DAMN SOUND, YOU IDIOTS!
GET OFF THE STAGE!
YOU!
ALL OF YOU!
THIS PARTY AIN'T OVER YET!
SOMEONE MESSED WITH THE SOUND SYSTEM TO RUIN OUR NIGHT.
SO I HAD NO CHOICE BUT TO PUT MY NEWER SKILLS ON STAGE.

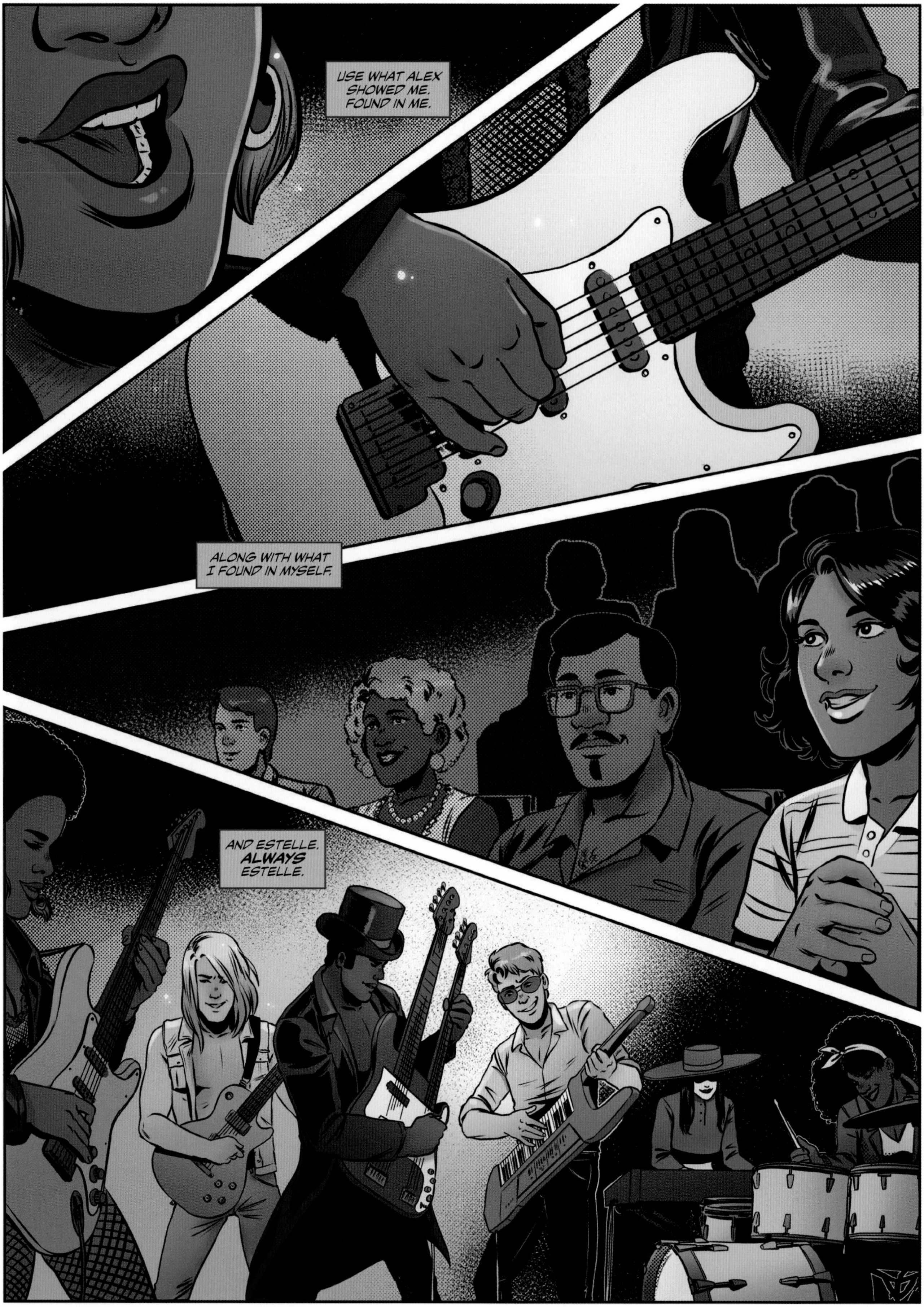
USE WHAT ALEX SHOWED ME. FOUND IN ME.
ALONG WITH WHAT I FOUND IN MYSELF.
AND ESTELLE. **ALWAYS** ESTELLE.

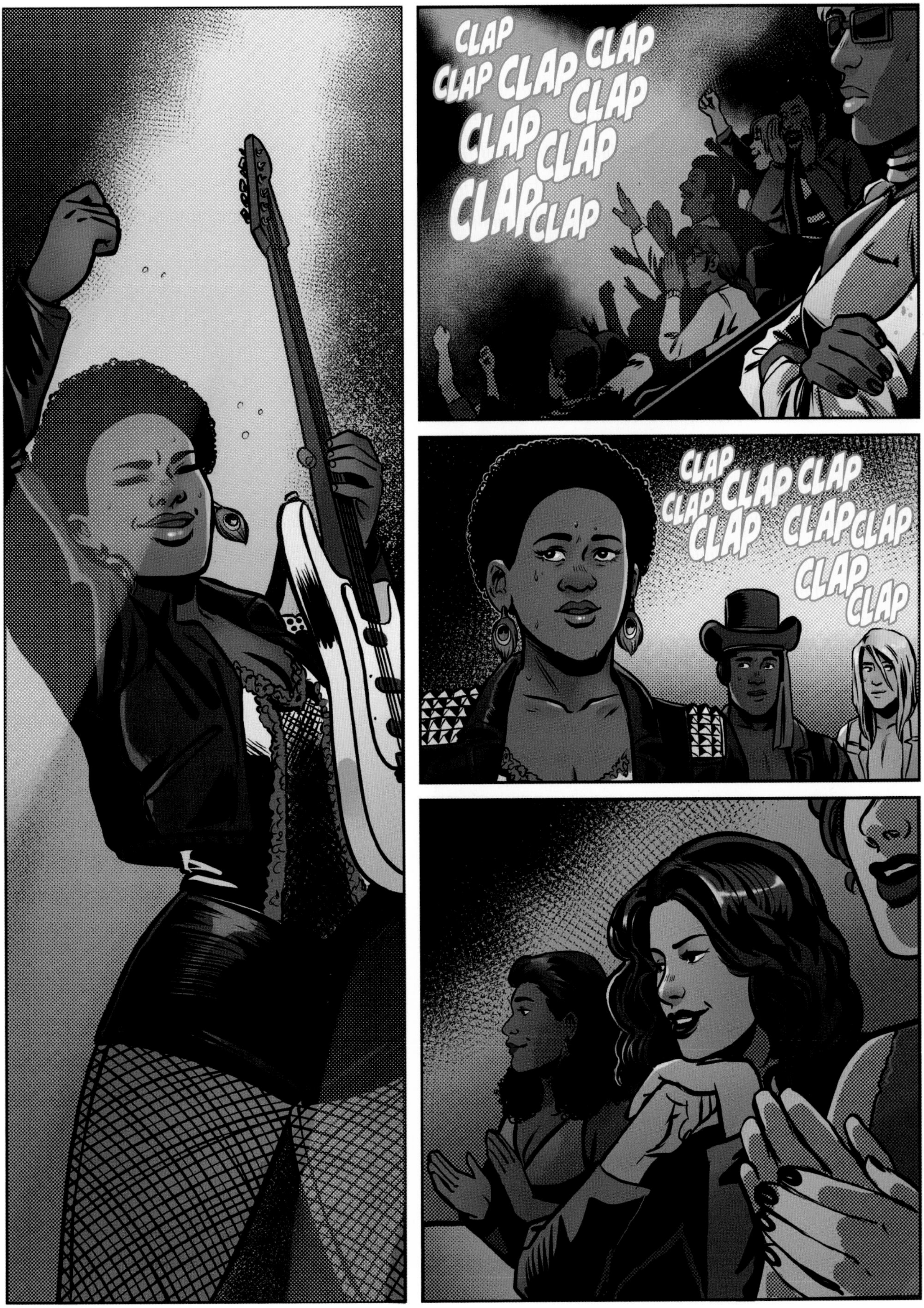
CLAP
CLAP CLAP CLAP
CLAP CLAP
CLAP CLAP
CLAP CLAP
CLAP
CLAP CLAP CLAP
CLAP CLAP CLAP
CLAP
CLAP

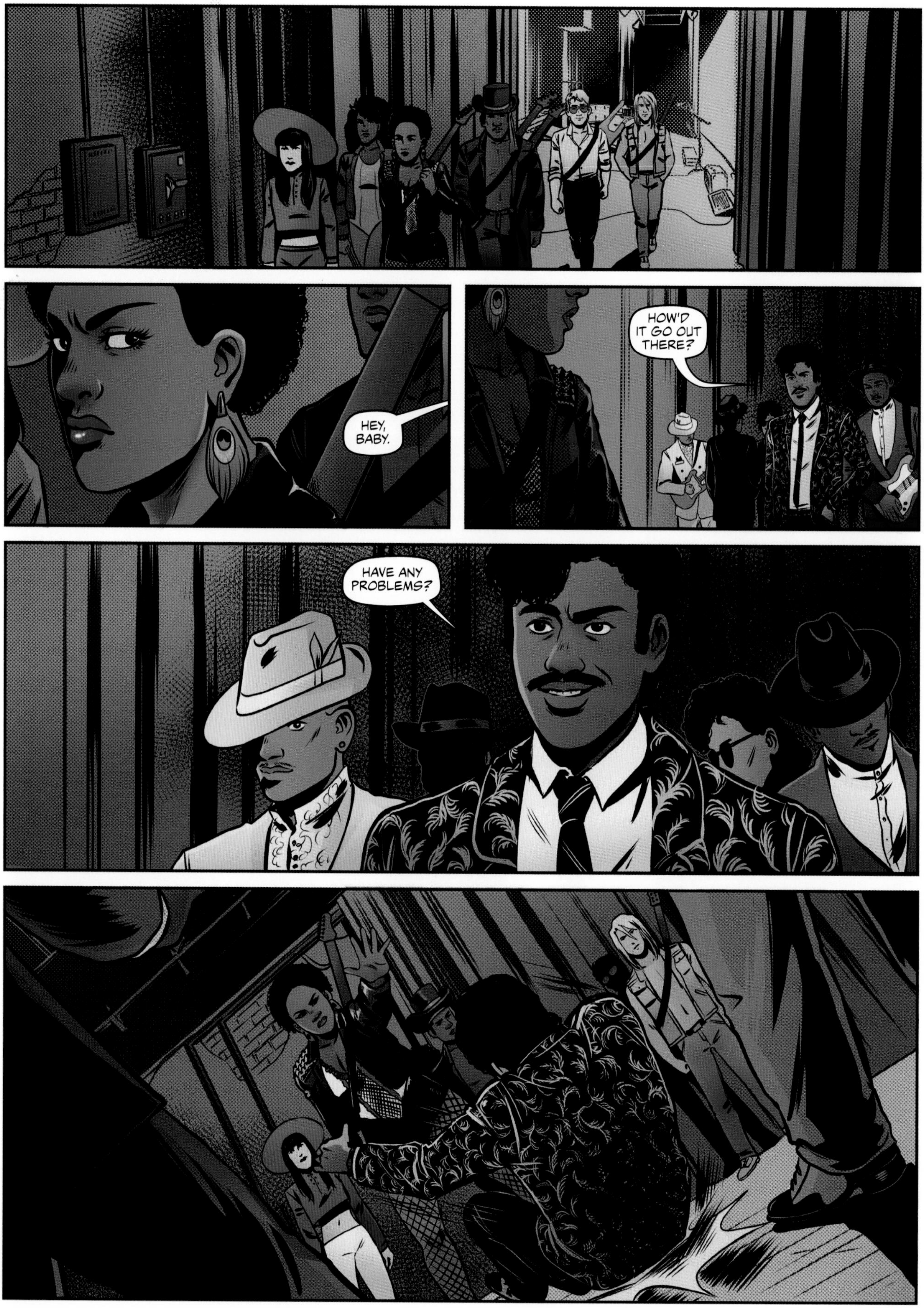
HEY, BABY.
HOW'D IT GO OUT THERE?
HAVE ANY PROBLEMS?

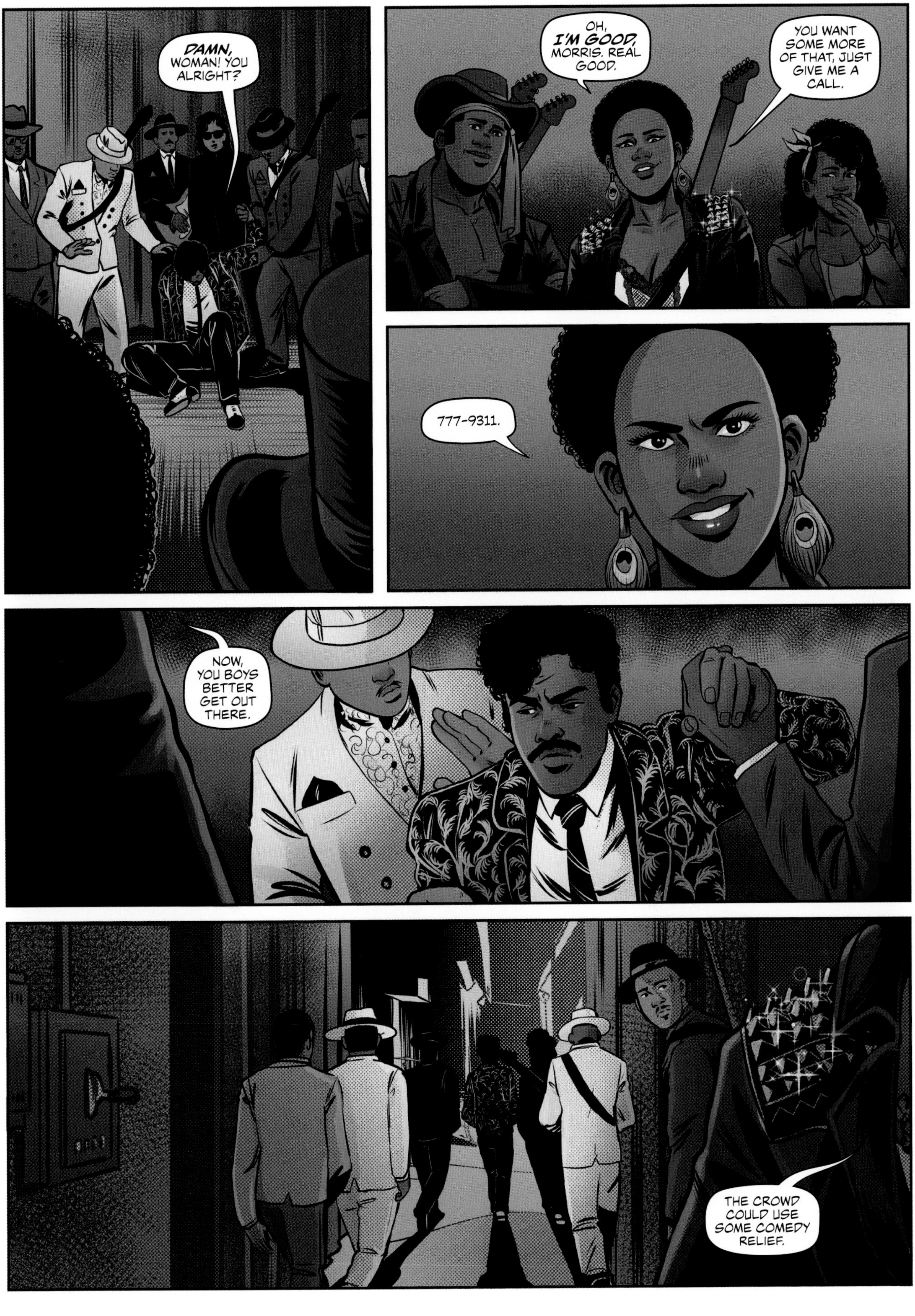
DAMN, WOMAN! YOU ALRIGHT?
OH, I'M GOOD, MORRIS. REAL GOOD.
YOU WANT SOME MORE OF THAT, JUST GIVE ME A CALL.
777-9311.
NOW, YOU BOYS BETTER GET OUT THERE.
THE CROWD COULD USE SOME COMEDY RELIEF.

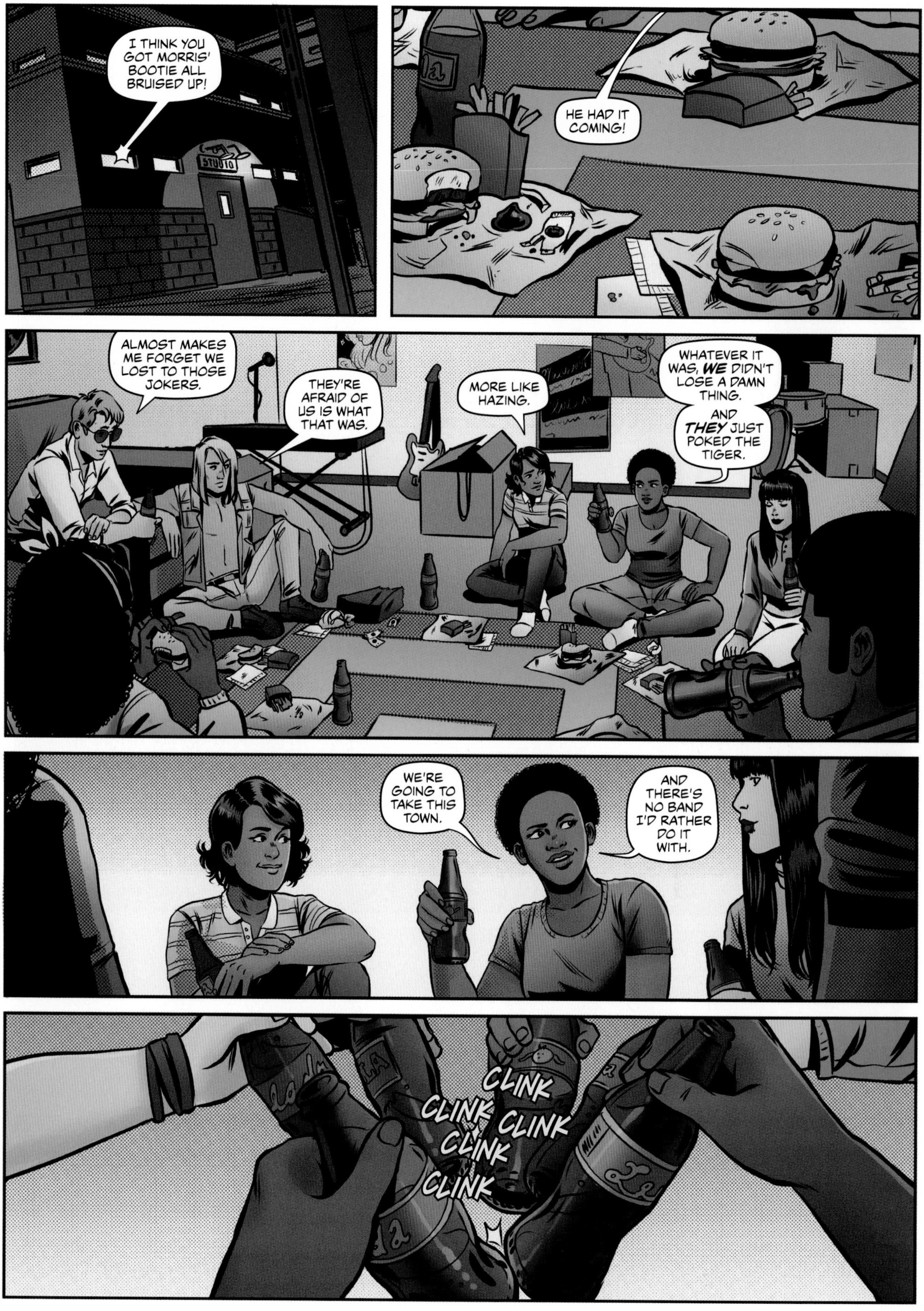
I THINK YOU GOT MORRIS' BOOTIE ALL BRUISED UP!
STUDIO
HE HAD IT COMING!
ALMOST MAKES ME FORGET WE LOST TO THOSE JOKERS.
THEY'RE AFRAID OF US IS WHAT THAT WAS.
MORE LIKE HAZING.
WHATEVER IT WAS, **WE** DIDN'T LOSE A DAMN THING.
AND **THEY** JUST POKED THE TIGER.
WE'RE GOING TO TAKE THIS TOWN.
AND THERE'S NO BAND I'D RATHER DO IT WITH.
CLINK
CLINK CLINK
CLINK
CLINK

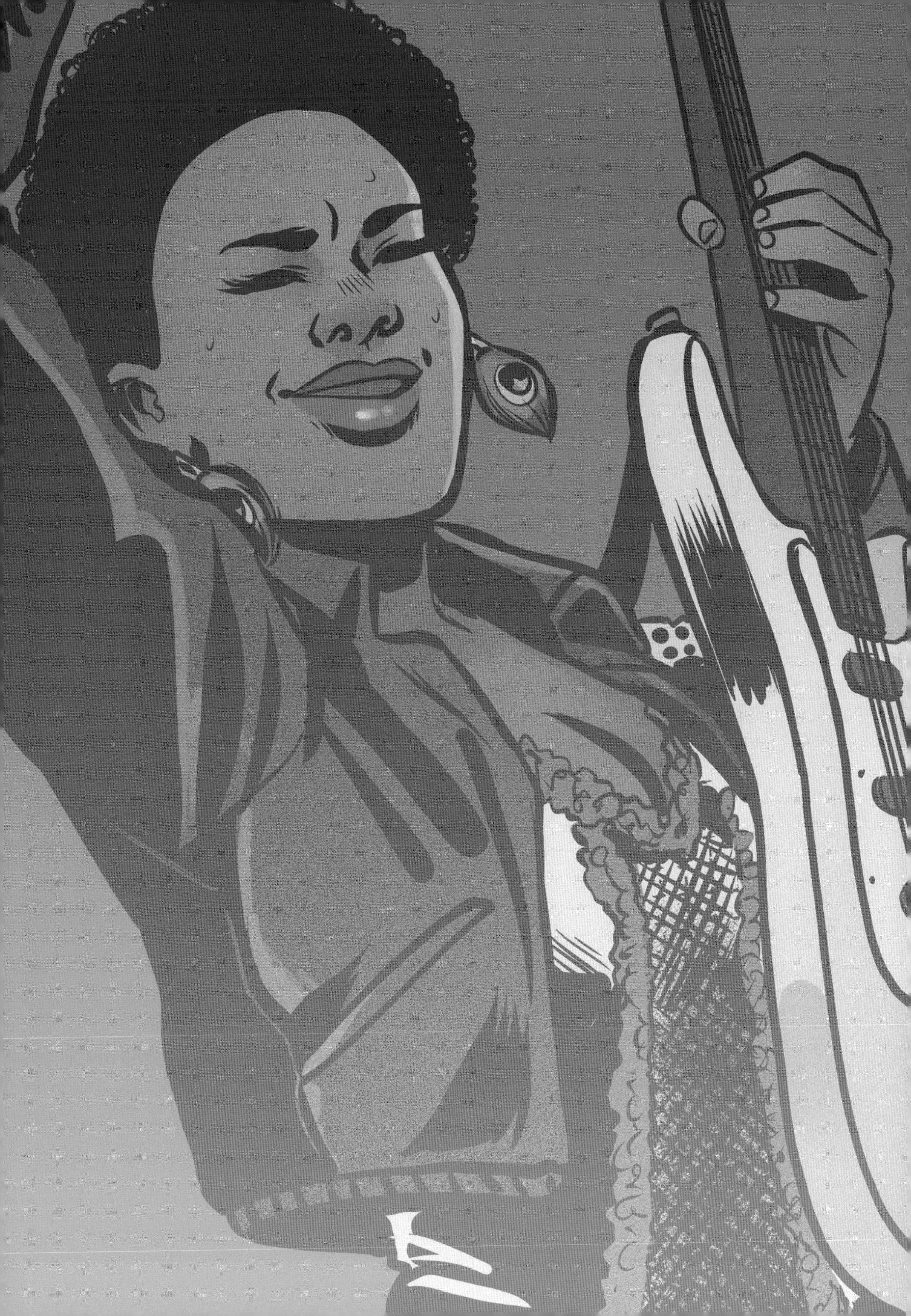

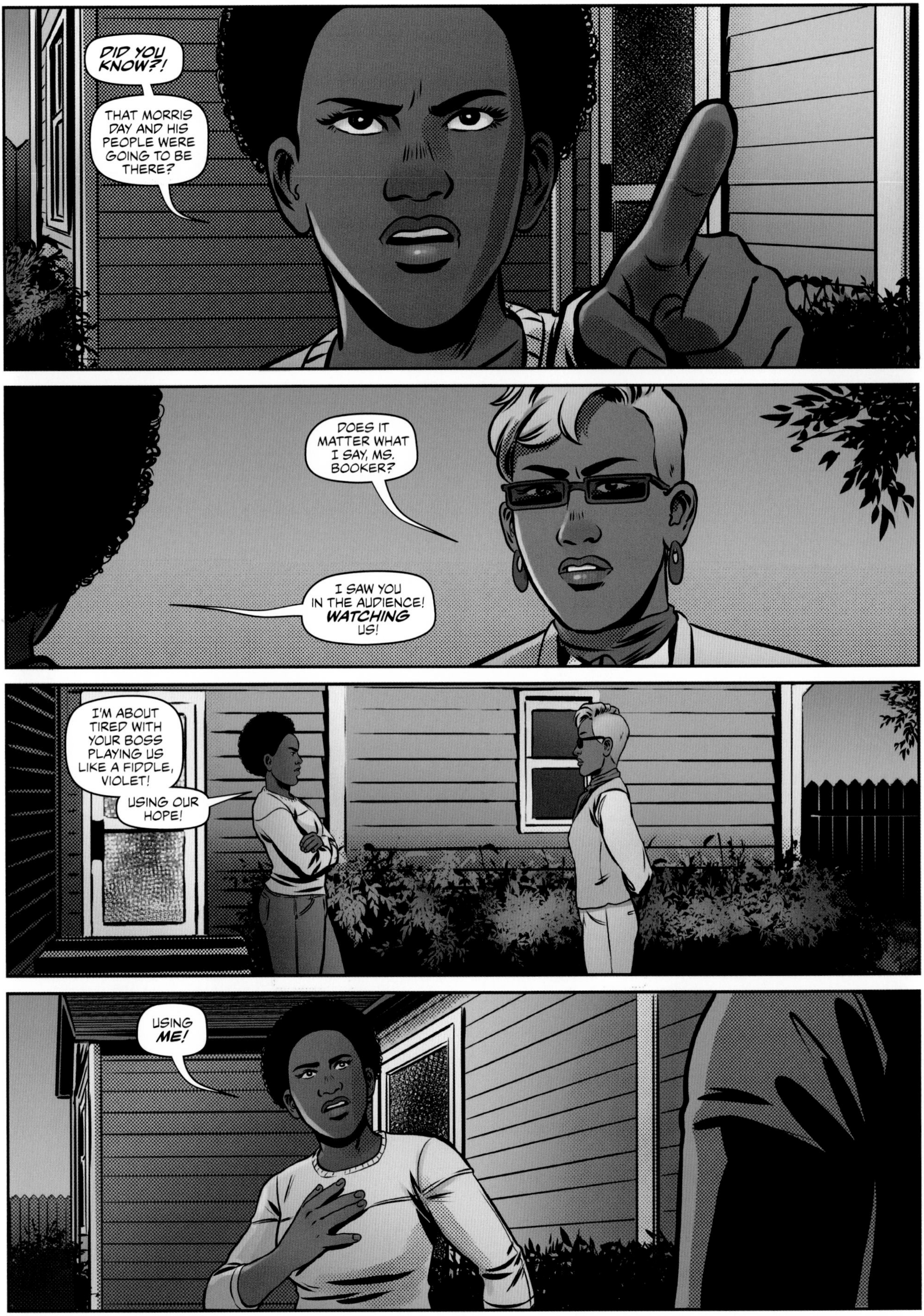
DID YOU KNOW?!
THAT MORRIS DAY AND HIS PEOPLE WERE GOING TO BE THERE?
DOES IT MATTER WHAT I SAY, MS. BOOKER?
I SAW YOU IN THE AUDIENCE! WATCHING US!
I'M ABOUT TIRED WITH YOUR BOSS PLAYING US LIKE A FIDDLE, VIOLET!
USING OUR HOPE!
USING ME!

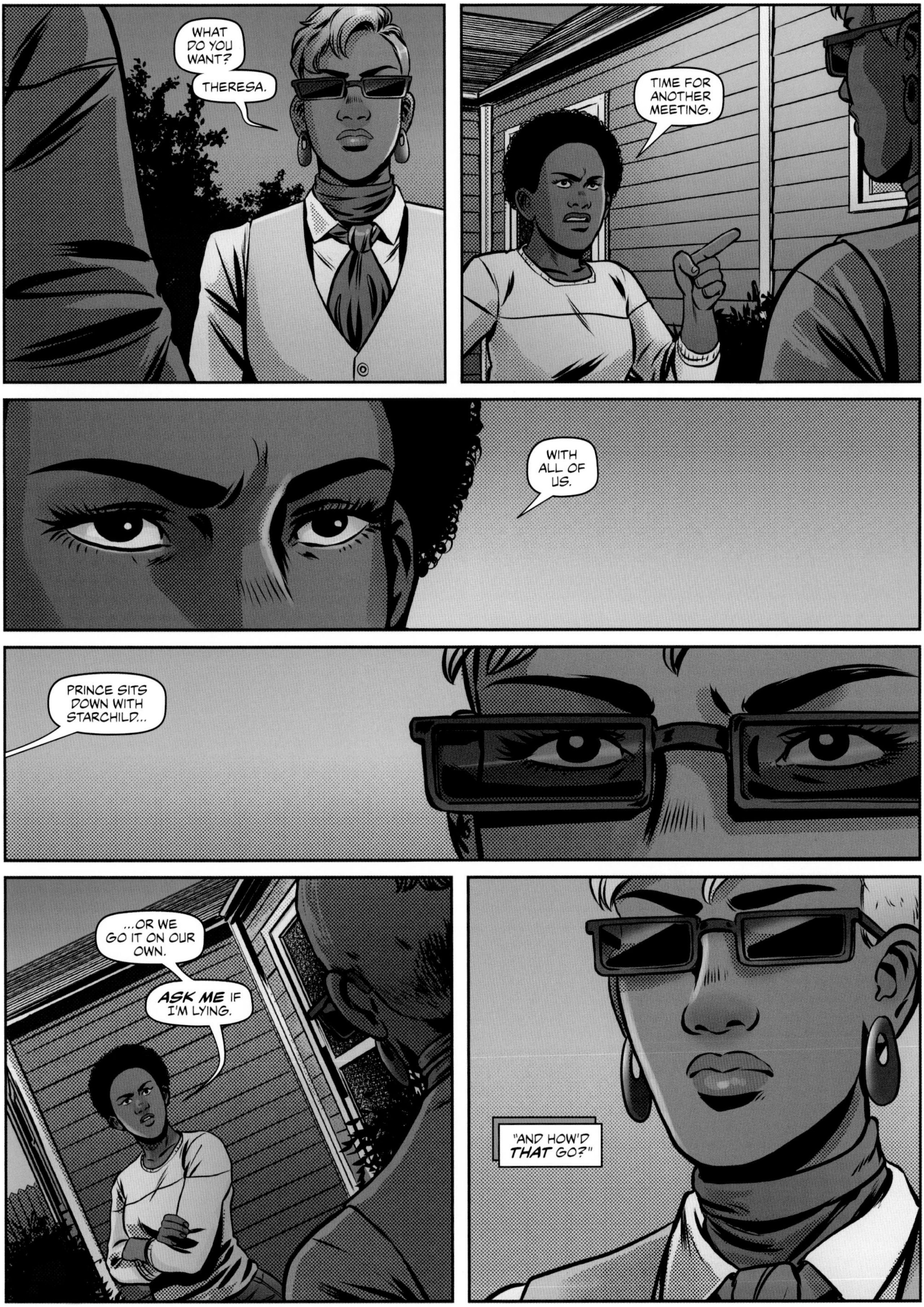

WHAT DO YOU WANT?
THERESA.
TIME FOR ANOTHER MEETING.
WITH ALL OF US.
PRINCE SITS DOWN WITH STARCHILD...
...OR WE GO IT ON OUR OWN.
ASK ME IF I'M LYING.
"AND HOW'D **THAT** GO?"

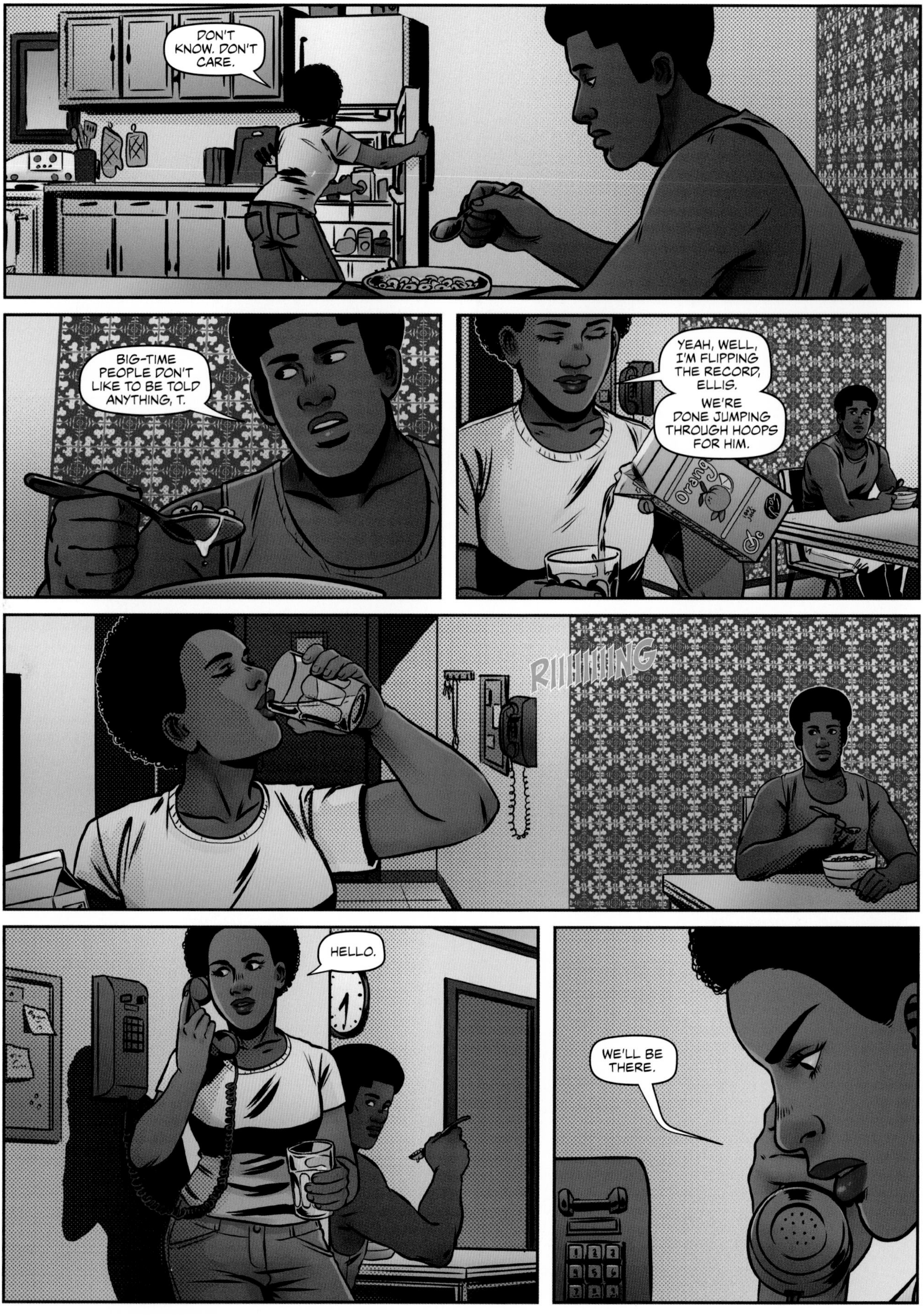
DON'T KNOW. DON'T CARE.
BIG-TIME PEOPLE DON'T LIKE TO BE TOLD ANYTHING, T.
YEAH, WELL, I'M FLIPPING THE RECORD, ELLIS.
WE'RE DONE JUMPING THROUGH HOOPS FOR HIM.
RIIIIIIIING
HELLO.
WE'LL BE THERE.

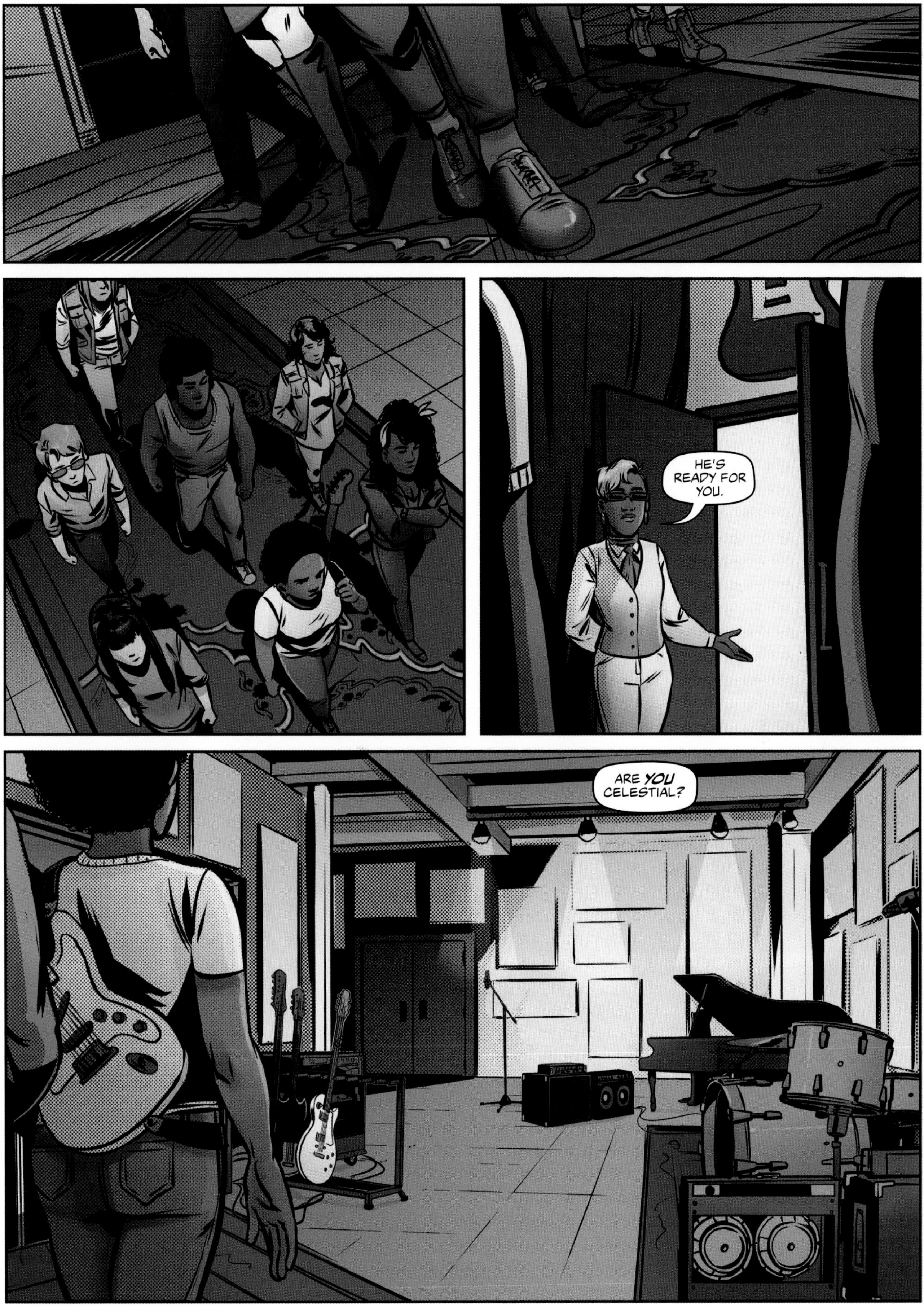
HE'S READY FOR YOU.
ARE YOU CELESTIAL?

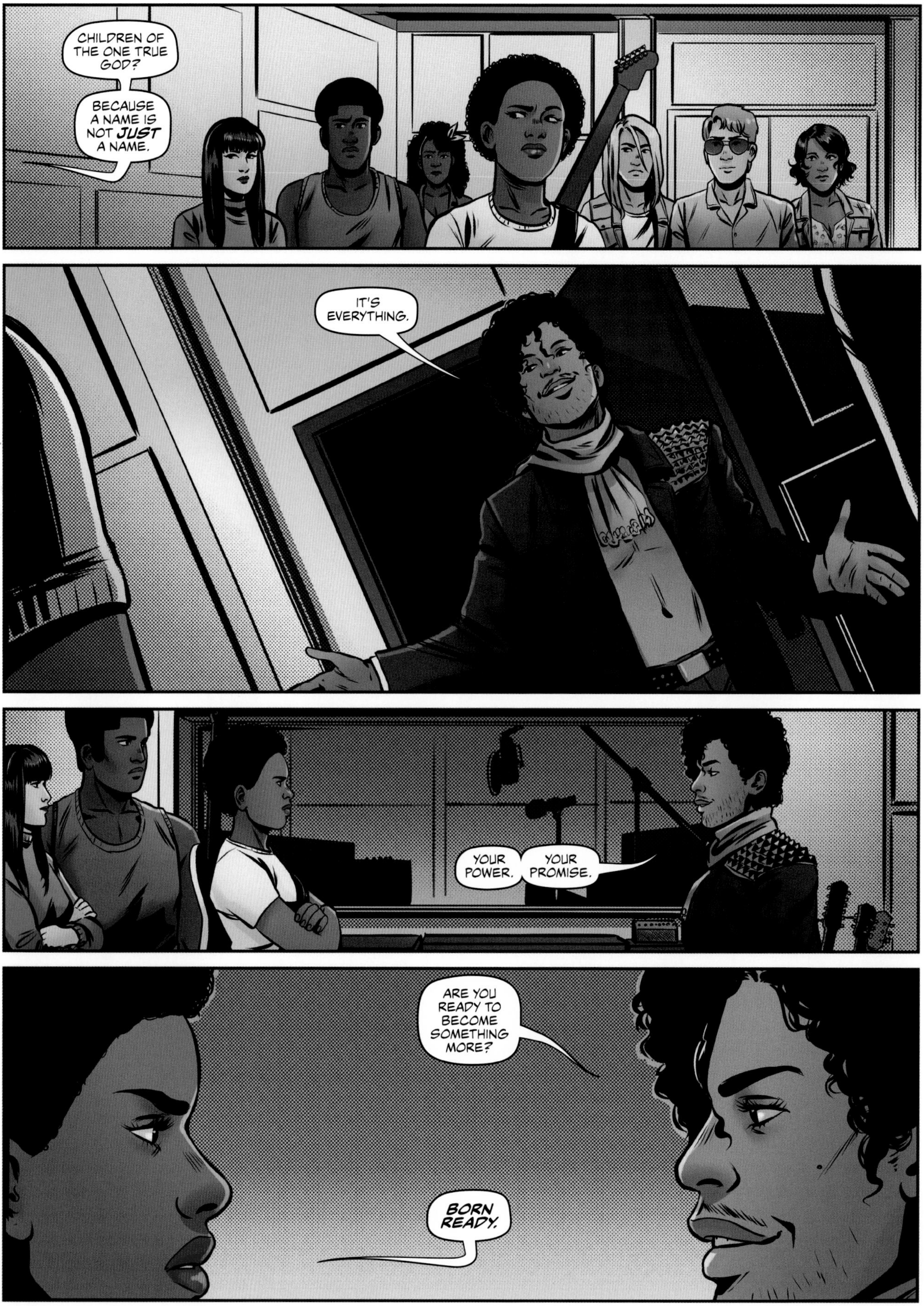
CHILDREN OF THE ONE TRUE GOD?
BECAUSE A NAME IS NOT *JUST* A NAME.
IT'S EVERYTHING.
YOUR POWER.
YOUR PROMISE.
ARE YOU READY TO BECOME SOMETHING MORE?
BORN READY.

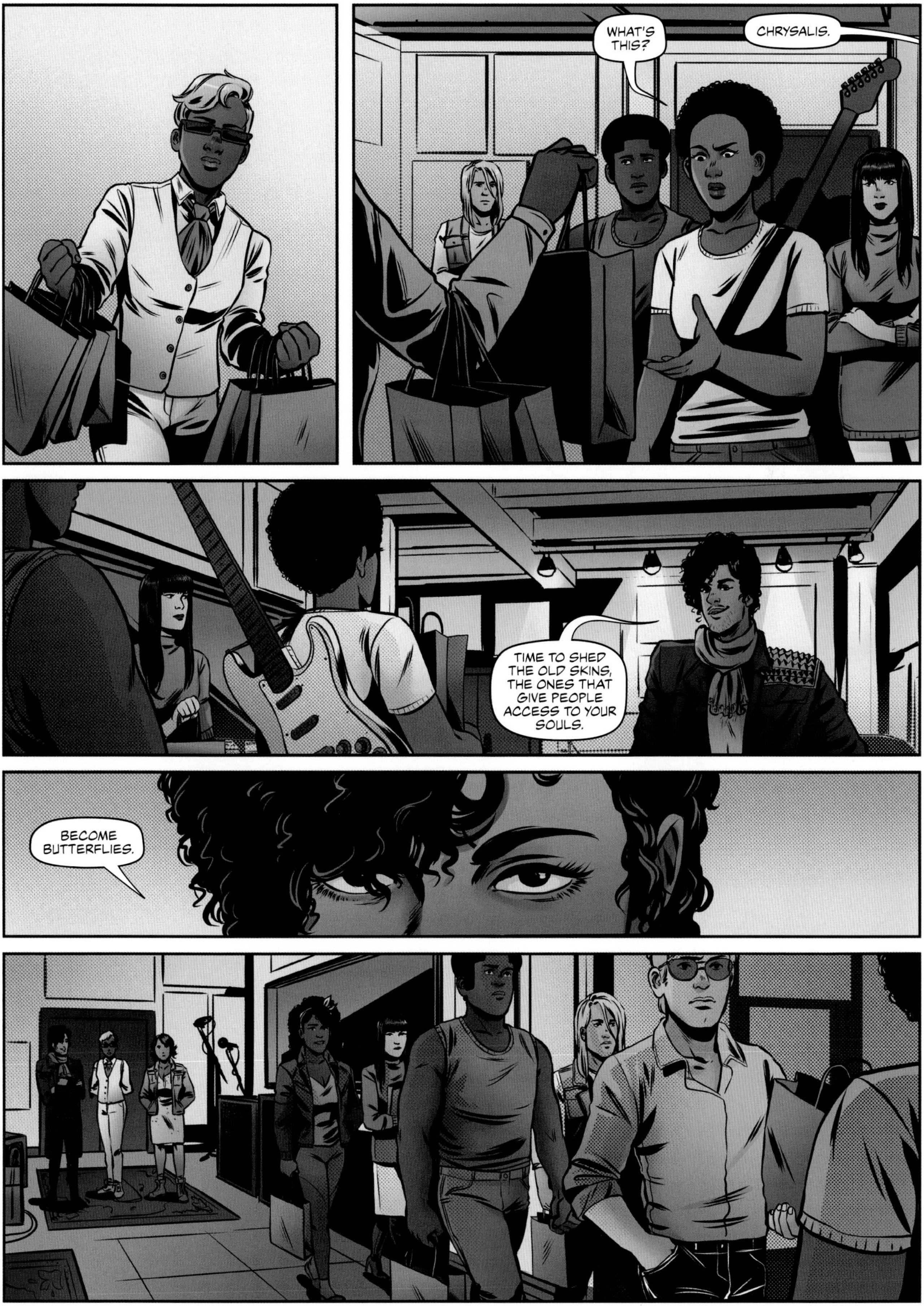
WHAT'S THIS?
CHRYSALIS.
TIME TO SHED THE OLD SKINS, THE ONES THAT GIVE PEOPLE ACCESS TO YOUR SOULS.
BECOME BUTTERFLIES.

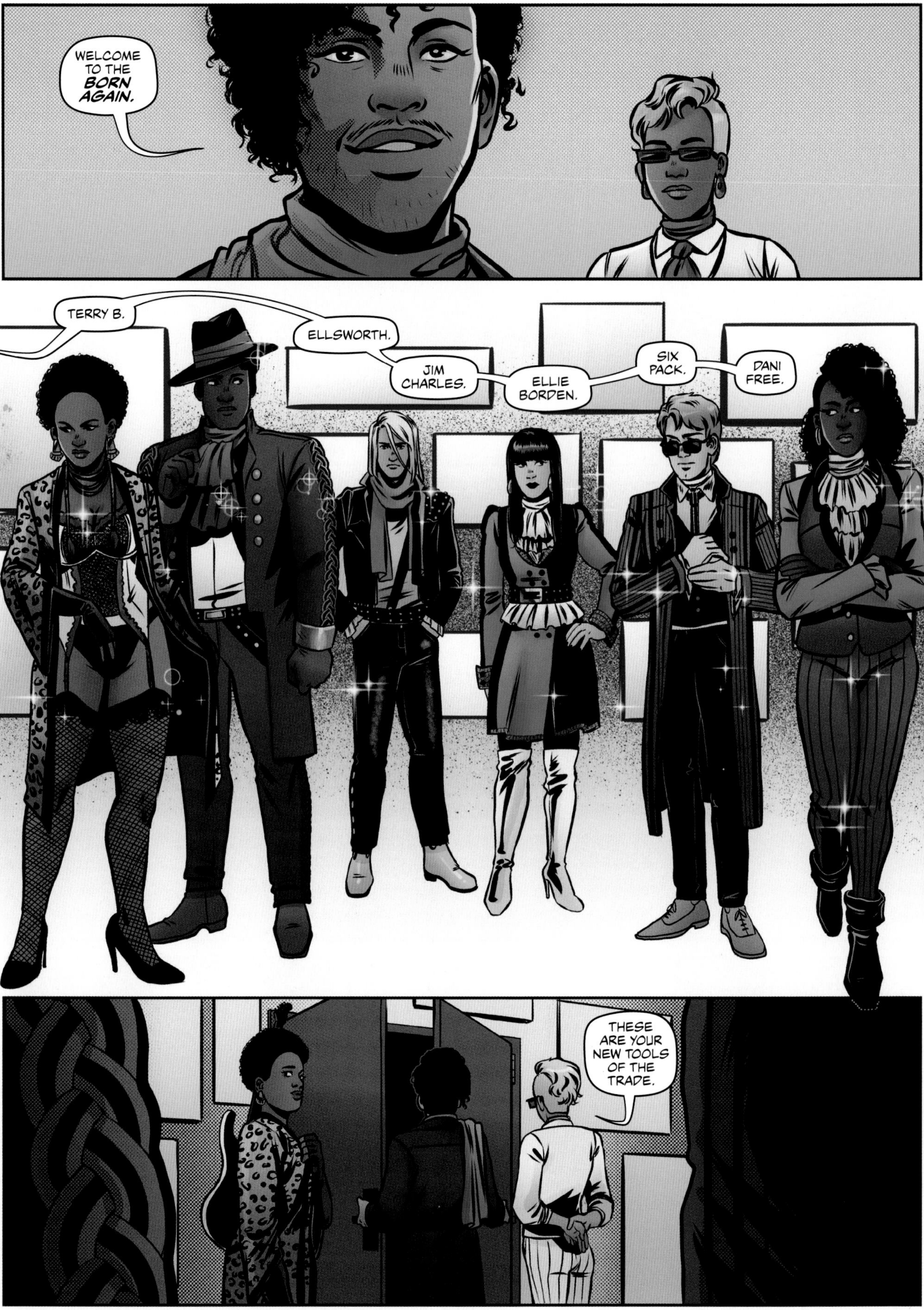
WELCOME TO THE *BORN AGAIN.*
TERRY B.
ELLSWORTH.
JIM CHARLES.
ELLIE BORDEN.
SIX PACK.
DANI FREE.
THESE ARE YOUR NEW TOOLS OF THE TRADE.

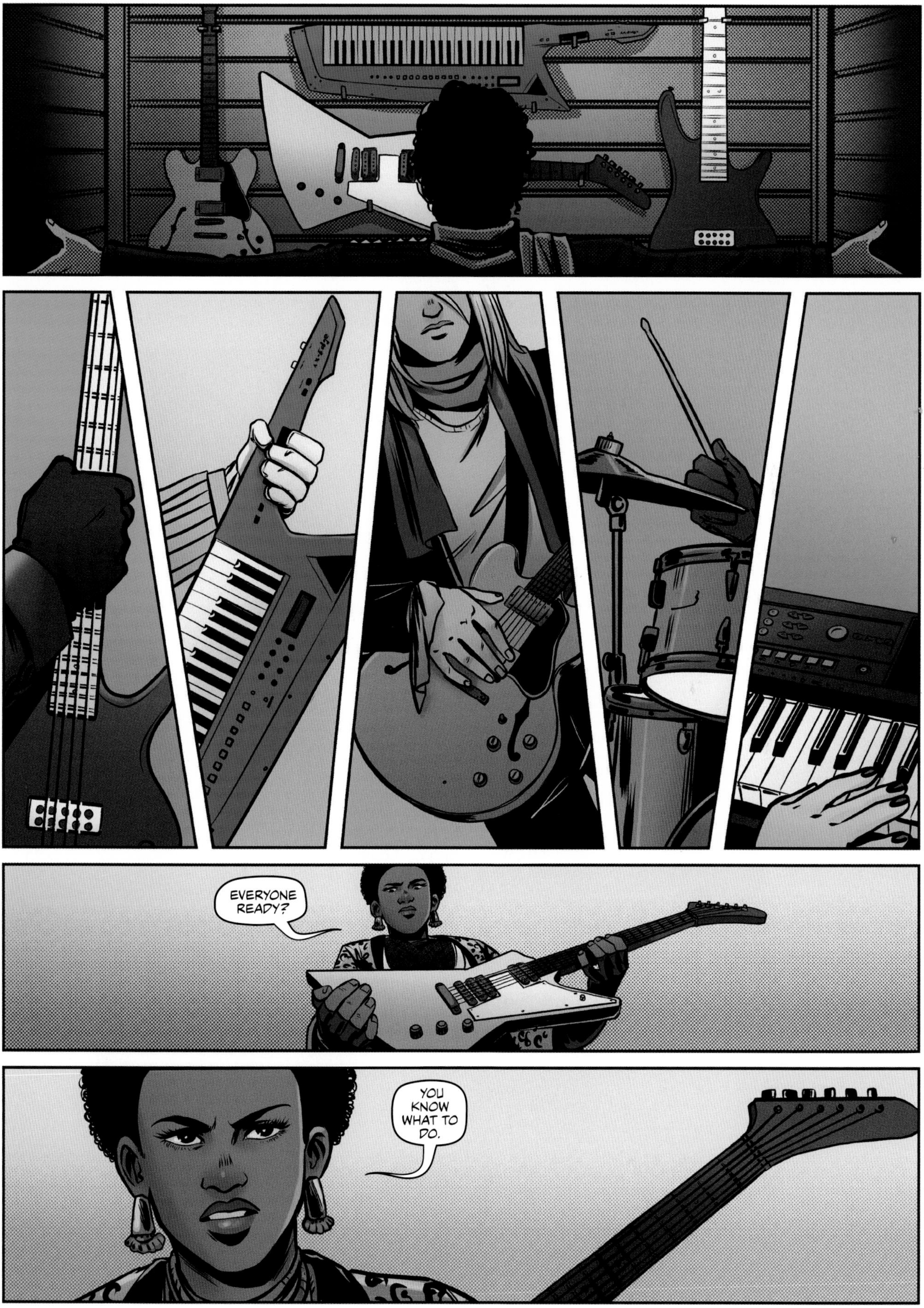
EVERYONE READY?
YOU KNOW WHAT TO DO.

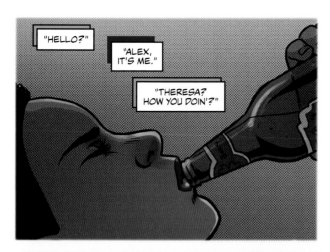

"HELLO?"

"ALEX, IT'S ME."

"THERESA? HOW YOU DOIN'?"

"NOT GOOD."

"I'M SORRY, HONEY."

"IT WAS... I FEEL SO..."

"...HUMILIATED!

"AND I DON'T KNOW *WHAT* THE HELL WE'RE GOING TO DO NOW."

"LET ME INTRODUCE YOU TO SOME PEOPLE. HELP GIVE YOU SOME PERSPECTIVE."

"YOU'LL LET OL' ALEX DO THAT?"

VERNON ANDREW BOOKER

1928-1977

YES.

SET IT UP.

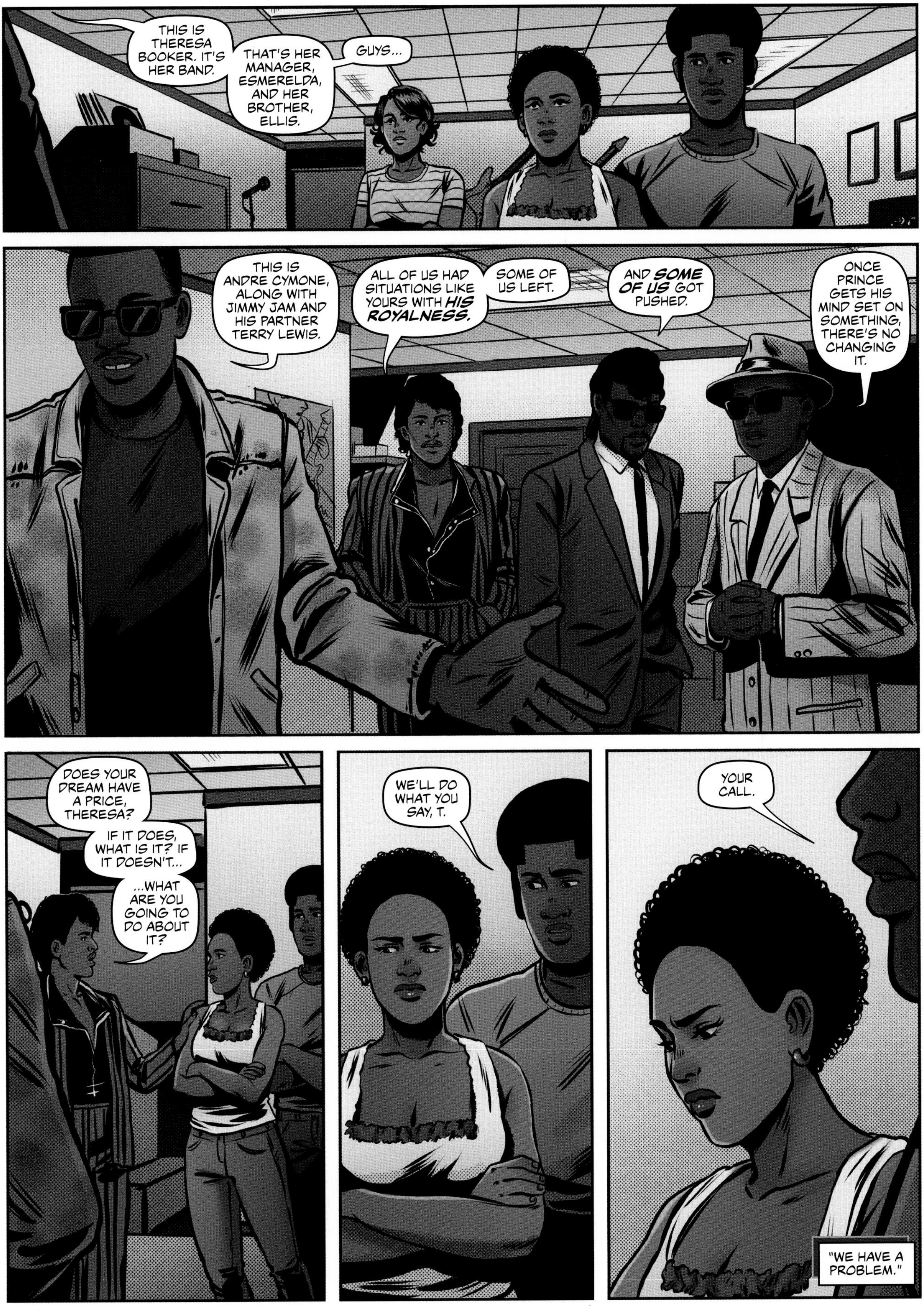
THIS IS THERESA BOOKER. IT'S HER BAND.
THAT'S HER MANAGER, ESMERELDA, AND HER BROTHER, ELLIS.
GUYS...
THIS IS ANDRE CYMONE, ALONG WITH JIMMY JAM AND HIS PARTNER TERRY LEWIS.
ALL OF US HAD SITUATIONS LIKE YOURS WITH ***HIS ROYALNESS.***
SOME OF US LEFT.
AND ***SOME OF US*** GOT PUSHED.
ONCE PRINCE GETS HIS MIND SET ON SOMETHING, THERE'S NO CHANGING IT.
DOES YOUR DREAM HAVE A PRICE, THERESA?
IF IT DOES, WHAT IS IT? IF IT DOESN'T...
...WHAT ARE YOU GOING TO DO ABOUT IT?
WE'LL DO WHAT YOU SAY, T.
YOUR CALL.
"WE HAVE A PROBLEM."

PRINCE'S IDEA OF STARCHILD-- AND *MY* IDEA.

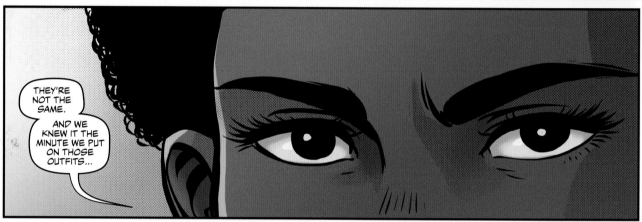

THEY'RE NOT THE SAME.

AND WE KNEW IT THE MINUTE WE PUT ON THOSE OUTFITS...

...LOSING OURSELVES IN THE PROCESS.

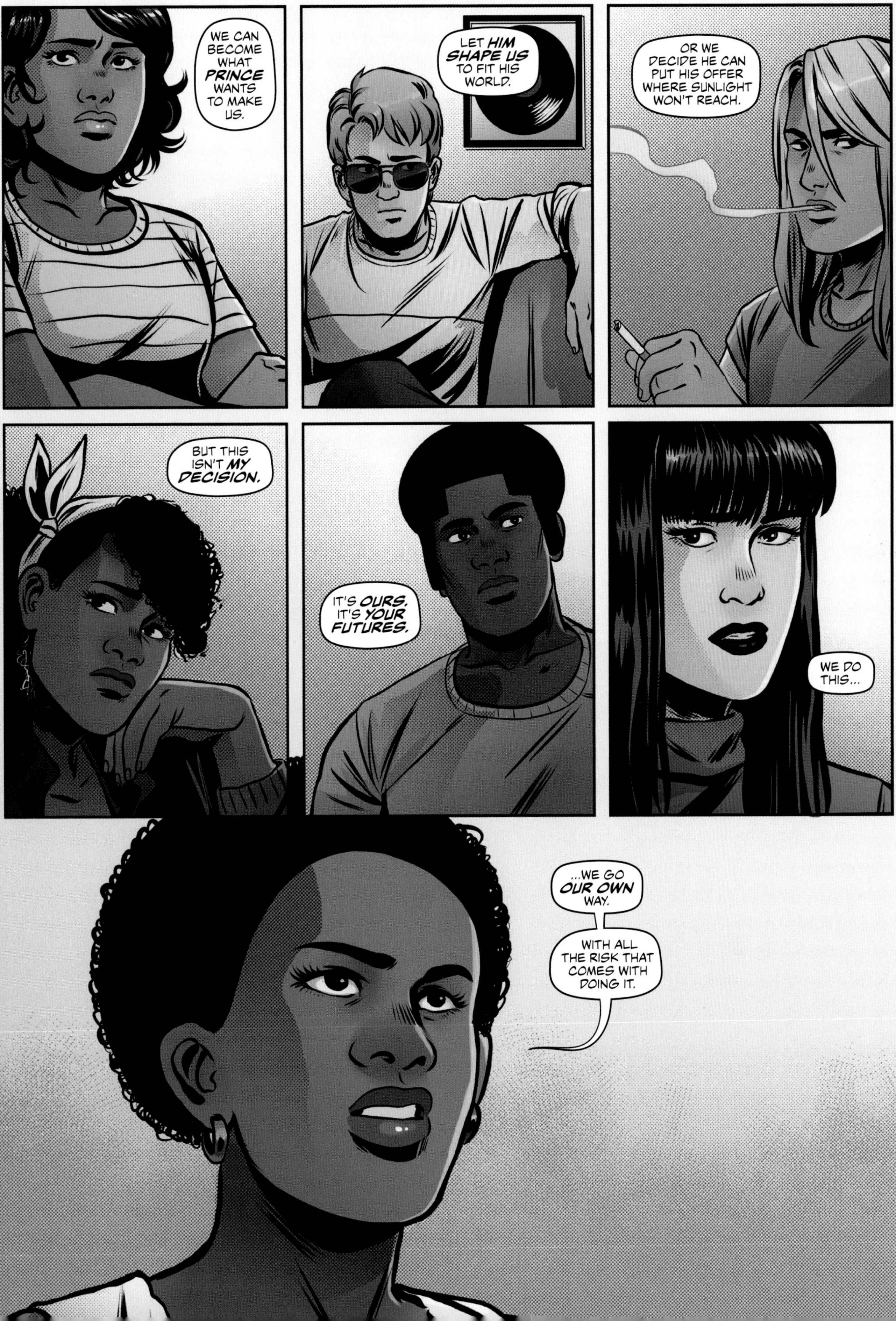

WE CAN BECOME WHAT PRINCE WANTS TO MAKE US.
LET HIM SHAPE US TO FIT HIS WORLD.
OR WE DECIDE HE CAN PUT HIS OFFER WHERE SUNLIGHT WON'T REACH.
BUT THIS ISN'T MY DECISION.
IT'S OURS. IT'S YOUR FUTURES.
WE DO THIS...
...WE GO OUR OWN WAY.
WITH ALL THE RISK THAT COMES WITH DOING IT.

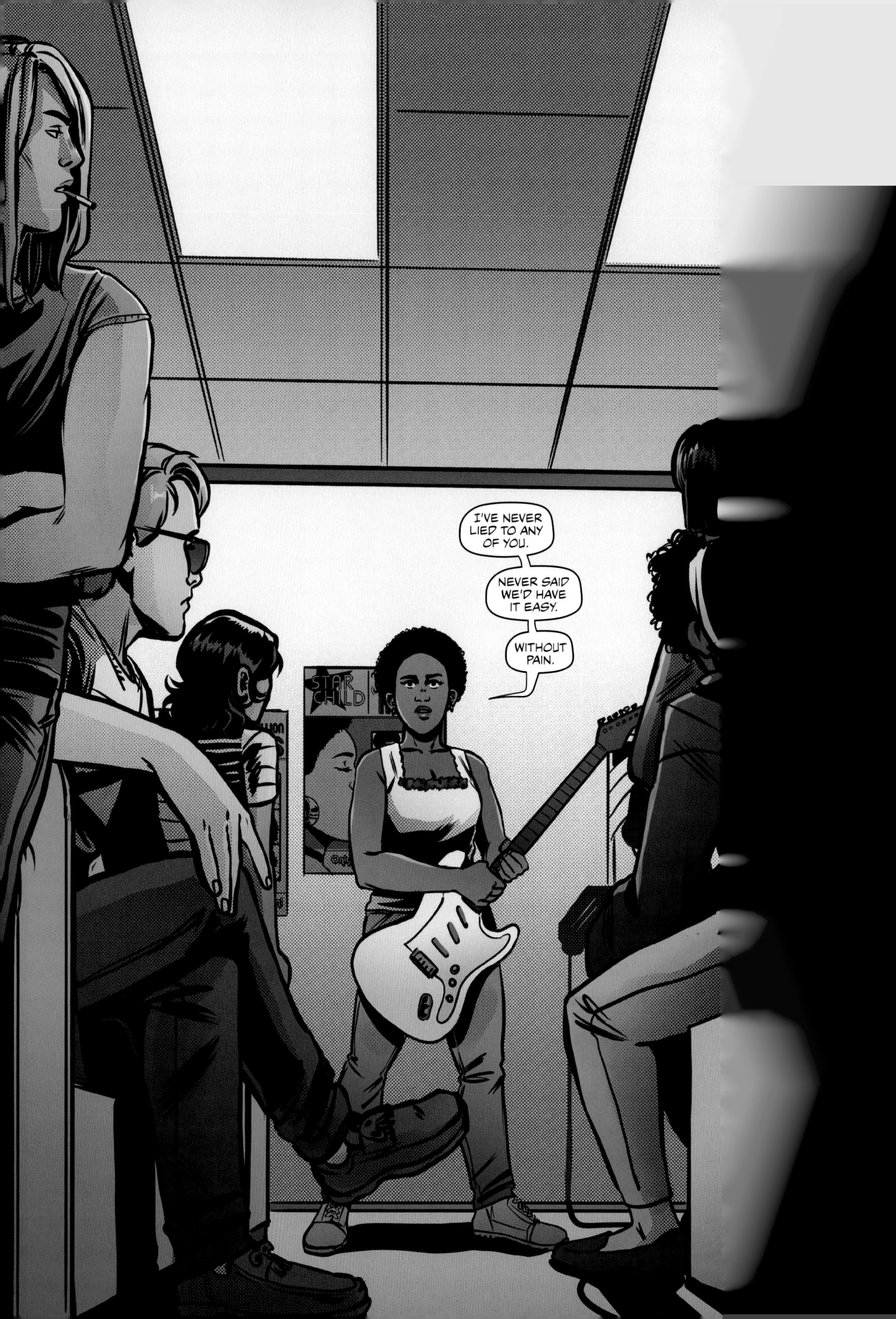
STAR CHILD
I'VE NEVER LIED TO ANY OF YOU.
NEVER SAID WE'D HAVE IT EASY.
WITHOUT PAIN.

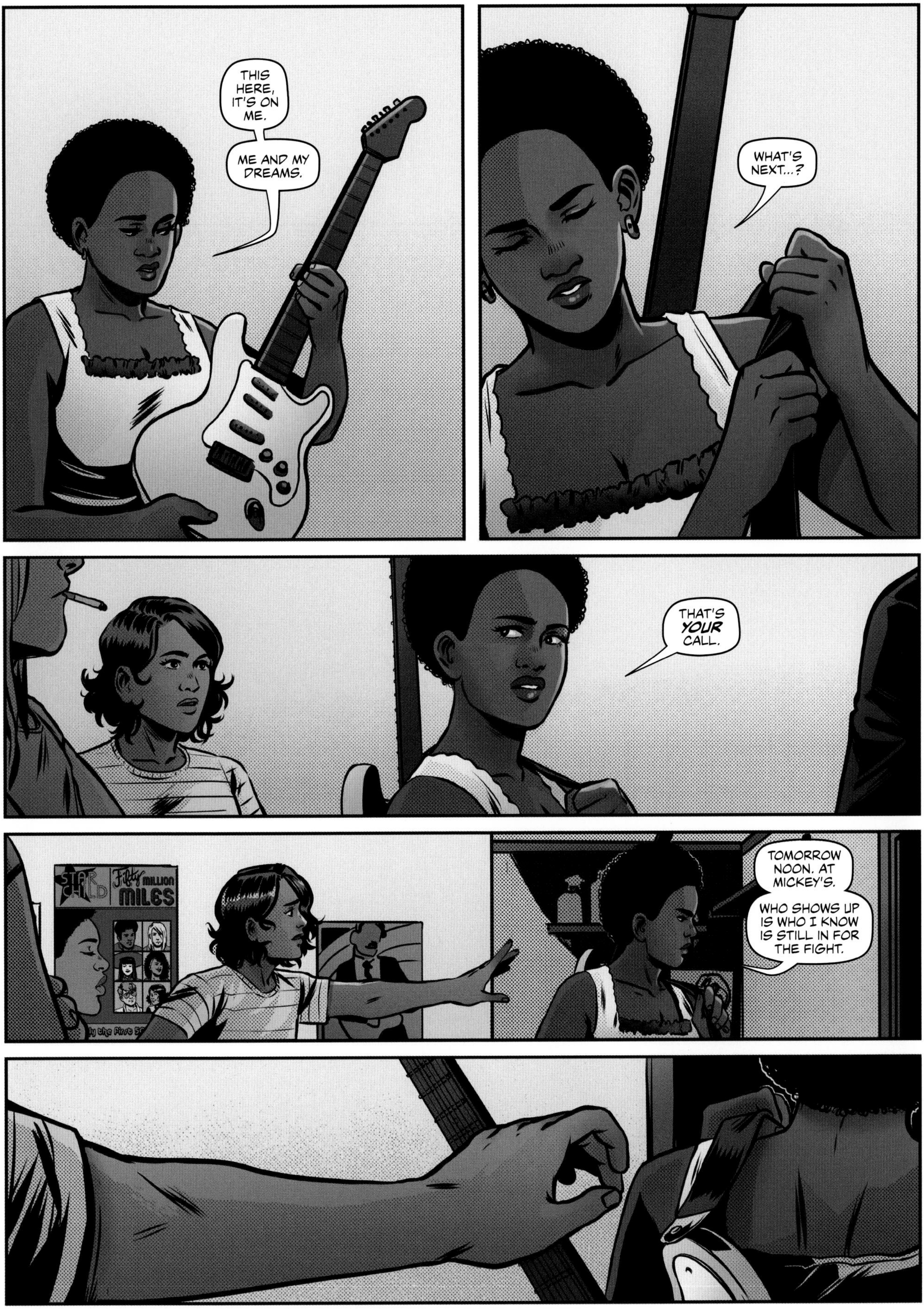
THIS HERE, IT'S ON ME.
ME AND MY DREAMS.
WHAT'S NEXT...?
THAT'S *YOUR* CALL.
STAR CHILD
Fifty MILLION MILES
TOMORROW NOON. AT MICKEY'S.
WHO SHOWS UP IS WHO I KNOW IS STILL IN FOR THE FIGHT.

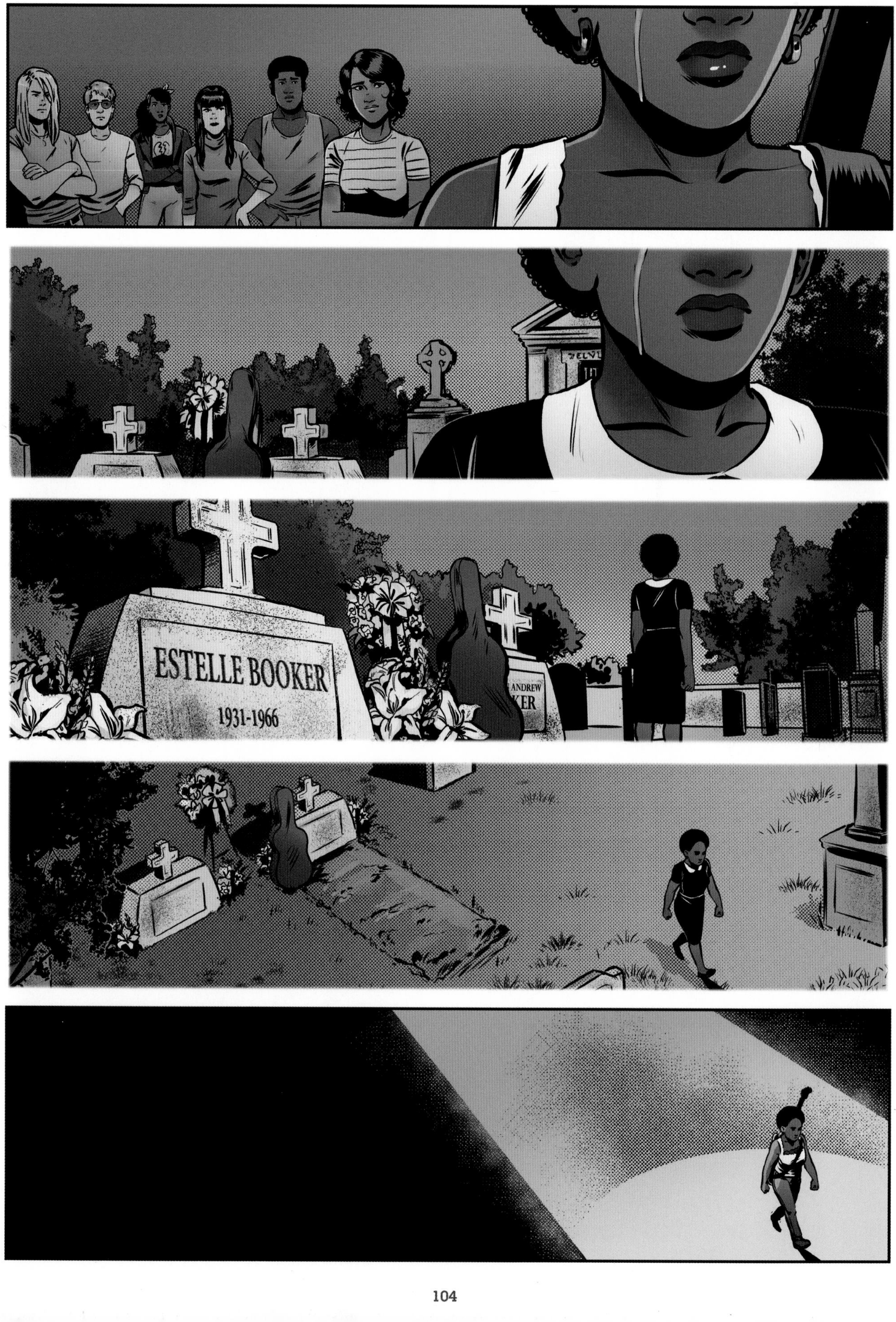
ESTELLE BOOKER
1931-1966
ANDREW
KER

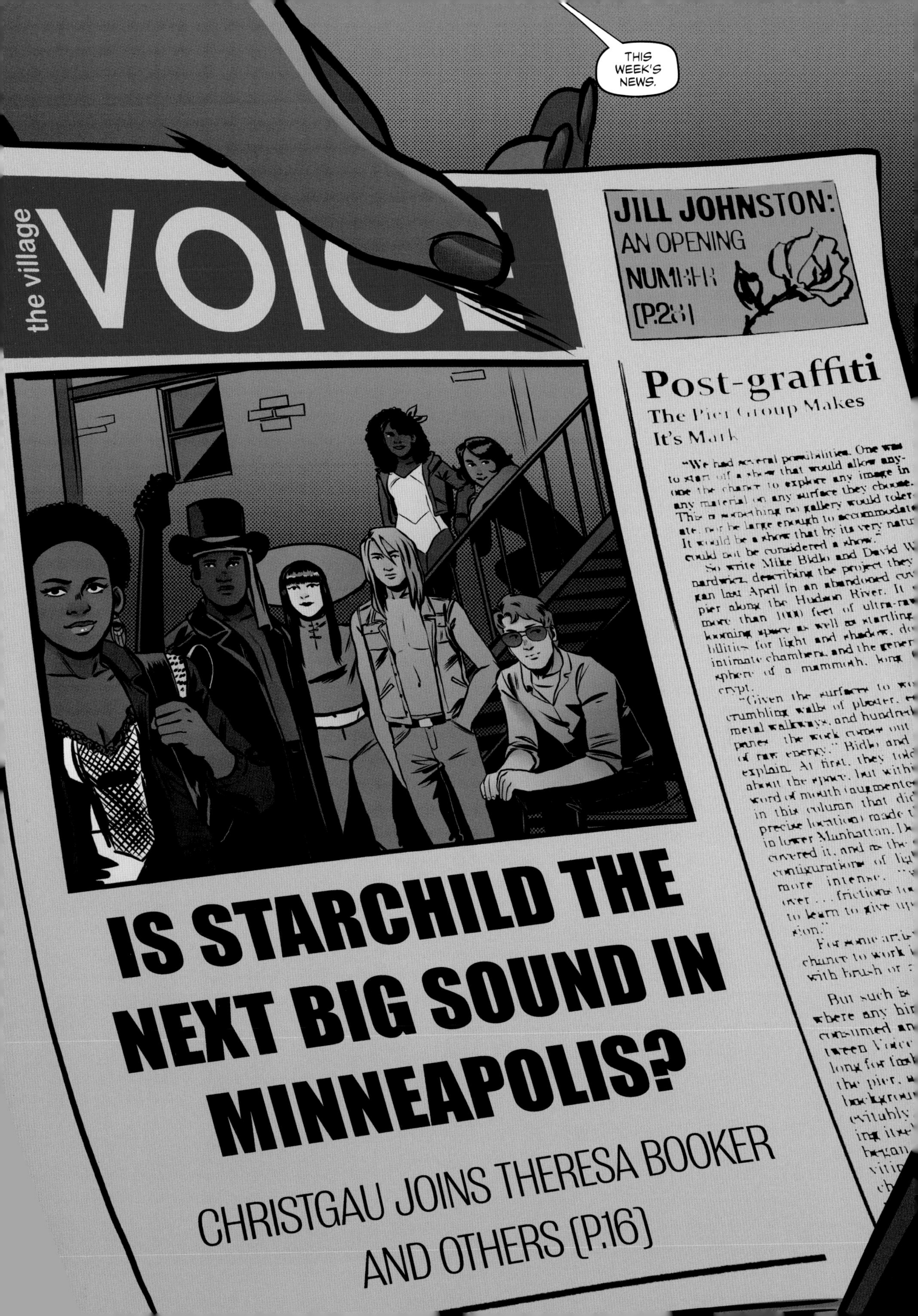
THIS WEEK'S NEWS.
the village VOICE
JILL JOHNSTON: AN OPENING NUMBER [P.28]
Post-graffiti
The Pier Group Makes It's Mark
IS STARCHILD THE NEXT BIG SOUND IN MINNEAPOLIS?
CHRISTGAU JOINS THERESA BOOKER AND OTHERS [P.16]

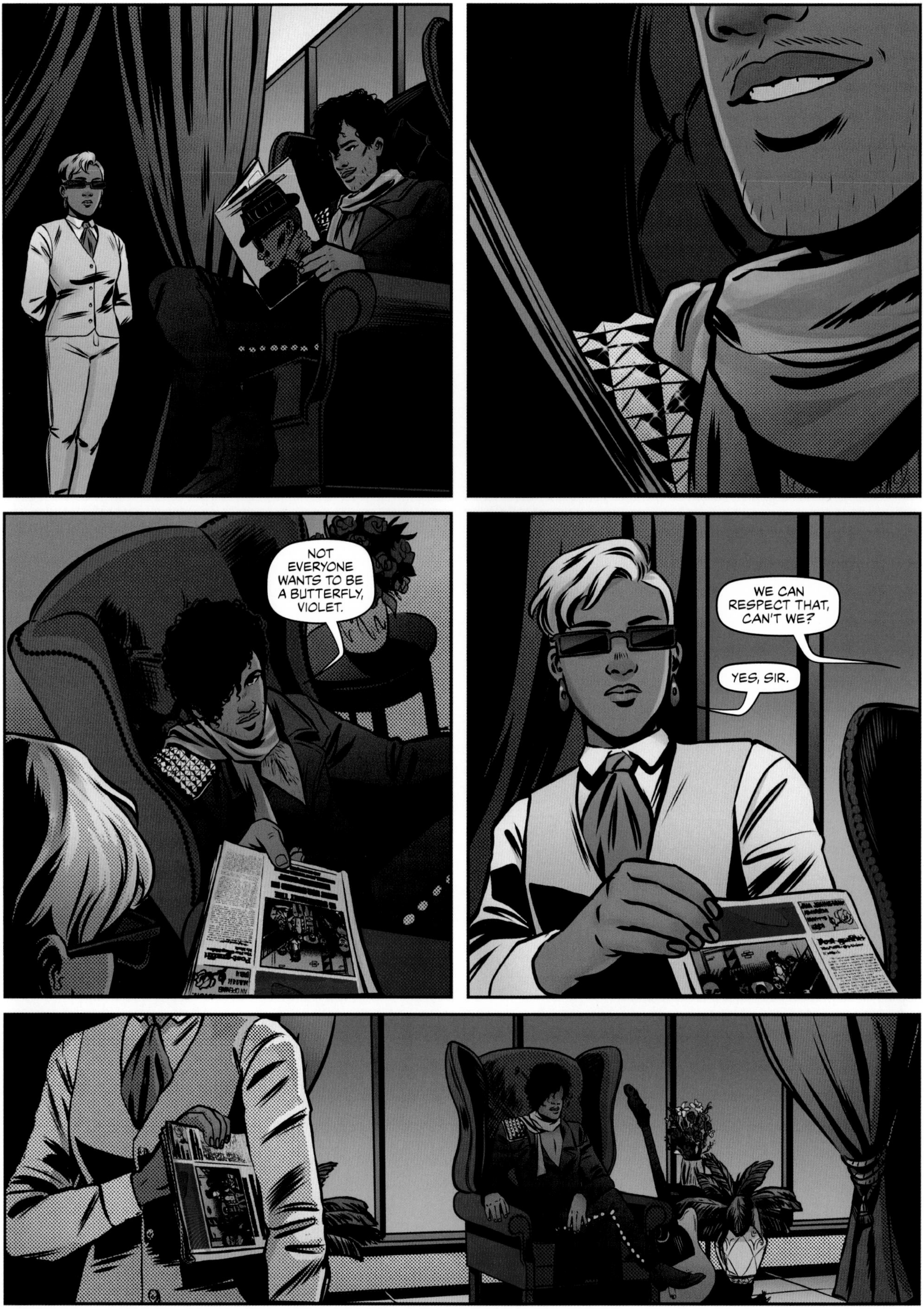

NOT EVERYONE WANTS TO BE A BUTTERFLY, VIOLET.
WE CAN RESPECT THAT, CAN'T WE?
YES, SIR.

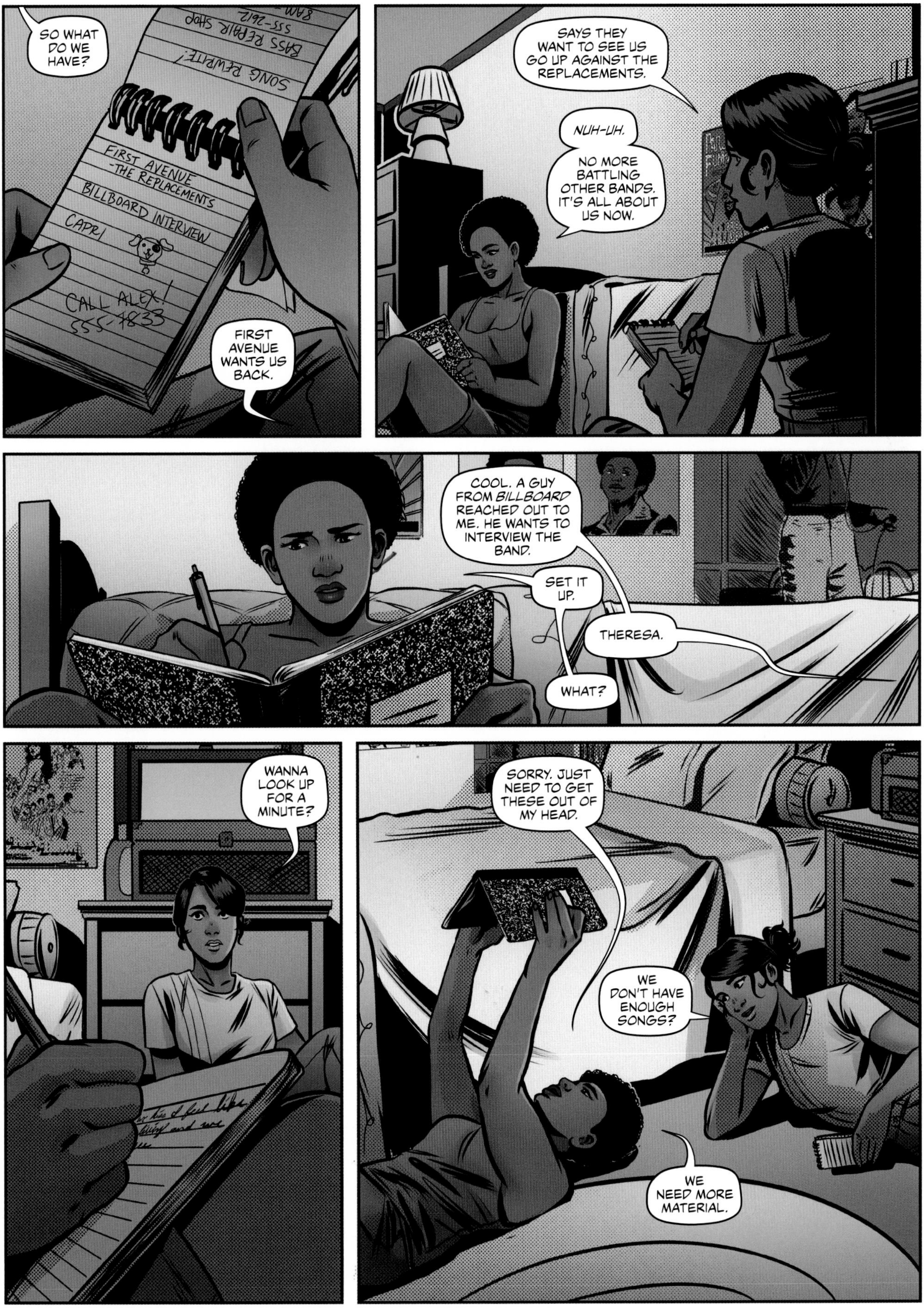
SO WHAT DO WE HAVE?
SONG REWRITE!
BASS REPAIR SHOP
555-2612
FIRST AVENUE -THE REPLACEMENTS
BILLBOARD INTERVIEW
CAPRI
CALL ALEX!
FIRST AVENUE WANTS US BACK.
SAYS THEY WANT TO SEE US GO UP AGAINST THE REPLACEMENTS.
NUH-UH.
NO MORE BATTLING OTHER BANDS. IT'S ALL ABOUT US NOW.
COOL. A GUY FROM BILLBOARD REACHED OUT TO ME. HE WANTS TO INTERVIEW THE BAND.
SET IT UP.
THERESA.
WHAT?
WANNA LOOK UP FOR A MINUTE?
SORRY. JUST NEED TO GET THESE OUT OF MY HEAD.
WE DON'T HAVE ENOUGH SONGS?
WE NEED MORE MATERIAL.

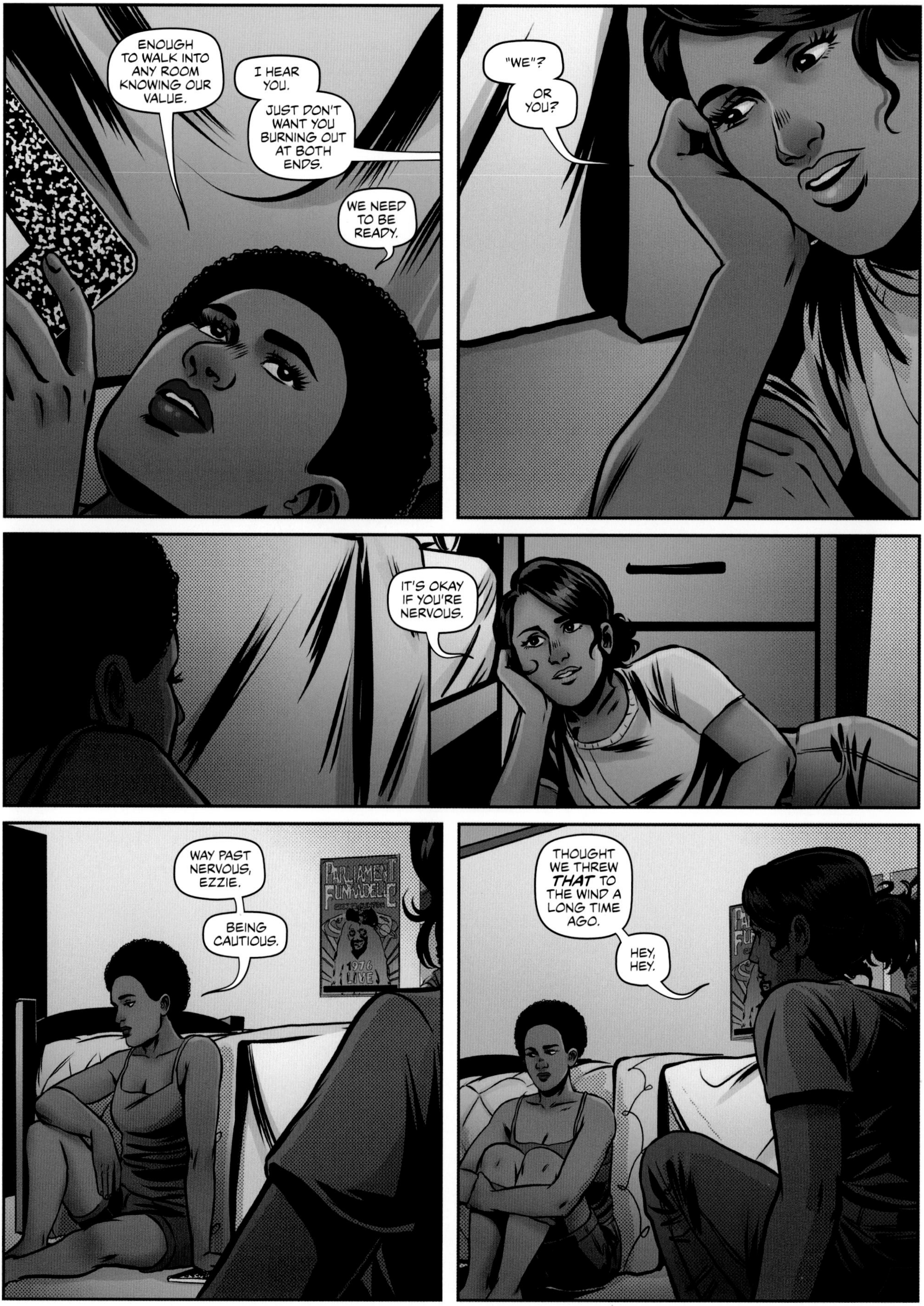
ENOUGH TO WALK INTO ANY ROOM KNOWING OUR VALUE.
I HEAR YOU.
JUST DON'T WANT YOU BURNING OUT AT BOTH ENDS.
WE NEED TO BE READY.
"WE"?
OR YOU?
IT'S OKAY IF YOU'RE NERVOUS.
WAY PAST NERVOUS, EZZIE.
BEING CAUTIOUS.
PARLIAMENT FUNKADELIC
1976 LIVE
THOUGHT WE THREW *THAT* TO THE WIND A LONG TIME AGO.
HEY, HEY.

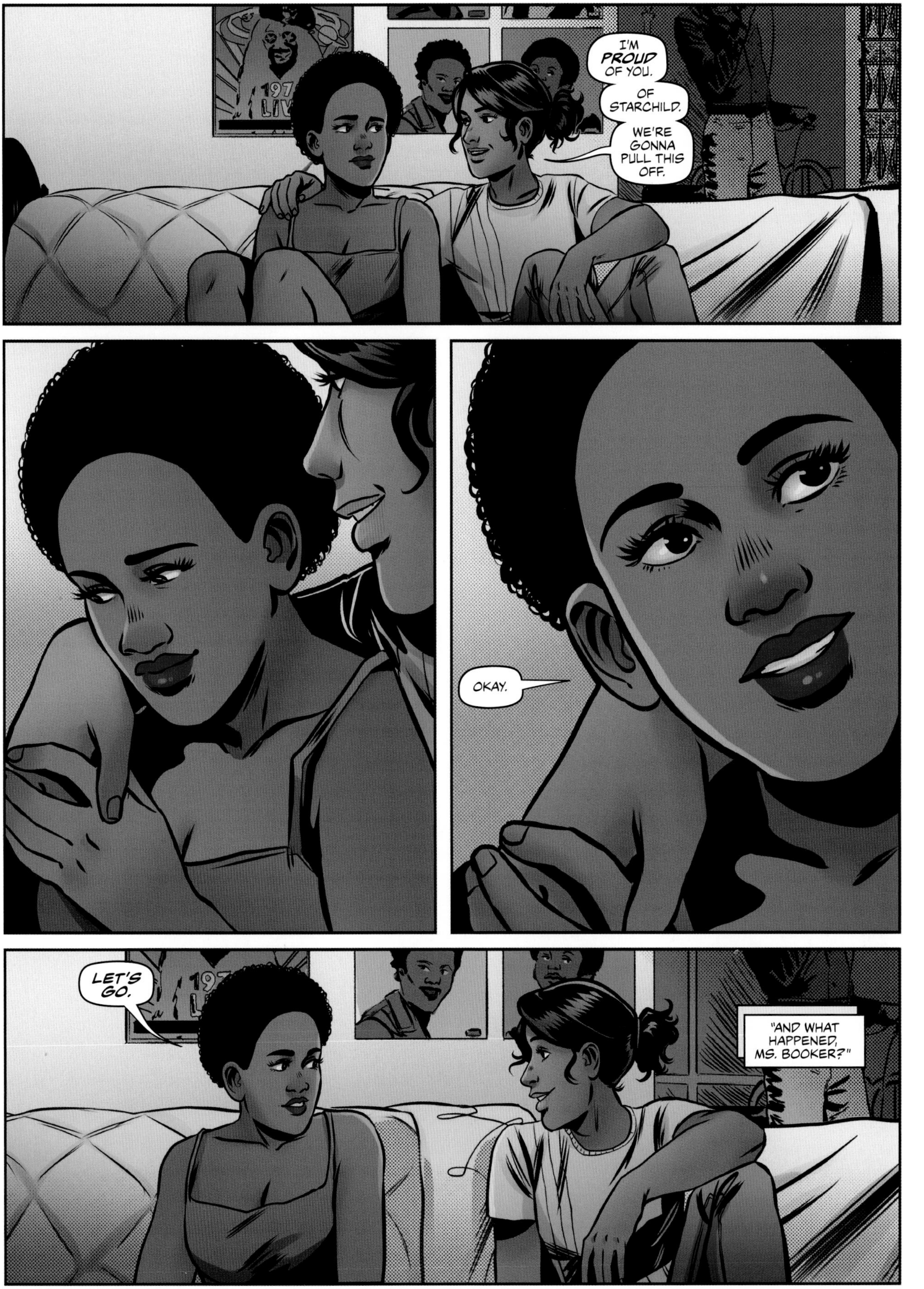
I'M *PROUD* OF YOU.
OF STARCHILD.
WE'RE GONNA PULL THIS OFF.
OKAY.
LET'S GO.
"AND WHAT HAPPENED, MS. BOOKER?"

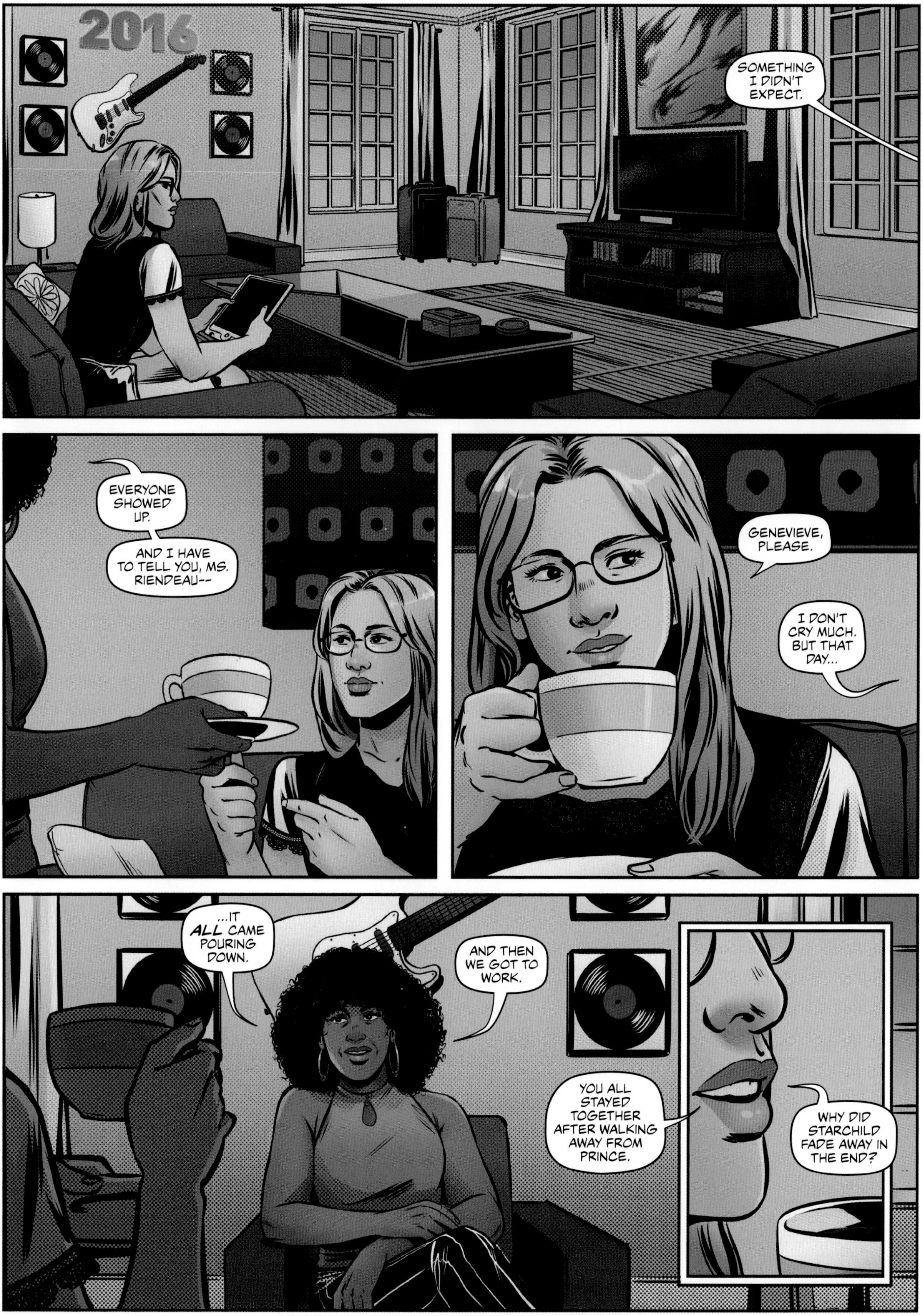
2016
SOMETHING I DIDN'T EXPECT.
EVERYONE SHOWED UP.
AND I HAVE TO TELL YOU, MS. RIENDEAU--
GENEVIEVE, PLEASE.
I DON'T CRY MUCH. BUT THAT DAY...
...IT ALL CAME POURING DOWN.
AND THEN WE GOT TO WORK.
YOU ALL STAYED TOGETHER AFTER WALKING AWAY FROM PRINCE.
WHY DID STARCHILD FADE AWAY IN THE END?

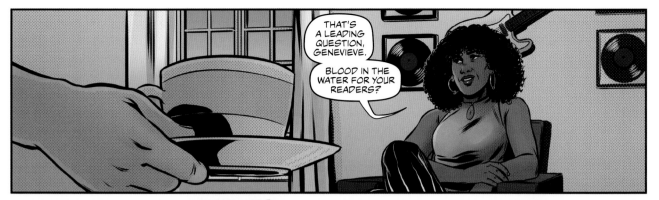

THAT'S A LEADING QUESTION, GENEVIEVE.

BLOOD IN THE WATER FOR YOUR READERS?

I'M NOT HERE TO EXPLOIT YOU, THERESA.

BUT WE'RE DEALING WITH THE UNPLEASANT FACT THAT PRINCE HAS DIED...

...AND EVERY PERSON WHOSE LIFE HE TOUCHED HAS BECOME A TETHER FOR THE REST OF US.

WE'RE ALL SUFFERING FROM THE LOSS OF HIM.

IT'S A RELIEF, YOU KNOW.

TO TALK ABOUT THIS. *ALL* OF IT.

"MY TIME WITH STARCHILD...IT WAS PRECIOUS."

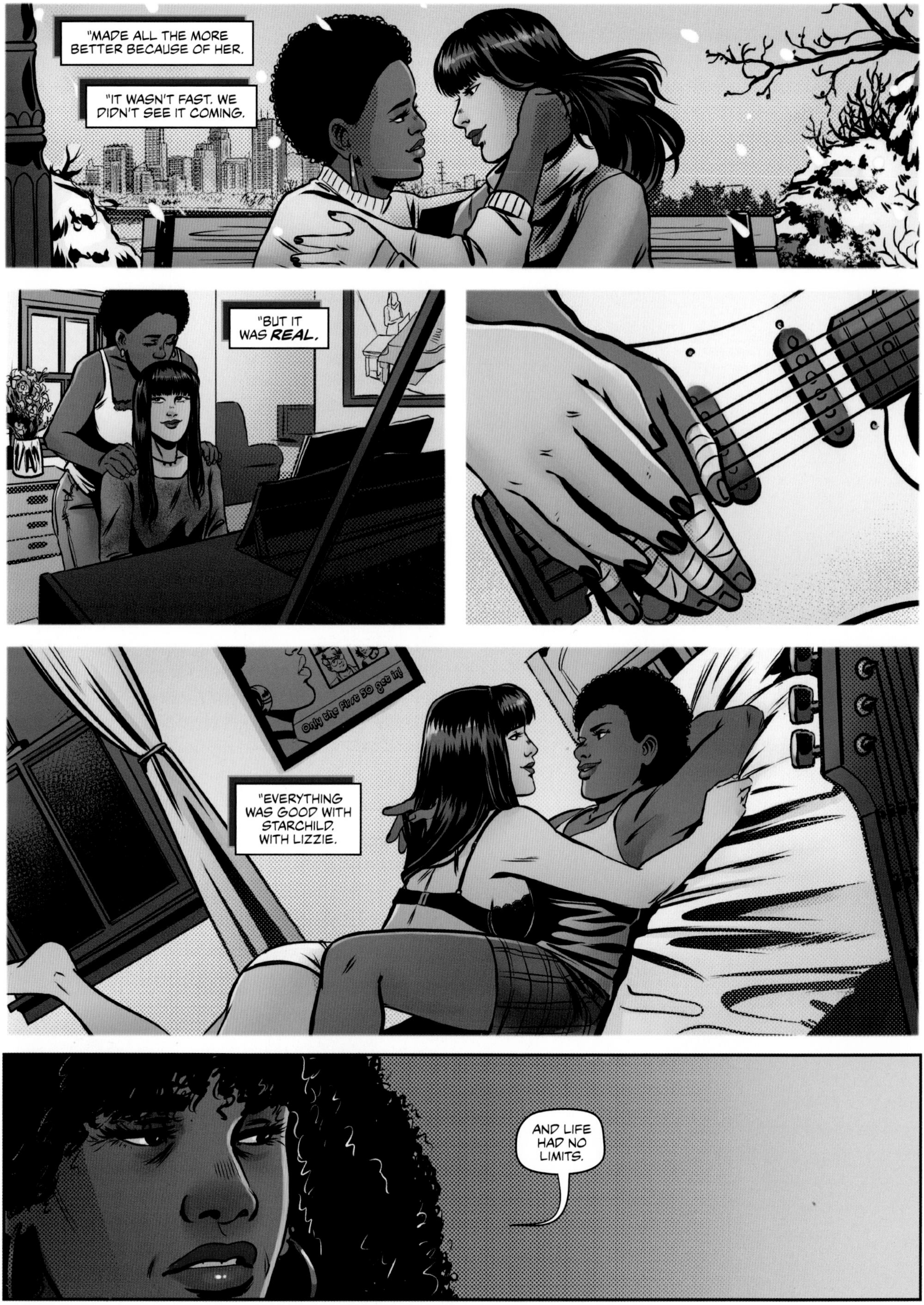
"MADE ALL THE MORE BETTER BECAUSE OF HER.
"IT WASN'T FAST. WE DIDN'T SEE IT COMING.
"BUT IT WAS REAL.
Only the First 30 get in!
"EVERYTHING WAS GOOD WITH STARCHILD. WITH LIZZIE.
AND LIFE HAD NO LIMITS.

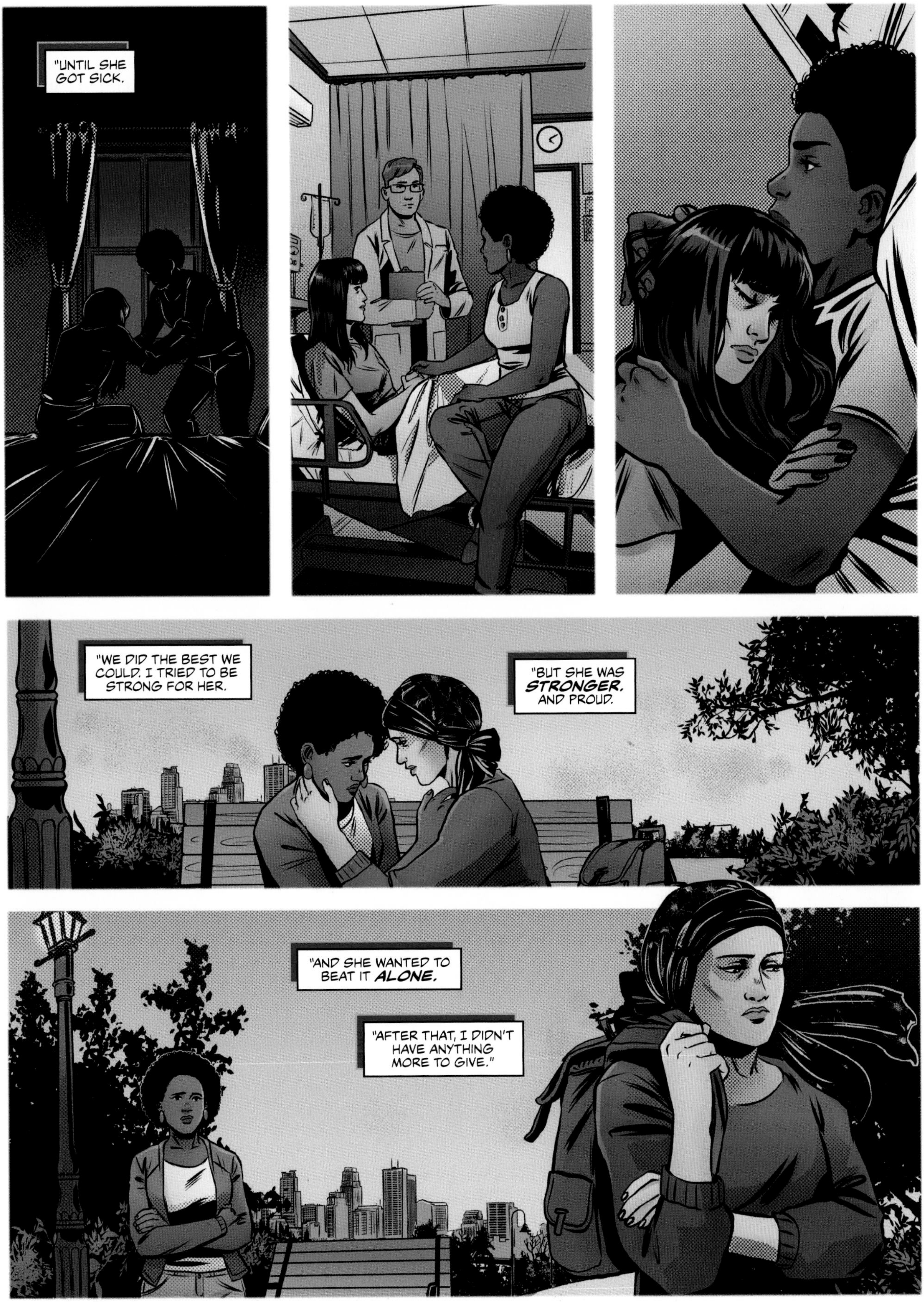
"UNTIL SHE GOT SICK.
"WE DID THE BEST WE COULD. I TRIED TO BE STRONG FOR HER.
"BUT SHE WAS STRONGER. AND PROUD.
"AND SHE WANTED TO BEAT IT ALONE.
"AFTER THAT, I DIDN'T HAVE ANYTHING MORE TO GIVE."

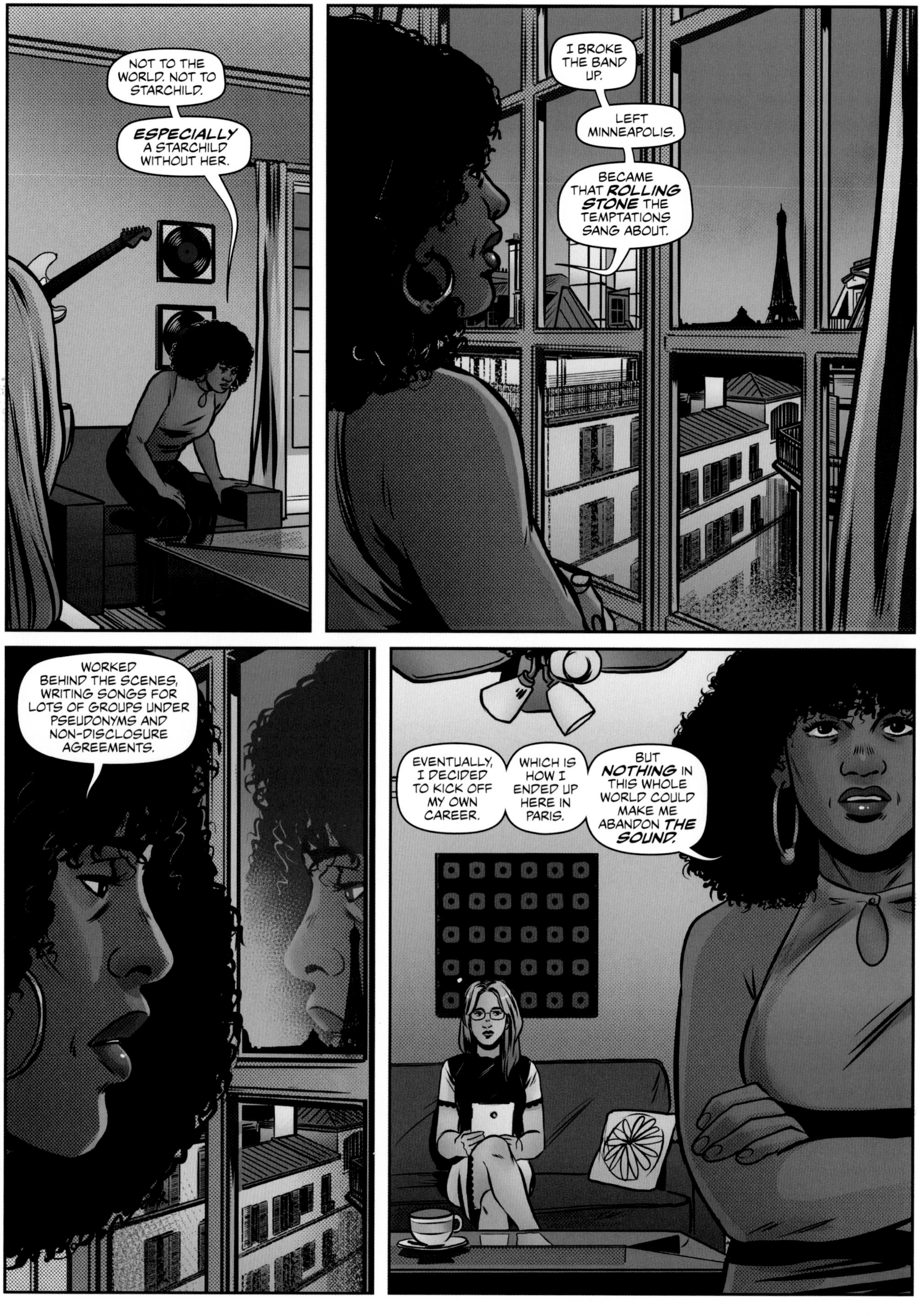

NOT TO THE WORLD. NOT TO STARCHILD.
ESPECIALLY A STARCHILD WITHOUT HER.
I BROKE THE BAND UP.
LEFT MINNEAPOLIS.
BECAME THAT ROLLING STONE THE TEMPTATIONS SANG ABOUT.
WORKED BEHIND THE SCENES, WRITING SONGS FOR LOTS OF GROUPS UNDER PSEUDONYMS AND NON-DISCLOSURE AGREEMENTS.
EVENTUALLY, I DECIDED TO KICK OFF MY OWN CAREER.
WHICH IS HOW I ENDED UP HERE IN PARIS.
BUT NOTHING IN THIS WHOLE WORLD COULD MAKE ME ABANDON THE SOUND.

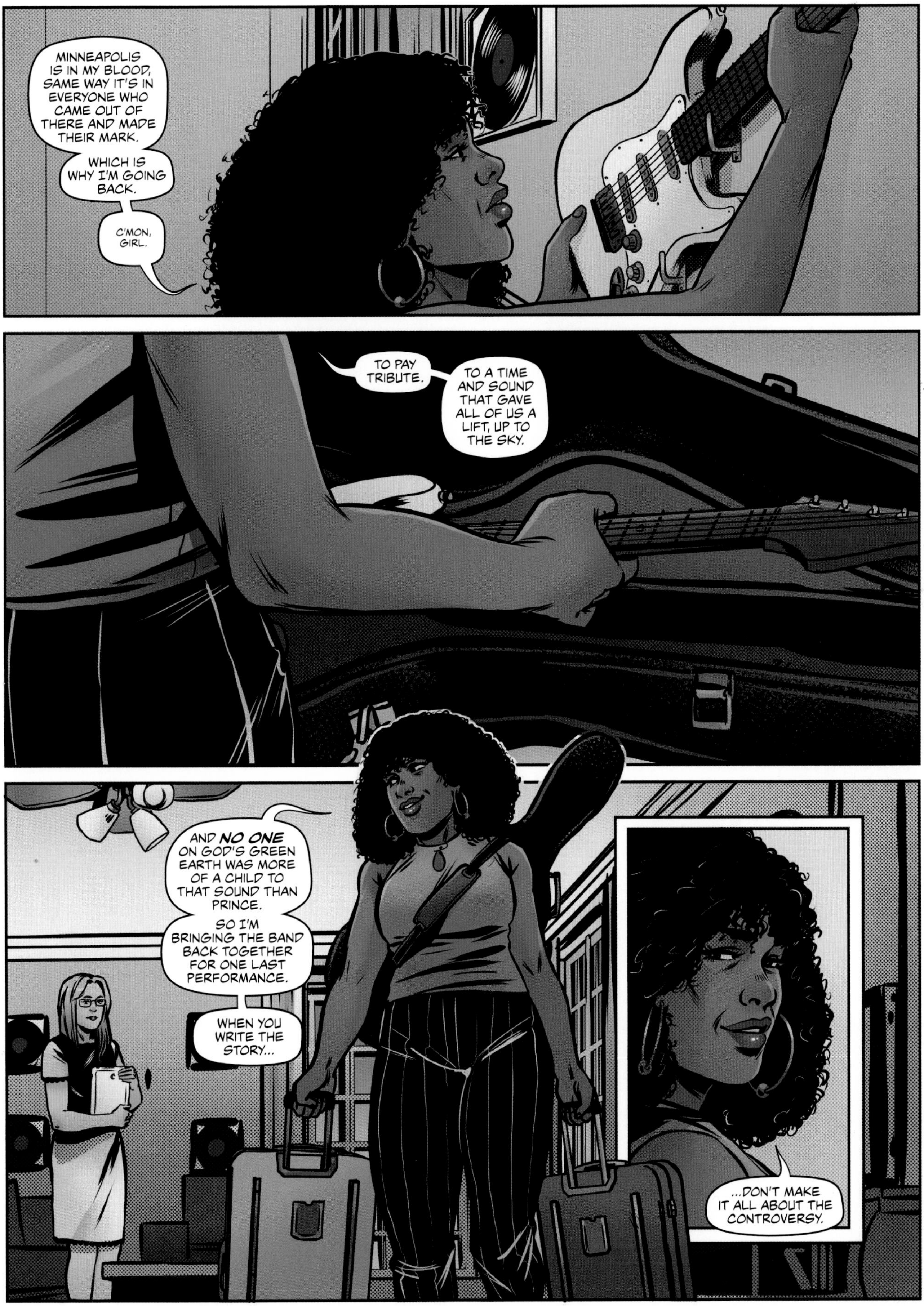
MINNEAPOLIS IS IN MY BLOOD, SAME WAY IT'S IN EVERYONE WHO CAME OUT OF THERE AND MADE THEIR MARK.
WHICH IS WHY I'M GOING BACK.
C'MON, GIRL.
TO PAY TRIBUTE.
TO A TIME AND SOUND THAT GAVE ALL OF US A LIFT, UP TO THE SKY.
AND **NO ONE** ON GOD'S GREEN EARTH WAS MORE OF A CHILD TO THAT SOUND THAN PRINCE.
SO I'M BRINGING THE BAND BACK TOGETHER FOR ONE LAST PERFORMANCE.
WHEN YOU WRITE THE STORY...
...DON'T MAKE IT ALL ABOUT THE CONTROVERSY.

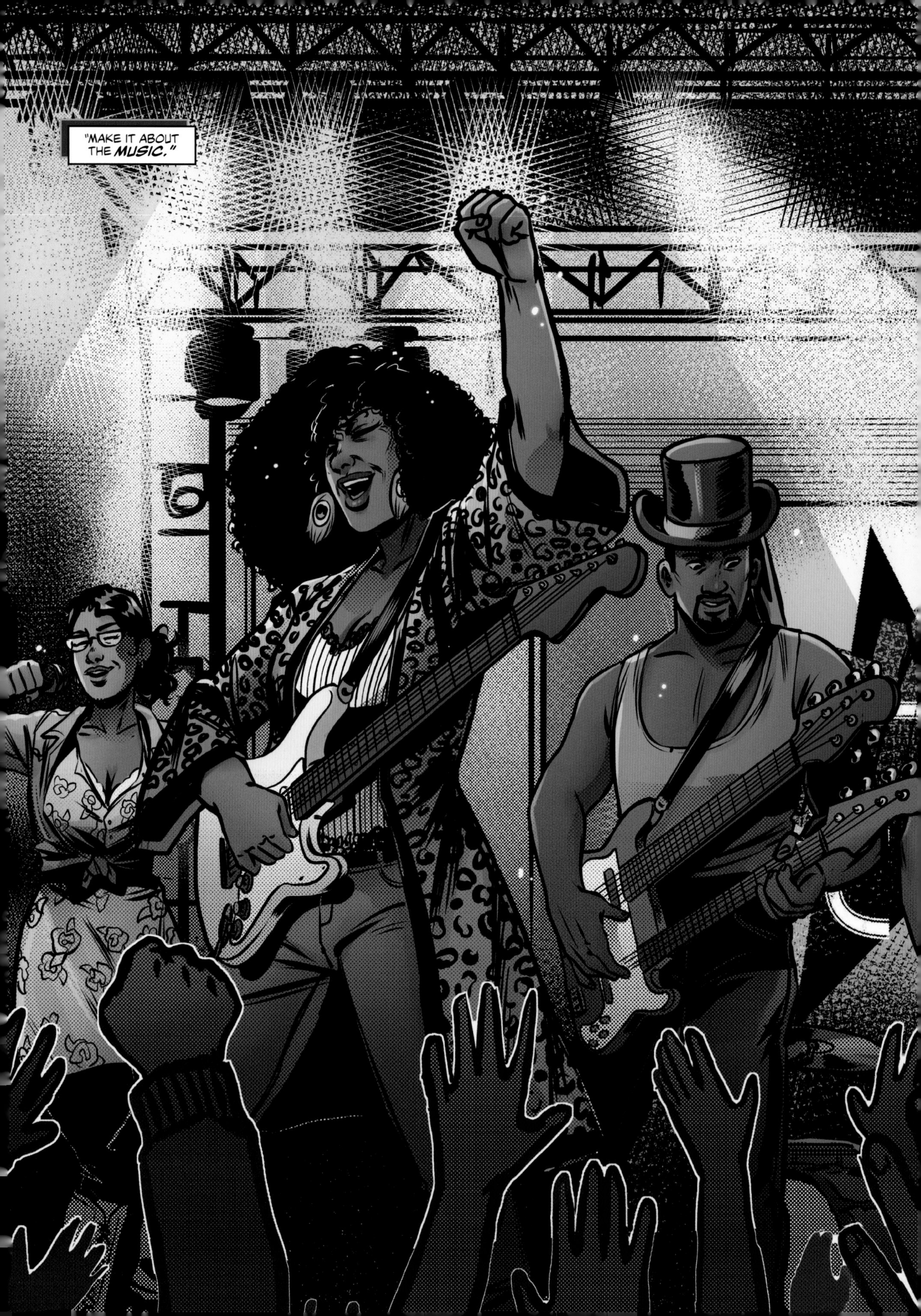
"MAKE IT ABOUT THE *MUSIC.*"

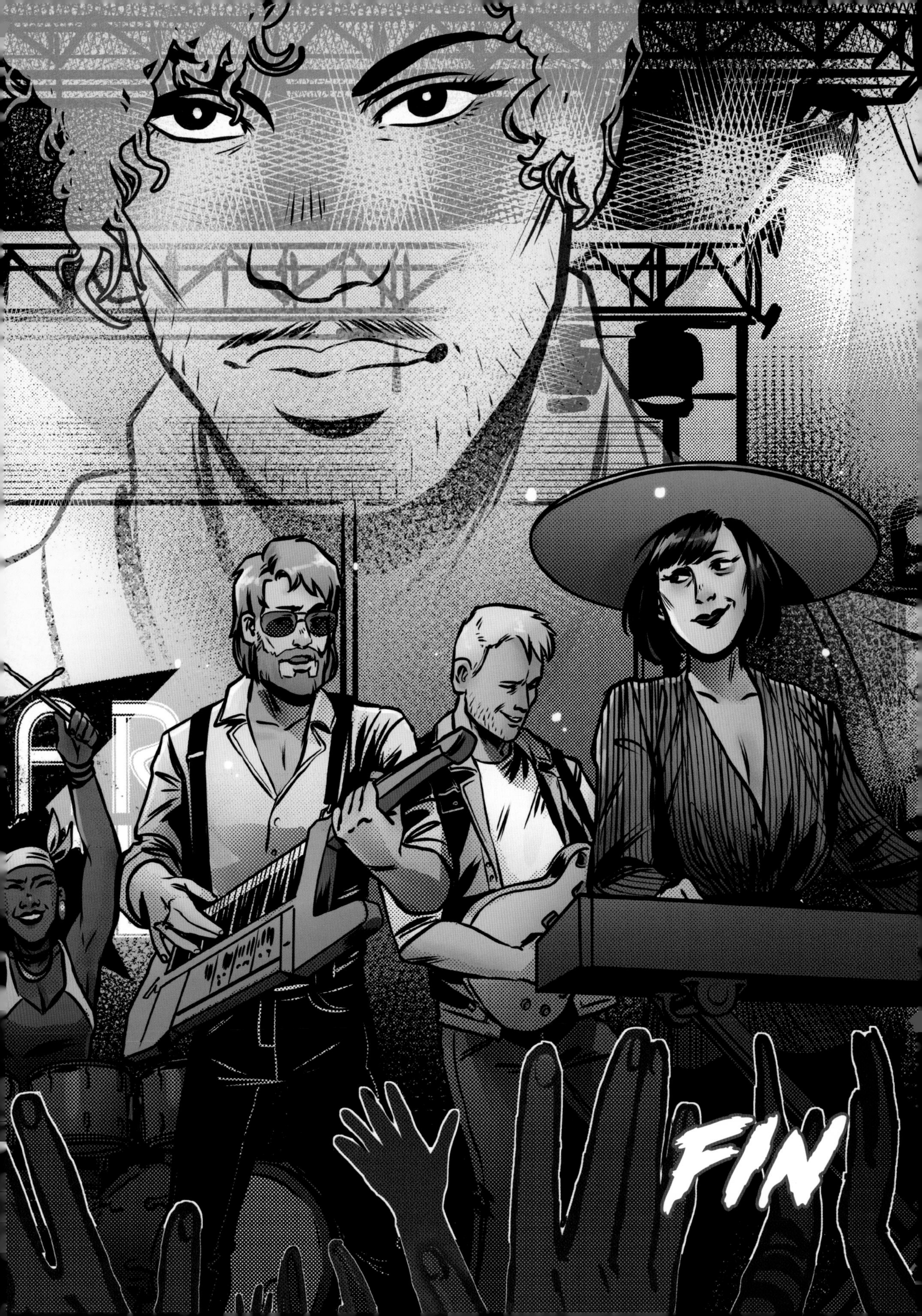
FIN

BEHIND THE MUSIC

AFTERWORD
By **Fabrice Sapolsky**

"May U live 2 see the Dawn." **These words were featured on many Prince records. It was as much a spiritual message from a very religious man as an invitation for his fans to join "the family." The Purple Family. I guess after reading and enjoying this graphic novel, you're now a member, too.**

Let's be honest. It's almost impossible to do justice to an artist like Prince Rogers Nelson in a few pages. Hundreds of books (including his unfinished autobiography[1]), articles, and blog posts have been published about an artist who could easily be considered as the biggest musical genius of all time. Through four decades, Prince delivered an amazing body of work: thirty-nine official studio albums under his name (or his symbol), another fifteen produced for other artists, dozens of contributions to the careers of a wide range of performers, and a legendary vault allegedly full of a thousand unreleased tracks. He was more than just a musician or an entertainer.

First, he never let anything or anyone stand between him and his dreams. He may have been slightly shorter in height—5'2"—than a lot of his friends, but he had the confidence of a seven-foot giant. Prince could school you at basketball. Prince was funny and very popular with the ladies. Prince could play fifteen different instruments. Prince would make a huge impression on everyone he was close to. Prince was unique. And the world had to take notice.

[1]PRINCE – *The Beautiful Ones*, Penguin Random House (2019)

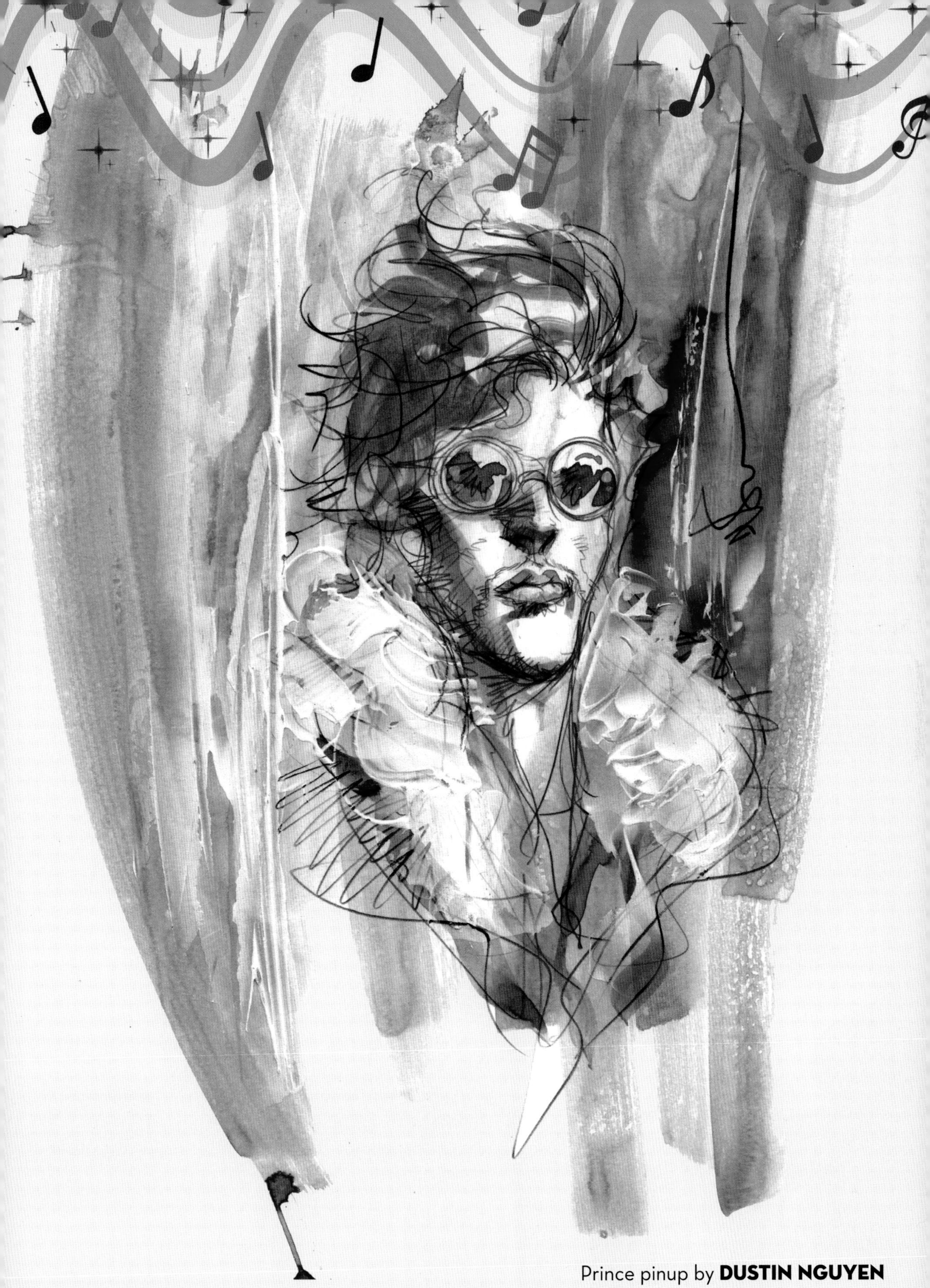

Prince pinup by **DUSTIN NGUYEN**

LITTLE PRINCE OF MINNEAPOLIS

In the early 1970s, Minneapolis wasn't really known for its R&B, soul, or funk flavor. The state of Minnesota was mostly famous for being Bob Dylan's and Judy Garland's home state. Being a predominantly Caucasian town, Minneapolis didn't even have a Black radio station in those days.

This didn't stop the younger generations from playing music and idolizing the biggest Black American artists like James Brown, Al Green, or Jimi Hendrix. Beginning bands spilled out of high schools and colleges. Prince's first band, Grand Central, was formed in 1971. They would play (mainly covers) at various venues in the Minneapolis area and "battle" other local bands such as Flyte Tyme (who counted among their number Jimmy Jam, Terry Lewis, and Alexander O'Neal). Famously discovered by producer Owen Husney, who managed to have Prince signed at Warner Bros., the 17-year-old prodigy went on to record his debut album, *For You*, on his own terms. The album wasn't a commercial success, but nothing could stop the "Kid from Minneapolis."

As time passed, Prince became inseparable from his hometown both literally and figuratively. The signature style he developed, quickly dubbed the "Minneapolis Sound," was a brilliant mix of funk, pop, rock, soul (and even rockabilly) that became inescapably associated with the city as Prince began expanding his influence by producing other local acts.

While many of his peers left the rough winters of Minnesota for greener pastures in New York, Atlanta, or Los Angeles, Prince never left his hometown. One of his famous quotes says it all: "I will always live in Minneapolis. It's so cold, it keeps the bad people out."

THE SOUND OF MUSIC

Many music historians believe that the 1999 album (from 1982) represented the pivotal moment when Prince started his journey to become an international sensation. Certainly, the 1980s brought two major elements that propelled him to new heights: advancements in music technology, and MTV.

With 1999, Prince ventured into new territories musically, aided by tech such as the famous LinnDrum machine. The LM-1 became Prince's second-most relied-upon musical companion (next to his guitar) and refined his sound in a way no other instrument could.[2] The machine became so associated with Prince that when he stopped using it in the 1990s, fans immediately recognized its absence.[3] Other bands and musicians, in an attempt to capture Prince's sound, went on and bought their own LM-1s, but they never could replicate what Prince achieved.

The rise of Music Television (MTV) also brought Prince to the next level. The channel, founded in 1981, was quickly criticized for its lack of diversity. Released in December 1982, the "1999" single became the first video to be featured in heavy rotation by a Black artist. Prince understood the power of videos. He filmed all his performances and had a small film crew responsible for documenting his life that followed him everywhere.[4]

[2]Prince used the machine heavily on 1999, *Purple Rain, Around the World in a Day, Parade, Sign o' the Times, Batman, Graffiti Bridge,* and countless non-album tracks.
[3]He ended up bringing it back by popular demand (and in a limited capacity) in the last years of his life, on albums like *Rave Un2 the Joy Fantastic, MPLS Sound, 20Ten,* and *Hit n Run vol.1 &2.*
[4]Morris Day, co-founder of The Time and frequent Prince collaborator, stated in his autobiography, *On Time,* (2019) that his first job at Prince's camp was being "the video guy."

50 SHADES OF PURPLE

A Gemini, Prince had distinctly different sides to his personality. He could be very shy and quiet with people he didn't know but extremely talkative and funny with those he trusted and allowed into his inner circle. And of course, he was a beast on stage. Over the years, he created multiple aliases, personae, and characters[5] that helped him express his bottomless creativity—largely to the benefit of others.

Prince's artistic generosity as much as his influence was what inspired this story and its characters. In earlier drafts of the script, Prince was physically absent, the idea being that his presence would permeate throughout. Ultimately, it was decided with the writers, Hannibal Tabu and Joseph Illidge, to make the connection between Starchild and Prince more explicit to underscore his passion for grooming new talent for success, pushing them to be the most creative version of themselves. That decision became the key to making *MPLS Sound* a sincere love letter to "His Royal Badness" and the gifts he gave the world.

[5]Prince signed songs as Jamie Starr (or The Starr Company), Alexander Nevermind, or Christopher. He performed as Camille (his female alter-ego), Tora Tora, and, of course, his unpronounceable Love Symbol.

Unlike many musicians who hit it big and never looked back, from the very start of his career, Prince was dedicated to working with and helping other musicians and continued to mentor young performers across his three decades in the limelight. Vanity, The Time, Janelle Monáe, and Sheila E. are only a few of the artists who benefited from Prince's guidance and insight. He also worked with several bands throughout his career: Grand Central, The Revolution, The New Power Generation, and 3rdEyeGirl. In 2010, he was named one of *Time* magazine's most influential people in the world, and it is entirely possible that this will be his ultimate legacy. It's certainly the one we honor here.

R&B/Funk connoisseur Fabrice Sapolsky is an independent immigrant writer-artist-editor. He's the co-creator of Marvel's Spider-Man Noir and has launched two creator-owned graphic novels, *One-Hit Wonder* and *Intertwined*. He lives in Los Angeles, where he recently founded FairSquare Comics to publish graphic novels from under-represented categories of creators, starting with *Noir Is The New Black*, a collection of Noir stories from Black American writers and artists.

CHARACTER DESIGNS

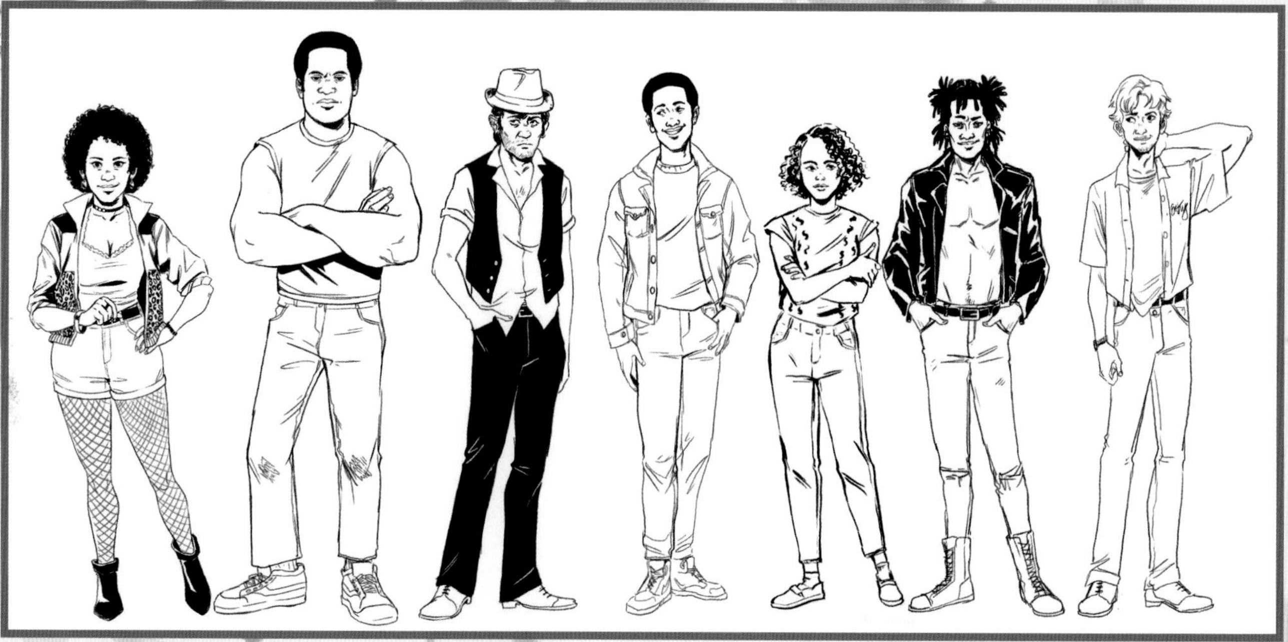

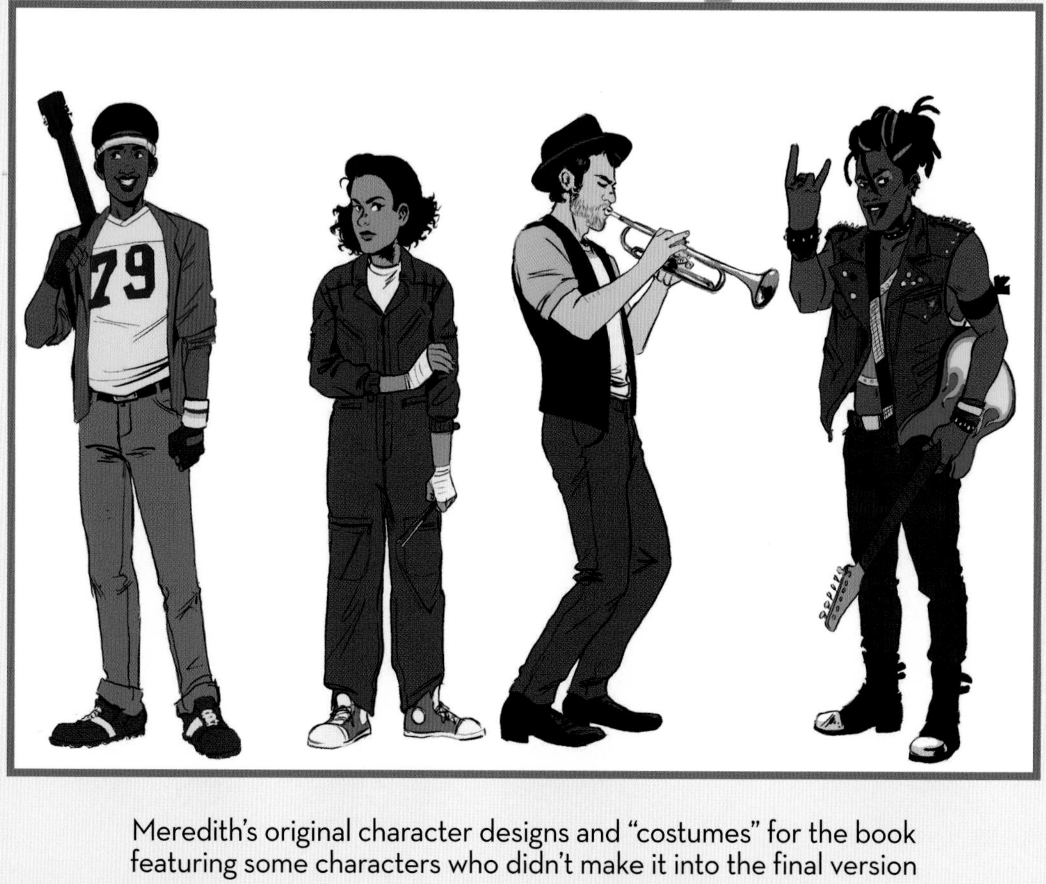
79

Meredith's original character designs and "costumes" for the book featuring some characters who didn't make it into the final version

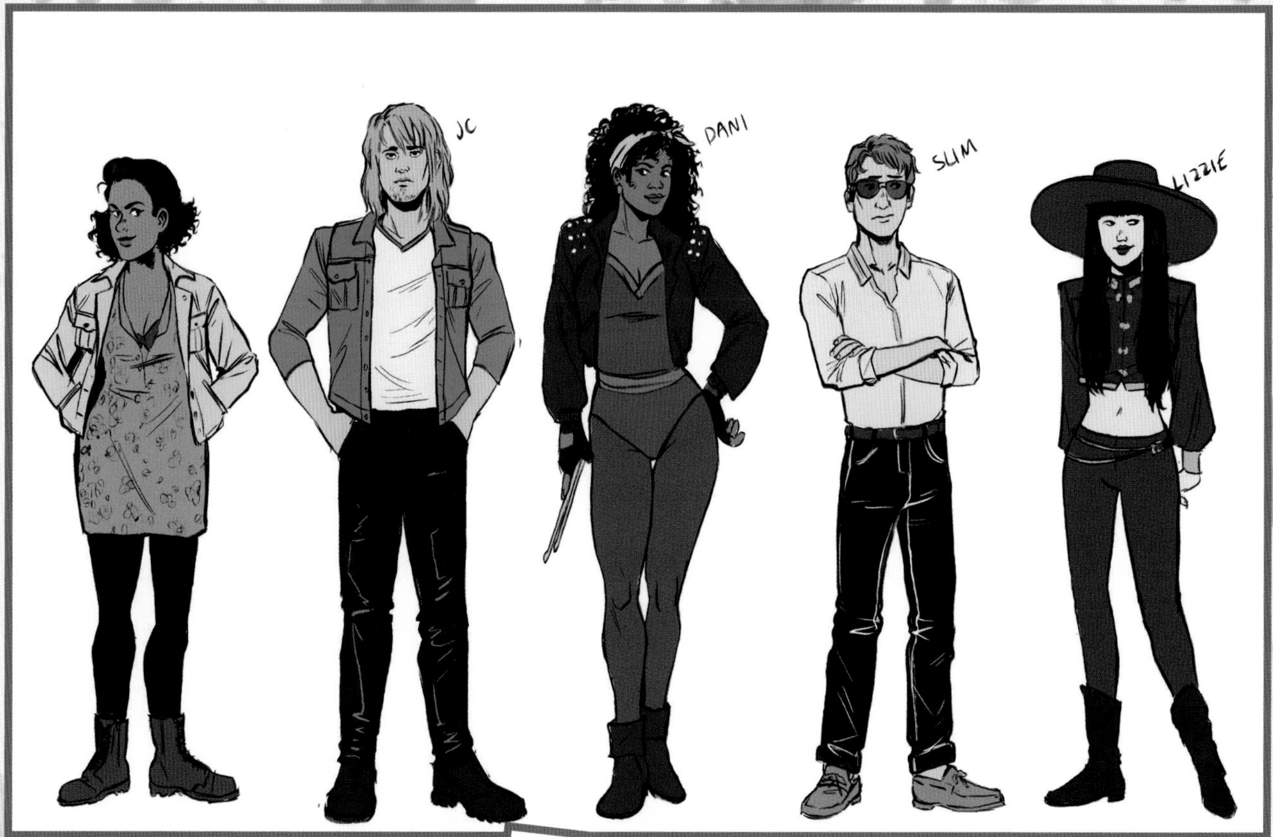
JC
DANI
SLIM
LIZZIE

Meredith's revised designs for the cast of ***MPLS Sound***

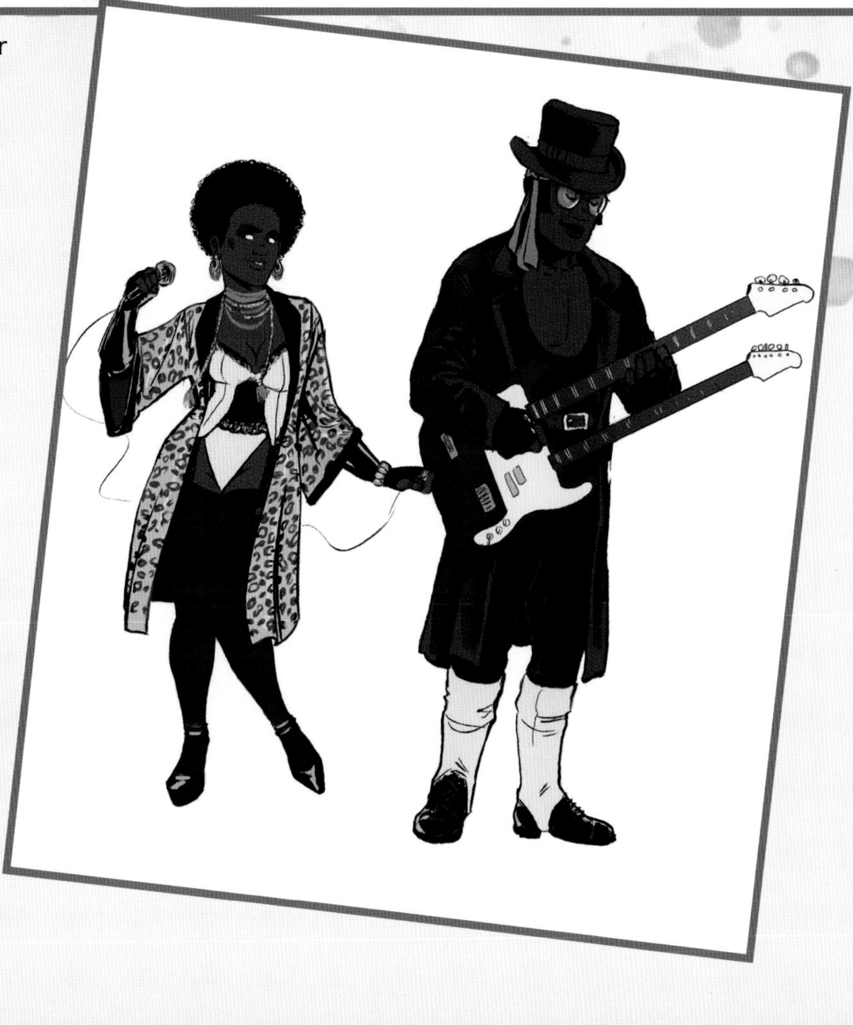

Theresa and Ellis costume designs

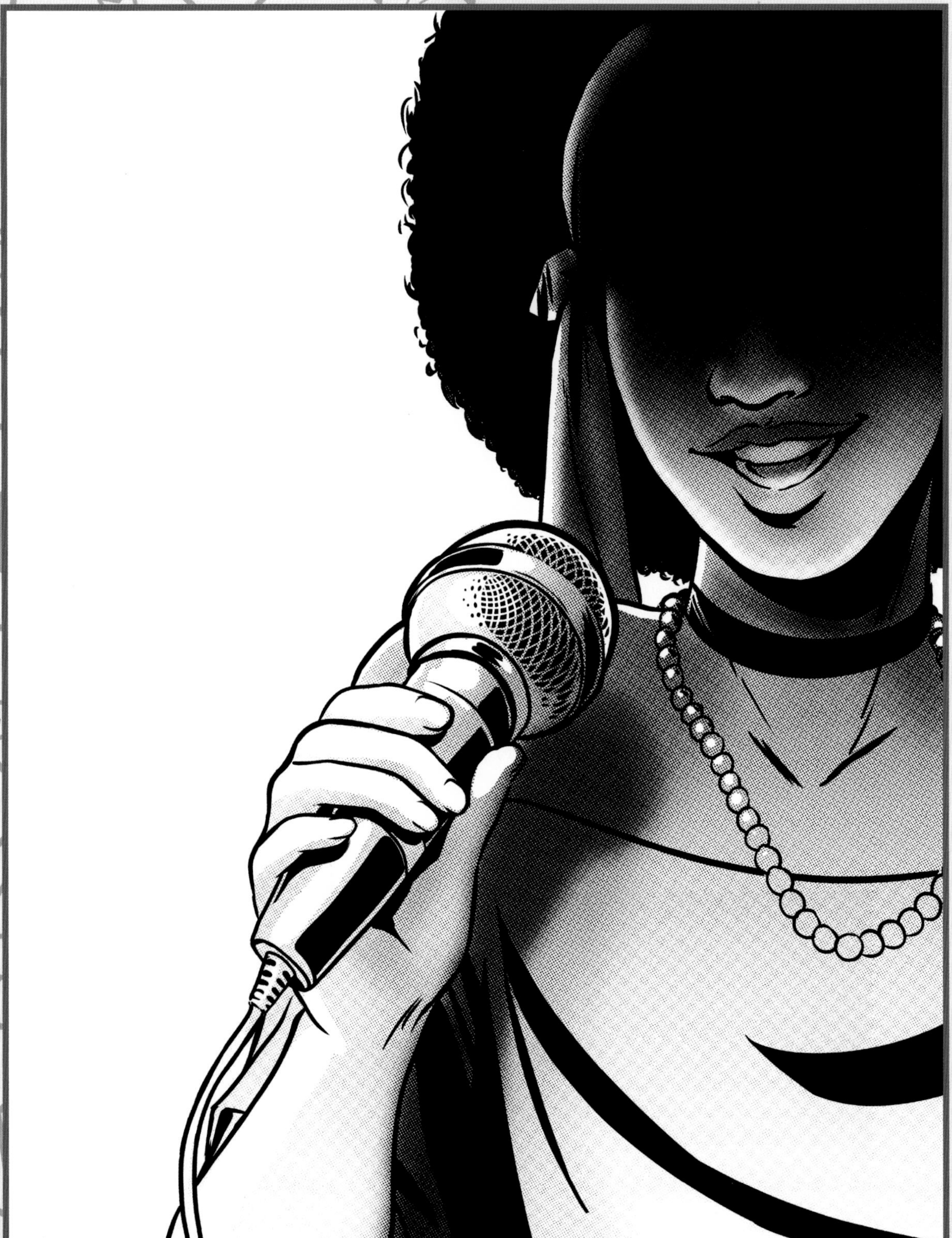

An unused page by Meredith featuring Theresa

COVER PROCESS

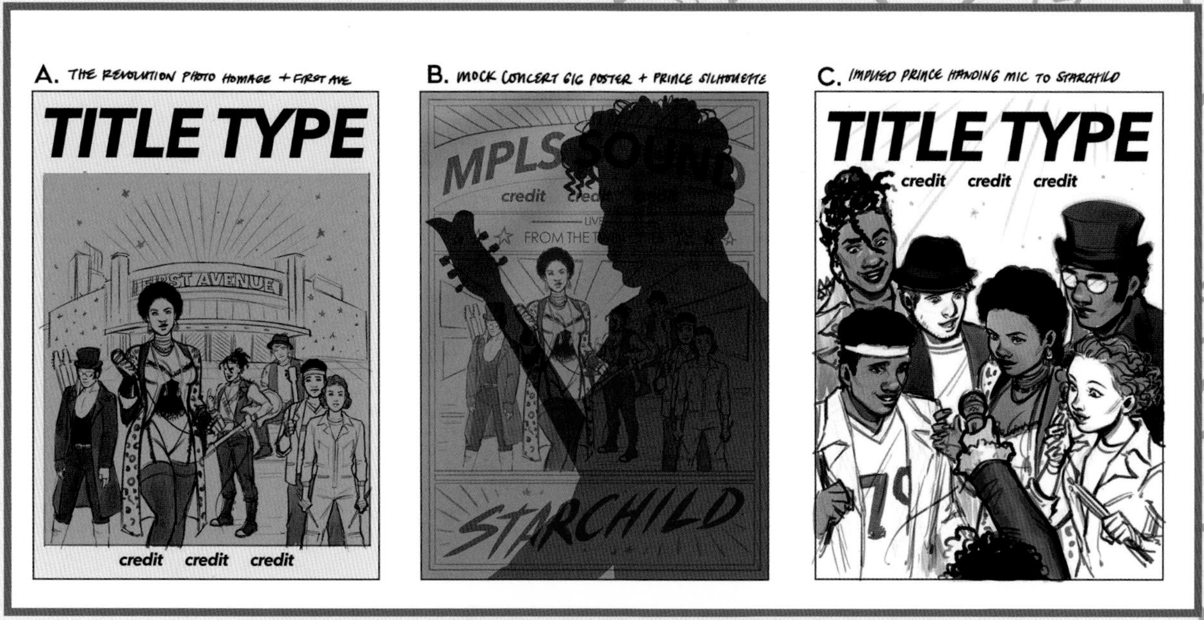
A. THE REVOLUTION PHOTO HOMAGE + FIRST AVE
TITLE TYPE
FIRST AVENUE
credit credit credit
B. MOCK CONCERT GIG POSTER + PRINCE SILHOUETTE
MPLS SOUND
credit
FROM THE
STARCHILD
C. IMPLIED PRINCE HANDING MIC TO STARCHILD
TITLE TYPE
credit credit credit

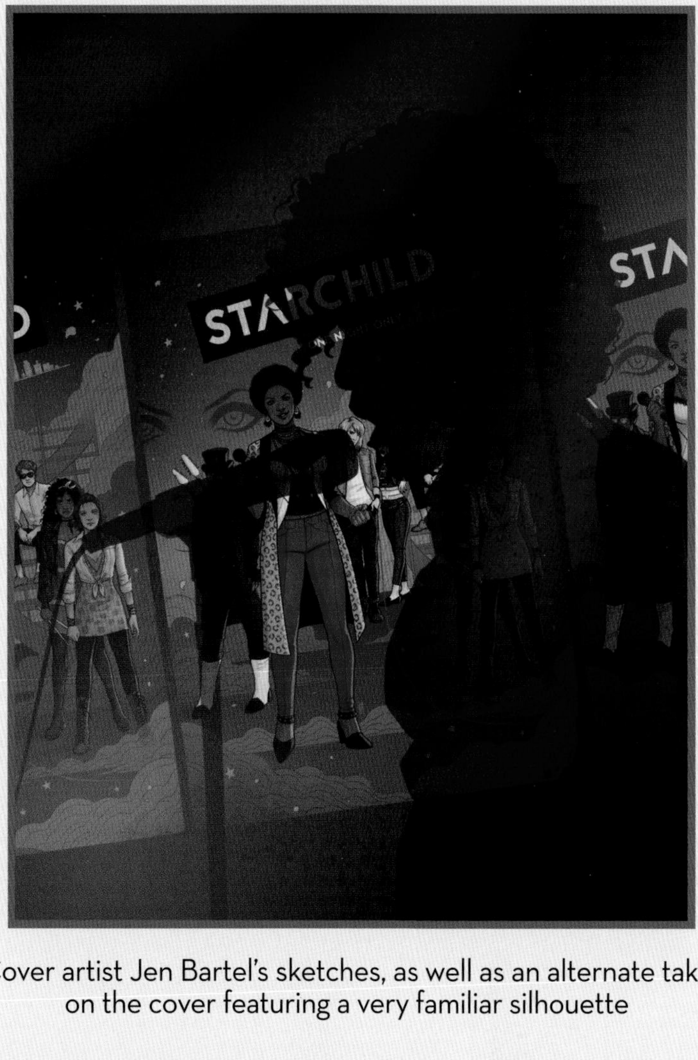
STARCHILD

Cover artist Jen Bartel's sketches, as well as an alternate take on the cover featuring a very familiar silhouette

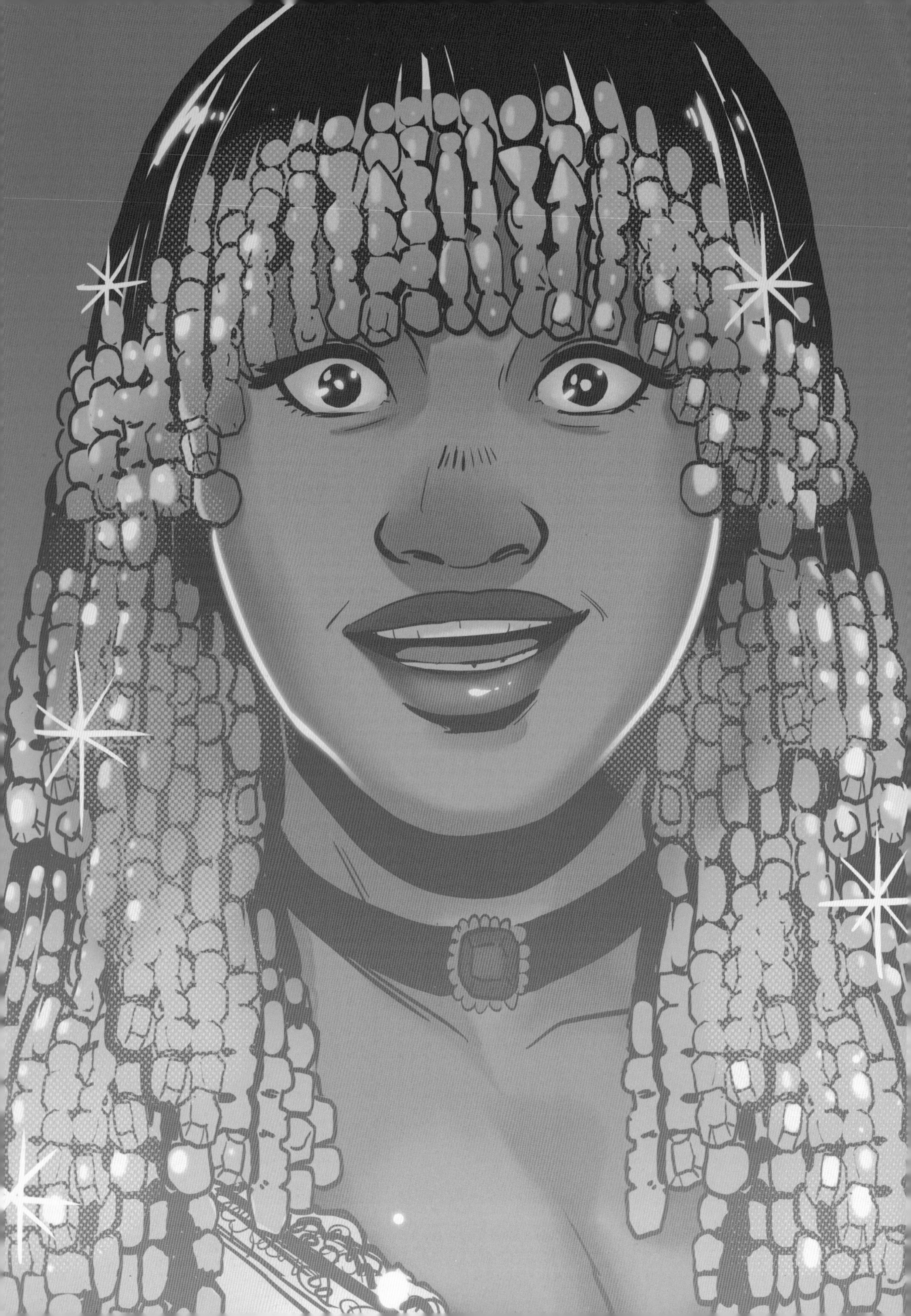